CARNIVAL KISS

"Imagine being forced to watch a magnificent sunset from the top of a ferris wheel," Maj said.

"Yes, imagine," Noah answered. "It cost me a pretty penny to get the operator to do that."

"You bribed him?" Maj turned quickly and set their swing to rocking.

They watched the sun go down. The sound of the merry-go-round music seemed louder, and she felt the bang of cymbals vibrate through her chest. She shivered.

"Cold?" he asked.

"A little. How long can it take to fix this thing?"

"Anywhere from ten minutes to an hour."

Maj said nothing, and her nervousness grew. There was a tension between them, man-to-woman, woman-to-man tension. They sat motionless except for the slight rocking of their swing, waiting. Waiting for what? she wondered. But she didn't have to wonder long.

Noah's four fingers rested on her lower lip, then slipped softly around her jaw and tilted her head back. In her vision his face grew blurry in the gathering darkness and in its closeness as it drew nearer hers. And then his mouth closed over hers, warm, tender, inviting more as it drew away . . .

OUT OF THE BLUE

GARDA PARKER

ZEBRA BOOKS
KENSINGTON PUBLISHING CORP.

To Aunt Muriel

*and to my women friends — fifty, over and
under — who have given me love and support
through my own half century:*

*Carole, Char, Chipper, Fran, Gloria, Heather,
Janice Kaye, Linn, Marge, Molly, Pam,
Pauline, Sharon, heroines among many . . .*

*and to my dearest friend with all my love,
my daughter Tamara*

ZEBRA BOOKS

are published by

Kensington Publishing Corp.
475 Park Avenue South
New York, NY 10016

First printing: July, 1992

Printed in the United States of America

ACKNOWLEDGMENTS

The author wishes to thank the following for their valuable contributions to the writing of this book:

Bob Milner

Bob Taylor, President
Airpower Museum
Ottumwa, Iowa

Maria Greene

Nancy Adamy, CSW

Tom O'Donnell

"Major" Bowes
Covewood Lodge
Big Moose Lake
Eagle Bay, New York

Sally & Paul Smith, Proprietors
The Moose Mart
Big Moose Station, New York

Bird Seaplane Base
Sixth Lake
Inlet, New York

Jiminy Cricket

and David Worden.

"Like a bolt out of the blue,
fate steps in . . ."

Chapter One

At the living room window in a second floor apartment in Brooklyn, Majesty Wilde methodically dunked a tea bag into a black-rimmed china cup, and peered through a shiny new aluminum screen and the budded branches of a maple tree down to the street below.

Buoyed by the freshness of late April breezes, the brownstone-lined neighborhood took on an air of awakening after a long sleep. Filmy curtains flapped outside open windows. People in unfastened jackets spoke to each other as they passed, offering uncustomary eye contact and an occasional smile. Blended strains of classical, salsa, and rock music floated in the air, softening the wail of distant sirens. From the bakery on the corner drifted a cinnamony aroma as the baker placed a wooden sign on the sidewalk advertising fresh hot cross buns.

Spring at last. Maj breathed deeply, feeling she

hadn't noticed spring in years, at least not in the almost two since Jack had been killed.

Behind her Nan Doyle clattered a cup on the coffee table. "God, I feel like I've been hibernating half my life. I hate winter. I hate being cold, and I always eat too much. How're you doing? Have you had sex yet?"

Maj turned from the window and smiled. "I'll get used to it." She answered the first but avoided the second question.

"Get used to which?"

"Being Majesty Wilde again."

Nan stretched out and settled her ample form comfortably on the dark blue overstuffed sofa, and propped herself on her elbow. Her short dark hair curled softly around her face. She dipped one knee over the other, and in her pink sweat suit appeared to be posing for a Rubens painting. Across the cozy room Maj dropped into an art deco-styled chair covered in a muted mauve and blue print fabric, and tucked her stocking feet up under her tweed skirt.

If anyone else came in, it might have looked as if Nan were the client and Maj the psychotherapist, instead of the reverse. Maj couldn't remember when their relationship had changed from therapist/client to friend/friend, and moved from Nan's office to one or the other's living room. On this day they were meeting at Nan's place. Maj's choice. She knew she would feel the natural emergence of spring in Brooklyn more than she would in her own apartment in Manhattan.

Nan had ceased to charge Maj a fee when a true friendship had developed between them. On several occasions their discussions turned to Nan's own complicated life, especially the time following her second divorce. Sex was a topic she brought up often in their times together, and Maj wondered in good humor for whose benefit she did it.

"You're avoiding the sex question again." When Maj raised her eyes in a mock disdainful frown, Nan returned to Maj's first comment. "Well, after all, you were Mrs. Jack Thompson for almost thirty years. It'll take some getting used to being single again. How do you feel about it?"

"Blurred, as if I've put on a new skin over an old body." Maj plopped the tea bag in the bowl of the spoon, wrapped the string around the wet bag twice, pressing it dry with the handle, then set them both next to the saucer.

"And?"

"And?"

Nan looked expectantly across the room toward Maj. "Yes. I sense an *and* in your voice. Or maybe it's a *but*."

Maj sipped the tea, then pulled back quickly as it burned her upper lip. "But . . . I'm restless. And I'm tired. And I just passed my fifty-first birthday, but for the first time in my life I don't have a list of things to do."

Nan nodded. "That happens to widows sometimes, especially childless widows."

11

Maj drank, her gaze resting unseeing on the beige dhurrie rug in front of Nan's sofa. Her regret over her childlessness hung unspoken between them. But that wasn't by choice. At least not her choice.

"I'm over that," Maj said, a hint of surprise in her voice. "Being a widow, I mean." She knew she said that too easily, and she looked up quickly for Nan's reaction. Would it seem too soon after Jack's death to Nan, as it did to her, that she didn't miss his presence?

"And you're feeling guilty about not feeling guilty about how fast you came to that conclusion, aren't you? Like maybe you think you didn't love him as much as you should have?" Nan cast nonaccusing dark eyes on Maj's face.

Maj studied her left hand thoughtfully. "I don't know if I stopped loving him or not, or, if I did, just when it was. Maybe we were a habit with each other, I don't know. Once in a while I thought about what it might be like not to be married, or at least not married to Jack." She turned her wedding ring around and around. "But then I'd get scared, I guess, just thinking about it. I mean, where would I go? What would I do? I had no money of my own. Jack took care of the finances. I guess it was easier for me to stay with the habit rather than try to break out on my own. It wasn't that bad."

"Have you thought about moving out of that apartment yet?" Nan asked. She stretched out, her head resting on the plump arm of the couch.

"I wouldn't know what to do with all our things, or even how to move them."

"That's what movers are for. All you have to do is make decisions on where things go."

"But all apartments are expensive. At least I know this one." Maj drained her teacup. "Maybe I could take on another job to make the financial burden easier."

"You're making excuses, and you're in a rut, my friend. Have you made any plans at all?"

"Plans? Plans for what?"

"Remember how we've talked about goals, and . . ."

". . . and bringing joy and pleasure into my life every day," Maj finished. She loved Nan's theory; she just had difficulty putting it into practice.

"Well, what have you written in your journal?"

Maj reached for the tapestry-covered journal in her black leather bag. A square pale blue envelope came out with it, caught inside the cover. She dropped it in her lap, opened the journal to a paper-clipped page, and read aloud.

"Today ended almost two years of paternity hearings, and began the resumption of the use of my maiden name. Oddly, that last was my own choice, the first choice it seemed since the spring I turned fourteen. Granddad offered to give me money for the twin sweater set I wanted (all the girls in my high school class were wearing them), or give me a flying lesson in his open-cockpit biplane. I was torn. I wanted the sweater set badly, in the new color. Aqua, they called it. Carole Ann, my best friend, said it would set off what she called my honey-gold hair, and reflect the little flecks of green in my blue eyes, and make the boys notice me.

"Granddad was always doing that, offering me fishing over dolls and flying over sweaters. I opted for the flying lesson. I can still feel the vibration of the propeller cutting through the wind and shimmying through my feet glued to the pedals, up my legs and body, down my arms to my white-knuckled fingers clamped around the stick as if choosing up sides for a softball game. Imagine me, piloting an airplane, soaring into the blue . . ."

Maj stared down at the page, swept away in the memory.

"I can," Nan said, "I can see you soaring into the wild blue yonder."

Maj came back to the present. "You couldn't soar in that old Stearman. Basically you just vibrated and bumped through the air over the Adirondacks shouting to each other through a tube or over your shoulder through the noise of the engine and the wind in your ears."

Nan laughed. "Did you ever get it?"

"What?"

"The twin sweater set."

"Oh, yes. Mother got it for me for Christmas that year."

"And did it do what Carole Ann said it would?"

"I guess. Jack noticed me. Of course, that was after Carole Ann showed me how to stuff my bra with Kleenex so my chest would stick out. Womanly, she said it was, womanly."

"An, those were the days, weren't they?" Nan grimaced.

"I was pretty flat-chested in those days. Mother refused to buy me a padded bra." Maj smiled, thinking back again. "I wasn't a woman, I was a girl, she said. Although, after my embarrassment at the junior prom, she gave in."

Nan shifted her head, interested. "What happened at the prom?"

"Aunt Muriel lent me her old prom dress. It was strapless, and Mother said I was too young for such things. Aunt Muriel talked Mother into letting me wear it. It was aqua, too. Aunt Muriel's only a few years older than I, so it wasn't too out-of-date as far as hand-me-downs go. I felt very grown-up and sophisticated wearing it. I can almost feel the netting and bust stays scratching me under the arms. Funny how all the girls ignored those red chafe marks we sported that night. Aunt Muriel was bigger in the bust than me, so of course Carole Ann came to the rescue armed with a box of Kleenex."

"Of course," Nan said. "Thank God for friends like Carole Ann."

"Well, I wasn't so sure about that then. I was doing the bunny hop, and my carefully placed Kleenex padding worked its way up and out and perched along the top of my fabricated cleavage."

Nan laughed out loud.

"You may laugh," Maj said, watching Nan's pink sweat suit bounce, "but I was mortified. Especially when one of the Kleenexes fell out. Kleenex didn't come in colors then, only white. Stark white. Glaring white. The-better-to-notice-it-in-the-low-lights-of-the-Charlotte-High-School-gym white. The easier for Jack Thompson, big man on campus, I might add, to retrieve it and hand it to me."

"Sorry." Nan stifled more laughter. "What happened?"

"I went to the girls' room and blew my nose and wiped my tears in my chest padding."

"Ah, the scars of a teenager."

"Yeah. Tell me, doctor, do you think I'm marred for life?"

"Do you still stuff your bra?"

"Of course not!"

"Cured of the dreaded teenage-girl-with-the-flat-chest syndrome of the fifties," Nan pronounced.

"Thank you. It's a good thing I don't pay you for this kind of therapy."

Nan sat up and wiped her eyes with a tissue from a nearby Kleenex box. They both laughed when she waved its obvious whiteness.

16

"So, what else did you write in your journal today?"

"Nothing."

Nan watched her friend's face carefully. "You didn't write anything more about the last hearing?"

Maj closed the journal. Absently she picked up the blue envelope and tapped it against her cheek. Her mood darkened.

"I couldn't do it, couldn't write it. I can still barely think about it."

Nan nodded. "Want to talk about it now?"

"I don't know," Maj whispered.

Nan waited. "What's the boy's name?" she urged.

Maj knew Nan would do this, would draw it, no, *drag it* out of her. And she knew she wanted Nan to do just that. She swallowed hard, and plunged in.

"John Bryce . . . Thompson. His mother calls him . . . Jack."

Nan let a breath out. "How did he look?"

"Like Jack. Same stocky build, same small brown eyes, same rust hair. He's even starting to style it like Jack, moussing it and blowing it dry into a perfect helmet. I always hated that." Maj closed her eyes and leaned her head against the chair back. "I guess I'm over the shock of their appearance at the funeral, and her introducing the young man as Jack's son. I think I'm into numbed acceptance now."

"Do you believe the woman?"

"The judge obviously did," Maj replied, a tone of weariness in her voice. "He said her proof substantiated beyond a shadow of a doubt that he was Jack's son. And in case that wasn't enough, there's the line on Jack's life insurance policy naming him beneficiary. I got the Manhattan apartment I can't afford on one salary, a yellow vintage Mustang convertible which he kept at the hangar and which I was never allowed to drive, and a huge amount of credit card debt. Jack liked to live well."

"I asked if *you* believed her," Nan pushed.

Maj's eyes became shiny, but she didn't cry. She took in a sharp breath. "Yes. I think I have all along, even though I didn't want to."

"I know."

"I mean"—Maj sat up straight and her voice took on an edge—"Jack was the one who didn't want children. We were too busy working to get somewhere, he said. Children would get in the way, he said. He knew I understood, he said. But *he* never understood anything. Never understood what happened to me after—"

"I know," Nan said again to soothe.

Maj clamped her eyes shut. "I was eighteen when I married him. Barely more than a baby myself, at least emotionally."

"Do you believe he loved you?"

"I believe he loved being a hotshot corporate pilot. I understood about his obsession with flying. After all, Dad was an airline pilot, and Granddad had been a dust pilot in the thirties. Jack made me feel . . . invalidated, or something, because I was a secretary in an ad agency. But he liked the money I handed over to him every week."

"But you've liked your work, your career, haven't you?"

"I'm an administrative assistant now," Maj said in a matter-of-fact voice.

"And does that make you feel 'validated'?" Nan pushed again.

"Jack always said I didn't work hard enough. He thought I should've undercut some of the other agents and taken on the clients myself. I was never going to succeed, he'd say. Well, I guess I wasn't good enough to succeed, or something. I never had the energy to undercut anybody, or acquire clients of my own. Truth is, I didn't want to."

"Hey, you've worked too long and too hard to let that low self-esteem baggage latch onto you again," Nan said, chastising Maj.

"I know. I didn't mean that the way it sounded. I didn't aspire to be an advertising agent. I just wanted a good job until I had my family. Maybe that's what I thought being validated meant. Being a wife and mother. Now Jack's gone, I'm no longer a wife, and it's too late anyway for me to have a baby. In a way, it's still his choice, isn't it? He controlled our married life, and somehow even after death he controls my single life." Maj examined her thoughts for a moment. "Maybe that's not fair to say. Time controls me now. Time past, time present, and time future. Now I'm fifty-goddamned-one, and too old for much of anything."

"You're not too old for a lot of things. And besides, you don't look a day over thirty-five."

Maj looked skeptical.

"I mean it. And you know it. Your eyes are a lovely blue and your hair is still what Carole Ann would call honey-gold."

"I wear bifocals"—Maj squinted—"and I have crow's-feet." She lifted the loose curls that fell over one side of her forehead and leaned over. "Look at this hairline. Gray lurks under here!"

"So what's a little strain of silver in a gold mine? And I prefer to call those added features near the eyes character lines. You earned every one of those, so just wear them proudly. And look at that figure! You're probably still as trim as you were when you met Jack. I, on the other hand . . ." She ran her palm over her rounded hip.

"You are voluptuous," Maj put in, "and I am fifteen pounds overweight."

"Aren't you running? I remember you said you ran a few miles every day to keep in shape. God, what an awful sport running is. Every person I've ever seen doing it looks to be in pain. How can that be fun?"

Maj laughed. "It was fun, sort of. I didn't run every day. Just a few times a week. It kept me in shape. And I worked off a lot of stress, I think."

"It has to be good for something. And it's clear your bust filled out." Nan laughed, pointing toward Maj's crisp white blouse.

Maj dropped her chin. "Yes, and now it's going down!"

"Everybody's a critic," Nan chided. "At least you've dated. I haven't had a date since the guy from Radio Shack installed my fax machine and stayed for a beer because his van wouldn't start. That was almost two years ago. I'm thinking of calling back for repair service!" Nan threw up her hands in mock despair.

"If you think going to the launderette with Ernest Bauer and folding sheets is a date . . ."

Nan lowered her voice seductively. "He's the regional director of your ad agency, and they were *his* sheets, after all. He was definitely making overtures to you."

"He's old enough to be my father . . . well, maybe my older brother. And besides, the sheets were green plaid cotton, for heaven's sake."

"Would it have made a difference if they were black satin?" Nan spread her hands.

"You are impossible." Maj laughed. "Dating. What a concept at my age. Some of the women at the office have fixed me up. I even hate that term, fix up, as if I've broken down, or something. What disasters! I'm just not ready for that yet, I guess. Next relationship, if there is one, I choose first. I'm not letting anybody choose me. I'll pay attention to my head. I'm not eighteen anymore."

"What about sex?"

"All right, I knew we'd have to come back to that sometime. What about sex?" Maj asked back.

"Don't you want it?"

"Want it?" Maj cocked her head to one side.

"Yes, want it. Crave it. Desire it. Get horny, for God's sake."

"Nan Doyle, you sound like you've been reading Shere Hite's reports again."

"Don't avoid this line of questioning, Ms. Wilde. It's healthy to want sex."

Maj thought for a minute. She'd remembered wanting Jack to make love to her when they were first married. And she remembered the act always left her feeling that something was missing. Well, Mother always said sex was something a man had to have and a wife had to endure. Somehow she'd always hoped it could be more than that, but she guessed Mother was right.

"You must fantasize." Nan looked at Maj. "You have fantasized. Haven't you?"

Maj looked down and felt her cheeks warm. Damn! She still blushed. Not too old for that.

"Yes," she said tentatively.

"Good! Tell me about it."

"Nan!"

"I'm not being a voyeur, if that's what you're thinking. Consider this part of your therapy. Or consider it giving your friend something warm to think about later tonight."

Maj laughed. "Well, once after I saw the *Ed Sullivan Show* I thought about Elvis Presley asking me out on a date."

"A date? I don't mean a date. I mean, right

down to the last crinoline under your poodle skirt. Doesn't Mel Gibson give you a twinge in the pit of your stomach? Or below?" Nan gestured to exactly the spot she meant.

"Who?"

"Who! When was the last time you saw a movie?"

"I told you, I don't date."

"All right, all right. Paul Newman. Robert Redford. Any of those make your heart go pitty-pat?"

"Oh, yes." Maj smiled. "And I remember watching old black and white John Wayne movies on our little television set with my mother. She thought he was the handsomest man she'd ever seen. So I told her I thought so, too, because I knew she had a crush on him. I felt funny knowing that about her, and worrying Dad might find out. And I did think John Wayne was pretty handsome. But then Elvis Presley exploded into my life, and he was all I thought about. Carole Ann and I stood in the drugstore and read every magazine that even mentioned his name. We pooled our money and bought a forty-five record of 'Heartbreak Hotel.' Whenever it was my turn to keep the record overnight, I played it constantly. That's when I thought I knew what being in love was all about. He stole my heart. I had pictures of him all over my bedroom, even on the ceiling. Those eyes, bedroom eyes, my mother called them, and she said they were dangerous. But it was his lips I liked."

"Did you say hips?"

"Those, too." Maj smiled. "Okay, I admit it. I dreamed about being in bed with Elvis."

"Great! What did you want him do?"

"Do? God, Nan, the man's dead. Let him rest in peace."

"Dead? Hardly. I have a client who saw him in Macy's last Christmas. Besides, even if he is dead, he's still thinking about sex. And you should, too."

"I do. Once in a while. I like to call it making love, though. Love and sex have always meant the same things to me."

"Call it whatever you want, just get it."

"I thought you were in business to help people."

"I am. I'm trying to help you find sex."

"There's a word for people who do that, and I don't think 'psychotherapist' is it." Maj laughed. Then she grew thoughtful. "I really don't know why I did that, change my name back to Wilde. I mean, what's the point?"

"I truly believe you just want to start over. Or you will when you take off that wedding ring."

"Why?" Maj waved her left hand. "I sure don't have another fifty years to do it all again. I don't even know if I have twenty years of energy just to keep moving." She tapped the envelope against her cheek again.

"God, you do need a change! Okay, what's in the envelope?" Nan motioned toward it.

Maj looked at it as if for the first time. "It's a birthday card from Ada and Sam Ferguson."

"Who are they?"

"Partners of Granddad in the West Wind Lodge."

"Oh, yes, the place at Large Elk Lake in the mountains you went to in the summer."

"Big Moose Lake."

"I knew it was named for some woodland creature. Your parents went with you, too, right?"

"Mother always did. Dad, too, sometimes, when his schedule permitted." Maj stopped for a moment. She remembered one night at the West Wind hearing her mother tell Grandma that she knew Dad was having an affair, had more than one. Mother was always stoic in front of other people, but this time Maj had seen her cry.

"And did the Fergusons' card disturb you for some reason?" Nan asked.

"A little, I guess. Grandma and Granddad took Ada and Fergie in after the war. They worked first for food and a roof over their heads, and pretty soon the four of them were as close as a family. The West Wind had been one of the Great Camps. A railroad builder constructed it for his family and friends, and then went broke. So Granddad bought it and turned it into a vacation lodge. Fergie and Ada put their life into it along with him and Grandma, and they became partners. They've thought of me as their granddaughter, too."

"Are they ill?"

"I'm not sure, but I sense something is wrong. They were a lot younger than my grandparents, but now they're getting old, of course. They asked me to visit them soon, sounded urgent in a way. I feel bad about not seeing them for so long. After I was married I still wanted to go up for visits, but Jack never wanted to. I let them know when he'd been killed, and they wrote right back and told me to come up if I needed time to myself. But what with working, and the hearings, I've never had the time."

"Well, I think you should make the time," Nan said. "It would do you good to get a change of scene. I think a visit to the Adirondacks is just what the doctor ordered. All that clean air without Manhattan-style chunks in it. Trees, lakes, a resort vacation. Who could ask for anything more? Except Mel Gibson in a sleeping bag, maybe."

Maj smiled. "I'll think about it."

"Don't think about it, just do it. Pack your bags tonight. Go back to the place where you felt loved, were adventurous."

"Me, adventurous?"

"Of course. Remember, you chose flying lessons over an aqua twin sweater set."

"I did, didn't I?" Maj smiled.

"Yes, you did. Think of yourself in that plane, free as a bird, looking down on the earth, completely in control of that powerful machine. You're a superwoman!"

Maj laughed with her friend, then sobered. "Except for one thing."

"Now what?"

26

"I've never soloed."

Nan stared at her, then grinned. "Then it's high time you did, isn't it?"

Five days and several arguments with Nan later, Maj arrived at the West Wind in the yellow Mustang with a small bag of clothes for a one-week vacation from the ad agency, and without the ring she'd been wearing on her third finger left hand for three decades.

A tearful reunion with the wiry Fergie and failing Ada, and finding the once-splendid lodge and adjacent cottages in acute disrepair, left her emotionally drained. In bed that night by ten o'clock in one of the musty-smelling guest rooms, she was unable to sleep.

She sensed Fergie and Ada were holding something back, but not their unabashed delight at seeing her again. In the total blackness of the mountain night Maj felt loved, no, cherished. The ascent up into the mountains that day, and the impact of feeling their unconditional love, softened the armored defenses she knew she'd built over the years.

The next morning Maj grabbed an old yellow slicker hanging on a peg by the back door and stepped out onto the porch. She started carefully down the slippery steps, and ambled through the six o'clock moisture-laden air across the expanse of lawn toward the wooden dock. Watching steam rising and blending into the mist from the black coffee she carried in a mug, she inhaled deeply, then opened her mouth and tasted the air.

At this end of Big Moose Lake, the cove lay under a blanket of morning fog, surrounded by a bank of red spruces, balsam firs, sugar maples, and towering white pines so dense their tips appeared black against the mist. Their pungent tangy aroma, mixed with damp Adirondack duff, hung in the air.

Somewhere a loon wailed, and without thought Maj called back as she had when she was a child, then moved in the direction of the lonely sound as if it were a commiserating soul.

At the tilted dock, bleached pale gray by years of sun and water, she lifted one white sneaker to the first weathered board and tested her weight. It gave a little, but held. She lifted her other foot, her full weight now on the dock. The slight shifting of it gave her the feeling she'd just stepped onto the first layer of a cloud.

A third of the way down sat a metal lawn chair, the kind she remembered painted in bright primary colors lined up in front of Danbury's hardware store in the mountain hamlet of Pinewood. The coat of red paint on this one was chipped and faded, and the metal underneath blended with the silver-gray morning. She started carefully toward it.

Lowering her backside toward the seat, she knew that in a few seconds she would feel cold wetness through her jeans just the way she'd felt it through her threadbare dungarees when she was eight years old and Grandma told her not to sit on the chairs before they were wiped with a beach towel. Under her weight the chair swayed back on its curved frame, catching her off balance just the way she remembered, but this time the dock swayed with it. Its underpinnings had shifted, caved, mired, needed shoring up just like her own.

Slipping back her hood, she let her hair absorb the mist. It stuck in wet ringlets to her forehead, and she felt a little naked without the mask of makeup she usually wore to the office. She sipped the coffee, savoring its richness mingled with the spicy-sweet taste in the air of lake and pines and earth, and let her eyes drift across the expanse of mist-swirled water toward the granite faces of the towering, solid Adirondacks.

The loon wailed again, as if checking to see if she was still there. She didn't respond, not wanting to break the utter peace of the morning. Vaguely she was aware that her backside was wet and cold, but she didn't move. She just sipped, breathed, stared against the fog, and listened to the quiet, the blessed quiet.

Then a pair of blue jays landed in a tree near the shore and set up a busy squawk as they went about their morning food hunt. A chickadee responded and was joined by three more, ducking their little black caps among the dripping branches. Maj heard the drone of an airplane from somewhere she couldn't determine. She looked toward the sky and guessed the rest of the mountain creatures must be waking. The sun was trying its best to burn through the fog.

The drone of the plane grew louder, then the engine seemed to skip. Maj's senses sharpened. She determined by the low-pitched vibration that it was a small plane, propeller-driven. The drone grew louder, nearer.

Maj stood slowly, then started to back herself toward shore. A dark shadow passed through the sun's narrow rays, and then she heard a splash. There was the whoosh of weight skimming over the lake, then the roar of the engine before it was shut down. A seaplane. She felt the wake from the plane's landing splash under the boards beneath her feet.

Just as she took a step onto shore, something bumped the dock. She heard a sickening crack as the boards pulled away from the pilings, and then the old familiar sound of pontoons scraping over the stony shore. She misstepped. The coffee mug dropped out of her hand and went to the bottom of the lake, and she fell into the wet stones. She crawled quickly up the lawn, then turned around.

Righting herself, she sat up and saw a dark figure wading through the lifting fog. Motionless she sat on the ground as the figure emerged from the mist and materialized into a man.

A tall man.

A man in cowboy boots, slim jeans, a leather

jacket, something resembling a white scarf at his neck.

A man with broad shoulders, a sculpted face topped with dark, damp hair that clung to his forehead — Lord, it was John Wayne as he appeared in *Flying Tigers!*

Chapter Two

Maj stared as his long strides brought the man near her and into the clear.

He stopped in his tracks. "Good God, you scared me to death!" He took another step toward her and hunkered down. "Are you hurt?"

Maj shook her head, gingerly rubbing the hip she'd landed on. "I scared *you?* Who are you? And what did you think you were doing?"

"Noah Decker, ma'am." He stood and extended a hand. "I was just coming in for breakfast. I live here."

Maj paused just a moment, then grasped his hand and let him pull her to her feet. He was holding her hand longer than polite greeting would deem reasonable, and she felt its warmth on her clammy palm.

"And may I be bold enough to ask the same of you?" He tilted his head to get a clearer look at her lowered face.

Maj looked up. Her eyes lingered on the band over his left chest pocket. It was stamped LT. N. DECKER. She let out a small breath, shaking herself mentally for making sure it didn't say J. Wayne. She knew her mother would think the resemblance as uncanny as she did. She raised her eyes past the square jaw, the straight mouth with a strong lower lip, the classic nose, and into eyes the same deep chestnut brown as his leather jacket.

"It appears you are bold enough, Mr. Decker." She sounded uncustomarily bold herself, and softened to her usual courteousness. "Majesty Thom—Wilde. I'm visiting."

"Pleased to make your acquaintance, Majesty Tom Wilde." He smiled with his eyes as well as his lips, and the corners of his mouth tilted provocatively over straight white teeth. "I hope it will be a long visit."

She withdrew her hand from his, which seemed reluctant to release it, and felt she must be blushing.

"Just Maj will be fine." She tried to sound businesslike, then remembered something he said. "Did you say you live here?" When he nodded, she said, "I didn't see you last night when I arrived."

"Stayed in the cabin I'm building a few miles down the lake." He motioned south with a toss of his head. "I lost all track of time and

33

it got too dark for me to fly back."

"Ah, then I was right. You've just destroyed this dock with what I presumed to be an airplane." Maj brushed wet duff from her slicker and jeans, attempting to hide her embarrassment over her quick remark, a remark that seemed to come from someone else's mouth, not her own.

Noah looked over his shoulder. "Appears like it. Needed fixing anyway. I just hope I didn't do much damage to the airplane. It's getting harder and harder to keep patching the fabric."

"Sounds like you make that kind of landing rather often," she observed, surprising herself at her own easy teasing of a man she'd known for a scant few minutes.

"I guess it does, doesn't it?" He smiled, neither confirming nor denying the allegation.

The morning brightened, clear and windless. Blue jays scolded above as if warning them away. Noah walked back to a lime-green single-engine plane on pontoons bobbing against the dock. He tightened tie-downs on the side of the fuselage to what was left of two dock pilings.

"Piper Cub . . . no, Supercub, isn't it?" Maj asked, raising the side of her hand to shade her eyes against the climbing sun.

"Right. How'd you know?"

She caught the surprise in his voice, and smiled. "I've been around that kind of plane before." She walked back to the edge of the lake and peered out into the water.

"Thinking of going fishing?" Noah asked from behind.

"You could say that. My coffee mug was another casualty of your landing."

"I'll look for it when I fix the dock. "It's the least I can do."

"The least," Maj said good-naturedly, looking up at him.

His eyes held hers for the moment.

"Well . . ." she said, and turned toward the lodge.

"Yes," he said, following her.

They were almost to the back porch when Sam Ferguson pushed open the squeaky screen door. "Well, Noah, I see you overshot the runway again."

"Guess so, Fergie. Looks like dock repair has just jumped to the top of the to-do list."

"Right after we get to that white pine in the side yard. It's threatening to go in the next windstorm, and I fear the roof will go with it."

"Right. I'll get my saws and we'll take it down. Shame to see that old thing go."

"I know. I remember when the top of it didn't go above the second floor balcony." Fergie shook his head.

In the lodge kitchen Noah headed toward a cast iron stove that took up three-quarters of the

35

back wall. Maj heard wood crackling in it, and her eyes followed the black stovepipe up the wall toward a tin plate that surrounded the exit hole. It was black with ancient soot, not shiny as it once was, but she knew the smoke curled blue out of the chimney just as it always had.

The room was cluttered with hanging chipped yellow enamel pots, blue painted crocks sprouting cooking utensils set upon linoleum-topped counters over white cupboards with red wooden knobs. Dark green plastic pots of plants waiting for transplanting lined a windowsill.

It was a kitchen in disrepair, but lived-in and clean. Homey. Maj loved it.

Noah hefted a gallon-size blue graniteware pot by the top and side handles and poured coffee into a heavy stoneware mug. The way he seemed to be so at home was very apparent to Maj.

"May I replace what you lost in the lake?" He grinned in Maj's direction, extending the mug.

"Thanks." As she walked toward him, her knees felt as if water had settled in them somehow. How could that be? She was certain she hadn't been hurt from the fall.

"I see you've met," Fergie said in his customary raspy morning voice. He shrugged off a red and black buffalo plaid jacket, and thumbed up an overall strap that had slipped down his arm. The red knit cap he'd been wearing drooped over a peg by the door leading to the attached woodshed, but its lasting impression could be clearly seen in the whorls of damp gray hair around his head. His chin sprouted a week-old scruff of beard, but Maj remembered his beard always looked that way, never longer, never shorter, always a week old.

"Where's the love of my life this morning?" Noah called toward the dining room. "Still lying abed like a princess?"

"Feeling poorly this morning," Fergie said in a low voice.

Ada Ferguson came through the door with a labored step. A diminutive woman crippled with polio as a toddler, she never let it keep her from getting around in the morning to start the coffee and make the beds. Her hair, thin and a bit unruly, was styled as it was during World War II when she'd worked in a munitions plant, parted in the middle and swept up in bobby pins to form soft rolls at her temples and the back of her neck.

"Good morning, gorgeous!" Noah circled her waist gently with a long arm and bent down to kiss her soundly on the mouth.

"Go on with you, Noah Decker." Ada pushed him away with a good-natured pat at his chest, but the color in her cheeks and the smile in her eyes told Maj she loved every second of Noah's affection.

He's out-and-out flirting with her, Maj thought with a twinge. Who was this man was who seemed as much a part of the Fergusons' life now as she'd been as a child? Was she jealous of the obvious closeness they'd formed among them, a closeness she'd been missing? Yet, she had to admit his flirting with Ada wasn't as offensive to her as what she'd seen other — all right, she had to say it — pilots do at cocktail parties.

"Oh, my, Maj honey, it's so good to see you in this kitchen again looking fresh as ever." Ada opened the industrial-size scratched white Gibson refrigerator and took out a clear glass jug filled with orange juice. "Now see what you've done, Noah? Made me forget my manners. Maj honey, this is Noah Decker."

"They've met." Fergie slurped his hot coffee.

"But not been formally introduced," Noah said, watching Maj. He drew in a breath, pulled himself up to full height, and held out his hand. "Noah Decker, soon to be neighbor, semiadopted son of Mr. and Mrs. Ferguson here, and not a bad guy to know, so some people tell me." His smile was dazzling, and Majesty thought if she waited a moment a rhinestone might sparkle from one of his teeth. He was almost too charming to believe.

She let out a tense breath, tilted a slight smile to one corner of her mouth, and reached for his outstretched hand. "Majesty Wilde, visitor again after too many years, semiadopted granddaughter of Ada and Fergie, and a fine woman to

38

know, so my friend tells me." She flashed him an equally dazzling smile.

"Wonderful," he responded, "just as long as that doesn't make us semirelatives. That would be a rotten shame." He held eye contact with her until she dropped hers.

"Been staying with us awhile," Ada went on as if no one had spoken a word, gesturing with the juice jug in her hand. "Building a cabin down the lake. We told him he didn't have to do that, he had a home right here at the West Wind long as he wanted it, but he wouldn't hear of it. Said he needed a new home now that he's back, and went right to it. Handy as anything, he is. Wait till you see it, honey."

"Stop waving that juice around, woman, and pour the damned stuff," Fergie muttered.

"Why, he's done a lot with this place," Ada went on, ignoring Fergie and pouring juice into four squat glasses that matched the strawberry design of the jug. "If it hadn't been for him, the place would've fallen in on—"

"No need for that now," Fergie cut in. "You gonna cook breakfast or do I have to go down to Pinewood for one of them McBiscuit things?"

Maj caught the look that passed between Ada and Fergie. It wasn't anger; it wasn't reproachful. It was silent communication with honest understanding. God, how she loved these two, and how she loved knowing how much they loved each other. For all the gruffness Fergie displayed, and all the ignoring of her husband Ada seemed to show, none of it had dimmed the glow of their regard for each other. If only every couple in the world could experience that kind of closeness. Maj felt a stab of regret in the pit of her stomach for a moment.

"Junk food. Did you hear The Man?" Ada threw up her hands in despair. She always called him "The Man" when speaking to others. "The minute those gold arches went up, he started complaining. He'd nohow eat one of those things in the morning, or anytime, for that matter . . ."

"I'm on my way now, woman, if you don't start cooking." Fergie was standing, thumbing up the ever-drooping overall strap and heading for his jacket.

"Just sit yourself down and don't get snippy with me, Samuel Ferguson," Ada instructed, "breakfast will be on in a jiffy."

"I'll help," Maj offered, and started for the refrigerator.

"You will not," Ada stopped her. "You just sit and visit with Noah and The Man."

Maj knew better than to argue with Ada. Small but feisty, that's what Granddad always called her. She took her coffee and set it down on the square table, then dragged up a red painted curved-back chair. She ran her hand over the wood tabletop, feeling the smoothness of years of use and scrubbing, and the dark lines from knife cuts and rings from hot casseroles.

A cat the color of butterscotch announced his entrance into the kitchen with a guttural meow.

"Morning, Clawed." Ada greeted the cat as if it were another member of the family.

Clawed curled around Ada's good leg till she gave him a bit of bacon. Showing gratefulness, he chewed the bacon with his eyes closed, then jumped up onto Noah and curled up in a comfortable ball in his lap, lapsing into a contented purr.

Maj felt another pang of jealousy in her chest. She'd never seen this cat before, but watching him and the old couple she adored interacting so easily with this stranger, Noah Decker, made her feel out of touch, as if she'd lost something dear.

"Where'd you learn about airplanes?" Noah asked, breaking into her thoughts. He stroked the cat and scratched its ears in a way that told her he'd done it at least a hundred times before.

Maj looked at him and felt shyer than usual, yet not tongue-tied. Butterflies had already started tumbling inside her, and while she wanted to dismiss them to unaccustomed altitude and sharp air, she knew those weren't the only reasons she was feeling unsettled.

She drew in a short breath. "You mean like yours?" When he nodded, she continued. "Up

41

here. You know Buss Bird over on Sixth Lake? Friend of Granddad's. Mr. Bird gave me my second ride over the Adirondacks. He showed me little lakes that no human had ever seen from the ground. I felt like I'd been flown to another planet."

Noah smiled appreciatively. "I've felt like that. I tried to get to one of those lakes once. I wanted to be the first human to swim in it. Never made it, but that's okay. I really didn't want to.

"Why not?" Maj asked, interested.

"Because then that would be one less spot left truly wild. We've already lost too much of that in this world as it is."

Maj watched Noah as he spoke. She'd thought he had a brashness about him, rather like her father and Jack, and that had set her on edge. Yet here he was in Ada's kitchen, flirting with her as if she were a girl and her soaking it up.

He stroked the cat with a gentleness that belied his large hands, and talked about leaving a lake untouched by human steps. They love him, even the cat loves him, she observed, and he honestly loves them. She could feel it. She was fascinated. And fearful. No apparent reason for the fear, but nonetheless she felt it.

"Where are you from?" Noah asked.

"I've been living in Manhattan."

"Speaking of another planet," he laughed lightly. When she didn't rise to the remark, he added, "What, no defense of the big city and all it has to offer?"

"Not me," Maj said, relaxing into her chair. "Should I?"

"That's what usually happens if I say something disparaging about New York City. Same thing with Los Angeles."

"Do you often say disparaging things about Los Angeles?"

"I guess I can't say too much. I lived there for more years than I should have."

"Then you're just visiting here, too?"

"No, I'm here to stay. Right back where I started from."

"You were born here?"

"Not too far away. Lake Placid. You?"

Maj twirled her coffee mug. "Rochester."

Noah gave her a level gaze. "And we've established you're just visiting."

A silence fell among them. Fergie tilted back his head and downed his orange juice in one gulp. "Not much'll be left wild like that if it keeps up around here like it's going," he said, setting the glass down hard on the table.

Maj looked up. "Why? What's going on around here?" She watched Fergie's frown deepen.

"First it's flat hotels—motels they call them—and then it's them damned gold arch things, and the next thing you know it's a shopping center—outlet mall they call it. Place is turning

43

into a goddamned Disney World."

"Watch your language," Ada chided Fergie.

"That's progress," Maj said evenly. "It's happened everywhere. There's no stopping it."

"Progress!" Fergie boomed. "Progress, my foot! It's ruination. It's ripping down the trees, and covering up deer feeding meadows with black tar. Parking lots for all the damned cars that flow up here. Everybody's selling out. Big money to be had, they think. Shafer's Drugstore is now some big-name pharmacy that sells garden tools at discount. Danbury's having a helluva time keeping his old hardware store going because of it. The Sugar Bowl's gone, you know, where your granddad took you for those chocolate sodas you liked. Had to make room for a supermarket. Everything in it's too perfect, all lined up like ducks in a shooting gallery. Hardly know anybody that works there anymore. I tell you, it's a crime, that's what it is."

"Watch your blood pressure," Ada soothed him without turning from the stove.

"And you can blame the whole damned destruction on Gerald Morris." Fergie ignored Ada's admonition.

"Who's Gerald Morris?" Maj asked.

Noah's eyes went heavenward. "Now you've done it," he whispered.

Maj looked at him with an unspoken "what?" in her eyes, but she didn't have to wait for the answer. Fergie let loose with a flood of epithets about Gerald Morris throwing his money around like some big hotshot, buying up everything in sight, saying he means to turn everything in the mountains into a big glitzy resort, and everybody'd get rich and live like kings instead of like hicks, the way they'd been doing all their lives.

Well, he'd never get his grubby hands on the West Wind as long as he had breath in his body, Fergie declared, and he didn't care how many millions the son of a bitch offered, and what was wrong with the way they'd been living anyway? It had been good enough for Maj's grandparents and good enough for him and Ada and everybody else around here, and once J. P. Morgan had stayed at the West Wind just the way it was and it was good enough for him, wasn't it? So, who in hell did Morris think he was anyway?

"Breakfast is ready," Ada announced, and set a platter of crisp bacon and steaming pancakes in the center of the table.

"Does this Morris want to buy the West Wind?" Maj asked with concern, taking two pancakes and passing the platter to Fergie.

"Buy it?" Fergie fumed, plunging his fork into a stack of three pancakes and sliding them onto his plate. "Hell no. He wants to steal it! The man's a lousy thief."

He slathered on a scoop of butter. Watching it melt over his pancakes, Maj wondered if she should ask what his cholesterol count was, but then thought better of it.

Ada took a small stoneware pitcher and filled it from a big plastic jug on which was printed PURE ADIRONDACK MAPLE SYRUP, then poured the deep brown liquid over the pancakes on Fergie's plate. She touched his shoulder gently before sitting down opposite him. She sent a troubled look to Maj, who sent one full of questions back to her.

Noah set down his fork and steepled his fingers over his plate. "The West Wind hasn't enjoyed the halcyon days it once did, as I'm sure you have determined," he began, looking squarely at Maj. "Times change. There's a matter of a hefty bill in back taxes, and Morris has bid on the property for payment of what's owed. There hasn't been enough money here to offset his bid, and, well, I'm afraid it's only a matter of time before he'll get the place. He's offered on several occasions to buy it . . ."

"Over my dead body," Fergie muttered. "We're staying put."

"Well, now, if we have to move, we have to move," Ada said quietly, but she kept her eyes on her plate and absently moved a piece of bacon around with her fork.

"Move? What do you mean move?" Maj's voice cracked, and wondered how it was Noah Decker knew more about the West Wind's plight than she did. The notion rankled her.

"If Morris takes the place, he has made it clear there will be no room for Fergie and Ada to be here," Noah answered for them. "He's tried to convince them that this will be in their best interests. He says he'll remove their financial burdens and give them enough for the property as a pension. He's even thinking of building a senior citizens' home in the village."

"Pension." Fergie slammed down his fork. "The way Henry and I worked this arrangement, we had no need for a pension. We planned we'd always have the place, always live here, always keep it going. Somebody in the family would always have a home here, and an income, and no way in hell will I let that bastard take it away from us." He rubbed his chest and frowned, then took Ada's hand. "And we will not live in any old folks' home. We'd rather be dead than that."

Ada looked up quickly into his eyes, then back down to her plate.

Concern leapt into Maj's eyes, and Noah placed a slightly restraining hand on her arm.

"It's not his heart, don't worry. He's just anxious," he said quietly. "We try to work it off, though, don't we, Fergie?" Noah tried to lighten the mood.

"More pancakes, honey?" Ada passed the platter to Maj.

"No thanks, Ada," Majesty managed to say

through a gulp of coffee. "I'm not much of a breakfast eater."

"Well, bein' up here will change that'," Fergie vowed. "That big city livin's what kept you the skinny little thing you are."

"Oh, Fergie, I'm not skinny." Majesty smiled at him, then felt the tops of her ears burn when she caught Noah's frank appraisal.

"Gotta get some color in those cheeks of yours instead of that rouge stuff you came in here with last night. Good old Adirondack air will do it 'fore long. You can count on that." Fergie scraped up all the syrup on his plate with a last piece of pancake.

Majesty turned her face toward the window to cover the heat of flush that spread up from her throat at the mention of her color, or lack of it.

"Samuel, now, you stop that. You're embarrassing the girl!" Ada scolded. "Don't let it bother you, Maj. He don't mean no harm." She gave an affectionate pat to Majesty's cheek.

"If I let you have your way, Fergie, I'd be a blimp inside of a month, or at the very least look like a lumberjack!" Maj chided him with good nature.

"Got something against the way lumberjacks are built?" Noah asked with a somber expression.

Majesty's smile faded, and she looked toward Ada and Fergie for some sort of assistance.

Ada broke in with a throaty laugh. "Noah's got

the sawmill and lumber company just outside of Pinewood."

A question she'd had all morning came back into Maj's mind, and she could no longer contain it. "What do you have to do with all this, Mr. Decker? What's your interest in the West Wind?"

"Noah's our friend, honey," Ada said with affection.

"I can see that," Maj said with a flare of temper, then fixed softer eyes on her beloved Ada. "But how do you know him? He seems to be a fixture here. What do you know about him?"

"As I said, Noah's in the lumber business, dear, down in the village. He's been helping out here, fixing the roof, and those old water pipes upstairs."

"The lumber business." Maj thought for a moment. "Is it possible he has more than a neighborly interest in the West Wind himself?"

"Maj," Fergie said firmly, "Noah's our friend, as Ada said. His only interest's been in helping us. Don't even think it's any more than that."

"Excuse me," Noah spoke brightly. "I'm still here, in case you've forgotten. If there's something you want to know about my interests, Maj, just ask me."

Maj turned hard eyes on Noah. She didn't know this man at all, but he'd certainly insinuated himself into the Fergusons' lives. Even the cat trusted him. There was no way for her to be sure he wasn't just as devious as this Gerald Morris they'd been describing.

"Your business must be good in these difficult economic times, Mr. Decker. You own an airplane."

"It's worse than that. I own two and fly three. And I wish you'd call me Noah. It would bring this conversation back to the friendly way in which it started."

"Three airplanes. I see. Seems a bit extravagant to me."

"One of them's always breaking down, and I have to have at least one I can count on at all times."

"The quicker to check on every corner of your corporation's empire, I suppose?"

"Corporation? Hardly. I'm a volunteer emergency medical technician. Flying over this terrain is a way of keeping track of campers and hikers."

Ada perked up. "Since Noah's been here, there's been a lot less people being lost or hurt bad."

Maj felt a little sorry for having been so harsh about the airplanes. Still, she had no reason to trust this man as completely as the Fergusons appeared to.

"And how long have you been here?" She refused to seem on friendly terms by using his first name, so she didn't use any.

"I was away for all of my adult life," he said,

smiling, "but then I saw the error of my ways and came back. This makes my second full year here this time."

"And in that time, Mr. Decker, you've managed to acquire a lumber business and three airplanes. You're rather enterprising." Now Maj was surprising herself at her temerity. Where was it coming from?

"You give me much too much credit, *Miss* Wilde," Noah said shortly. "I inherited the lumber mill and an old tail-dragger airplane from my father, and one was donated to the local medical team. I maintain it. I bought the Supercub used, my major expenditure the first year. The lot for my cabin is on family property as well. In fact, I've been accused of being spoiled and having everything handed to me. If it hadn't been for Gerald Morris and his tarnished reputation, I'm sure I would have suffered much more maligning from the Adirondackers than I have."

Noah took a deep breath and continued. "As for the West Wind, my repair work here is barely enough payment for the temporary roof over my head, leaky though it is, and good home cooking. Regardless of how things appear to you, I came back here empty-handed. Fergie and Ada decided I wasn't a derelict or a crook, and took me in my first night at Big Moose. They've considered me a friend, a happy event for which I feel truly honored.

51

"And now that you know my life story, I really hope there is nothing more you care to ask me, because that is the longest speech I've had to make since I was a flight instructor in the Marine Corps." He gave her as even an eye as she gave him.

Knowing she'd just been soundly put in her place, and feeling almost as if she'd deserved it, Maj relaxed in her chair and looked at the old couple.

"I'm sorry . . . Noah. It's just that, well, these two people mean so much to me. I'm concerned that others might take advantage of them. Perhaps I came on too strongly. I can see now that you didn't deserve the inference in my questions."

"Apology accepted, Maj." He held out his right hand. She smiled and grasped it in a gesture of truce. Once again he held it longer than necessary. "Isn't this where we came in?" He grinned.

She gave a small fleeting smile and withdrew her hand. "I'd like a more detailed explanation of things, if you feel like talking about it," she said toward Fergie and Ada.

"All right, honey," Fergie answered, "but can it wait a day or two? It's just good having you here again. Like old times. Let's enjoy that and let you relax a bit. You've been having some tough times yourself."

Maj laughed. "Agreed. I feel like wandering around my old haunts anyway. I'm glad to see most of the cottages are still standing. And the carriage barn." She cleared the table and ran water for the dishes.

"You go ahead, honey. I'll take care of those." Ada patted her back.

Maj turned and hugged Ada. She felt her friend slump slightly toward her and, when she leaned back, saw the tears in her old gray eyes.

Embarrassed, Ada fumbled for her handkerchief and hastily wiped them away. "You've been sorely missed, my girl," she said quietly. "It feels good to have you back."

"Me, too," Maj said, and kissed the pale cheek.

Chapter Three

Outside the Coffee Cup diner in the mountain hamlet of Pinewood, Noah dropped some coins into a pay phone and dialed eleven numbers. As his call went through, he shrugged out of his leather jacket and slung it, hanging from his index finger, over one shoulder, and leaned against the diner wall. The morning was warming, and the climbing sun felt good in contrast to the still-cold breeze he felt against his blue chambray shirt.

He let the phone ring twelve times. No answer.

He frowned, and stood up straight. He took in a long breath and squared his shoulders as if preparing to do a nasty job. Then he slapped the switchhook, retrieved his coins, dropped them back into the slot, and dialed another eleven numbers. At the second ring he heard the click at the other end of the line.

"Adrienne Blackshear," came the efficient voice in his ear.

Noah paused for a moment. "Blackshear, is it now?" he said more acidly than he meant to.

"Who is this?" Adrienne replied crisply.

"Noah Decker, your husband, remember me?"

"What do you want, Noah?" Adrienne's voice carried irritation clearly.

Noah pictured Adrienne seated in her high-tech chair behind her brass and glass desk in her glass-walled corner office on the top floor of Blackshear Associates, the construction and interior decorating firm founded by her father. Beyond the windows the Los Angeles smog would lie like a gritty dark cloud.

She'd be wearing a shell-pink silk blouse tucked firmly enough into a pale gray skirt to reveal the lace of her satin bra; her slim legs would be crossed at the ankles at the side of the chair; her gray suede pumps would be poised on the thick pale carpet like a ballerina. Her perfectly shaded ash-blond hair would be swept back and caught by a pink and gray silk hair twist, set off by perfect gold earrings from Fortunoff's.

"I haven't heard from Kimmie lately, and I was wondering if you have." Noah tried to sound as friendly as he could bring himself to be.

"The United States postal service probably isn't aware people live in that godforsaken place you've chosen to run to," Adrienne said icily. "But give them time. Once they bring back the Pony Express, or should I say moose express, perhaps you'll receive some mail, at the very least a notice about a quilting bee or a carnival."

"You have no idea how it delights me to hear you haven't changed a bit in the five years since I've seen you, my dear," Noah said sarcastically.

"Nor you," Adrienne bit off. "Jumping out of airplanes, living in caves. Everyone here is still astounded that you gave up your vice presidency in the company."

"I'm building a cabin in the mountains, not living in a cave." He sighed wearily. Interesting how a conversation with Adrienne could be the same even if it happened only once a year. "And you know that anyone who really knows me understands why I left, why I came back east."

"To your roots, of course. And the hillbillies."

Noah chose to ignore her biting remark and return to the reason he felt compelled to call her. The operator interrupted, asking for more money.

"Bill it to this number," Adrienne said in her superior tone. "The sound of coins jangling into my ear is intolerable. I know you do it on purpose, Noah. You could have used your credit card, but of course you had to do one more thing to irritate me."

"I gave up credit cards long ago."

"Right about the time you gave me up, no doubt."

"I didn't give you up, Adrienne," Noah said as he had so many times before. "We've been over this a dozen times. It was natural for us to part. Our lives didn't mesh. Or I should say my life-style didn't mesh with yours no matter how much you and your father tried to manipulate me."

"We gave you everything you could ever want," Adrienne sniffed. "Everyone thought we were the perfect couple. *I* thought we were the perfect couple. What else brought us together, if not the plans we had for the company?"

"Lust brought us together, and you know it, Adrienne."

"You had that before we were married," she snapped, "so why did we bother to get married?"

"Have you talked with Kimmie lately?" Noah wasn't interested in continuing old conflicts.

The only thing he and Adrienne had in common was their daughter, or actually the conception of their daughter. There the commonality ended. Noah had known the child had been in the way, at least where Adrienne was concerned.

She'd failed to mention when they were engaged that she never wanted to have children. He'd always wanted two.

He'd caught her in time to save the baby from being aborted, and Adrienne never let him forget it. Thinking back over it too many times, he felt he'd probably been unfair to both Adrienne and Kimberly, and felt responsible for how his wife had treated their daughter. But he'd have sold his soul to the devil to get her to have the baby.

In a way, he had.

He'd promised her, and he fulfilled that promise, to play the role of her husband in public the way she wanted it—dashing, handsome, a vice president in her father's company. He'd hated it. He'd taken on the private-dwelling construction arm of the company and, to Adrienne's constant aggravation, tended to spend a lot of time with the builders, masons, electricians, and plumbers. Lowbrow, she called him. And he hadn't cared.

"No, I haven't heard from her," Adrienne said impatiently. "I've been traveling a lot lately. The board held its annual meeting in Acapulco, and Daddy wanted me to stay on a few days with him there. I sent her a check almost two months ago, and she hasn't had the courtesy to even write me a thank-you note."

"How gauche of her." God, how it irked him that at forty-five years of age she still called her father Daddy.

"Well, no matter what you think, she's rude. And you've never been any help with her."

Adrienne launched into her usual speech about giving Kimberly everything money could buy, and the girl was not grateful for her privileges. Everything money could buy had meant stuffy boarding schools and acquiring perfect manners. Anything to get her out of the way, he guessed, and he still chastised himself for not bucking Adrienne on some of the decisions she'd made about their child. He always wondered how much Kimmie sensed her mother's detachment.

Silently he let Adrienne get out her barbs. After all, it was her nickel.

Across the street he saw Fergie's thirty-year-old red Ford pickup pull up in front of Danbury's hardware store. The pickup's paint was dull, but not the pride he knew Fergie felt for it. It probably hadn't reached fifty thousand miles on the odometer yet. Fergie eased himself out of the driver's side, and Noah saw Majesty Wilde jump out of the passenger side.

Adrienne was still haranguing as Noah watched Maj walk out into the street, shade her eyes with her hand and look around, then up toward No Name Mountain. She'd been at the West Wind almost a week, and he hadn't seen much of her. They'd passed each other in the kitchen a couple of mornings, exchanged polite greetings, but that was it. No real conversation. Hard to believe they lived together.

He caught himself at his last thought. They lived in the same lodge, that's what he meant.

He supposed she still didn't completely trust him, even though he'd been spending more time at the lodge puttering with Fergie and fixing the dock than he had down at his own cabin. Construction on that had virtually come to a halt since he met Majesty Wilde.

And he'd been wondering a lot about her. Was she married? Did she have kids? She had an athletic gait to her, he noted, watching her stride toward the lot where the Sugar Bowl used to be. Her jeans made her look leggy. He liked that. She wore a black turtleneck and a pale blue sweatshirt that he knew had SAVE THE ADIRONDACK RAILWAY on it because he had a red one just like it. Ada must have given it to her as a gift, just as she had given him the one he had. Maj's hair blew in the breeze, catching the sun's rays on its loose waves that made it look like a golden cloud settling around her shoulders.

She and Fergie wrapped an arm around each

other's waist and headed into Danbury's. Noah felt a strong urge to catch up with them, but there was still Adrienne droning in his ear.

"Well, are you going to say anything to her about that?"

"About what?" Noah snapped to Adrienne's question.

"About Kimberly's idea of staying in Saratoga this summer and working."

"I don't see anything wrong with that. She's nineteen."

"She wants to work as a waitress at the race-track! A waitress, for God's sake! Haven't you been listening?"

For a split second Noah wanted to tell Adrienne the truth about what he'd been doing while she was talking. Fortunately he thought better of that notion. "It's good, honest work, and I think she should be encouraged to do it."

"You would."

"Look, Adrienne, you know I'd love to stand here in the street like this and chat with you all day, but I have some shopping to do."

"Oh, in need of a new ax, are you, dear?"

"How'd you guess?" he answered with a grin he knew she probably sensed. "I'll try Kimmie again later. If she calls you, will you tell her I've been trying to get in touch with her?"

"I'm not sure I will talk to her. I'm off to Chicago in the morning. Not sure when I'll be back, and . . . well, you understand."

"Oh, yeah, Adrienne, I've always understood. Don't concern yourself with Kimmie. I'll get to her. Have a nice trip."

"Noah?"

"Yes."

"Are you seeing anyone?"

"No more than usual."

"Don't be flip," Adrienne snapped. "I just wondered, that's all."

"I didn't know you cared."

"I don't!"

"Then why ask? I never ask you."

"It isn't any of your business. Some marriage this has been."

"It was once, Adrienne, it was once."

Adrienne was silent a moment. Noah heard her let out a small sigh, then, "Goodbye Noah. Say hello to Kimberly for me if you reach her. Remind her about the check." Click.

Noah turned and hung up the phone slowly. He stared at it a moment, then turned and crossed the street toward Danbury's.

"How about a get-reacquainted tour of the Adirondacks this morning?" Noah asked Maj brightly when they came out of Danbury's. She carried one small bag and Fergie dropped a green-handled hoe and matching garden rake into the bed of his truck.

"In Fergie's pickup?" Maj asked, skepticism evident.

"No, in my airplane. It'll take the high peaks better." He grinned at Fergie.

"You mean one of your little planes?" Maj asked carefully.

"Small aircraft, yes," Noah said nodding, "but there's room for a wing and an engine. And two seats, of course."

"I'm well aware of the components of most airplanes. I just don't think I'll have time today. Maybe some other time."

"Go on and go with him," Fergie urged. "You'll get to see parts of these mountains no human foot has ever stepped on."

"Now, Fergie, don't push the city girl if she's afraid," Noah threw over his shoulder as he turned to walk back to his own pickup.

"Who said anything about being afraid?" Maj shot toward his back, hands planted firmly on her hips.

Noah spun around, a wide grin lighting his face. "Great! Then it's a date. See you at the West Wind dock in one hour." He whistled as he crossed the street, then jumped into his blue pickup.

Maj could still hear his whistle as he drove past them.

At the West Wind dock Noah handed Majesty up and into the right-hand seat of the high-wing Supercub. He pulled her seat belt snugly across her middle, then settled his long frame into the left side of the two-seater and buckled his own belt. The gentle bobbing of the light aircraft as it rested on aluminum pontoons in the water gave Maj's stomach a surge of queasiness.

"If something happens to me on this ride, Fergie, keep the Mustang," she called out with a nervous laugh as Fergie closed her door down.

Noah switched the key on, and with a cough the propeller started to turn until it was spinning almost invisibly, and the engine purred like a well-oiled lawn mower. Needles jumped and held on the instrument panel. Noah wound a small lever over their heads. Maj remembered it being called the trim tab, and she likened it to winding a toy top. He used the radio to speak to someone; Maj could not guess who, since there was no control tower to be seen.

They taxied out onto the lake, scattering a flotilla of ducks into a great flurry of splashing and flapping wings. Maj looked wistfully out of the thin Plexiglas window on her side and sent a nervous wave to Fergie who stood on the dock grinning widely and waving his extended arm vigorously.

To be nervous in an airplane was new to Maj. She'd grown up with planes, flown in them to vacations with Jack. She'd never been afraid to fly in her life. She sent a cursory glance toward Noah. Maybe it wasn't the aircraft she was afraid of. Maybe it was the pilot.

And maybe she'd been away from the mountains too long. Living in Manhattan gave her an ingrained distrust of everyone. Remembering how it had been at Big Moose when she was a child, she knew how relaxed and trusting her family had been about everyone and everything.

They idled at the end of the lake for a few minutes as Noah turned this dial and twisted that lever and tapped yet another instrument, pulled back and pushed forward on the half wheel in front of him, and tested the pedals under his feet.

"What are you doing?" Maj asked in a shaky voice over the vibration of the engine.

"Flight check, making sure everything works," Noah responded, donning a pair of gold-rimmed sunglasses.

"It does, doesn't it?" she came back urgently.

Noah was silent for a short moment that

seemed to Maj like an eternity. "Mmm-hmm," he responded at last. "Ready?"

"Oh, sure," she mustered, watching him and thinking how much he would remind her mother of John Wayne in *The Fighting Seabees*. She hoped he didn't have a streak of barnstorming in him.

The airplane surged forward, gaining speed as it moved toward the pine grove that rimmed the end of the lake. Straightening up on the pontoons, it lifted quickly and climbed rapidly, just skimming the tops of the pines. Maj's stomach sank along with the land that fell away below them. Rugged mountaintops studded with huge gray boulders and dark trees loomed on either side of them.

"Is this as high as it will go?" she asked over the engine's humming vibration, not certain if she really wanted the answer or not.

"Oh, no, it'll make several thousand feet, but you can't see anything closely from up there except an occasional Canada goose. I want to make sure you can see a lot. It's a great day for a ride. Look at that sky! Not a cloud in it."

"Not a cloud," she reiterated in a low voice, eyeing the walls of stone and trees on both sides of the airplane. "I feel as if I'm flying down a hallway. How do you avoid the errant mountain that may spring up ahead now and then? Or geese caught in the engine? Or, God forbid, another airplane?"

"I stay in my own lane," he said, looking around.

"I'll try to be comforted by that," she replied, staring straight ahead.

He smiled toward her. "You're not really scared, are you? I thought you'd flown a lot." She didn't answer and kept her eyes riveted in front of her. "I'd think anyone who's ever ridden in a New York City cab wouldn't be afraid of any moving vehicle." Still no answer. "Majesty, you'll never see anything if you continue to look straight ahead. Anything worth seeing is out your right window — and directly to your left," he added with a teasing smile.

She turned her head carefully toward her left shoulder and saw his dazzling smile beneath the dark glasses. Then she turned back to the front windscreen.

"This thing is made of nothing more than fabric and aluminum, isn't it?" She worked at keeping her voice even.

"That, and a few other things."

"How old is it?"

"Around forty years."

"Is it safe at that age?"

"About as safe as anything over forty can be."

He grinned, then quickly checked the instruments.

She looked at him as if she knew he'd meant that remark to be more personal than mechanical. He thought about asking her the same question. Not that her age would matter to him. He was quite suddenly aware that he wanted to know everything about Majesty Wilde, everything there was to know, or at least what she was willing to share.

This inquisitiveness about a woman was alien to Noah. He didn't remember feeling this way about Adrienne, and he knew he never had with the three or four women he'd had short affairs with since they'd been separated. Since he'd returned to the Adirondacks, he'd been singleminded about building his cabin and maintaining his airplanes, too busy to give any thought to women anymore.

"When was the last time you flew over these mountains?" He knew he was fishing now.

"When I was a kid," she said distantly, "with Granddad and Mr. Bird. That seems like it happened in somebody else's lifetime."

"I know the feeling," he said, banking the plane toward down left.

Maj grabbed the hold bar in front of her.

"You are rather afraid, aren't you?" He didn't tease her, just observed in a matter-of-fact way.

68

"I was fourteen when Granddad let me take over the controls of his beloved Stearman. I loved that old bi-wing, too."

"That thing was probably less sturdy and safe than this one."

Maj looked over at him. "You're right, I suppose. I guess I didn't know enough to be scared in those days. Now that I think of it, the wings were made of wood, and the rest was cloth."

"You're right. Cedar, in some cases, and cotton."

"Granddad was like a kid with a new bike when he bought it from some barnstormer he knew. Seemed like he took forever restoring it. It was red and silver. He called me the Red Baroness that day . . ." Her voice trailed off.

"Those were uncomplicated times, weren't they?" he put in, cocking an eyebrow toward her.

"Yes, sort of between a lot, and before anything else."

"What was that, 1960 . . . ?"

"No 1954." She gave him a sidelong glance and watched him mentally calculating the math. "I'm fifty-one. You could have asked me outright how old I am."

He grinned sheepishly at being caught. "I thought women were touchy about admitting their age."

"I'm not."

He smiled again. That was refreshing, guile-less of her.

"What about you? Are you touchy about your age?" she asked.

"Only in that I wish I wasn't forty-nine. Thirty-nine would be nice, wouldn't it?"

She didn't respond for a moment, then, "It wasn't any better than now."

He caught a note of fleeting sadness in her voice and responded brightly, "I'll take that as a compliment."

"Why should you?" Maj looked at him inquis-itively.

"Didn't you just say something to the effect that it doesn't get any better than this?" He ges-tured toward the open sky, the passing moun-tains, trees, and lakes below, and then toward the two of them inside the cabin.

She smiled. "A tiny bit conceited of you, I think."

He laughed. "Accurate self-appraisal, I think. Admit it, you're loving this."

Maj snapped her head around. "Do you know Nan Doyle?"

"No, should I?"

"Maybe not," Maj said, laughing, and came back to his comment. "I'll admit I don't remember seeing this part of the mountain range before."

"Well, your Adirondack education is sorely lacking. Best way to see all of these mountains is from up here."

"I usually prefer to leave this location to the birds."

"You have flown on a jet, haven't you?" He looked over at her.

"Of course."

"Well?"

"Well, I was surrounded by steel and other people. Are you paying attention to your driving?"

He grimaced at the last word. "Of course. I'm a good pilot. Between the Marine Corps and private flying I've logged more than ten thousand hours without so much as a ding."

"I'm impressed."

"You should be."

"I meant that."

"Only time I ever got in trouble was when I had to land a Waco in a cornfield south of Old Forge."

"How could you do that on pontoons?" She gave him a doubtful frown.

"It was winter and I had skis on the airplane. Of course, there was the time over in Fulton when I was forced to land on a highway during a stunt show."

"Stunt show?" Maj asked with a catch in her

71

voice. "You're telling me I'm currently riding with a stunt pilot?"

"Un-hunh."

She grabbed the door handle as if about to take leave of the aircraft. "Why were you forced to land on a highway? What about cars?"

"The drivers knew enough to pull over. I mean, if you saw an airplane coming at you, you'd think about pulling over, wouldn't you?"

She looked at him as if any response would be a stupid one. "Did you do that for the heck of it, or was there a method to your madness?"

"Had a lady wing-walker strapped up top who got sick and passed out. If I hadn't landed I'd have lost her."

What could Maj respond to that? "Un-hunh." She looked at him askance.

"Un-hunh. You don't believe me, do you?"

"I'm trying to," she said evenly.

He stared straight ahead, then pulled back on the wheel and the nose of the aircraft pointed up into the clear blue sky as several rugged mountaintops rolled away beneath them.

Maj relaxed a little. He was right, she was actually enjoying the ride. She didn't know where her fear had come from at first, or why it did. The mountains below them now looked as if they were covered in a quilt of green velvet in the crisp spring morning. Every now and then a

72

small hidden lake emerged like a blue-white rough-cut diamond in the dense forests. The ride with Buss Bird came back to her.

"It truly is breathtaking, isn't it?" she observed, more to herself than to him.

"Sure is," he agreed. "Most out-of-staters think only of the city when they think of New York. I wish I could show everybody this wonderful wilderness. Great fishing and swimming in those lakes down there. And the animals. Black bears, and deer, and coyotes, fox—did you know we may have more kinds of snakes than any other state?"

"I didn't, and I'm not overjoyed that you told me that." She spun her head toward him to see if he was serious about the snake fact.

He laughed, and she was also surprised by how much she liked the deep, genuine sound of it. She ran her eyes over his form in the seat behind the half wheel. From his leather-booted foot resting on a rudder pedal, she let her eyes travel up his pant leg, where the soft, faded denim stretched over a long, muscled calf and thigh, and molded to his slim hip. For a moment her mind continued around his hip, and she pictured the fabric over his trim, muscled buttocks. She blinked her eyes and jerked her head forward. Nan would be proud of her for even thinking this!

Noah hummed to himself. He was clearly a happy man lost in the joy of piloting the small aircraft over his beloved mountains.

Slowly Majesty drew her head around to assess him again. His jawline was sharply angled, and she noticed the pale gray streaks brushed back along his hair at his temple.

All he needed was a soft dark cap with a peak and a white chiffon scarf and he'd look every bit like the romantic Dennis Morgan in one of her mother's favorite old movies, *God Is My Co-Pilot*. She smiled and tilted her head with warm amusement.

Suddenly the airplane banked sharply to the right and the nose dropped. Yanked from her thoughts, Majesty shrieked, grabbing the top of the instrument panel to hold on.

"What's happening?" she yelled over the engine's roar.

"Just wanted you to see the huge herd of deer down there in that meadow." He pointed past her and out the window.

"You could have warned me before you tipped us out of the sky!"

"No time. Just spotted them myself."

With a sudden sharpness the engine stopped, the propeller wound slowly down until it barely turned, and the airplane was silent. All Majesty could hear was the light sound of wind whistling outside the aircraft, and the thumping of her heart in her ears inside. Terror gripped at her stomach and choked off her breath.

"Are . . . are we going to crash?"

Noah laughed. "No, I just cut the engine so we could get down a little closer and not scare the deer too much."

"Well, you scared the bejeebers out of me! Start it up again," she ordered.

"Stop worrying and take a look, and then we'll get up and out of here."

She did look, and never had she seen so many deer together in her life. They grazed docilely in the meadow like a herd of cows, their white tails flicking downward as they ate, or straight up with their finely tuned ears as they became aware of the aircraft overhead.

Noah reengaged the engine and pulled the plane's nose up. They soared up and over the trees like a kingbird in search of insects.

Majesty caught her breath. "How can you do that, turn it off and on like that?"

"It's just like a car."

She looked at him, doubting the validity of those words.

"I think I'll have to give you more flying lessons so you won't be so concerned about the performance of the machine."

"I won't be here long enough for flying lessons."

Noah raised his eyebrows slightly, and leveled off the airplane. Suddenly a tiger cat scrambled out from under the right seat and flew into Majesty's lap.

"What in the world?" she shrieked.

"Orville! Well, you sly dog, er, sorry—cat!" Noah laughed. "Always sneaking a ride!"

"This is your cat?" Majesty asked, incredulous.

"Well, he eats my food." Noah reached over and scratched the cat's ears.

"And he's not afraid to fly?"

"Orville? Hah! He's not afraid of much of anything. Found him in here one day about a year ago. I was leveling off over Indian Lake, and out from under the seat came this tiger who nonchalantly climbed up beside me and went to sleep. He adopted me, and I've been with him ever since." Orville curled up in Maj's lap and made himself comfortable. "Although something tells me he's considering defecting."

Maj scratched Orville's ears. "Does he fly often?"

"Yes, usually uninvited. Got a lengthy frequent flyer record. Travels light, you'll notice."

She smiled. "Yes, although I suppose if I look, I'll find a box of cat litter under the seat."

"If you do, after that last turn and the scare I put into both of you, I think you'd find a sign over it saying *occupado!*"

Laughing, she stroked Orville's streaked fur, and the sound of the cat's purr rivaled in contentment that of the airplane's engine. Two old people, two cats. Noah Decker was racking up a few pluses, she calculated.

Maj watched as the Fulton chain of lakes spread out below them.

"You'll be back for another vacation, won't you?" He looked over at her. She thought his voice sounded almost hopeful that she'd return. He scanned to the left below the aircraft.

"Most likely not," she answered. "At least not to stay for any length of time."

"But what about the Fergusons?"

"Yes, I know. I'm hoping they'll sell the West Wind. It's too much for them now. I'm sure they could find a nice place to live in a town where they'll have people around them."

He snapped his head back to her, a frown creasing his forehead. "Strikes me the person they want most around them is you, and the place they'd most like to be is the West Wind. I haven't seen them this happy since I've known them, and you're the reason."

She let a glance skim over him, then looked out over the mountains. "I know they're glad to see me, and I'm thrilled to see them. But the place can't support them anymore. It can't even support itself. I can't afford to help them out. It's just not practical to try to keep the place. There's no income now, and it doesn't look as if there ever will be again."

"Not practical," Noah said dully, and banked the airplane left to start the return over a different route. "Ever think of leaving Manhattan? Or wouldn't that be practical either?"

She stared hard at him for a moment, then answered. "I have . . . expenses. I have to work, have to keep my job."

"What do you do?"

"I'm an administrative assistant in an advertising agency."

"Do you love your work?"

"Love it?" She thought for a brief moment. "It's all right."

"Just all right?"

She didn't look at him. "It's a necessity."

"What about the rewards? Pride? Satisfaction?" When she didn't answer, he went on. "Now, up here in the Adirondacks, everything is a reward. The work is pleasurable, a joy."

Maj could hear Nan saying, *You must bring joy and pleasure into your life every day.*

She thought for a moment, absently stroking Orville's fur and wondering what it could feel like to know absolutely that you love where you are and what you're doing.

"You love it up here, don't you?" she observed.

"Best life I've ever had."

"Well, then I'm sure it will always reap rewards for you."

"Not the way people gobble up the land and spoil it all."

"How could they spoil it all? There's so much of it. Look at it!" She swept her hand over the panorama in front of them. "And all those deer we saw, and the other animals you spoke of. They'll always be around."

"We no longer have native wolves, moose, or lynx and other wildcats."

"Why not?"

"Civilization pushed them away." He deliberately flew over a construction crew cutting a wide swath in a mountain in preparation for a new ski tow.

"But skiing is a good way to enjoy the mountains," Maj countered.

"Agreed, as long as there aren't too many ski slopes and too many big hotels. That herd of deer you saw could disappear into thin air."

"Listen, I've heard there are so many deer around that people have seen them wandering through backyards as near to Manhattan as Westchester."

"Ah, the famous 'upstate New York.' Probably took a wrong turn on the thruway on their way to the Catskill Game Farm," he said sarcastically.

"You're overdramatizing the situation, or, at the very least, exaggerating." Her voice took on a sharp edge.

"I don't think so," he replied, tight-lipped.

"It's pretty up here, but I can't imagine droves of city people flocking here for recreation. Not everybody likes to camp out, you know."

Noah's head spun around toward her, and she was glad he wore sunglasses so she couldn't see what was in his eyes. She hadn't meant the words to come out as they had, but it was too late to take them back now.

He turned his head to the front, then picked up the radio microphone. "Piper one nine two three Able Mike returning to Big Moose."

A crackling voice came back over the radio and gave an affirmative response. Noah pushed in on the half wheel, and the aircraft began to descend. Clearly they were of differing opinions at the moment, and the flight and the discussion had come to an end.

Noah set the plane down smoothly until the

pontoons skimmed over the water like skis on snow. They drew toward the shore and he cut the engine, sending the plane toward the dock with a whoosh of waves and rocking it against the wood pilings. Fergie stood in the same spot, waving, as if he'd never left.

Noah took Orville from Maj and helped her out of the plane. She stood on the dock for a moment, her knees quivering and her legs still sensing the engine's vibrations. It took a moment to set her equilibrium straight before she could walk toward Fergie.

"Well, how was it?" Fergie called out to her with a wide grin.

"Fabulous! What an incredibly clear sight from up there!" she called back to him brightly.

"Sight may be clear, but the vision is still clouded," Noah said in a low voice behind her, holding Orville and scratching his ears.

"What?" she spun around.

"Here's your charge, Fergie. I'm off." Noah turned back toward the airplane.

Majesty stood in stunned silence at his curt departure. She wasn't exactly sure how it had happened, but she had made Noah angry with her. Her brow creased.

"Thank you, Noah, for the sight-seeing tour," she said in as friendly a tone as she could.

He didn't say anything as he climbed back

into the Supercub. Fergie and Maj watched the airplane taxi out onto the lake and take off.

"Isn't he something?" Fergie asked proudly.

"Oh, he's something all right," she answered, and headed toward the back porch. *I just can't figure out what yet, that's all.*

Chapter Four

Maj had puttered and poked through drawers and cupboards and closets all week, looked over and repacked old toys, and even spent a couple of evenings putting a one-thousand-piece jigsaw puzzle together with Fergie.

She pored over old photographs and clippings while Ada happily identified this person or that one, the memory of whom escaped Maj. Reading diaries and listening to the old couple spin stories, Maj believed she'd absorbed the history of an era. Her own era as well.

Sharing memories with Ada and Fergie was the purest joy and pleasure she'd experienced in recent memory, and she could tell they loved every minute of it, even the few tears their conversations occasionally evoked. Nan would be proud of all of them, she thought.

In more than one instance Maj wished she

could go back to those times when she was carefree, cared for, and curious about everything. Why did growing older have to mean childlike curiosity disappeared? Yet, during the week at the lodge that's exactly how she felt. Curious. And youthful. Maybe she'd discovered the secret to eternal youth. Be eternally curious, carefree as far as reasonable responsibility would allow, and unconditionally cared for, as she was by Ada and Fergie. She added another ingredient—to unconditionally care for others, as she did for them.

Noah Decker figured in the picture, she had to admit. He laughed in all the right places when they told him a story, and they watched his back when he left the room as if one of their points of light had dimmed. Maj admitted to herself one night, as she sank down into the feather pillows, that he made her feel something, something that only a teenager should feel. As soon as she had it figured out, she'd gain control over it and stop watching his back as closely as Fergie and Ada did.

She'd been so engrossed in seeing everything all over again, touching it all, being a part of it all again, she hadn't wanted to deal with the nervousness she felt when they passed each other in the kitchen in the mornings and engaged in meaningless small talk.

Saturday afternoon, the day before she'd planned to return to Manhattan, Maj walked through the central hall of the lodge on her way to her grandfather's study. That was one of the last places she wanted to poke through. The other was the old carriage barn, but it was padlocked shut and she kept forgetting to ask Fergie to unlock it.

A clunky black phone on a mission oak desk in the lobby rang loud and long, making Maj smile. There was nothing light and sophisticated about that phone or its ring. Everything about it was substantial, just like her life had seemed every summer at West Wind. She picked up the handset and decided to answer as Granddad had taught her.

"Good day. The West Wind Lodge can make it so. May I help you?"

"That is sickening!" came the voice at the other end. "Maj, is that you, or some backwoods version of you?"

"Nan, hi! Yes, it's me. What are you doing?"

"Nursing a sinus headache. I can see yours must have cleared, or . . . you've had sex, haven't you? Tell me everything! Don't spare any erotic detail!" Nan panted heavily into her mouthpiece and, laughing, Maj held the earpiece away at her end.

"Is that all you think about? No, I haven't had sex. What I have had is a great time here with Fergie and Ada and a lodge full of memories and souvenirs."

"Then you should have this god-awful sinus headache."

"Not possible. The air's too clear here. Unless, of course, you're allergic to pine trees, sunshine, dewdrops, the wail of loons . . ."

"Stop, please! If I want flora and fauna, I can go to the Brooklyn Botanical Gardens. Except I'm allergic to some weeds or something they have over there. When are you coming home?"

"Tomorrow," Maj answered, wistfulness evident in her voice. Saying it out loud underscored how relaxed she'd felt all week, how at home she'd been with everything.

"Good."

"Good? Then you've missed me and my woes." Maj laughed.

"No. Yes. I mean, I have missed your company, and I'm dying to tell you the latest in my existence. But, good that you have one more night and the possibility of getting laid."

"Nan!"

"Try not to sound so shocked. I've been telling you this for almost two years. It would do

86

you a world of good. So, have you met any gorgeous hunks of mountain men who want to drag you off to a tent and ravish your body?"

"I don't think so," Maj answered quickly. But a fleeting picture of Noah Decker emerging from the mist her first morning at West Wind flashed into her mind, lingered, then faded.

"You don't *think* so? Ah-ha, then you have met one, haven't you? I knew it, I just knew it." Maj could almost see Nan with the phone cradled between her ear and shoulder while she rubbed her hands together in glee.

"Tons of them." Maj laughed.

"Name them," Nan ordered.

"Abe Danbury at the hardware store."

"Sounds honest, but old."

"Hovering around eighty, I'd say."

"Older men can be nice, but as far as sex goes, that may be stretching a bit. No pun intended. Go on," Nan urged.

"Mmm, let's see." Maj stalled, not wanting to mention Noah's name, as if saying it would make Nan think his presence was auspicious. Or was she worried she might think so herself? "Oh, yes, Bobby Maynard at the Super Duper."

"Uh-hunh, I can tell that's a sixteen-year-old checkout clerk. Probably has a cute little butt.

87

Younger men can be nice, but can get you into a lot of trouble. Stop holding back."

"That's about it. Oh, except for Fergie's friend Noah."

"Noah." Nan cogitated. "Nice, but sounds a bit biblical. Probably bearded and good with animals."

Maj didn't say anything for a moment, then, "Yes, cats." She didn't have time to stop the break in her voice.

"Well, a man who likes cats can't be all bad—wait a minute. I caught that."

"What?"

"That little hitch in your voice."

"Hitch? I didn't hitch my voice."

"Well, then it caught in your throat of its own accord. This Noah isn't a bit biblical, or bearded, is he?" Silence. "Maj? Spit it out!"

Maj breathed into the mouthpiece. "No, he's not bearded or biblical, I guess."

"What's he look like? Describe him, and don't leave out one sexy detail."

"John Wayne. Why are you so interested?"

"In *True Grit* or *Flying Leathernecks?*"

Maj laughed.

"What's so funny?" Nan demanded.

"He's a pilot."

"Pilot? How romantic. Or not, given your experience. So, do you?"

"Do I what?"

"Know this Noah John Wayne in, shall we say, the biblical sense?"

"Nan! For God's sake!" Maj grew irritated at her friend.

"No, dear, for your sake," Nan came back unflappably. "Come on, give! Have you been to his house? Or his tent, or at least his hangar?"

Maj couldn't stay irritated with Nan for long. "In a manner of speaking, I've been to his home. At least his temporary home."

"Great! What's it like?"

"Like the West Wind Lodge."

"He lives in a" — Nan's voice trailed into thought — "*the* West Wind Lodge. That's it, isn't it? You're living with him in the lodge! Breakthrough!"

"Not the way you think. He's staying in the lodge, this *big* rambling lodge, temporarily. He's a friend of the Fergusons. They live here, too," Maj added quickly.

"So, what's he like?"

What's he like? Maj let the question sink in. "I don't know exactly. We haven't really talked about much except Adirondack Park. He's very interested in keeping things wild."

"Sounds good to me. The wilder the better!" When Maj didn't respond, Nan softened her tone. "Sorry. What do you think about him?"

Think about him. Nan's words gave credence to the fact that Maj had been thinking about Noah Decker. In fact, if she were honest, she'd have to admit she'd been thinking about him, wondering about him, every day since she'd met him.

Not that she'd wanted to think about him at all. In the beginning he reminded her too much of the kind of men she wanted to forget — all surface, no depth. But that assessment had faded in a few short days. Nothing she could clearly define was instrumental, but something certainly had been.

When he came into Danbury's hardware the day she was there with Fergie, he'd laughed over Fergie's tool inspection and his complaints about how "they don't make stuff like they used to." Maj had loved the genuine warmth in his friendly teasing. He talked her into buying a canvas barn jacket, and she did it knowing full well she didn't have a barn and it wouldn't be appropriate attire for anything she did at home.

Home. Manhattan seemed the farthest thing from home. At least it had with Noah Decker standing there handing her a barn jacket. And he'd kidded her about her sweatshirt with the Adirondack Railway slogan on it. Said he had one just like it in red, and complimented her on her good taste in clothes.

"Maj? I know what you're doing," Nan's voice intruded. "You're taking time to make something up so I'll quit asking about this Noah guy. You should know better than that. Is he nice? How old is he? Is he, shudder, married?"

"He's very nice to Fergie and Ada." Married? Maj hadn't heard if he was or not. He didn't seem married, but she'd learned that wasn't any indication one way or another.

"Let me help. Pick a number between sixteen and eighty."

Maj thought a minute. "Forty-nine, I think he said. Somewhere around there."

"Perfect," Nan pronounced.

"Perfect for what?"

"For you, of course!"

"Me? Be serious, Nan. I'm fifty-one. You said younger men would get me into trouble."

"What's a couple of years? And I can tell you're considering him. Brown or blue?"

"What?"

"His eyes. Brown or blue?"

"Brown," Maj said quietly, "chestnut brown."

"Hair?"

"Of course."

91

"I'm not asking if he's bald. What color is his hair?"

It sounded to Maj that Nan would drag a description of Noah Decker out of her no matter what it took. But she sensed more than that. Nan was making her think about Noah as a man, and she knew she'd been trying not to. He was a *pilot*. Not like those she'd known before, she would have to admit that. He was different. Very different.

"All right, I'll get this over with," Maj said with a light laugh, "or you'll grill me like a police sergeant until I spill everything."

"Success! Go on!"

"He's tall, well over six feet, has dark, thick hair with a tendency to curl when it's wet. He's very trim, broad-shouldered, laughs like he feels good about most everything. And . . . there's something else about him that I don't quite understand."

"For someone who isn't looking, you've just given me an interesting shopping list. I like him so far. In fact, I think I'm in love!" Nan gushed. "What don't you understand?"

"I think there's something secretive about him, something he doesn't talk about. I've seen him by the dock at times, staring at the mountains, or skipping rocks, or idling a stick through the pebbles on the shore."

"A brooding male. Powerfully attractive."

"Oh, I don't know about that. I haven't been with him enough to know if he's brooding about anything. Hey, I've got some work to do here. I can't stand around analyzing a man I hardly know and will never see again."

"I'd remedy that last situation if I were you. How are your friends? Is everything all right with them?"

"Well, they've aged, that's for sure," Maj said, grateful to change the subject from Noah Decker. "Although Fergie seems as hearty as ever, and as cantankerous. Seems there's a developer badgering him to sell the West Wind. Fergie is determined not to. I'm afraid he'll have to sell. There's a long-overdue tax bill facing them, and he doesn't have the money to pay it. I wish I could help. This place hasn't brought in any real income in years as far as I can see. I don't think they have any choice but to sell."

"You sound sad about that."

"I am. The place has meant so much to them, and to me. But time pushes on and changes things."

"I'll say. Well, kid, I'll be glad to see you. Just a minute!" she called to someone other than Maj. "I've got to go, too. The Radio Shack guy is here to look at my fax. Listen, kid, make your last night in the jungle a memorable one, so we'll have lots to talk about on Monday. Okay? Gotta run, he's pounding the door down. I've always loved an impatient man!" She hung up.

Maj laughed and dropped the heavy handset into its cradle. She shook her head. For all Nan's bravado, she knew her friend was as lonely as she'd been the last couple of years. Suddenly she realized she'd been lonely longer than just since Jack's death. She'd been lonely for at least half of their married life.

Married. She realized she hadn't answered Nan's question about Noah's marital status. She had no sense of it. Yet, as she told Nan, she did sense something secretive about him. What?

A knock at the front screen door jolted her out of her thoughts. She went around to it.

"Yes?"

A portly man in an impeccably cut navy blue suit opened the door and stepped into the foyer. Maj could smell his strong cologne from several feet away, and she had to stifle a sneeze.

"Gerald Morris." He held out his right hand to her and smiled with practiced intensity. "Is Mr. Ferguson around?"

"Mr. Ferguson isn't here at the moment.

Something I can help you with?"

"You must be Majesty Wilde," Morris said thoughtfully. "Sam spoke of you, and so have several others in the village. You've made quite an impression on the locals, and I can see why."

"Fergie has spoken of you as well," Maj said coolly, ignoring his other remarks.

"I have no doubt. Then he's told you I've made an offer on this old place?"

"Yes, he has."

"I'm sure you understand how things are. Sam said you'd find a way to take care of things."

"He did?" Maj was truly curious about his last comment.

"Yes, he said you were a smart city girl, and when you came up here you'd know the right thing to do, and he and his wife would do whatever you told them to."

"He did?" Maj asked again.

"Yes, indeed. And now that I've met you, I think he's right. You look like a smart girl. I'm sure you'll make a decision that's right for everybody. This old place is an eyesore, in the way of development in this area. Now, I've tried to be reasonable with Ferguson"—Morris opened his briefcase and took out a sheaf of papers—"but he won't consider my offer. I'm sure you know how bull-headed he can be."

"Yes, I do," Maj said, taking a suspicious step back from Gerald Morris.

"I've made them an offer that will solve all their financial problems, as you'll see right here." He pointed to a column of figures on the third page. "This is the delinquent tax bill due on the property. That and the cost of repair and maintenance . . . well, you can see how impossible it is for people the Fergusons' age. My offer would wipe out their debts and give them something to live on."

Maj thought for a moment. "Yes, but nothing to live for," she mused.

"I beg your pardon?"

"Nothing, Mr. Morris. Would you let me look at these papers today? I'll get them back to you later. I'm returning to New York tomorrow anyway."

"Of course. I see what you mean. You'd like to act quickly. I can see we think alike." He leaned toward her. "I knew you were a smart girl. Perhaps you'll be able to make them see the wisdom in selling to me."

Maj leaned back. "As an intelligent *woman,* I can assure you, Mr. Morris, I will discuss your offer in great depth."

"Well, then, I leave it in your capable hands, Miss Wilde," Morris gushed. "It's been a pleasure to meet you, and I know we'll be doing business together."

An errant breeze came through the screen door and swept another wave of his cologne into Maj's face. She turned her face and put a finger under her nose to stifle another sneeze.

"I'm glad I met you," she mumbled, and closed the heavy inside door before Morris had even stepped to the other side of the screen one.

What a distasteful man, she thought. No wonder Fergie didn't like him. She threw the papers down on the foyer table and went down the hall to her grandfather's study. Morris's words disturbed her. Fergie had told him she'd take care of everything once she got there. She couldn't have known about that, of course, but she didn't feel capable of taking care of her own life very well, let alone those of two other people and a mountain lodge.

Henry Wilde's study was as dark as she remembered, owing to the dense green window shades left over from the war days of the forties. Piles of books and papers were heaped onto heavy oak furniture. Dominating the room was a huge postmaster's rolltop desk, an appropriate piece since he'd also served as

97

postmaster in a village whose name she couldn't remember.

Maj sneezed. "Whew," she breathed, "guess I'd better get some of the dust out of here before I dig into all these papers."

She lifted the two dark shades and opened the windows. Circulation of fresh air in the room stirred the dust even more and sharpened the musty scent of damp walls and books. Maj sneezed again and rubbed her eyes.

She pulled the chain under a green glass shade on a brass desk lamp, pleased that the light bulb was still good. As she moved a few things around on the desk, the corner of a faded photograph poked out from under a ledger. Carefully she slipped it out and took it to a window to have a better look. Four faces in the crackled black and white photo smiled up at her. Carl and Maria Wilde, her parents, stood smiling broadly with her grandparents, Henry and Anna Wilde, in front of the West Wind Lodge.

Majesty smiled back wistfully. At least the outside of the main lodge with its red spruce siding hadn't changed too much over the years. She'd felt comfortable when she'd driven into the driveway that first night, almost as if all the years hadn't intervened.

Maj went behind the desk and dropped into her grandfather's swivel chair, her elbow resting on its arm. She pushed the back of one sneaker down with the toe of her other one, then reversed the procedure, and kicked her feet out of them. She picked up a stubby yellow pencil, pressed the eraser against her temple, and sighed while she played the fingers of her other hand over the heavy spine of the green ledger.

Rubbing the back of her neck, she let her eyes roam lazily around the room. Everything was covered with dust, from the books and bookcases to pictures hung on the faded papered walls and the wide plank floor. The drapes should be discarded, she observed. Washing them would be a disaster since she could tell the only thing holding the fabric together was the dirt of time.

A dull headache began to capture more of Maj's attention. She got up from the chair and stretched, then walked barefoot to a window. A breeze wafted in, at once filling the room with the aroma of balsam and damp earth from an overnight rain. Breathing deeply, she held the scent, then let it out slowly. There certainly was something about the Adirondack air that gave her a sense of well-being. Perhaps it had already cleared her lungs and bloodstream of all the impurities of Manhattan. The headache was probably a withdrawal symptom.

She dropped back into the chair, threw her feet up onto the desk, and crossed her ankles. Blowing dust off the top first, she opened the ledger and smiled at the neat rows of figures and precise entries inscribed in her grandfather's hand. Flipping through the pages, she read his notes on when each piece of furniture was acquired, each repair made, each outstanding debt paid. And as she came to the end of the ledger, the story of the dissolution of an era was told in dwindling numbers and entries and low bottom lines. Then Fergie's handwriting took up the task, and the figures were more often than not preceded with a minus sign. The many erasures and cross-outs told Maj of his frustration and the steady losses to the West Wind and the Fergusons.

"Anybody home?" Noah's rich baritone voice slipped into the room before he did.

Maj jerked her head up quickly and her eyes shifted toward the door with an excited expectancy at his entrance. Her reaction to his arrival awakened a blatant fact — she liked his voice, his laugh, and had even hoped for more conversation with him, even if they appeared to disagree.

"What's happening back here?" he called again.

A silent answer formed in Maj's mind, *Damned if I know*, but she didn't say it.

Noah cocked his head around the door, a dazzling smile forming quickly. "Wow!" he exclaimed, stepping in and beaming down on her. "You look right at home behind that desk. Looks like it was made for you to take it over."

Briefly she wondered if he was hinting for her to stay. She lifted her legs off the desk, stood up and walked to the front of the desk.

Noah watched her, noticed her erect carriage and her movement, fluid with feline gracefulness. He caught himself. He'd been thinking about Majesty Wilde every day since they'd met, and that wasn't good for him. He'd numbed himself against such feelings for so long that it sent him into a state of confusion when the full impact of what was happening hit him. Against his better judgment he was intensely attracted to her. What good would that do? She'd be leaving soon. Leaving.

What would keep her here?

He wondered what kept her in Manhattan. A man?

"So," he said, lightening his momentary

dark mood, "find any skeletons in the file drawers?"

"Was I supposed to?" Maj leaned back on the edge of the desk, crossed her arms at her chest, and crossed her bare feet at her ankles. A lock of hair flopped down over one eye, and she sent a column of breath through side-tilted lips to lift it away.

"You never know," Noah said, watching her and obviously enjoying what he was seeing. "I hear most everybody's got some hidden somewhere."

"Oh? Does that mean you have some, too?" A nervous smile played at the corners of her mouth.

"If everybody's supposed to have them, I must have them, too." He walked toward the window. "I was wondering if you, well, it's your last night at West Wind, and I was wondering if you had any specific plans."

"I was going to spend it with Ada and Fergie, but they've gone to Tupper Lake. The daughter of some old friends of theirs called for them to come. An emergency of some kind. I hope everything's all right. They said they wouldn't be back until late."

Noah turned around. "Well, then, it appears you might be at loose ends. I'd like to make up for the less than happy ending to our airplane ride the other day. There's a firemen's field day down in the village. Sickening rides, disgusting food, rigged games of chance, that sort of thing. I was wondering if you'd like to join me for supper there?"

Maj looked down at her wriggling toes, and a warm smile touched her lips. "Well, when you make it sound so attractive, how can I refuse? I'd love to dine out with you, Mr. Decker. What might be the manner of dress?" She glanced at her jeans, pale blue turtleneck, and navy tweed blazer.

"I think, Ms. Wilde, other than your feet, you might be overdressed, but I promise not to show my embarrassment."

"I'll just primp a bit," she said, sitting down on a dusty carton and putting her sneakers back on.

When she stood up and turned around to shut off the desk lamp, Noah spotted two perfectly round patches of dust on her jeans clinging to her backside.

"How's that?" Maj turned around, smiling.

"Perfect." His lopsided grin gave away his next intention. "Except for one thing."

"What?"

"Allow me." He took a bandanna from his jeans' back pocket, turned her around, and started brushing off her backside.

103

"Hey! What are you doing?" Maj spun around.

"Removing a little bit of imperfection from something otherwise perfect. Shall we, then? Your limo awaits." He offered his arm.

Maj knew her color had deepened at his interesting compliment. But she liked his words, and decided to enjoy them without a return comment.

She crooked her arm through his, and he escorted her out to his pickup.

Chapter Five

"The days are getting longer," Maj observed as they swung atop a Ferris wheel that had jammed and kept them aloft for already over ten minutes.

They'd ridden the merry-go-round, smacked each other into gales of laughter in the bumper cars, stuffed themselves with hot dogs, beer, and paper cones full of french fries with vinegar sprinkled on. They'd played quarter toss and hook the milk bottle, but had avoided the chukaluck wheel. At the shooting gallery Noah had shown his prowess and won a tiny stuffed skunk. Maj had taken the rifle and won a big chartreuse stuffed dinosaur.

"I'm glad," he said, surveying the carnival field. "Summer's my favorite time of the year."

They watched the pink and mauve sky start to go deep gray as the sun went behind the peaks.

"Imagine being forced to watch a magnificent sunset from the top of a Ferris wheel," Maj said quietly, cradling the skunk in the palm of her hand.

"Yes, imagine," Noah answered, cradling the dinosaur on his outside arm. "It cost me a pretty penny to get the operator to do that."

"You bribed him?" Maj turned quickly and set their swing to rocking.

He laughed. "That would be a cheap trick. Anyway, every year the same show troupe does this field day event, and every year the Ferris wheel gets stuck. I do marvel, though, at the odds of it happening just when you wanted it to." He slipped his arm behind her over the back of the swing.

They watched the sun going down. It sunk so fast, Maj thought it looked as if someone had pulled its plug. The rest of the carnival lights twinkled on, bright, some chasing, some missing. The sound of the merry-go-round music seemed louder, and she felt the bang of cymbals vibrate through her chest. She shivered.

"Cold?" he asked.

"A little. How long will it take to fix this thing?"

"Anywhere from ten minutes to an hour. Depends on if he has to go get Mr. Danbury to

106

open the hardware so he can get a tool."

"You're kidding!"

"Yes, unfortunately."

"Unfortunately? You like being stuck up here?" Maj looked at him with good-natured curiosity.

"Tell me what would be better than being atop a Ferris wheel at sunset with a beautiful woman in your arms."

Maj stared at him. He'd just complimented her again, said she was beautiful. She'd never been called beautiful in her adult life. She shivered again.

"Here." He cupped his hand around her far shoulder and brought her close to his chest. Then he put his palm against the side of her head and lowered it onto his shoulder. He snuggled her against the dinosaur. "How's that?"

Nerve-wracking, she thought. "Typical," she said.

"Typical? What do you mean?" he said, laughing.

"All teenagers do this on Ferris wheels at carnivals."

"Do you feel like a teenager?"

I'm nervous as one, she thought. "A little," she said.

"Good." He laughed again. "Why?"

107

Maj thought about what she should say, could say. She heard Nan's voice in the back of her mind saying, *Go on, it's your last night in town. Throw caution to the winds and say whatever you feel like, do whatever you feel like!* Maj had never done that kind of thing, allowed herself enough freedom to be spontaneous. She'd always worried about what other people might think of her.

But maybe Nan was right, as usual.

"Okay," she ventured, "I feel as if I'm on a first date with the most popular boy in school. It makes me a little nervous."

"Don't be nervous. I wasn't that popular till I got my braces off."

"Braces? You wore braces, too?" She lifted her head and looked at him.

"Oh, no, I've just destroyed a part of my mystique, haven't I?" He put on a mock pout.

"That wonderful smile is man-made?" Her voice was animated, full of fun.

"Afraid so. But, here now, no teasing. You've just admitted you wore braces, too." He touched her lower lip with one finger, and the laugh left him.

Maj said nothing, and her nervousness grew. There was a tension between them, but not one born of differing opinions. This was man-to-woman woman-to-man tension. They sat motionless except for the slight rocking of their swing, waiting. Waiting for what, she wondered. But she didn't have to wonder long.

Noah's four fingers rested on her lower lip, then slipped softly around her jaw and tilted her head back. In her vision his face grew blurry in the gathering darkness and in its closeness as it drew nearer hers. And then his mouth closed over hers, warm, tender, inviting more as it drew away.

They both let out a sigh between them.

"I've been wanting to do that for days," he whispered. When she didn't say anything, didn't protest, he drew her to him and kissed her again, fully, more warmly than before, more insistently than before.

Maj shivered. "I—I don't know what I'm supposed to say right now."

"I'm not sure I do either." The Ferris wheel jerked forward a few inches, then stopped abruptly, setting their chair to swinging. She grasped his jacket. "At least I know you won't run away." He laughed, and the tension of the moment was broken a little.

The Ferris wheel jerked again, then started a vibrating descent. Maj laughed to lessen the intensity of her shaking nerves. As they came around the platform, the attendant lifted the bar and they swung out and down the ramp.

"Hey, mister," the attendant shouted, "thanks for the ten bucks. I hope I stalled it long enough for you!"

Maj stood stunned for a moment until Noah hooked her arm and took her off on a run toward the parked pickup.

On the dark road along the lake as they drove back toward the West Wind, Maj looked over at Noah. He hummed while he drove.

"You actually bribed that guy to stall the Ferris wheel with us on top, didn't you?"

"That's affirmative, ma'am. Are you mad at me?"

Maj smiled in the darkness. "I guess I should be. That was pretty fresh what you did up there."

"You didn't seem to mind a bit." He hummed louder.

She hadn't minded the kiss. In fact, she'd enjoyed it. It had felt good, stirred things in her she'd forgotten to feel for years. She wondered how it felt to him.

"Did you mind?" she asked quietly, and couldn't believe her own boldness.

"Mind? I enjoyed it thoroughly. I wish now I'd given the guy twenty bucks!"

Maj felt good about his response, secretly pleased. He pointed the truck down a side road she hadn't seen before.

110

"This isn't the way to the West Wind," she said, concerned.

"Nope. But it's a better way."

"Why?"

"You'll see."

The road bumped and wound and ended up at the shore of the lake. The moon cast a silver swath across the black expanse to the shore.

"This is beautiful," she breathed. "Where are we?"

"My good woman, haven't you ever been to the submarine races before?"

"The submarine races! Noah Decker, you back this truck out of here right now!"

"So you *have* been to the submarine races before!"

"I have not! But I've heard about them."

"All the more reason to stay. Everyone should, at least once in their lives. Don't you think?"

Maj hugged the dinosaur to her chest. "That's for teenagers. Teenagers seem to need to find a place to—"

"Make out?" Noah grinned at her.

"Make out! Now *you* sound like a teenager!"

"Good! Now, where were we when we were so rudely interrupted?" He pushed the dinosaur down to the floor and gently pulled her toward

111

him. "Oh, yes, I remember now," he whispered, then lowered his mouth to hers.

Maj pushed away from him, not as firmly as she thought she should have. "Noah, we aren't teenagers."

"Yeah, and aren't we lucky?" He sighed. When she didn't respond, he slipped his arm from her shoulders and rested it on the seat back. "You're right. We're two . . . adults." He left out the word *consenting*. So far he was the only one who was consenting, and the last thing he wanted to do was pressure her into something she didn't want to do. Relax, he told himself. Just be with her. "This is a beautiful place. We should just enjoy the sight, right?"

"Adults," Maj echoed, but she couldn't deny the fluttering in her stomach, or the tingling in her fingers. Or the desire for him to kiss her again.

He draped his forearms over the steering wheel and looked out at the moon. Maj stole a glance. Moonlight bathed the side of his face, and she saw his jaw flexing.

What was she supposed to do? Let him take all the liberties he wanted to? Or should she insist he stop? Should she tell him she didn't kiss on the first date, let alone anything more? What was she supposed to say? Was she just supposed to ask him to kiss her again? Was she supposed to tell him what she wanted? That's what all the psychology books said—tell him what you want, tell him what makes you feel good.

God, Maj thought, I've never done that in my life. I never told Jack that I wanted to be held, to be kissed tenderly, that I wanted him to stare at me in a way that told me he couldn't get enough of looking at me. That I wanted to make love slowly, tenderly, to make it last all night like it did in romantic stories. How does a woman tell that to a man? She shivered.

Noah turned toward her. "Majesty, I don't know how to say what I want to say to you so you won't think I'm saying it just because it's your last night here." He turned back toward the window. "That felt like the most awkward thing I've ever said to a woman. Maybe I *am* acting like a teenager."

Scared but somehow relieved that he'd apparently been thinking almost the same things she had, Maj suddenly realized she wanted him to say anything he wanted to just because it *was* her last night here. She put a hand on his arm. He jumped slightly.

"Just say it," she whispered.

He let out a long breath and placed a warm

hand over hers, where it rested on his arm. He turned and stared at her a long time, so long Maj's shaking turned from being cold to being on the verge of shattering with . . . what? Fear? Fear of what? Her own deep-down desire for a man? This man? She knew now she wasn't afraid of Noah Decker, she was afraid of Majesty Wilde!

She started to withdraw her hand, but he held it fast. "I . . . I want so much for you to understand. . . ." he started. "I want us to make love."

Maj was certain her heart stopped beating. Her breath lodged in her lungs which ceased to release it or take any more in. Did men always say what they wanted straight out? Jack hadn't. At least not with her.

"But only if you want to," he rushed on. "Oh, I don't mean here, in a truck. But the way I feel about you right now, it wouldn't matter where it was. Jesus, I'm saying this badly, I know. I want it to sound to you the way I really mean it, and I'm messing this up, but—"

Maj turned her hand so they were palm to palm. She felt a shaking in their hands, and knew this time it was as much him as it was her. A pleased warmth calmed her fearful cold. If he was as scared as she was . . .

well, he couldn't be *that* scared.

"I'm not very practiced . . . I mean, I haven't . . . I don't . . ." She couldn't find the right words. How did you tell a man you haven't had sex in countless months, and when you did have it, it was over soon and you didn't know how you were supposed to feel, or what you were supposed to do?

"Don't think about that." His laugh was shaky. "I've had sex about as often as a Democrat gets to be president!"

His joking, true or not, eased Maj's tightly strung nerves. "I haven't had it in so long, I'm probably recertified as a virgin," she said with an unsteady voice, and was almost mortified at her words.

He laughed deeply, not mockingly. Pleasantly, the way she liked. "We were meant to be together tonight, I think," he whispered, looking into her eyes. "Would it be fresh of me to ask if you'd consider coming home with me?"

Maj looked back into his eyes, trying to read something she didn't know herself what she hoped to see there. Honesty. She could tell that. Desire. Desire? Should she allow herself to think that he desired her? Could he see the desire in her eyes, the desire for him she knew she was feeling deep inside?

"Of course it would be. And I suppose it

115

would be shameless of me to go with you." She took a deep breath. "So I feel compelled to ask if you'll still respect me in the morning?" she teased to hide her growing tension. Did nice women do this? Did they feel like this when they were about to "do it" for the first time outside of marriage?

"I promise to respect you in the morning, and I could extend that to the afternoon, if you'd stay," he said warmly, squeezing her hand.

Maj turned to look out the window. "I also feel compelled to ask what Fergie and Ada will think?" she said quietly, watching the moonlight float provocatively over the gently lapping water.

"I'll tell them we ran out of gas," he said seriously but with a trace of teasing in his voice.

"That story's been told to parents since the beginning of civilization"—she laughed—"and none of them ever believed it. But I'm sure they'll believe anything you tell them, no matter how outlandish it sounds."

Noah started the engine, then turned back to her. "I'd like to hope you'll believe what I tell you, too. I have a feeling it will be nothing I've told to anyone ever before."

* * *

For twenty wordless minutes they rode side by side in the pickup, feeling every bump in the road, every nerve in their bodies. Noah gripped the steering wheel. Maj stroked the dinosaur. The skunk rested in the pocket of her tweed blazer.

After a while Maj noticed that they'd passed no other cars on this road. Not another soul. No one. She felt the desolation of the night and her aloneness inside. Noah's decision was made. He'd told her he wanted to make love with her. She'd said yes. Yet, at this very moment she believed herself to be like the stuffed chartreuse creature in her lap. A dinosaur when it came to man-woman relationships.

What had possessed her to give in to him at that moment? Wait, that wasn't fair. She hadn't given in, she knew that. She'd come to a decision of sorts herself back at the lake. Who was it for? For Nan? So Nan could tell her now all her problems would magically disappear once she'd been in bed with a sexy man?

She didn't have to look at him now to know that Noah was definitely a sexy man. She could feel it, feel him without touching him. Feel him feeling her without his touching her. It was powerful. And frightening. She should tell him to turn around, take her back to the West Wind. It was only about nine o'clock, a perfectly respectable time to be getting in.

Too late. The hood ornament on his pickup led the way into a cleared area, and looming ahead was a log cabin. A dark log cabin.

With a bed in it. A bed on which she . . . and he . . . were about to lie down. Together.

For a moment in the dark Maj looked over at the man next to her. Noah Decker. A man she'd known less than a week.

Noah dropped the transmission into park and slid out of the truck. He came around and opened the door for Maj, and took her hand to help her down. She was stiff, trembling. All the way home in the truck he'd thought about what the rest of the evening would be like. The two of them together.

He was behaving like a teenager. No, that wasn't so. He was being the most honest adult he'd ever been in his life. He'd felt lust many times, but nothing like what he was feeling now for this woman. He'd been thinking about this moment since the first morning they'd met. This was definitely lust, and something more.

God, but he was scared.

It was important to him to please Maj, to make everything perfect for her, make every moment they were together exquisite for her. Looking at her stepping tentatively down from the truck, he felt awkward, worried that he would somehow fail.

"This is where I live," he said brightly, "or at least where I will live someday. It's a bit rustic right now, so don't expect a palace. But at least the roof is on and it's watertight, and warm with the fireplace."

He knew he was babbling as he led her toward the door, but he wanted to quell her nervousness. Or was he just trying to calm himself? God, what was going on inside him?

Inside the cabin Noah stopped her by the open door. "It'll take me a moment to light the lantern. Wait here."

She did, shivering more from her own confused senses than from the damp night. He struck a match and lit the lantern. The glow emanating from the glass chimney cast a soft burnished aura over the plank walls. Noah took her hand, drew her into the room, and closed the door.

Closed the door.

Maj turned and looked at it, then back toward Noah, who was lighting a fire in the stone fireplace. The dry wood crackled and flamed, adding more light to the room. She looked around at the framework of what would soon enclose his life.

"What do you think?" he asked.

"About what?" she answered too quickly.

"This"—he waved his hand around the expanse of room—"or at least what it's going to be."

"Oh, it's . . . it's going to be great. That is, when you finish it. I mean, not that it isn't great now, but I mean, when you do more—this isn't coming out right, is it? I feel as if I'm insulting your work, and that's not what I mean at all." Her chin dropped, and she stroked the dinosaur's nose frantically.

He laughed warmly. "I do know what you mean. I suppose it's difficult for a city girl to imagine what a finished mountain cabin will look like. As finished as any mountain cabin ever is."

"On the contrary, I can imagine very well." She laughed, too, hoping to hide her apprehension.

Noah sensed what was going on inside her. Hell, it was going on inside him with as much intensity. He'd thought of her being in his cabin, and now that she was actually there he hadn't reckoned for his senses to take off in such an erratic manner.

The faint aroma of her perfume reached him on a waft of air. He didn't know the name of it, but it smelled sensually unique among the heady mountain scent of balsam and crackling cherry wood that filled the cabin. The firelight lent her hair and skin the delicate amber sheen of wild honey and lit the midnight depth of her eyes like the shaft of moonlight had over the lake.

"You are beautiful." He couldn't help himself. The words tumbled out before he could think about them. He didn't want to sound glib lest she think he was coming on too fast. But dammit, she was beautiful, standing there in her jeans, turtleneck, and tweed jacket. She didn't move. He wanted her to speak, say anything, just end this awkward moment in which he felt as if he'd never been in the presence of a woman before.

"Noah . . ."

Thank God. He breathed out.

"I'm sorry," she said, turning toward him. "This was a mistake. Please take me back to the West Wind."

He didn't say anything for a long time. Her words sounded sad to him, lonely. Deflated. And he felt as deflated as last week's carnival balloon. But all he could think about was making her feel better.

"No, I'm the one who's sorry," he said. "I came on too fast, didn't I? I didn't mean it like that, but I'm not sure how to explain it to you."

"No, it isn't your fault at all." She raised her eyes, and he saw she meant it. "It's really mine. I shouldn't have said yes to something I'm not ready for. I guess I'm not cut out for . . . this. I don't know. I don't know what I think."

Gently he took the dinosaur from her hands. His knuckles brushed the back of her hand, and even that merest of touches set her nerves on edge. Maj jumped. She was growing nauseated.

"May I make a suggestion?" His voice was husky.

Wordlessly, she looked at him.

"How about if I make us some hot chocolate, and we sit in front of the fire and discuss the nature of modern technology and how it relates to old-fashioned Ferris wheels? I'm certain it would provide an interesting discourse on how the same event shared by two people could be experienced very differently. What do you say?"

He lit a lantern in a nook, which, when the wick was turned up, showed the beginnings of a cozy kitchen.

Maj relaxed a little. What had she been so afraid of? After all, she was an adult woman in control of her own actions. When Noah smiled, his face reflected only appreciation of her, not disappointment or accusation.

She found her voice and felt the obvious relief in it. "That sounds very enlightening. Perhaps we might even discuss the effects of bribery on modern technology."

"Too complicated for me at this time of night. Let's just concentrate on making hot chocolate on a Coleman stove. It's a much safer subject, at least for me."

A light tapping came at the door. Maj jumped, and her eyes fixed on Noah's face. Caught. She'd been caught in this man's cabin by someone who would know exactly why she was there.

"Would you mind getting the door?" Noah asked over his shoulder as he pumped the propane tank on a small green camp stove.

"Should I?" Maj asked tentatively.

"I think so. He won't stop knocking unless you do."

Maj's nose wrinkled inquisitively, but Noah offered nothing in the way of explanation, only a cryptic smile.

She opened the door slowly. No one was there. Something furry slipped by her ankle, and she stepped back quickly.

"Hi, Orville," Noah called to the tiger cat hurrying toward him. Orville muttered a feline greeting.

Maj shut the door, hand over her heart. The furry thing slipping by her foot had given her a chill. At least it wasn't a human who could make snap judgments and talk about it in the drugstore in the morning.

Noah set a saucepan of water on the stove, pried open a can of tuna with his Swiss army knife, flaked it with a fork onto a gray stoneware saucer, and set it down near the framework of a cupboard. Orville dove into it, meowing and muttering with every bite.

"That's the most vocal cat I've ever heard. He talks with his mouth full." Maj laughed.

"I know. I really should teach him some manners, but he won't allow it. That's what I like about him. He is who he is, and I can do nothing but accept him. The same way he accepts me. Warts and all."

Noah unearthed two tin mugs from a cardboard box of wrapped utensils, took a container of cocoa from another box, went back to the first for a spoon, then scooped into the cocoa and put some in each mug. The water was steaming now, and he poured and stirred in the mugs till the smell of chocolate filled the air and mixed with the balsam.

"Sorry, no marshmallows."

"Well, that does it," she chided him. "How can you expect me to stay here now, what with a cat that talks while he eats and no marsh-mallows for the hot chocolate? Really, it's simply not done." She sniffed and took on a haughty air.

"Oh, but surely I've redeemed myself with these lovely matching cups." He handed one to her.

"True. I've always loved blue with white speckles. All right, maybe just a sip."

He gestured toward the pile of quilts and blankets in front of the fireplace. She hesitated.

"You just can't get good help these days," he continued joking as if he hadn't noticed her hesitation. "I've been expecting my ecru velour sectional for days now, but no sign of the delivery people." He dropped down onto the pile, pulled off his boots, and invited her to join him. He drew up a half log. "Good thing the coffee table arrived in time, isn't it?"

Maj looked around a little more. She didn't see a bed anywhere, although there did seem to be a loft of some kind suspended over the far end of the cabin. There could be a bed up there. Or not. He did say it was still in its rustic state, and she could corroborate that now.

She relaxed and dropped easily down next to him, careful not to touch him. She wasn't sure if that was so as not to give him the wrong idea, or if touching him would make her dissolve. They sat staring into the fire, silently blowing and sipping the chocolate, and thinking. Orville walked across Maj's lap and settled himself between them in the blankets.

Without looking at her, Noah said, "Can we talk about this?"

Maj didn't have to ask what he wanted to talk about. "I'm sorry," she said at last. "I didn't mean to disappoint you."

"There's no need for an apology. I want us to talk about it only because we both seemed so sure of ourselves back there at the lake."

She giggled. "Submarine races. Really!"

He looked at her. "What about them? I thought they were particularly exciting this evening."

She turned toward him. "You couldn't see a thing out there!"

"Of course not. They were submarines!"

"Whatever got that started anyway? I remember that from high school."

"I think it was devised by some intelligent sixteen-year-old who hoped there might be better things to do if his date got bored looking for submarines in the dark."

Maj stopped smiling. "And we didn't keep with the original idea, did we?"

"Sure we did. Or have you forgotten already? We kissed. People are supposed to kiss at submarine races. You knew that, of course."

"Oh, of course." She drained her cup and set it on the log coffee table. "I'm fifty-one years old." That came out as if she were trying to explain or make excuses for her behavior. Only it didn't do either, and she knew it, and it just didn't make any sense that she'd said it.

"You know I'm forty-nine. Now that we've established the numbers, what difference does that make?" He paused. Then, "Oh, I get it. You've got something against being with a younger man, haven't you? Let me assure you, I'm pretty grown-up." He wiggled his toes inside his Ragg socks, then looked at her and laughed lightly at his childlike action.

Maj reached into her jacket pocket and brought out the little stuffed skunk. She set it on the log with her mug.

"So that's it, hunh?" he said, nodding his head toward the skunk.

"What?"

"Just because you won at the rifle shoot, you think you're too superior to be with such an inept shot, right?"

Maj leaned back in the pile of quilts and blankets, and Orville let out a grumbled protest against the destruction of the nest he'd built between them.

"Thanks, Noah," she whispered.

He laced his fingers behind his nape, dropped his head back as far as it would go, and stretched his feet toward the fire. "You're welcome. For what? Those great kisses?"

"You know for what," she said, and agreed in her mind that those were great kisses.

He did know. "It has to be right for both people," he said quietly, "or it isn't right for one."

"Thank you again," she whispered. "I've never heard that before." She looked at him as the firelight danced over his face. His gentle response touched her in a new way. Remembering Jack in bed, it never mattered to him whether she wanted to make love or not. It only mattered if he did. Especially if he was going on a trip that would last several days. He always wanted to "get one in" before he left.

Noah was quiet for several long minutes. "Do you really have to leave tomorrow?"

"Yes."

"Will nothing I say convince you to stay?"

"Nothing could. I have to go. I have no choice. I have a job, obligations."

"Yes, I know." He unlaced his fingers and sat up. "They need you, you know."

She sighed, thinking of Fergie and Ada.

"Yes, I know, and I wish I could help them, but I don't have enough money. I have all these bills of my husband's. . . ."

His head jerked around, and she thought she read something akin to real disappointment in his eyes. "You're married."

"I was. He died almost two years ago."

He let out a breath. "I'm sorry."

Don't be were the first words in her mind. She was shocked at her own response, and grateful she didn't speak it out loud.

"Are there children?"

The inevitable question. "No."

"No? That surprises me. I think you would make a perfect mother."

Noah's voice sounded distant to Maj. Should she tell him the story of why she was childless? No. That was past, and explanation would only renew the empty feeling she'd never succeeded in filling. And besides, women shouldn't tell men that kind of thing.

"I really should go, Noah. I have a long drive ahead of me tomorrow."

Noah set his cup next to hers on the log. He turned and carefully picked up the snoring Orville and set the cat on the other side of him. Then he moved toward Maj.

"It's a shame, you know?"

She knew. She didn't want to say it. But

that didn't stop him from saying it.

"I wish there were time for us to get to know each other more." His fingers picked up locks of her hair and sifted it through them. "I think there could be a lot to discover, interesting things to talk about."

He was moving closer to her. His fingers brushed the back of her neck and she felt shivers go up to her crown and down her arms. Now his hand was moving around the other side of her head, brushing her cheek, his fingers cradling her chin.

"Will you look at me, Maj, please?" Gently he urged her face around.

She did look at him and knew instantly it was a downfall of sorts. She felt her face moving toward his, knew her lips were headed for his, and she didn't want to stop them.

He whispered, close to her mouth. "I was desperate to touch you tonight, be close to you. But I know now we won't make love. And it's our loss, but it's all right. We'll both have a year's worth of fantasizing material. I believe you'll be back."

Before she could say anything, his lips closed over hers, soft, clinging, tasting as if she were the only flower on the mountain with precious nectar to sip. One hand was in her hair, cradling her head and gently moving it against his mouth, the other hand held her jaw, urging it closer. He released her lips and caught the swollen fullness of them in the firelight. A small groan escaped his throat, and he pulled her into his arms, kissing her fully, a complete lush kiss with insistent exploring tongue.

Maj felt the foundation of her reserve crumbling, her strength weakening. Tension left her muscles. She uttered a small sound of surrender and gave her lips openly, fully, like the first full bloom of a spring tulip catching a refreshing rain.

And then his hands splayed across her back. Hers went under his arms and clutched his shoulders. His chest pressed into her breasts, her breasts pressed into his chest. He lowered her onto her back on the quilts, and she did not resist. Their lips clung, tasted, nipped. Tongues caressed, explored, demanded. He stretched his full length over her, pushing her body deeper into the quilts, and she felt him hard against her. He reached for her hands and pushed her arms above her head, holding them down with his palms to her palms, and did not release her mouth.

Maj lay tense, filled with desire for him, with apprehension for herself.

He drew his mouth away from hers then, and they lay panting face-to-face, chests heaving, breathing ragged, gazes locked in mutual longing. The scent of chocolate, balsam, burning logs, and her perfume mingled between them. And then his stiffened body relaxed. He lowered himself gently over her, stretched to kiss each palm softly, lingeringly.

Then he dropped his lips to her ear and whispered to her gruffly, "I could take you here and now, fast and furiously. I want you, Maj, so much, I'm afraid I would tear us both apart."

Maj tensed beneath him, every nerve, every fiber alive with electrical current. She wanted him; she could admit that to herself. Alien thoughts, alien words to allow to enter her mind. She knew she would let it happen if he continued. And she could also admit to herself Nan had nothing to do with what she was feeling.

These feelings were all hers.

He eased away from her. "I'd better get you back before I make you a prisoner in this cabin, Majesty Wilde. And before I do something I would not respect myself for in the morning. When you're ready, I hope I'm the one you'll want." He sat up, and his gaze burned into hers. "I promise you this, all you'll have to do is tell me you want me, and I'll be there so fast, your head will swim. When you think of me, you'll know how much I want to make love to you, know that I'm ready to give you all the pleasure you can stand. And you will think of me, won't you?"

Joy and pleasure. Nan had said she should bring joy and pleasure into her life every day. Yet here she was in the presence of a man who professed he was ready to give her exactly that, and she couldn't let it happen. What was stopping her? What was she afraid of?

She had no answers for either of them.

Maj allowed herself a long, slow, relaxing breath, and stood up. "I think it's best I go back to the lodge now."

He nodded agreement and scooped up the truck keys from the mantel. "One question."

"All right."

"What's that perfume you're wearing?"

"Obsession."

He emitted a short, hard breath through his nostrils, then opened the cabin door and escorted her out.

Chapter Six

When Maj stepped into the kitchen, Fergie and Ada were sitting at the table drinking tea, somber expressions on their faces.

"Was that Noah's truck we heard leaving?" Fergie asked.

"Yes, it was." Maj's back was to them as she busily made a cup of tea for herself.

"Funny he didn't come in," Ada said. "Is he coming back?"

"I think he planned to stay at the cabin tonight," Maj said, making up his excuse. "He took me down to the firemen's field day in Pinewood, and I think the excitement was too much for him." She tried to sound light. When she turned back to the old couple, she noticed their serious expressions hadn't changed. "Is something wrong? Is it your friends?"

Wearily Ada got up and took her cup to the

sink. Fergie sighed and didn't look at Maj. "Yes," he said after a long pause. "Emma and George Rodgers, you remember them, don't you?"

Maj thought for a moment. "George Rodgers. Of course. He had a that little grocery store next to the Texaco station. He used to give me a Tootsie Roll Pop whenever I went in there. He'd never let me pay for it even though I showed him I had my own money."

Fergie smiled. "I'm glad you remember him. After they moved to Tupper they figured everybody here forgot them."

"Is he sick? He's not . . . dead?"

Fergie lowered his shaggy head and shook it. "No, he's not dead, but he'd be better off if he was."

"Fergie, what happened?" Maj put a hand on his arm.

Ada walked out of the room, and Maj saw her wipe her eyes with her ever-present handkerchief.

"George lost the store quite a while back. Emma got sick, out of her head now and then."

Maj felt her throat constrict. "Alzheimer's disease?"

Fergie nodded. "He had a lot of doctor bills and no insurance, and now they're out of money. A decision was made for them. Put Emma in a nursing home because she can't take care of herself and it's getting hard for George to do it." He shook his head. "The daughter says she can't take them in. She's too busy with her own family. George wouldn't be able to go with Emma to the nursing home because he's able to get around all right."

Fergie dropped his head again, and a sob racked his shoulders. When he looked up, tears were streaming down his ruddy, lined cheeks. "George got a gun and . . . and he shot Emma. She's dead. He tried to kill himself, but it didn't work. He's in the hospital in a coma. And I hope to God he never wakes up. The police said when he comes to, he'll have to go to trial. Can you believe that?"

Fergie cried like a baby then, and when Maj tried to comfort him, he pulled away and stood up, holding on to the chair and rocking back and forth.

"The best thing for George is to die. What's he got to live for? He and Emma were everything to each other. They've been in love for over fifty years. All he wanted to do was take care of her, make her happy. And he couldn't. She knew she was a burden to him, and it broke her heart."

Fergie blew his nose in a red bandanna.

"The nursing home wanted to take what little he had left to take care of Emma, and then take her away from him, too. I don't blame him for what he did. I'd have done the same thing if I was him." He wiped his eyes on the sleeve of his green flannel shirt. "He's my best friend, and by God, I hope he dies. If he doesn't, I'll kill him myself. That's what he wants. There's no point to his living now, old and lonely and penniless. Somebody's got to help him help himself."

Maj said nothing. There was nothing she could say. She felt helpless in the face of Fergie's outpouring. He turned away from her and started in Ada's direction. Broken, exhausted, he climbed the stairway to their bedroom, and she could do nothing but watch. And she believed him. If George Rodgers survived this evening's ordeal, Fergie would do his friend the supreme favor. He would kill him. She dropped her head on her folded arms and let her own tears come. And she prayed for George Rodgers never to awaken.

In the middle of a sleepless night Maj heard the phone ring downstairs. She heard Fergie's low voice. It was a short conversation. She met him in the hallway as he trudged back up the stairs. His face answered her unasked question.

"George died, didn't he, Fergie?"

The old man nodded. Maj went to him, put her arms around him, and rubbed his trembling shoulders. When his emotion subsided, he stepped back and looked at her.

"It's been pure pleasure having you with us, honey. You don't know how much it's meant to both of us. It's like having the old days back again with you humming and laughing around these old walls. We hate seeing you go."

"I know, Fergie. It's meant a great deal to me, too. I wish so much I could stay longer, but . . ."

"You can't, honey, we know. But maybe you can come back next year if we're still here. We'd like that."

"What do you mean, if you're still here? You've always been here. Why wouldn't you be here?" Her own adult voice sounded like that of her child's voice, high-pitched and shaky, as if she might suddenly cry.

"Someday we won't be." Fergie hugged her hard. "Well, you better get some sleep. You got a long day tomorrow, and I have a lot of work lined up. Keep busy, we keep busy. Best thing. 'Night, honey."

Maj got back into bed and pulled the quilt up under her chin. She stared up into the dark above her and let images of her mother and father, Granddad and Grandma, and Ada and Fergie drift by. It was all passing out of existence. Fergie and Ada and the West Wind were all that was left of those times. In a few years all of them would be gone, too.

She turned her face into the feather pillow. Oh, to be five years old again instead of fifty! To start over again instead of just maintaining.

How could she help them? She sensed they had wanted to rely on her, but understood that they shouldn't, couldn't. What did they expect of her? Nothing. And they never said one word to make her feel guilty about that.

She'd felt guilty on a regular basis during her married life with Jack. Somehow she'd always felt inadequate where he was concerned. Never doing enough, never giving enough, not smart enough, not sophisticated enough, not sexy enough, not anything enough.

Growing up, no one had expected anything of her other than to be happy. Then why had she felt a low, nagging sensation of being unhappy for so long? She was healthy. Had an uneventful childhood. Married her high school boyfriend. Had an abortion in a doctor's clean office, not in a seedy back room like one of her friends who ended up with a massive infection. Became a widow and learned her husband had a long-term affair while they were married which produced a son. Never had children because her husband said he didn't want any.

Stop! Don't think about that!

Funny how half a century could be synopsized like a book report for a sophomore English class. What did it really say about what was between the covers? Nothing . . . and everything.

What had she expected of herself? She guessed nothing. Only since she'd been talking professionally with Nan did she learn people should set goals and expect certain things of themselves. But it was too late for that now. Three quarters of her life was over. At least three quarters. What more could anyone expect but to live out the rest of life keeping even?

Maj tossed in bed, couldn't get comfortable, couldn't find that womblike nest she'd made in this wonderful old bed all week long. All she felt were lumps in the mattress. Her head ached.

She thought of Fergie and Ada again. Something as monumental as the tragic death of friends at this stage in their lives, and they didn't ask anything of her. She had simply listened.

Her eyes sprung open. Fergie . . . he wouldn't think of doing what George had done. Would he? She'd sensed a quiet desperation about him when he'd gone to bed after the phone call. Oh, no, he wouldn't, couldn't. But she recognized Ada was growing weaker no matter how much she tried to conceal it. And Fergie put in long, hard days keeping the lodge in the best shape he could.

She knew Noah helped them a lot. A stranger came to their aid. The West Wind had been their pride and joy, their life. They would surely lose the lodge if something didn't happen soon. And if they lost the lodge, they would have nothing to live for. . . .

Maj sat up. She dragged the quilt up to her chin. *She* had to make something happen for them. Soon.

Now.

She looked at the clock. Five A.M. She had to get some sleep. Tomorrow—no, today—was Sunday. She never could remember if Sunday was counted as the end of a week or the beginning.

The grating whine of a power saw sliced into Majesty's sleep like the cut of a razor blade. Groaning, she turned over in the brass bed to a cacophony of creaking springs, and pulled the thick patchwork quilt up under her chin.

Her head ached. Sunday morning, after a Saturday night like she'd never before experienced in her life.

She nestled her head farther into the oversize feather pillow. Every muscle and bone in her body protested movement. Her shoulders and back ached the most. Tension. Stress.

She thought of the Fergusons. Ada and Fergie in the kitchen talking and making breakfast. Ada and Fergie mourning the deaths of their friends. And she thought of George and Emma Rodgers, and her throat ached.

She thought of Noah. Noah on the Ferris wheel, Noah in his cabin. Noah's arms around her, his lips on hers, the smell of him, the hard and soft feel of him.

The power saw droned on in the background of her thoughts. Maj squinted toward the clock on the night table. The night table. She'd looked at it but hadn't really seen it until then. Made in the Adirondack twig style, it was earth brown, rustic, enduring.

Her eyes shifted back to the clock. Seven-fifteen, or thereabouts. Had she really been asleep for two hours? The night hadn't existed for her, and the past hours she'd lain in the bed were merely extensions of one of the longest days in her life.

Abruptly the whine of the saw stopped. She

heard shouts, followed by the ripping sound of a tree trunk and a loud thud, then another sound like ripping fabric, then a quieter thud.

Alert now, and alarmed, Maj bounded out of bed and ran to the window, yanking the pull and sending the dark shade snapping to the top. From her spot in the second story window she could see Fergie's back, see him push his visored red cap up off his forehead, scratch his head, and lean on a long-handled ax. His gaze was fixed across a felled tree, but she couldn't see anything beyond. Then he looked up toward her bedroom window.

A sickening thought flashed through her mind. She ripped her blue-flowered flannel nightgown up over her head and threw it on the bed. Quickly she pulled on jeans and jammed her feet into her sneakers, turning down the back of one in her haste, and wincing in pain as it rubbed hard over her heel. She fumbled with the hooks on her bra. Unable to get it fastened, she tossed it on top of the nightgown and pulled on a turtleneck sweater.

She ran down the stairs to the kitchen, past Ada, and out the back door, turned the corner by the woodshed, and ran alongside the building. Rounding the corner, she stopped short. Her mouth dropped open.

There in the middle of the gravel driveway sat Jack's yellow Mustang convertible, a tall white pine wedged in the cradle of its caved-in white vinyl top. She opened her arms and ran toward it as if to embrace a hurt child, but stopped abruptly at the sound of a slow-ticking rip as the tree slipped farther, wedging itself firmly between the metal ribs of the vinyl top, then folding them down in what seemed like slow motion.

Maj stood still in disbelief. Then she came out of her shock.

"Fergie!" she wailed, and a flock of blue jays that had retreated to the top of the trees at the first roar of the saw's motor left the grove entirely.

"Now, honey . . ." The old man started toward her, stepping through broken branches, crunching needles and twigs under his green rubber boots. His baggy gray pants caught on a sharp branch, and he fell headlong into the tree, his buffalo plaid jacket mixing into the pine green in a crazy-quilt pattern. "It was an accident," he sputtered through branches, scrambling to regain his balance.

Noah moved deftly over the fallen tree, picking his way carefully through the thick branches. Maj stepped into it as well. Fergie's arm flailed about like a red and black flag.

144

Noah grabbed at it several times, finally making contact at the same time Maj did, and the two of them helped him out of the tangle.

"Are you all right?" Maj's voice was full of concern.

"I'm okay, really, honey," Fergie said, working at catching his breath. "It was an accident, honey. Gosh, I'm sorry." He patted her back.

Satisfied that Fergie was unhurt, Maj stared at the flattened convertible top cradling the tall pine tree.

"I'm really sorry, Maj." Noah looked over his shoulder at the Mustang. "We should have moved your car, I guess, but I thought it was out of harm's way."

Fergie slipped his arm around her shoulders. "I'm sorry, honey" was all he could manage. He adjusted his cap nervously, a helpless look on his face. He stared at the ground, clearing his throat as Noah stood appraising the damage to the Mustang. Its yellow paint shone hopefully bright through the tangle of pine branches under the upwardly streaming morning sun.

Noah wondered why Maj didn't explode with anger at the situation. For some reason, he wanted to see her angry, wanted to see how she reacted in anger. He looked from her face back to the Mustang. It was a mess, he'd grant that. The color of the damned thing reminded him of the yellow mustard they'd squirted on their hot dogs at the firemen's field day. She'd have a good excuse now to have it repainted.

Maj leaned into the crook of Fergie's arm, her gaze and thoughts fixed on the Mustang. The last thing she had was extra money to pay for the damages. She didn't even know what the insurance would pay for.

Standing there with pine branches and chips around them, the Mustang all but buried under what looked like a small forest, Maj felt numb. She didn't know what she was feeling about what had happened to Jack's car. She'd never thought of it as her car, anyway, before now.

Now. Now, when it would be worth a fair sum of money because of its age and, up to this moment, mint condition. Now it could have truly meant something to her besides transportation out of Manhattan.

"How could this happen?" She leveled her gaze on Noah. "I thought you were an expert lumberman. You must have cut down hundreds of trees. You know how they fall, know how to place the cuts properly so they fall exactly where you want them to. Don't you?"

"Yes, ma'am." Noah avoided her eyes, and

with his hands in his pockets rocked back and forth in his boots. "Try to stay calm, Maj," he said. "I'm sure things look a lot better under that tree than they do above it. I'm sure it can be repaired." He smiled and winked then, trying to ease her mind. "Good thing it's a pine tree, not a redwood."

"Trust me, I am *very* calm—for me." Maj kept her eyes on him.

Noah looked over at Maj and resettled appraising eyes on her. She wore a rose turtleneck sweater cropped at the waist, and it easily occurred to him that she wasn't wearing a bra. He had to force himself not to stare at her breasts, not an easy task for him.

She stood taut like a coiled spring, jeans flowing in two columns of dark blue down her long legs. Her uncombed hair tumbled around her shoulders, and one unruly lock dipped in a deep wave over her left eye. She looked like she'd just fallen out of bed, all rumpled as if she'd been routed out of a comfortable nest.

But it was her eyes. Noah was fascinated the way they changed in color from blue to almost dark violet with green glints. He thoroughly enjoyed the whole picture.

His voice went soft with apology. "The trunk was split in two places—windstorm a few days ago, as Fergie said—and we thought we were, that is, *I* thought the tree would fall in a different direction than it did. Fergie warned me. . . ."

Maj listened to his explanation without reaction. Then a sharp breeze made her acutely aware of her bralessness. The cold air caused her nipples to stand erect and rub against the nubby yarns of her sweater. She was positive they were visible through the weave, but could not bring herself to look down and verify the fact, nor call attention to the possibility. Her calm control started to crumble.

"Please," she said, backing away, and wishing she were inside the kitchen, "just get the tree off the car. I'll have to think about what to do." She turned around and walked quickly toward the back door, knowing her face was flushed. She'd had a hell of a night deciding what she'd do about her departure from the West Wind, and now this. And all before her first cup of coffee.

Majesty bolted into the kitchen, letting the spring-loaded screen door slam behind her. Ada held out a mug of steaming coffee, which she accepted gratefully, warming her hands around it and sipping the hot liquid gingerly. She sank down in a chair at the table and leaned back.

"A tree fell on my car," she sighed.

"Oh, dear, I'm sorry," Ada said, sitting down with her. "Is it bad?"

"I don't know. I hope not. I need that car."

Ada rubbed Maj's arm lovingly. "I know, honey. I know you're eager to get started on the road for New York."

Maj stared straight ahead. "It was worth some money, but now . . ."

"It can probably be fixed." Ada got up and went slowly to the refrigerator. Hand on the door, she turned around and said with a hopeful voice, "Maybe you can take the train, or go to Placid or Saranac and rent a car. Then when yours is fixed, you can come back and get it." She poured a glass of orange juice and set it in front of Maj. "Here, drink this, honey, you'll feel better. Breakfast'll be ready soon as you clean up."

Majesty dutifully drank the orange juice, distracted by the myriad of thoughts working in her mind. Then she heard Noah and Fergie coming up the back steps. She pushed herself out of the chair and started out of the kitchen. Passing a small oak-framed mirror by the door, she caught a glimpse of her reflection. Her hands flew to her hair.

"Oh, my God!" she whispered hoarsely. "Look at me!" Puffy face, red-rimmed eyes, and hair in snarled disarray greeted her. And

149

her nipples were definitely visible through the sweater. The renewed flush of embarrassment crept up her throat and over her face, and she ran upstairs.

Twenty minutes later, freshly sponge-bathed and dressed in pale gray trousers and a forest-green turtleneck, Majesty walked downstairs. The aroma of frying smoked bacon curling out of the kitchen like beckoning fingers quickened her step. She entered the kitchen briskly.

Noah sat at the table engaged in serious conversation with Fergie and Ada, leisurely polishing off what looked like a three-course breakfast. He stood up when she came into the room and smiled warmly at her, the side of his sensuous lips quirking in a provocative smile.

"Well, good morning," he said with feigned formality negated by the sparkle of amusement in his eyes as he assessed her. "You look very familiar to me. You resemble a wild lady I met earlier this morning in an, ah, interesting sweater."

Maj tried to check a grin that threatened to curve her lips as she walked toward the table, but was unsuccessful. Fergie loudly cleared his throat while studiously picking pine needles from his pants.

She sat down and touched Ada's arm. "I'm

sorry, Ada. In all the excitement I forgot to ask how you're feeling this morning? I feel bad about George and Emma."

"I'm all right, honey." Ada patted her hand. "It's all for the best, I think."

There was nothing more they could say. The ensuing moments of silence underscored Ada's words for all of them.

Noah finished a cup of coffee, then pushed his chair away from the table and stood up. "I'll go out and have a look at your car and see what we can do about it. I know you're eager to get started." He stared hard at her. "You are eager, aren't you?"

"Very," Maj concurred. "I'll be in Granddad's study if you need me. There are a few things I want to look over."

Ada wiped the corner of her eye with her apron, then busied herself putting away the breakfast things. Fergie cleared his throat, and grabbing his jacket and cap, followed Noah out the door.

In the study Maj read over her grandfather's ledger and journal again. Then she looked into the distance and thought about Fergie and Ada. Their eyes were as red and swollen this morning as hers had been. She knew they'd been awake all night talking about their friends.

151

And maybe they'd been talking about themselves, too.

Ada and Fergie. After her grandparents were gone, they had stepped in to fill the void, offering their love and support. She remembered how they helped her through the death of her parents, driving more than six hours in that old pickup to be with her each time. Maj knew those were the longest and hardest trips they'd ever taken.

Except maybe for the one to Tupper Lake last night.

Could she make a similar journey for them?

A light knock at the open door broke her reverie. "Didn't mean to interrupt, honey." Ada stepped into the room. "The menfolks got the tree off your car. They want you to come out and see."

Maj closed the ledger. "Thanks, Ada, I'm coming."

Noah met her in the kitchen. He ran a hand through the shock of hair over his forehead before he spoke. "It's not as bad as it could have been," he told her, sounding like a doctor diagnosing an illness. "It's drivable, I believe, but since we didn't have the keys, we didn't try the engine. Looks as if the damage is confined to the top and a few scratches to the paint."

Majesty followed him out the screen door onto the back porch. Ada followed, bracing her hand on her crippled leg as Maj had always remembered her doing.

When they reached the forlorn-looking Mustang, Fergie was brushing pine needles off the hood and, using his own bandanna, was wiping away spots of sticky sap that had oozed out of the tree and clung to the paint in several places.

Majesty walked around the car, running a hand over it now and then. She saw no dents, but plenty of scrapes and scratches. She peered through the torn vinyl roof over the mangled ribs that had once held it in place. Mentally she figured a completely new tree could be reconstructed with the amount of debris that covered the seats and carpet.

She dug in her pocket for the keys, got in, and tried the engine. It started immediately.

"Well, I guess it's not the end of the world." She smiled at Fergie's audible sigh of relief. "The top is a terminal case, but it can be replaced. It may be difficult finding the right color paint to match the original though."

Noah stepped around to the driver's side and leaned his elbows on the lowered window. His face was only inches from hers. "A color like that could take years to find," he said softly.

"You'd want to be here to try samples just to be certain you get the right one."

"I would, wouldn't I?" Maj said, her gaze caught in his.

"You take that top into town tomorrow, Noah," Fergie said, coming over to them. "Joe Mason's the best around. He'll fix 'er up just like new. You won't have to worry about a thing, honey."

"Looks like I'm marooned, doesn't it?" Maj asked, still looking into Noah's eyes.

"Looks like it." He grinned. "Good thing you're not alone, isn't it? I mean, so far away from home, and everything."

Home. Maj came to her senses then. "I've got to make some phone calls and let people know what's happened."

She turned the ignition off, but Noah did not make a move to let her out of the car. He just smiled at her, and she thought she detected a note of triumph in his eyes. She caught his scent on a morning breeze, a combination of dew-washed grass and leather and Ivory soap. Curious. Ivory soap on a rugged outdoorsman like Noah Decker.

"Does this mean you're staying a spell? You can take the truck if you have to go someplace," Fergie volunteered loudly, clearly a happier man than he'd been all morning.

154

"Yes, I'm staying a spell, Fergie." Maj pulled the keys out of the ignition and tripped the door handle. "You'll have to move," she said to Noah, "if I'm to get out."

"As long as you don't get away," he whispered. "Allow me." He bowed and opened the door for her. "I'd say it's too bad your trip back to New York is being delayed if I really meant it. Which I don't. But I will say it's too bad about the damage to your car, which I do."

"Yes, it is too bad, isn't it?" Maj said evenly.

"Which one?"

She didn't answer.

That afternoon, after a long session of arguing with herself, Maj called Nan. She told her everything that had happened, about George and Emma, and her car. She didn't say anything about the Ferris wheel and events in Noah's cabin.

"So, what did you do to make this lumberjack pull such a great stunt?" Nan bubbled with excitement.

"Stunt?"

"Yes. Isn't it possible he dropped a tree on your car just to get you to stay?"

"Of course not. He's pretty unpredictable, but he'd never do anything that despicable."

"Despicable? Who said anything about despicable? I think it's a romantic idea." Nan sighed. "Are you sure you didn't do anything to cause this, ah, act of nature?"

"Don't be ridiculous. I didn't do anything."

"Nothing at all?"

"Nothing at all."

"I'm very sorry to hear that. You've had a whole week."

"Oh, Nan, for heaven's sake!"

"What?"

"Don't act so innocent. I know what you're hinting at."

"What is it you think I'm hinting at?" Nan asked, feigning indignant innocence.

"Sex, of course. What else?"

"Indeed, what else is there?"

Maj decided to ignore that question. "As soon as I figure out what I'm going to do, I'll call you back, okay?"

"I have a suggestion."

"I've heard your suggestions before, so don't give me the same ones." Maj laughed lightly.

"Stay there."

Maj didn't respond. She looked down at the faded West Wind tourist brochures on the foyer table, fanned them out, then closed them into a pile.

"Maj?"

"I heard you."

"You've already thought of that suggestion, haven't you?"

Maj hesitated, then she said, "Yes. But how can I possibly do that? There's my job, the bills, the apartment and my things, and—"

"Bullshit!"

"What do you mean bullshit? God, Nan, look at the mess I'm still cleaning up back there. How can I take on another one?"

"I don't know. You're right. How can you take on another mess? I mean, you have so much here to cherish, so much that means everything to you," Nan said with a deliberate thoughtful edge.

"Well, I don't exactly *cherish* what I have there. I mean, most of it I could sell. That would bring a little money."

"Yes, it would, but your job is very important to you, and all those wonderful people you work with. You'd miss them. How much money do you need?"

"I wouldn't miss them, and they wouldn't miss me. There's about fifteen thousand owed on the taxes on the West Wind. Then it would take a lot more than that to get the place ready for business again. I wouldn't know where to start."

"Yeah, that sounds like a huge undertaking. Too bad you don't know anyone who could help with the fixing up."

"Well, Noah is pretty good at it. And I'm sure there are people in town who could—"

"Sure! So your biggest problem to start with is paying off the debts here, then raising the money for the taxes and getting a loan for the rebuilding." Nan's voice had suddenly taken on a rush of enthusiasm.

"Wait a minute." Maj drew out the words slowly. "Did you just turn this whole conversation around so that I talked myself into staying up here?"

"Who me?"

"Yeah, you. I must be insane to even think about such an idea."

"Then don't think, just do it!" Nan pushed. "You know you want to, don't you?"

Maj drew in a sharp breath. "All right. Confession time. I knew it before I got out of bed this morning. I can't leave Ada and Fergie. I don't want to leave them. They need me and I want to give them all the time and resources I have. I know now that they and the West Wind mean everything to me. I guess I just wanted you to tell me I was making sense."

"Consider it done."

"But how can I . . . ?" Maj ran a trembling hand through her hair.

158

"By letting your friend help you out. I'll call the ad agency for you in the morning. Tell me what you want saved in that apartment, and Dave and I will pack it up and ship it to you. We'll sell the rest and raise some money for you."

"Dave?"

"The Radio Shack guy. That's what I wanted to tell you about. Well, that can wait! What else? Bank accounts?"

"Checking, and minuscule savings."

"What about that classic Mustang? Why don't you sell the damned thing? That should bring something."

"Remember the little item of the tree through the convertible top?"

"Stroke of genius! I can't wait to meet this Noah guy!" Nan gushed.

"It was an accident, Nan," Maj shouted into the phone.

"Call it an accident, call it fate, call it whatever. But this is exactly what you need to get your life back on course, sweetie."

"Yes, or put me on welfare for the rest of my life."

"Hey, it's the American way! Now, don't worry about anything here. I promise I can take care of everything. You just put things into motion up there, okay?"

"Okay. And thanks, Nan, for talking me into something I knew I wanted to do. You're a good friend . . . I think."

"You know I am! I'll be in touch." She hung up.

Maj sank down on the floor by the registration desk, and pulled her knees up to her chin. She'd done it now. The last vestiges of her sanity had come crashing down with that white pine laying in a heap in the Mustang.

Fifty-one years old and starting a whole new life as if she had fifty-one more to live it.

She stood up, stretched, and took a deep breath. What did it matter if there were fifty years, or ten years, or even one year? No matter how many, she'd make them good years for Ada and Fergie.

And it would be the best time of her own life. She knew it.

What a difference a week made!

Chapter Seven

"I thought there used to be a town near here," Majesty mused Monday morning as Noah drove her car along a winding mountain road. She wore a long pale blue chiffon scarf wrapped around her head and black framed sunglasses, à la Grace Kelly.

The convertible top had been removed and was piled in an ungainly heap in the backseat.

"You're thinking of Mount Kidd, maybe. It died a painful death."

"Oh, that's right. Granddad always thought Mount Kidd would come back again someday. But I guess it never did."

Noah reached into his shirt pocket for his sunglasses. The sun had climbed high enough so that it penetrated the thick maples over their heads, sending strobelike rays into their eyes as they passed beneath them.

"You've made them happier 'than they've

been in years, you know," he said, and she didn't have to ask whom he was talking about.

"They deserve it."

"Took a lot of guts to do what you did. I admire you. Not a lot of people could quit a job and give up everything in one night, just like that." He snapped his fingers.

"Did I do a thing like that?" Maj laughed with a trace of incredulity.

"You sure did. It's a great feeling, isn't it?"

"Sounds like you've had a similar experience."

"I have," he admitted freely. "But mine was a selfish decision. I did it for me, and no one else."

Maj watched the road winding in front of them. "I'm not so certain mine wasn't selfish either."

"Oh?"

"Yes. I truly hope I can work something out for Ada and Fergie, but I think the move is good for me, too."

"Sick of the big city?"

"Mmm-hmm, I guess so. Sick of the treadmill. Sick of working for someone. Sick of just paying bills and not feeling anything, not doing anything that matters to me or anybody else." She gave him a fleeting glance, embarrassed at sharing such a personal confession to someone she'd known only a week. Yet, she was feeling curiously close to him.

"I know exactly what you mean," he responded quickly. "You just keep thinking there's more, you're worth more, can do more, make a difference. Simplification was the first move for me. After a run of some risky business being a stunt pilot. Have you ever read Thoreau? He had the right idea, I think."

Maj stayed silent in thought for a few minutes.

"What really happened, Noah? I mean to the West Wind and Mount Kidd?" She turned toward him and shaded her eyes with her hand. "I remember some of the wealthy people who used to stay at the lodge. Granddad loved to talk about when Rockefeller—I forgot which one—stayed up in the blue room on the second floor. That was the only room with a private bath, as I remember. Everyone else was obliged to go down the halls to community bathrooms."

Suddenly Noah hit the brakes and the Mustang slid to a screeching halt as a deer bounded across the road in front of them. Noah shot a protective right arm across Majesty's chest. Two more deer crashed out of the woods, white tails waving high, and bobbed to the other side after the first one.

"You all right?" He turned quickly toward her.

"Yes," she responded breathlessly, and looked down to where his arm still rested across her chest. "I'm wearing a seat belt."

Noah quickly brought his arm away and clamped his hand to the steering wheel.

Maj watched the deer disappear into thick underbrush. "They were so beautiful—and so close."

"They're particularly plentiful along this road," Noah told her. "You never know when one might decide to cross, and where there's one, there are always at least two more." He put the car in drive and pointed it back on the road.

"I guess I'd forgotten how often we would see deer when I visited as a child, or how close they always seemed to be." She rushed her words. "I used to think I saw sadness in those velvet-brown eyes. I always felt sorry when Granddad would write how he bagged a deer and told how tasty the venison was or was not, depending on the year."

"Sometimes it's easy to forget things when you're away from them." Noah looked at her

164

for a moment, then drew his eyes back to the road. "I always hated venison. Hated even the smell of it cooking. Guess that's why I was never a deer hunter. Small game is all I've ever hunted."

"What, no women?" Majesty's question came out too quickly and too flippantly, she thought in the split second after it left her lips. What made her ask that?

Noah paused a moment before answering. "A few. Nothing important."

He made a left turn onto a road that was the same as the other—tree-lined, narrow, and winding. The sun shone brighter, but the air was still crisp and cool.

"You?" Noah sent her a brief glance.

"Me?"

"Yes. Ever hunt? Has there been another man since your husband died?"

"Not so anyone would notice. Same luck as you," she answered, then quickly returned to the original subject. "What about the luck of Mount Kidd?"

"Nothing left to keep her going. Once the lumber and iron ore were exhausted, the people left, too."

"But all these trees . . ." Majesty waved her arm, indicating the trees on both sides of the road and ahead up the mountains as far as they could see.

"Too far away to haul, for one thing, and too expensive. Mount Kidd's story is the same as so many others up in the northwoods, Maj. Boom to bust. Railroads, steamboats, tanneries, wealthy vacationers with their great camps and yachts — all a faded memory. Lumber and iron ore companies built them and the same companies destroyed them when they exhausted the resources and moved on. What brought the people in at first took them out at last. Like everything else, progress changes things. There's always someone else with more money to offer than most people can refuse, even if they wanted to stay."

Majesty stared straight ahead. "Like Gerald Morris?"

"Like Gerald Morris."

"You mentioned your family has been here a long time."

"Un-hunh. My grandfather started a lumber mill here in the late twenties on property his father and grandfather owned and cleared in the 1800s."

"I never knew you when I used to come up here summers. At least I don't remember you. I don't mean that as an insult," she added hastily, lest he think she thought he was a for-gettable person. He certainly wasn't that.

Noah smiled in silence. Maj pressed on. "Did your grandfather have anything to do with the decline and fall of the Mount Kidd empire?"

"Nothing," came the clipped reply. "He was one of the ones who stayed and taught his sons to work at rebuilding the land. If anything, his partner, Morris, had a lot to do with the death of Mount Kidd — and of my grandfather."

"Morris? As in Gerald Morris?"

"His grandfather and my grandfather were childhood friends, and later partners in the lumber mill. Big difference in them was that Morris was a get-rich-quick-and-get-out sort of a guy who didn't care who got hurt in his wake. My grandfather, and yours, too, were men with strong work ethics and compassion for the land and resources. They wanted to give back as much as they got out of it. But, not everyone cares that much, sorry to say."

A complex of buildings on the right side of the road caught Maj's attention. As they drew closer she saw a large wooden sign lettered in red: *Decker & Son Lumber*.

"Decker," she read. "Is that your place?"

"Yep."

"You have a son?"

"No." He laughed. "At least I don't think so!" When she did not respond, Noah went on. "It's generational. Decker was my grandfather and son was my father, then Decker was my father and son was me. Now that Dad's gone, it's just me, Decker. No son, and no possibility of my daughter going into the lumber business. Maybe someday there'll be another grandson again."

He has a daughter. That piece of news hit Maj like a falling pine. She wanted to ask about a wife, but thought better of it. "Where is she? Your daughter, I mean?"

"Second year at Skidmore. Now that you're staying, you'll get to meet her. We've been talking about her coming up for a visit sometime." He pulled the car to a stop. "We're here," he announced.

Maj looked around, twisting in the car seat. Noah had pulled the car in front of a ramshackle building with an ancient round red and white Texaco gas pump standing guard at the end of a porchlike overhang.

"We're where?"

Noah turned off the engine, honked the horn, and looked over at Maj. "Joe Mason's garage. You do remember why we were coming here, don't you?" He made a sweeping gesture over the backseat filled with the mangled convertible top.

"Oh, I remember very well." She gave him an amused sidelong glance.

A bent old man shuffled out from around the back of the building. He passed a small metal sign that proclaimed the establishment to be the Mason Garage and Body Shop. Majesty's eyes went heavenward. Joe Mason couldn't know a thing about repairing a classic Mustang convertible unless, of course, he worked closely with the first Henry Ford. As she watched the old man slowly approaching them, Maj felt that idea was not entirely out of the realm of possibility. Jack would be mortified to think of such a person touching his beloved car. She smiled to herself with amused irony at the thought.

"Hi, Horace," Noah stood up in the car, bracing himself over the windshield and waving a greeting to the old man. At the mention of his name, Majesty exuded a sigh of relief, thankful that this man was not Joe Mason.

"Joe around?" Noah asked in a loud voice.

"What?" Horace answered in a gravelly voice, cupping a hand to his left ear.

169

"Is your grandson here?" Noah called out more slowly. Majesty was not at all surprised to find that this was yet another person's grandfather involved in a family business.

Horace shook his wiry white head. "Diner. Gone to the diner for coffee." He wiped his brow with a faded blue bandanna. "Thet you, Noah?"

"Yes, it's me, Horace."

"Didn't recognize ya in thet car. Sure is bright, Noah."

"Sure is, Horace."

"Looks t'need work, though," Horace observed, pointing at the pile in the backseat and running his bony hand over a few scratches. "You'll be needin' Joe."

"You got that right, Horace. You say he's at the diner? We'll go find him."

"Wait, Noah. Where's your manners?" Horace took small halting steps toward Maj's side of the car. "You didn't introduce me to your lady friend here. Is she a new one?"

Majesty rather enjoyed seeing Noah blush a deep crimson at the old man's question. "Uh, no, Horace. I mean yes. She's new, I mean, she's new up north." He added hastily, "Well, she not really new up north exactly. She's . . ." He pulled his hands away from the edge of the windshield, noticing sticky pine sap showing in black lines on his palms.

"Perhaps you should let me handle this since you seem to be having so much difficulty," Majesty said quietly. She turned to the old man and smiled warmly, holding her hand out over the door. "I'm Majesty Wilde, Mr. Mason, Henry Wilde's granddaughter." To Noah she said in an aside, "I'm a quick study."

The old man accepted her hand in a surprisingly strong grip. "You don't say," he said with amazement. "Where'd you come from, girl?" He held on to her hand, shaking it in an exaggerated slow movement.

"New York, sir. New York City."

"You don't say," Horace Mason repeated.

"Yes, sir," Maj replied, trying gently to extract her hand. He held on to it with both of his.

"Wal, don't thet beat all?" Horace croaked. "Henry's granddaughter." He looked her over with small shining gray eyes. "Henry's granddaughter. You hear thet, Noah? She's Henry Wilde's granddaughter!"

"Yes, I know, Horace." Noah wiped his hands on a handkerchief.

"Fergusons know you're here, girl?" Horace squinted close to her face.

171

"Yes, they do, Mr. Mason. I'm staying with the Fergusons at the West Wind Lodge."

Horace let go with one of his hands and scratched his thatched white head. "Don't thet beat all?" He stared into space for a brief 'moment. "I'll be sure an' tell Joe you was here."

"We'll find him at the diner, Horace." Noah turned on the ignition.

" 'Less you wanna look him up at the diner," Horace added.

"That's a good idea, Horace. You'll have to let go of Majesty now so we can do that."

"Right!" Horace said, more quickly than he'd said anything before. He let go of Maj's hand and waved them away.

As Noah pulled the car out onto the road, Majesty waved back to the old man. "Nice to meet you, Mr. Mason," she called, and was positive she could read his lips saying, "Don't thet beat all?" Smiling, she settled back in the seat and felt herself becoming more comfortable in the place that was a curious blend of fond memories and new experiences.

"How'd you get that name anyway? Majesty." Noah said with honest interest.

"If you laugh, you can never drive this car again," she chided.

"Is it that bad?"

"Do you promise or not?"

"Okay, I promise I won't laugh. Now tell me!"

"It's Granddad's fault. He wanted me named in honor of the mountains he loved."

"That's wonderful. It's a nice name, it suits you. Why do you think I'd laugh about that?"

"Well, it was tough growing up with this name. To this day I can't wear purple."

"What's purple have to do with anything?"

She took a deep breath. "I've never told this to a living soul. Not even my psychotherapist."

"Privileged information? I'm honored."

"Just remember your promise. When I was in junior high and I started to . . . ah . . . develop, I wore my favorite purple sweater to school one day. The boys started singing 'America the Beautiful,' and pointed at me when they came to that line about purple mountain's majesty. I wanted to die."

Noah burst out laughing.

"Hey, you promised!" She gave him a good-natured punch on his shoulder.

"I did, didn't I? I apologize. And furthermore, I apologize to you for all those misguided nasty boys who couldn't see how your name would fit you so beautifully when you grew up." He kept his eyes on the road.

173

As Noah drove the rest of the way into town, every now and then he stole a glance at Majesty, who was intently scanning buildings and stores and people on the sidewalks as they passed. She'd removed the blue scarf, and her hair blew around her face in gentle waves, moving enticingly as the speed of the car decreased. She is beautiful, he thought suddenly, as if it had just occurred to him.

"Seems the Morrises moved in and took over Pinewood when they left Mount Kidd," Maj observed.

Noah lazily emerged from his thoughts. "Hmm?"

"The Morrises. I said, it looks like they moved here and took over. Morris Hotel, Morris Department Store, Morris Park," she read. "What don't they own around here?"

"Decker and Son Lumber," Noah snapped, "and Danbury's Hardware . . . yet." He pulled the car sharply into a diagonal parking place in front of the Coffee Cup, the local diner. "This is where Joe is," he said more gently. "Got a crush on a cute waitress in here."

Majesty gave him a cursory glance. It sounded to her as if the Decker-Morris disagreement, or feud, or whatever it was, still lived in the younger generation.

174

Noah came around to her side to open her door, but she'd opened it and had stepped out before he got there.

"I can open that for you," he said, taking the handle and closing the door carefully.

"Thank you. I can open it too," Maj said, smiling.

"Hey, Decker!" A laughing voice boomed from the other side of the street. "Sinking your money into antique cars now?"

Noah ignored the barb and took Majesty's elbow to propel her into the diner.

"Friend of yours?"

"Not mine," he replied darkly.

"Decker!" The voice was closer now. "You really ought to build a garage at that cabin of yours to hide a flashy car like that! So out of character for you." He laughed as if he'd made the sharpest of jokes.

Majesty took instant offense at the tone and content of the man's words, and she spun around to face him, a caustic retort ready to spill over her lips.

"Gerald Morris, isn't it?" she whispered.

"Ignore him," Noah whispered back, and tugged on her elbow.

"Just who does he think he is?" she flashed back.

"Don't ask him. He's liable to tell you, and we'll be here all day."

The portly Morris made a beeline for them just as Noah's hand was on the diner door. He strolled around the front of the Mustang, then stopped near them and stood with his feet slightly apart. His upper lip curled at one corner like a sneer as his small gray eyes made a slow sweep of Majesty.

"Majesty, this is—"

"Gerald Morris," she cut in.

"The third," Noah finished. The word came through his lips with a bite behind it.

"We met the other day at the West Wind."

"Ah, yes, Majesty Wilde." Morris held out his hand. "Nice to see you again, and may I say that's a beautiful name for a beautiful lady. My friends call me Gerry."

Maj's hand was quite suddenly engulfed by his thick one, and she felt caught in a trap.

"Of which you have precious few," Noah interjected. "However, you should hear what his legions of enemies call him," he said near Maj's ear.

"Shame about your car, Decker. Now, if I owned a classic number like this"—his eyes shifted to Maj first and then to the Mustang—"I'd put a lot of money into it and keep it purring. Decker never was good at taking care of classic bodies"—he turned back to Maj— "cars *or* women. I hope we will become *very* close friends," he said suggestively, ignoring Noah. "May I entice you away from Decker and take you to a place more fitting of your beauty?"

Maj took a step back. "If you'll excuse us, Mr. Morris, Mr. Decker and I have business with someone inside this restaurant. Incidentally, you might be interested in knowing this particular classic body belongs to me." She gestured toward the Mustang, then turned toward Noah, linking her arm through his. "Shall we?" she asked sweetly, then preceded him toward the door, pushed it open, and went into the diner.

Maj slid into a green vinyl cushioned booth and snapped open a coffee-stained menu. Her face was moist, and little tendrils of hair clung near her cheeks. She was conscious of Noah's assessing look as he slid in the seat across from her. Taking a tissue from her bag, she dabbed under her eyes and over her lips.

"The morning air was so cold, who would ever think it could turn warm so quickly?" she said lightly. "I'll have to learn how to dress all over again."

After a long moment Noah said quietly, "You look fine. Dressed perfectly for riding in broken cars and giving weather reports." He needled her with good-natured lightness. "I'm sorry about the unpleasantness with Morris. I hope you're not too upset by it."

Maj's foot swung up and down impatiently under the table. "I'm not upset, I'm angry. He certainly has a high opinion of himself and a low opinion of women. Gerald Morris is the kind who gives himself away almost by the way he combs his hair and walks, or should I say swaggers?"

"Sounds like you've been acquainted with a few of his type."

She ignored his comment. "Could you call a waitress?"

"No need to, she's on her way," came his soft reply.

"Hi, Noah! Two coffees to start?" A waitress in a well-worn white uniform and red apron bustled over to their booth. Her bright gold curls bounced over her left eye as she held with anticipation a chrome pot and two mugs.

"Hi, Margie. Yes, thanks."

Margie poured the coffee with quick deftness while she answered Noah's questions about her parents. Maj wanted nothing but coffee, and

Noah ordered a jelly doughnut.

"Joe here?" Noah asked Margie when she brought his doughnut.

"In the back," Margie replied, indicating the kitchen door with a toss of her curls.

"When he's through out there, would you ask him to come join us for a bit?"

"Sure, Noah. He'll be right over."

Majesty sat silently drinking her coffee, lost in thought. Noah watched her carefully, trying to define her mood. Entirely conscious of his own stirrings, he couldn't define those either. He hadn't liked the way Morris eyed her, he knew that much. Morris always seemed to have a way with women. For the life of him, Noah couldn't figure out how any woman could stand being in the company of such an arrogant, unattractive—maybe it was the way he threw his money around.

But Maj reacted differently, self-assured, in control of herself. She'd put the son of a bitch in his place! He was proud of her. So what was wrong with him? Could it be jealousy he was feeling? That shouldn't happen. He hadn't the right to those kinds of feelings.

"Penny for your thoughts." He broke gently into the silence and took her hand in his.

"They're not worth that much," she re-

179

sponded dully, avoiding eye contact with him but leaving her hand where it rested.

"Morris does that to people."

"Does what? Acts like a conceited boor?"

"That's no act." Noah stared long and hard at her until she returned his gaze. Then he flashed a wide smile and gave a low laugh. "Comes naturally to a guy like that, and something tells me you know his kind well. Or maybe I should say *knew.*"

Before she could answer, a lanky, incredibly thin young man wearing a straw cowboy hat folded his long frame and slid effortlessly into the booth beside Noah. He stretched his legs outside the booth until they reached Maj's side, and crossed his scuffed motorcycle boots at the ankles.

"Noah. Ma'am." He tipped his hat but didn't remove it. "Heard you wuz lookin' fer me," he drawled with what sounded like an affected western accent. "What's up?"

"Joe, meet Majesty Wilde. She's staying at the West Wind with the Fergusons. Had a rather, shall we say, unfortunate accident with her car. We'd like you to take a look at it and see what you can do about it."

Joe nodded his head. "Saw you drive up. Figured you might be needin' my advice.

180

Thet's a sorry mess you got there, miss."

"I'm sorry to have to agree with you, Mr. Mason." Maj nodded. "Can you help me out with it?"

"I'm sure ol' Gerry Morris would like to help you out purty good. Right, Noah?" With a throaty chuckle Joe jabbed Noah in the ribs, then pulled out a pouch of chewing tobacco. He was still chuckling while he placed a brown wad in his lower cheek, then frowned when Maj didn't respond and leaned close to Noah. "City girl, ain't she? What's the matter, can't she take ribbin'?"

"Now, Joe, Miss Wilde's been having a difficult time." Noah spoke quietly. "I'm sure you can understand that. I've seen plenty of mornings when you couldn't stand the sound of a bird chirping! She has a lot on her mind. Right, Maj?"

Majesty remained silent, her eyes fixed on the sidewalk in front of the diner, where Gerald Morris stood talking to two men in dark suits. Noah's eyes followed her gaze, then shifted back to her face.

"Right," he answered for her, then turned back to Joe. "She's heard you're the best around here and would like your opinion on what can be done to fix up her car. Why don't

181

you take a look at it while we finish our coffee?"

Joe chewed his tobacco slowly while Noah spoke, all the time watching Majesty carefully. He continued to chew thoughtfully for a long time. "Right," he said, keeping his gaze on her. He unfolded his long frame and stood up, then scuffed his way out to the Mustang.

"It won't do to alienate people like Joe Mason right off the bat," Noah cautioned her. "He's more of a craftsman than he looks, not to mention he's the only game in town. You treat these people right and they'll knock themselves out for you."

Majesty drew her gaze back to Noah. "I'm sorry. I was just thinking. If I've offended Joe, I'll certainly apologize to him."

"He'll get over it," Noah assured her.

"You really don't like him at all, do you? Gerald Morris, I mean." Maj's gaze was steady. "It's fairly clear that he doesn't like you either. Is all this left over from the days of your respective grandfathers, or is there more?"

"What's past is past and nothing can be done about it. You're right, I don't like him. I don't like what he's doing to these mountain towns, and I don't like his type."

182

"What do you think that type is?" Maj watched Morris, now in conversation with Joe Mason in back of her car, through the diner window.

"Users." Noah's answer was quick and matter-of-fact. "His kind takes, and the only thing they ever give back is a lot of pain."

Maj pulled her gaze back to Noah. "You sound like someone who has experienced that kind of pain sometime in your life. Was Gerald Morris responsible for it?"

"I've discovered the present is always more interesting than the past." His comment was cold, and it was clear to Majesty that the subject was closed.

She turned her head back toward the window, and watched Morris with Joe Mason. "You know," she said as if her thoughts were forming at the moment she spoke, "I don't really care a whit about that Mustang. I mean, I have no sentimental feeling about it. But it's worth some money, and a classic car like that can mean a lot to someone who likes to collect things."

Noah tilted his head. "What are you saying? You don't want to repair it?"

"It's worth more in perfect condition," she said distantly.

"Exactly, that's why you have to get it repaired properly."

"Not necessarily." She looked back at him. "If you were a collector of say, antique or classic cars, what would you be willing to pay for a Mustang that age and that color?"

"I hate that color."

"Pretend it's metallic blue, or something. What would you pay?"

Noah gave it some thought. "Oh, it'd be worth maybe eleven or twelve thousand."

"That much, hunh?" She looked back at him and broke into a big smile. "Come on. And don't forget your offer!" She slid out of the booth, and motioned for him to follow as he sat there with surprise on his face.

On the sidewalk Maj took in a deep breath of the crisp spring air and walked toward the Mustang. Gerald Morris broke out in obviously insincere laughter at something Joe Mason said, then motioned that Majesty was coming up behind them. Joe turned around.

Majesty spun around toward Noah, who practically ran into her when she stopped. "Twelve thousand? You're offering twelve thousand for my pride and joy here? God, Mr. Decker, I thought you were going to make me a reasonable offer for it. That is an insult!"

184

"But," Noah started, then caught himself. "Look, *Miss* Wilde, face it, you're in a bind. You need money. All I'm trying to do is help you out. It's a good deal I'm offering. After all, it's going to cost me a bundle to fix this jalopy, you know."

"Jalopy? You, Mr. Decker, have no understanding of true class. Let me ask someone who obviously does. Well, Mr. Mason, what do you think?" Majesty was careful to keep genuine respect in her question to Joe. "What do you think of this beautiful classic car and Mr. Decker's pitiful offer?"

Joe kicked at a tire and spat a stream of tobacco juice toward the curb before he answered. "Wal, if this baby was mine, I'd sure think she was worth it. It's a purty big job, but I can handle it. Have to order the top special, and if I can get some matching paint, it'll look like the day it came off the line."

"And then what would be your opinion of how much it's worth?"

Joe scratched his head.

Gerald Morris grabbed his arm. "Here, Joe, let an expert in money matters take over. That little sweetheart would easily be worth thirteen thousand to a discerning eye like mine, Miss Wilde."

Maj shot a purposefully satisfied look toward Noah. "So you'd be willing to pay thirteen thousand, Mr. Morris?"

"Yes." Morris patted his girth and shot a look of triumph toward Noah.

"I knew I was in the presence of a man with an understanding for the finer things in life. You strike me, Mr. Morris, as a person who could write out a check instantly when he saw something he wanted. Am I right?" Maj smiled conspiratorially at him.

"I know what I like," Morris came back suggestively, "and I'm more than willing to pay for it."

"I admire a man who thinks with such acumen," Maj came back just as suggestively. Morris took her hand.

"Fourteen thousand!" Noah said, and stepped closer to them.

Maj turned and glared at him, speechless.

Noah stepped back. "And that's my last offer. Take it or leave it."

Momentarily nonplused, Maj quickly regained her composure and turned back to Morris. She gazed up at him and squeezed his hand. "What do you think, Mr. Morris? Has Mr. Decker more of an understanding of the true value of things than I? Or, heaven for-

186

fend, even of a man like yourself?"

Morris leered so obviously at Maj that Noah felt his fists doubling of their own accord.

"Decker hardly has an understanding of money. I would give you fifteen thousand without batting an eyelash, my dear." He rubbed her palm.

Maj's stomach churned, but she made herself squeeze his hand. She batted her own eyelashes. "Why, Mr. Morris, you are the one, aren't you? You've just made me an offer I can't refuse. I'll take it. And I must say I'm honored to know . . . *she*"— she wiped an imaginary tear from her eye and patted the scratched door of the Mustang—"will be in your very capable and loving hands."

Morris's jaw dropped. "Well, Miss Wilde, I wouldn't dream of taking your—"

Noah stepped in. "Well, Morris, I guess I have to bow to your business skills. Once again you've bested me in one of the sweetest deals around. Do me a favor and write the check right now so I can see it. I might as well be embarrassed right to the end."

When Morris hesitated, Maj looked up at him. "Thank you . . . Gerry," she whispered, "for helping me prove I know the right man when I see him. Perhaps someday I'll be in a position to return the favor." She winked.

Morris beamed, whipped out his checkbook and wrote a check for fifteen thousand as if it were fifteen dollars. Maj accepted it graciously, folded it, and placed it securely in her purse. She patted the hood in fond farewell to the Mustang, and turned to Morris, handing him the keys.

"Thank you, Mr. Morris, I know you'll take tender loving care of her. I'll have the transfer made out immediately." She turned back to Noah. "Mr. Decker, I'm not feeling very well. Would you mind taking me back into the restaurant for a glass of water? I want to leave Mr. Morris alone with her now."

Noah took her arm and turned her toward the Coffee Cup. Maj sent a wan wave to Morris, and let Noah lead her away, leaving Morris staring after her and Joe holding his hat and spitting tobacco juice.

"A little thick, wasn't it?" Noah muttered in her ear.

"Well, what about you? I could have kicked you when you came back with that counteroffer. I was sure we'd lose him then." They went to a back booth in the diner, far away from the street window.

"But we didn't, did we? Thanks to your eyelash batting." He mimicked her with batting of his own. "What was that all about?"

"That's the kind of thing a man like Morris responds to."

"You did it quite well. Lots of practice?"

Maj kicked him under the table, and he feigned deep pain. "I was almost sick to my stomach doing that. Putting the female gender on a car bugs the hell out of me."

"*Gerry* liked it." Noah wagged his shoulders.

"Didn't he though?" Maj laughed.

"I hope you noticed that I just managed to get us fifteen thousand dollars so the back taxes on the lodge can be paid," he said smugly.

"*You* got *us?*" she said with exaggerated irritation. "*I* had to do all the dirty work."

"Oh, yeah? And I'll just bet if Morris hadn't counteroffered, you'd have stuck me on the spot for the fourteen thousand. It was my quick thinking that upped the ante. Admit it!" He leaned back in the booth, arms folded across his chest, looking very self-satisfied.

"You scared the wits out of me with that! I had to think fast and butter that guy up!" Maj threw at him.

"What a team, right? We're one hell of a team! Morris has just paid the back taxes on the West Wind for us, and nixed his own deal to get the place by default!" Noah leaned across the table and held out his right hand.

Maj set her lips, and then a spate of laughter erupted from her. "Right! One hell of a team!"

She gave him her right hand, and he closed both his over it. He leaned over the table and gave her a warm kiss full on the lips. When he released her, she slanted her eyes around the room, slightly embarrassed by his display, yet feeling happy.

"Now," she said, "you'd better point me to the bank and the town clerk's office. I want to clear that debt first thing."

Noah stood up and bowed, then gestured the way toward the door.

While Maj opened an account at the Pine Valley Bank, then walked to the town clerk's office and paid the back taxes, Noah went down to the lumber yard and got his own pride and joy out of storage. He drove it around to the office and waited for her at the curb. Maj came out, and he honked the horn.

Maj burst out laughing. Noah sat behind the wheel of a dark blue 1967 Buick, a big boat of a thing that gleamed in the morning sun. He jumped out and stood beaming at the open door.

"Why am I not surprised?" she said laughing. "You probably have every shirt you've ever owned, too."

"You didn't look in my closet the other night, so don't make rash judgments," he teased. "Besides, I haven't built the closet yet."

"But I'm right, aren't I?" she teased back.

"About some things," he conceded.

He motioned for Maj to get behind the wheel. She protested, but he insisted.

"You might as well start getting used to driving it on these roads. After all, I can't be with you everywhere you go—unless, of course, you'll need me to fend off all the scoundrels you're likely to attract!"

That night when she slipped between the cool sheets on the high bed, Majesty felt bone weary. What a day. She amazed herself at how many on-the-spot decisions she'd had to make. But then she felt proud of herself for having made difficult decisions on her own for the first time in her life.

The car deal exhilarated her. That pleased her almost as much as seeing the tears in

Ada's and Fergie's eyes when she told them she wasn't going to leave them.

Sighing, she leaned back against the thick feather pillows at her back, and looked out the open window. The night was tar black. Nothing penetrated that blackness except the blended chords of peepers, the occasional voice of a nightbird, and a stray breeze rustling the trees.

It would be difficult to sleep, she knew. Not because it was too quiet. Not because it was nothing like Manhattan. Manhattan could be so loud it could keep you from thinking. But this quiet, this quiet could make your thoughts echo loudly in your head. This quiet made it clear just how much responsibility she had facing her now.

Maj clamped her eyes shut and tried to drift into sleep. Noah Decker's face floated dreamily across her mind, his full lips open in that enticing smile, his bottom lip quivering provocatively, his brown eyes glittering with gold dust, a rhinestone in his teeth blinding her with its brilliance.

Chapter Eight

Maj knew she couldn't let Nan handle all her personal affairs in New York, so she made a trip back by train, first calming the fearful looks in the Fergusons' eyes and assuring them she'd be back by the weekend. From the moment she blew into Manhattan, her week gusted up to a whirlwind.

Her boss said he was sorry to see her leave after so many years with the company, but she noticed how attentive he was to the young woman the temp agency had sent over to fill in. However, he did come through with a healthy check for unused vacation and an unexpected bonus. Inside of an hour she'd cleaned out her desk and thrown all but a silver picture frame into the trash. The frame had held a honeymoon picture of Jack and her in the Bahamas. She took one last look at their youthful faces, and deposited the photograph in the trash as well.

In the apartment she sorted through everything, threw out, packed what linens, books, and clothes she wanted and sent them to the West Wind via UPS, then called an estate buyer to come in and haul away the last vestiges of her adult life. All except for the pine writing desk she'd had since high school, and a white wicker chaise longue she and Jack had bought on a whim—their only whim, she remembered—in the middle of a particularly cold and snowy January. She placed those in storage until she could decide how and when to transport them to the lodge.

She closed out her checking and savings accounts, got back a damage deposit on the apartment, and with the money from the furniture sale paid off one of the three remaining debts owed since Jack's death. She wrote down everything in a journal, and read it over her last night in the city with Nan at her favorite restaurant, La Bonne Fondue.

"I don't believe I'm doing this," she said, a little breathless.

They were huddled over a simmering pot of cheese fondue, dipping and twirling French bread on long two-pronged forks, and drinking Chardonnay.

"Believe it." Nan slurped a long string of hot cheese. "You've come of age."

"By throwing away every shred of security I've ever known to take up residence in the north woods in a crumbling, debt-ridden lodge? What age? The age of unreason?"

"Stop letting your fears make you think like that. What you're throwing away is the false security of a job that chipped away at debts you were only partially responsible for, and kept you in the apartment where you lived with a husband who was distant during your marriage and who was still able to break your heart after he was dead. The place where you've been stagnating for years. What you're getting is a second life with people who love you in a place that will challenge your resources and creativity and give you something to look forward to, goals to achieve. Do you know how many people in this restaurant alone would give their eye teeth for just such a chance?" She stuck a marshmallow-size ball of fondue-covered bread in her mouth that puffed out her cheeks like a chipmunk.

"You sound like a psychotherapist."

"I *am* a psychotherapist. And I'm a forty-four-year-old jealous woman, too! I'd love to chuck it all and head for the mountains with some hot guy, and just live off the land and

195

the lakes and his body." Nan poured them each more wine.

Maj laughed. "You'd hate it and you know it! No French restaurants"—she waved her hand around the room—"no taxis, no Bloomingdale's, no Broadway, and no fax machines with Radio Shack repairmen named Dave."

"Really roughing it, eh?"

Maj laughed. "In a manner of speaking." She set her fork criss-cross along the white plate, drew her wineglass over the oilcloth-covered table close to her chest, folded both hands over the top of it, and rested the point of her chin on them. She grew serious and introspective.

"Spill it," Nan urged. "What's going on in your head?"

Maj took a deep breath and sat back against the booth. "I'm scared to death, Nan."

"About what?"

"About . . . everything. I've never done this before, any of this. I've never made real decisions for myself, let alone for people like the Fergusons. And I don't want them to know how scared I am. They're depending on me for so much. But, I don't mind that, you know? It's not a burden to be with them or try to help them out. I want to do it for and with them because I love them and believe in their dreams."

"I'm proud of you, kid. Those are the best reasons to help people. And to help yourself. I believe you'll find a way to make sound decisions for all of you. And you won't be alone doing it."

"Alone." Maj repeated the word. "I've been trying to figure out why I feel so alone when I have you and the Fergusons in my life. I never lived alone until Jack died, and even then I was surrounded by his furniture, his photographs, his souvenirs all over that apartment. Not to mention facing . . . his son . . . in a lawyer's office every few weeks. I never felt that I was alone without Jack somehow."

"Being alone with yourself is what you've been facing. That can be daunting to anybody, but it can be an enormously freeing experience, get you in touch with all the things Majesty Wilde left behind when she became Mrs. Jack Thompson."

"I know that. If there's something I've learned through these months with you, it's that. I guess maybe it's not the aloneness I'm worried about. It's the loneliness. Something's been missing from me, my life, for so long I didn't recognize its absence until now."

197

"Why now?" Nan sounded as if she knew exactly *why now* the moment she asked the question.

Maj took a swallow of wine. "All right, this is what you're waiting for, I know."

Nan smiled smugly.

"Noah Decker."

"God, I'm good!" Nan laughed.

Maj's smile was fleeting. "I'm afraid to even like him more than just as a friend." She ran a hand through a wave of hair curving over her forehead, and a frown rippled the space between her eyes. "I've been in love once in my life, and look how it turned out. I feel as if love comes from a spigot — cold, hot, or tepid — and someone else controls the faucets, not me."

"Then it's time for you to get control of that part of your life." When Maj looked skeptical, Nan shook her head. "I don't mean that you go out and pick some seemingly perfect man and decide you'll be in love with him and he'll be in love with you, and you'll live happily ever after. Life doesn't work that way. What I mean is that you *allow* love to flow from tepid to hot by keeping your hand on the faucet and turning it when you feel something bubbling up from the well."

"You mean like Noah Decker."

"Have you thought about him since you've been back here?"

"Who had time to think? I've been busier than bacon on a hot griddle, and just as jumpy." Maj lost a piece of bread in the fondue, then stabbed at it several times till her fork made contact and held it.

"My, what quaint mountain jargon. If I translate correctly, then you *have* thought about him. Am I right?" Nan cocked her head.

Maj sighed, dropped the fondue fork against the pot, leaned back against the dark wood booth, and twisted her wineglass around. "Only once a day, most of the day," she admitted.

"Cheers!" Nan touched her glass to Maj's.

"What makes you so excited about that?" Maj's tone was serious.

"What, you're not?"

Maj thought a moment before answering. "Well, yes . . . and no. It scares me a little to think about him, and think about—"

"Going to bed with him."

"Yes, that, too. But not just that. I'm not the free-wheeling dating kind. I think I'm a—" she used finger quotes in the air—"*relationship* kind. But I'm scared of that, too. And something else. Something ridiculous."

"What could be ridiculous enough about that to scare you?"

"I feel as if I'd be, well, cheating on my marriage, for some reason."

"Cheating on —" Nan dropped her fondue fork. It clattered on her plate, making other customers look over at them. "Listen kid, your husband showed you the real meaning of cheating on someone. Don't forget that part."

"I haven't. I told you it was ridiculous."

"It's just an old habit you're in, based on old morals and ideals. Some habits were meant to be broken, like static jobs and residual feelings from a less than ideal relationship. You have the opportunity of a lifetime to put the past behind you and turn your life around."

"I know, you're right."

"Then believe it."

"I'll try. You think I was crazy not to have gone to bed with him, don't you? I couldn't have just fallen into bed with him, Nan. I mean, I'm not built like that, and it's foolish to behave like that in this day and age anyway."

"I understand that. I don't advise sex for sex's sake. I tease you to remind you to at least think about that part of your life. You are attracted to Noah Decker, and from what you've told me about him, who wouldn't be? Is he attracted to you?"

"I can't answer that question." Maj felt her face warming.

"Why can't you?"

"It seems so . . . so, I don't know, conceited or something."

"Like something Jack would say, right?"

Maj nodded. "I don't know how many times he told me this woman or that had the hots for him."

"Maybe they did."

"I know they did. I saw it many times."

"And we know he had it for them, too, don't we?"

Maj's eyes filled, but she willed the tears back. "There were some I didn't think were any better than I was, or looked any better. I guess they were smarter, but—"

Nan's hand went up. "Enough of that. Let's go back to what I've been preaching at you for almost two years."

"I know, I know." Maj managed a chuckle. "Bring joy and pleasure into my life every day."

"Yeah, and don't forget *accurate self-appraisal*. That means, my dear, if you sense, or feel, or if the guy's got it written in red paint all over his chest that he's attracted to you, then you admit it to yourself and accept that he's got good reason and good taste. If you're attracted to him in return, then we've got a lot of hot water pressure potential here!"

Maj smiled, wanting to believe her friend.

"What about the ones attracted to you that you're not attracted to back?"

"It happens all the time. Be polite, but learn to recognize and accept what you're feeling and thinking and act accordingly. It's the same principle. Recognition, understanding, appropriate personal action. Simple."

"Oh, sure, real simple."

"Just like life in Jellystone Park, where you're going!"

"It's not that primitive! Promise me you'll come up for a visit. You can drive up there in a day. I'd love you to see the West Wind and meet Fergie and Ada."

Nan watched her friend's face. "And the tree-dropping Duke Wayne Decker?"

Maj smiled. "Him, too." She drained her wineglass. "I mean it about your coming up for a visit. Say you will."

"I don't know. The idea of meeting unconfined wildlife on the street, like a bear with an attitude, doesn't overjoy me."

"It would be a different experience for you. Could build character, as you always tell me. You could even bring Dave. And speaking of whom, what is it with you two?"

"Hell, I don't know. Other than a good romp in the bedsheets, I don't think beyond that. That's all I want right now."

"And you call yourself a shrink! How can you advise other people when you haven't got your own life on track?" Maj teased good-naturedly.

"I don't advise. I suggest. And as for me, remember, I prefer to call it"—she used finger quotes as Maj had—*"accurate self-appraisal."*

"Mm-hmm." Maj nodded, eyeing Nan with skepticism.

"Come on," Nan said, waving to the waiter for the bill, "let's go to my apartment for a giddy-girl sleepover, especially since you have no apartment to go to, and I'll take you to the train station in the morning." She rose and started walking toward the cashier near the front door.

"What, no Dave tonight?" Maj asked, following her.

"You can't do that every night!" Nan suddenly stopped and turned back to Maj. "Wait, I lost my head there. You *can* do that every night!"

Impulsively Maj threw her arms around Nan and hugged her. "I'm really gonna miss you, pal."

Nan's eyes filled, and she pushed Maj away in mock disgust. "God, what do you think these people are going to think? Remember where you are, will you?"

Maj laughed and steered her toward the door. "I prefer to remember it as where I've been."

Two mornings later on the dock in back of the West Wind, Maj rocked in the metal chair and sipped her coffee. Still in a state of disbelief, she allowed the gradual realization of the future impact of the events that had happened to her in the last two weeks seep in.

Once out of Manhattan, with every mile of railroad track slipping away beneath her, she'd experienced a chipping away of layers of her life. By the time she'd reached the station in the mountains where Fergie and Ada met her, she was left with a clean canvas upon which to paint the landscape of her future.

Everything hadn't just happened *to* her, she'd *made* them happen! She experienced a thrill sluice through her and reveled in it. For the first time in her life she'd made choices and decisions for herself without asking anyone else for permission, without worrying about how what she decided would affect other people.

Choices.

She understood now, more than ever, that she had choices.

She heard an airplane in the distance, its familiar drone drawing nearer. She smiled. Noah. It had to be. She'd arrived late the previous night, and he'd stayed up at his cabin, so she hadn't seen him. She sat still. The green plane emerged at the end of the lake and descended to a smooth-as-glass landing and taxied up to the dock. She felt the whoosh of water beneath the boards, and watched the plane turn in, roar alongside the dock and bump it, then shut down.

It was déjà vu all over again.

"Hey! You're back!" Noah called, waving as he dropped down on the dock. "Be right there!"

At the sight and sound of him, Maj felt her stomach clutching and her pulse pumping rapidly. He looked wonderful. Wonderful. As if she hadn't seen him in months. She watched him tying down the airplane, latching the door. And then he ran toward her, long jean-clad legs swallowing the short distance, cowboy boots slapping dew-heavy grass.

He hit the dock, making the whole thing sway. She had to take a step with one foot to hold her balance. He reached her and threw his arms around her in a bear hug, lifted her, and swung her around. The coffee in her cup swung around with them, leaving a brown circle on the gray dock boards.

"Wow, I'm glad to see you!" he said with a breathlessness she found endearing because it matched her own. And then he kissed her deeply in the warmest welcome she'd ever received.

He plunked her back down on her feet, and she pulled down the sweatshirt that had snaked up her stomach during his exuberant greeting. His welcome was even more enthusiastic than the Fergusons' had been, if that were possible, and Maj let its warmth wash over her. *Accept it, recognize it for the truth it tells.*

"I'm . . . I'm glad to be back. I think. I hope." She held his gaze for several long moments, and knew she was glad to see him, too. But she couldn't say it.

"Everything all right in New York?"

"Everything's all gone in New York." She laughed nervously.

He smiled. "Remind me to ask the chamber of commerce to welcome the newest permanent resident of Big Moose."

"Permanent. I guess so. I've certainly burned all my bridges. So, what do we call ourselves up here? Moosers? Moosites? Moosequiteers?" She laughed again, trying to calm her nerves.

"Lucky," he said quietly.

She concurred silently. Looking out over the lake, she thought herself the luckiest woman in

206

the world to be sharing space with birds, and fish, and animals, and wonderful people. She turned and looked beyond Noah's broad shoulder to the lodge, and seeing its sagging back porch, bare-patched roof, missing chunks of red spruce siding, weed-overgrown lawns, shrubbery gone wild, windows in need of paint and repair, she thought herself to be the least equipped woman in the world to cope with it.

"Don't worry," he said, reading her expression, "you made the right decision."

"I just don't know where to start," she said with a hint of despair in her voice.

"With a pencil and a pad of paper, a couple of county inspectors, and some construction experts. And in your grandfather's study. Nothing like a good dose of history to make sense out of the present."

"Do you always have an answer for everything?"

He thought for a minute. "Yep."

"Pretty sure of yourself, aren't you?"

"Not in everything." He stood, still keeping his gaze on her face.

He had a way of unsettling her that she tried to grasp and control but couldn't. And for some reason, she was beginning not to mind one bit.

* * *

"I haven't found a key to the padlock on the carriage barn, Fergie. Is there a way we can get in there?" Maj came into the kitchen just as Fergie was sharing lunch with Ada.

"Well, now, honey, you'll have to ask Noah about that. He's the one put the lock on it last year."

"Why would he do that?" She was more than a little curious. After all, it wasn't his barn.

"Stored some things of his own in there, I guess. Dunno. He tinkers in there pretty regular."

With perfect timing Noah came up the back porch steps and walked into the kitchen. "Having kind of a late lunch, aren't you, Fergie?" he asked, pouring himself a glass of orange juice and sitting down at the table. "It's almost your time for supper," he teased.

Before Fergie could reply, Maj spoke quickly.

"Why do you keep the carriage barn padlocked, Noah? Shouldn't Fergie have access to it since it does, after all, belong to the West Wind?"

Noah's smile faded slightly. He peered down into his glass, and then swirled the contents.

"Caught with a secret," he said. "Okay, the jig is up. I suppose I'll have to confess." He inhaled a sharp breath, placed both hands on

208

the edge of the table, and leveled a lingering look on each face. Amusement played at the corners of his mouth as he enjoyed their rapt attention. "I discovered a treasure in there, and I wanted to keep curious cats and other undesirables from finding it," he whispered.

No one said anything for a moment. Noah couldn't tell what they were thinking, but if he'd had to lay a wager who would speak first, he knew he'd have won a bundle.

"What kind of treasure?" Maj asked, laughing. "Something that will make Fergie and Ada rich and turn the West Wind back into its old glory?"

"Not possible," Noah said thoughtfully. "It doesn't belong to Ada and Fergie."

Maj's excitement turned to seriousness. "Now, you know, Noah, if you've found something of value at the West Wind, then it should be turned over to them. Every penny will be of great help to them."

Fergie stood up and picked up his cap. He wrung it over and over in his hands as if it were a mop filled with dirty water. Ada watched him and nodded her head. Maj caught an exchange between them that she couldn't read.

"Majesty honey, there's something I've been meaning to tell you," Fergie started, keeping his eyes lowered on the cap he still twisted.

"What? Is something else wrong?"

"Well, yes. And no."

"Go on, dear," Ada urged her husband. "Good a time as any to tell her."

"Tell me what?" Maj grew anxious.

"We ain't got a lot of money, that's true. But the big financial trouble ain't completely ours. Fact is, the West Wind ain't ours, neither."

"What . . . what do you mean, it's not yours? Whose is it?"

"The owner is probably not the one you would have chosen to run the place," Noah said. "I'm sure you'll have more trouble than you bargained for."

Maj looked out of the corner of one eye at him. Noah knew she figured it was him, but he didn't say more.

Fergie took in a deep breath and leveled his eyes on her. "It's yours, honey. You own this place."

Maj's jaw dropped open. "Me? I own it? But how?"

"Now, 'fore you get all worked up, let me explain why we didn't tell you before. Your granddad and I agreed, oh, a little while before he died, that we'd put it in your name. Remember I told you how he always wanted to keep it in the family?"

"Yes, but I thought that would, of course, mean you and Ada. You're his partners. You were always family."

"We always felt like it, too. Still do. The West Wind has always provided for us all. And it will again. Especially now that you're the innkeeper. He made a provision in the document that we were to take care of all expenses, even though the place was legally yours. It was to remain that way until such time as you wanted to take it over.

"We wanted to tell you before, but we were afraid you'd want to sell it, and we just couldn't let go. But then we almost lost it to Morris for the taxes. I guess maybe we thought we could hang on to it somehow, make a go of it so when you came back again you wouldn't want to sell."

Fergie grew breathless, and then wept openly, burying his face in his wrinkled cap. Ada got up and put her arms around him, rubbed his back, and whispered everything would be all right.

"The man didn't mean no harm by not telling you before now, honey. He only meant to do good," Ada said, unshed tears in her old eyes.

Maj watched the dear people for a mind-numbing moment. And then the full realization of what he'd said hit her. She stood up, went quickly to them, and threw her arms around them both, tears spilling down her cheeks. She hugged her face against Fergie's shoulder.

"You've done more good than you know," she whispered. "You've given me a new life, excitement I haven't felt since . . . since Granddad let me fly his airplane."

The three stood in a circle, arms around one another, tears and smiles on all three faces.

"I haven't felt this good in years!" Maj said, giving them each a squeeze.

"You've made us so happy, honey, just being here. And now what you've done about the taxes, and staying . . ." Ada was overcome. She hugged Maj and kissed her cheek.

Fergie plopped his cap with a playful tug on Maj's head. "We love you just like always, funny face."

"You haven't called me that since the summer I got that big goose egg on my forehead when I tripped on the dock in my bare feet."

"I'm glad you remember," he said, wiping his eyes with his shirt-sleeve.

Noah stood and was clearing away his lunch makings when Maj caught him wiping the corner of one eye. Her heart filled with even more emotion knowing that he was as moved by Fergie's speech as she was. She was searching for the right words to say to him when the kitchen phone rang.

"I'll get that," Noah said hastily, trying to cover his own emotion.

"Could I, please?" Maj asked gently. "It'll be my first phone call as owner of the lodge"—she looked over at Fergie and Ada and winked—"at least knowingly."

Noah smiled and make a sweeping gesture of deference. Maj lifted the receiver.

"Good afternoon, West Wind Lodge. Majesty Wilde, innkeeper, speaking." She smiled broadly at Fergie and Ada and Noah, who gave her smiling approval in return.

"Um, hello," a female voice said. "Is Noah Decker there?"

"Yes, he is," Maj replied. "May I tell him who's calling?"

"This is his daughter."

"Oh, yes. Just one moment, please." Maj cupped a palm over the mouthpiece and held the receiver out to Noah. "Your daughter's on the line."

Maj saw his face light with happy surprise as he grabbed for the phone. "Kimmie? I'm so glad to hear from you. Where are you, honey?"

Maj watched his excitement as he listened to his daughter for several minutes. His response to her softened the lines in his face and lit his eyes with a different sparkle. She felt all warm and soft inside as he talked with her, his parental voice changing with nuances of sympathy, concern, and pride, then excitement. Seeing Noah Decker, father, added yet another dimension to him for Maj, and she felt drawn to him even more powerfully, if that were possible.

Fergie touched her arm, and Maj flinched. She realized she'd been standing there, staring at Noah while he conversed with his daughter, making herself a part of his private conversation. She let Fergie draw her back into discussion with him and Ada about the arrangements Henry Wilde had made to provide for their welfare, and his investment for his only grandchild.

While Noah talked, she and Fergie took a slow tour through the main lodge, Maj seeing it now for the first time since she learned she owned it. A different kind of pride swept over her. She'd never owned property herself. Now *she* owned this wonderful piece of Adirondack history, and she would treat and preserve it with the respect it deserved.

They wandered room to room, remembering

times spent in all of them, Maj making mental notes of what would be needed to spruce them up. Everywhere there were antlers, deer, and moose mounted on walls or above fireplaces, and distinctive Adirondack-style furniture constructed of logs, twigs, and bark.

In the lounge next to the native stone fireplace stood a stuffed bear cub, caught in its adolescence and dusty with age. She smiled and checked the cub's left eye. Still missing. She'd picked it out when she was six years old and was positive she could still find it in her souvenir box packed among her things. She wondered how one cleaned a stuffed bear, and knew she'd have to learn how, since she meant to leave the cub right where he stood.

Between the expansive parlor and bark-walled foyer was a graceful natural arch. Fergie told her the original owner combed the forest for months, searching for just the right size and shape. No steaming or processing of any kind had been used to shape it.

Wide windows in all the public rooms afforded a panorama of lake and forest. On the first-floor screened porch that ran the full length of the back of the lodge sat a long line of identical green rocking chairs, arm to arm, for patrons to sit in as they watched water activity or just relaxed.

215

Maj hugged herself. This was truly her home.

"He never figured progress to roll in here with quite the speed it did, I guess," Maj mused as she and Fergie walked into the kitchen. Noah was still on the phone with his daughter.

"Progress to your granddad meant keeping ahead of the hedge growth." Fergie laughed, wiping his eyes as he watched her touching a wall here, a chair there, remembering and loving the place as he did.

"Oh, I don't know about that. Wasn't the West Wind the first lodge in these parts to upgrade to bathrooms in every room?" Maj asked with pride evident in her voice.

"You're just a tad off, funny face. The West Wind was the *last* place to go all bathrooms. I b'lieve that was about 1960, if I remember correctly."

"You probably didn't get a chance to notice while you were poking around upstairs," Ada put in, "but the Vanderbilt room is the only one without a bathroom."

"Why is that?"

"Your granddad said if it was good enough for the Vanderbilts to go without a bathroom, then it should be good enough for anybody else."

216

"So where did the Vanderbilts go?"

"Somewhere else that wasn't in the Adirondacks, I guess. We haven't see them for years." Fergie scratched his head again. "Funny thing, we never did rent that room much."

"Go on with you." Ada poked him.

Fergie gave her and then Maj a kiss on the cheek.

Noah hung up the phone and crossed the kitchen, heading for the back door.

"Noah?" Maj stopped him. "Is everything all right with your daughter?"

He turned around. Maj watched him struggle with some hidden turmoil, then relax. "The usual trauma of finals. But she's going to visit for a few days."

"How wonderful," Ada said. "I've been hoping I'd get to meet her sometime."

"Wonderful, yes" — Noah laughed — "but I haven't finished the bathroom in the cabin yet. Picture a nineteen-year-old girl coping with an outhouse!"

"Why don't both of you just stay here?" Maj offered. "The West Wind has more than one bathroom. She can primp to her heart's content."

Noah looked down and brushed his pant leg free of imaginary lint, then looked up with a playful smile at the corner of his lips. "What's

217

the possibility of reduced rates on the rooms?"

Maj smiled back. "I think that could be worked out. You have friends in high places at the West Wind."

"Then I accept your offer. When you all get through with this love-in," he said with his hand on the screen door, "I'll be out unlocking Majesty Wilde's carriage barn."

He turned and walked off the porch. Maj watched the proud set of his shoulders under the blue chambray shirt, the length of his legs beneath slim jeans, and a quick sense raced through her mind of the feel of both when they were pressed together in the quilts in his cabin.

Another thought filled her mind in stark fashion. Neither one of them had shared their pasts with the other, shared the events that had molded each life. Yet, in those moments, hearing the love in his voice as he talked to his daughter and then about her, she envisioned the loss of something she'd never actually had.

She turned back to Fergie and Ada. "So Noah's daughter goes to Skidmore, right?"

"I think so," Ada said. "One of those nice places."

"You've never met her?"

"No. Heard a lot about her, though. Noah thinks the world of her."

218

Maj finished cleaning up the lunch dishes and food. "Where is her mother?" She wanted to sound offhand, nonchalant, but she knew she hadn't carried it off very well.

"Not sure. Noah never said much to me about her. Has he said anything to you?" Ada turned toward her husband.

Fergie was adjusting his cap and grabbing his jacket. "What say we go see what's in the carriage barn?"

Maj tried not to think he'd avoided her question. It was probably just Fergie's usual act of being lost in his own thoughts.

"Be right there," Maj said, wiping her hands on a faded towel. She stepped out on the porch and stopped abruptly when she caught sight of Noah down by the dock.

Ada and Fergie came up close behind her. "Well, would you look at that," Fergie whispered in awe.

"What's the matter, Majesty," Noah called, "cat got your tongue?"

Chapter Nine

Moored by the dock at the end of the sloping lawn sat Henry Wilde's old Stearman biplane. With a fresh coat of silver and red paint, it bobbed in the water atop floats, the sun glinting off its wings making it appear for all the world like a dragonfly feeding at the water's edge.

Noah leaned casually with one arm against the lower blade of the propeller, one knee bent with the toe of his boot crossed over the opposite ankle, and pointing into the grass.

Maj's lips parted, and she wagged her head in suspended disbelief. A storm of memories washed over her, and through the rain of emotion that filled her vision, she saw once again Granddad landing by the dock. Saw him jump down and scoop her up in his arms and strap her into the front seat. Saw them taking off over the lake, over the trees, into the blue he'd said belonged to everyone.

As her vision cleared, she saw Noah looking a little like the Great Waldo Pepper and a lot like Henry Wilde.

"Where . . . ?" she started, and walked slowly down the stairs and across the lawn, Ada and Fergie close behind.

When she reached the wonderful old airplane, she touched its nose and petted it as she might have a beloved mare.

"How . . . ?" she started again.

Noah beamed as much as the plane did in its sunny spotlight. "I found her under a tarp in the carriage barn right after I got here. I didn't think anybody would mind if I worked on her. She was in pretty good shape, considering her age. Your granddad must have taken good care of her, and he'd done a lot of fine custom work. Her engine had seized, and the fabric was in sore need of repair. She ached for a new paint job and there were a couple of squirrel nests in the wings, as well as a few mice to contend with in the seats. I strung some new wire, and took the engine apart, and that's about it."

He watched Maj's face as he ticked off the repairs as if they were as simple as lacing a sneaker. When she didn't say anything, his enthusiasm waned. "You're not angry about this, are you? I mean, I know what I'm doing. I had training and extensive experience in the Marine Corps. I didn't alter it in any way. It's just like it was when Henry Wilde and his granddaughter flew it."

"So this is what you've been tinkering with all this time," Fergie said, looking over the bi-plane with a critical eye.

Noah nodded, holding his gaze on Maj's face. "And I cleaned up in the barn a little, and made kind of a workbench. But I didn't change much, honest."

"I don't know what to say," Maj whispered hoarsely.

Noah leaned around and made an obvious scrutiny of her face. "How about, 'I'm not mad at you for taking my airplane and fixing it up, Noah'?"

"My airplane?" She turned around quickly to face him. "I'm sorry . . . I'm just so over-whelmed . . . I'm not mad at all. I'm amazed. Thrilled." She couldn't keep her hands off the fabric, the shiny nose, or the wooden propeller. "And grateful. Granddad would be thrilled, wouldn't he, Fergie?"

Fergie and Ada stood on the dock arm in arm, just looking into the distance at the dark jutting Adirondack Mountains. As Maj watched them, her heartbeat quickened, and she swallowed hard. She knew what they were thinking.

She turned back to Noah. "Granddad would be ecstatic, Noah, and so am I. *Thank you* seems inadequate, but I can't seem to find any other words . . ." She struggled a moment, then opened her arms, palms out, empty-handed.

It seemed the most natural thing in the world to walk into each other's arms and hug closely. When they stepped back, they dropped arms, she feeling nervous and he smiling with pleasure.

Noah spoke first. "Actually, I should thank you."

"What for?"

"For showing me how to render you speech-less, for once!"

"Well, that's gratitude for you."

His smile turned from teasing to serious. "Honestly, I must thank you for not being up-set with me. Working on this plane has given me more pleasure than I can ever express. It never failed to make me feel good when I was feeling down, or exhausted, or . . . lonely."

Maj knew the last was an admission. She

didn't need words to understand the feeling of loneliness, but she wondered how a man like Noah Decker could ever feel lonely.

"It was a joy, a labor of love." He smiled.

Nan was right, she would love this man, Maj thought with a smile. *And so could I*. The last thought stunned her for a moment.

"How about we take her up for a spin?"

Maj looked surprised. "Is it airworthy?"

"Only one way to find out."

"You mean this would be a test flight?"

"Somebody's got to do it. She can't do it by herself."

"How do you know it'll even start?"

"I've had her running a few times when Fergie and Ada were away."

"But what if it can't get off the water?"

"Then we'll just turn around and drive her back here."

"But what if it *can* get off the water?"

"Then we'll fly!" He narrowed his eyes. "Are you afraid?"

"You've challenged me with that before," Maj said, surveying the distance past Ada and Fergie.

"It didn't stop you then."

Maj looked up into his eyes. His brown gaze locked with hers. *Trust* came into her mind.

224

She could trust him. She looked back at the airplane. But could she trust the Stearman?

"You'll need to dress more warmly than you are now. It's cold up there. Got a wool sweater with you?"

"Yes." She still felt tentative about going up.

"Good. How about some boots? Those sneakers aren't sturdy enough. Some gloves. And some wool socks. Have you got any of those?"

"No." Her uncertainty was growing.

"Fergie has some. Well, what are you waiting for? Get going! As my own grandfather used to say, time's a-wasting." Noah mimicked with two hands, pointing to the lowering sun and pushing her toward the lodge.

When she came back she'd donned a black turtleneck and the only wool sweater she owned, oatmeal tweed, oversized, and reaching her knees. She'd swapped sneakers for beat-up lug-soled brown boots she'd saved for years, and a pair of Fergie's gray wool socks pulled up over her jeans, their red circle borders resembling garters.

"Here, this will complete your outfit," Noah said. He handed her a dark brown leather jacket. "Found it in the barn. Do you think it belonged to your grandfather?"

"I know it did," she said, shoving her arms into the sleeves. She ran her hand over one, felt how years of daily wear had softened the leather.

"And you'll need this." He pulled a brown leather helmet over her head, flattening her hair so it fringed around her face. Then he adjusted a pair of goggles over her eyes and lifted the ear flaps. He laughed. "What did Fergie call you? Funny face, was it?"

"Thank you for the compliment. Both of you," she said warmly, quickly tucking her hair up all around and watching Fergie as he came toward them.

Noah helped her over the only place on the wing she knew was all right to step. She started to get into the front seat of the open cockpit, but he motioned her to the rear one.

"Granddad always said the pilot flew from the rear seat."

"I know. This is just for weight distribution."

"What do you mean by that?" she asked, suspicion evident in her voice.

"I'm not sure. I just made it up now." He tightened the belt harness around her. "You know how to use a gosport tube?"

"Do I ever!" He handed her the end of funnel-shaped object attached to a tube that led to a headset in the front seat. She remembered playing a telephone game with her grandfather, talking through the old hearing and speaking devices.

"Instructors don't usually do this, you know." He handed her another tube set that reversed the first.

"Do what?"

"Give a student the speaking end of the tube."

"Why not?"

"Lesson number one. They don't want them to talk back!"

He pulled on a leather helmet and goggles. Maj was impressed when he jumped into the front seat with an agility that belied his size. He moved with the grace of a dancer, and she was surprised when that thought crossed her mind. It seemed he surprised her on an almost hourly basis.

"Are we ready?" Noah asked.

"I don't know," Maj answered.

"I wasn't asking you," he came back. "I was asking *her*." He patted the fuselage.

Fergie went to work as Maj remembered he always had in the old days. He released the tie-downs, and carefully turned the propeller to horizontal and then up several degrees. Then he waited, poised with both hands on the upper prop blade.

Noah tapped the oil pressure and fuel gauges with his leather-gloved forefinger, and then repeated the procedure with the altimeter and airspeed indicator.

"Spark on!" Noah called, turning a black button.

"Contact!" Fergie called back.

He pulled down on the propeller blade with all his weight, then quickly stepped back. The propeller spun once, lacking gusto. The engine chuffed a wheeze like an old man catching his breath at the top of a long flight of stairs. The Stearman bobbed in the water.

"I don't think it's ready," Maj said thinly. She didn't want to sound worried or less than moderately confident, but she was hard pressed to keep trepidation out of her voice.

"Just napping," Noah said. He tapped the gauges again and turned the button back to its original position.

Fergie lined up the propeller once again. Noah turned the button once again.

"Spark on!"

"Contact!"

Fergie pulled the propeller down and stepped back again. The Stearman's engine fired and caught, the propeller putted a few seconds, then wound to a halt. The airplane bobbed a little harder, making small waves roll against the shoreline, the same shoreline where Maj now wished she was standing.

"Maybe it would rather continue napping," Maj said, "and maybe we shouldn't disturb it anymore."

"She's been a sleeping beauty for years. Time she woke up and got a new lease on life," Noah said, tapping the gauges and twisting the button off.

Maj silently fantasized Noah in the role of the handsome prince, awakening the sleeping Stearman with a tender kiss, bringing it out of its decades of hidden slumber. And then she thought of his lips upon hers, and what they had awakened inside her sleeping senses.

Fergie lined up the propeller once again. Noah turned the button.

"Spark on!"

"Contact!"

Fergie pulled the propeller down and stepped back. The engine fired, caught, inhaled, and exhaled like a marathon runner doing warmup exercises. Then the blades spun and gained momentum, the Lycoming engine roaring into a deafening purr.

With Fergie positioning the aircraft, Noah pulled out the throttle with one hand, and with the other on the stick edged the aircraft away from the dock. He gave it a little more throttle, and spun the tail around so the nose headed into the wind.

"We're off!" he called into the gosport tube, then pulled steadily on the throttle.

"God help us," Maj whispered into the wind, raising her eyes to the sky.

She sat with her hands clasped to the leather trim on the open cockpit while they roared down the lake. It seemed to take forever before they'd gained enough speed to lift off and skim the bank of trees at the end. She raised her feet instinctively.

Emotion rushed her senses. She opened herself to feel it all, hold on to the sense memories in the making. And then it came to her with the added rush of wind past her face— she'd been grounded too long.

"Who-whee!" Noah shouted into the tube. "What a feeling!"

Oh, yes, what a feeling.

Maj startled herself with how quickly she relaxed. She felt as if they were driving slowly on an imaginary highway barely above the treetops, a highway that would take them into a kingdom only birds could claim as their do-main. She looked out over Noah's shoulder, be-yond the Stearman's nose, and fancied herself on a journey to an unseen destination where no woman had ever before released her spirit.

Over an open meadow Noah pointed for her to look down. Several tiny lakes amid tall pines shone like antique silver brooches displayed on dark green velvet. Noah had indeed found a treasure, she mused.

Then the sheer pleasure of being in the open air, looking down on what felt to her like a brave new world, overwhelmed Maj. Her body aligned itself with the movement of the aircraft, and she was no longer a passenger. Rather, she knew herself to be part of a float-ing piece of the sky.

"Just like a Ferris wheel, isn't it?" Noah tubed.

She laughed and shouted over the roar. "Are you paying somebody to keep us up here this time?"

"Nope. We're on our own!"

Noah banked the Stearman around and headed back toward the West Wind. Pushing the stick forward, he put the aircraft into a de-scent, then leveled it off and buzzed Ada and Fergie, who stood on the dock, smiling and

231

waving, arms around each other. Then he pulled back the stick and the aircraft rose up over the trees like a hawk with an eye on its prey.

When they'd leveled off again, Noah picked up the tube and called to Maj. "Take the controls, granddaughter, she's all yours!"

"No!" Maj shrieked back. "I don't remember how."

"Just like riding a bike!" Noah called back. He threw both arms up over his head as an instructor would signal his student to take over.

The aircraft's nose started down. Maj froze for an instant, then grabbed the stick, planted her feet on the rudder pedals. The power of the engine vibrated through the stick up her arms and into her shoulders. Her hands, her feet, her mind, reacted once again as they'd been taught. She leveled it off.

The thrill of control! She was the pilot, mistress of the moment, and the sky was all hers.

In the front seat Noah raised a thumbs-up, then dipped his open hand back toward her. Her hands were tightly gripped around the stick, but she pried one loose and reached out to grasp his. He squeezed it hard and held it, and the three of them flew in concert for several joyous moments.

Sheer pleasure, Maj thought while they floated through the darkening blue sky hand in hand.

"We'd better head back," Noah called to her. "Sun's going down, and I think she's had enough for her first time."

"No, she hasn't!"

"I meant the airplane!"

"Roger!" Maj returned. "You take over."

"You're doing fine!"

"I don't know how to land!"

"Feel through it with me."

Maj placed her feet lightly on the pedals, and loosened her grip on the stick, holding it lightly in one hand.

Beneath her she felt Noah's feet in the controls. From his hand movement, she felt the fullness in the stick fill her grasp. He moved it, and the Stearman responded, making Maj's whole world tilt. His slightest touch of pressure relayed sensations and impulses through the stick into her hand and made the two into one with the aircraft, melded them with sky and air and earth below.

Their path was lit with setting sun, folds of mauve and gray cloud trails surrounded them like a quilt of eiderdown. Wordlessly they glided, idling, suspended on mutual wings, accompanied by the ethereal song of the wind in the wires.

Through her hands and the tingle in her feet Maj felt Noah take them on a descent out of the sky and down to a mirror-smooth landing on the lake. He pulled on the throttle, and she felt the last surge of power before they taxied to the West Wind dock. At the cut of the engine the propeller whirred down to a putt, then stopped.

In the ensuing quiet Maj and Noah did not move, rocking in slowing rhythm in the cradle of what had carried them aloft, each with a hand on the control.

Maj lifted the ancient goggles and saw clearly the breadth of Noah's shoulders, saw the yoke of his leather jacket ripple as he moved to unlatch his harness and seat belt. She released a tremor of breath as a shiver coursed through her blood, and sent a small electrical current to lift the downy hair on the back of her neck.

Maj moved then, unbuckling the belt and harness, elevating herself up and out of the seat, and dropping down to the dock. She guided the aircraft to the shore using a pair of grips mounted on the fuselage, then ran for the tie-down cables.

Noah extracted himself from his seat and dropped down to the dock. Watching Maj work filled him with a sense of pride. He felt high about their shared half hour alone in the intimate setting under the open blue roof of the world.

Breathless when she finished her chores, Maj walked back to him, whipping the leather helmet off. "Thank you," she whispered, her face flushed with exhilaration from her time in the sky.

He smiled and touched the side of her cheek with two leather-gloved fingers. "You're beautiful when you're excited," he said hoarsely.

Maj dropped her gaze almost shyly, then raised it to his. "I *felt* beautiful up there." She looked toward the darkening sky, laced now with fingers of rose and mauve as the sun sank behind the far peaks. "Is that all right to say?"

"Absolutely. You were wonderful!"

"It was wonderful," she breathed. "I want to do it again. Can we?"

"Of course! Whenever you want to! It's wonderful for me, too, you know."

He dropped his arms, encircled them under her backside, and lifted her off her feet, much to her surprise. Once again she was held aloft, this time pressed against his chest, and what she looked down upon was the light in his deep brown eyes. Then he let her slide to her feet as he lowered his lips to her smiling mouth and kissed her thoroughly.

Majesty gave her lips willingly, fitting them into his until every contour melded. She wondered in a fragment of a moment if his senses had gone as wild as hers were now.

When he released her, Noah's heartbeat went out of control. This was a warm, vital, alive, giving woman. He wanted to experience her, all of her, over and over again. He held her close again, held her gaze until her eyes slanted toward the back porch. Ada and Fergie walked across the lawn and were just about within earshot.

"Say," he said to Maj, lightening the moment, "did you gain weight or something?"

She stepped back and tugged on her turtleneck. "It's all these clothes you made me put on. I feel like a toad."

"Maybe you should take them off, then," he urged, winking.

"And maybe not," she shivered, and wrapped the leather jacket closer around her. Looking directly into his eyes, she added something she knew was shameful to say. "At least not here."

And she knew she held as intense a look of shock at her flirtatious statement as he did.

"How'd she feel?" Fergie asked Noah.

"Sensational," Noah answered, keeping his eyes on Maj.

Maj scuffed her foot in the lawn. "*She* feels wonderful, Fergie, and the Stearman was as exciting to fly again as it was in the old days. Noah let me fly it."

"Oh, dear," Ada said, "now, don't you go scaring me again."

Maj laughed. "I'm grown-up now, Ada. I think I can fly with a more level head than when I was a kid." She let her eyes glance off Noah. "At least I hope so."

"I don't know why anybody wants to fly anyway," Ada came back.

"Here comes the part about if God wanted us to fly, He'd have given us wings," Fergie said, hugging his wife's shoulders.

"Well, it scares the daylights out of me. Henry was bad teaching her things like that. She could get killed or something," Ada fretted.

"Noah wouldn't have let anything like that happen." Maj put her arm around Ada's shoulders.

"But you'll have to solo sometime," Noah said.

"Sometime," Maj echoed, and headed for the porch.

By the third week in May Maj felt as if she'd been "drug through a knothole backward" as Fergie'd been saying at the end of every day. Her life in Manhattan seemed now to have been lived by someone else entirely.

She had the county inspectors out, and following their guidelines contacted Moffett Brothers and the Frenchman General Contractors, the only builders in the area other than one of Gerald Morris's companies. She requested reports and estimates for getting the structure sound and bringing it up to code, and discussed with them restoration and remodeling and asked for drawings and cost breakdowns.

The Moffetts carried out their inspection slowly and silently, arriving early in the morning, making their greetings all around, and remaining at work for four hours, never more, never less.

On the final day Maj watched the twin brothers, who bore a curious resemblance to Tweedledum and Tweedledee, and their partner, a dark-haired French Canadian known only as the Frenchman, drive away.

Fenton Moffett, the oldest brother by seven minutes, drove a white Cadillac easily thirty years old. It was only right, he'd told her, because of his superiority in age. Foley Moffett, sometimes known as Moffett the Younger, drove a beat-up rusted station wagon of dubious make and color that he referred to as the Silver Bullet. In it he transported everything in the way of tools, ladders, and dropcloths, including a pair of sawhorses strapped to the top that were mottled with so many paint drips they looked like a piece of Jackson Pollock art.

The Frenchman arrived and left daily exactly fourteen minutes later than the Moffetts. His mode of transportation was a three-wheel all-terrain vehicle, at the back of which he towed a small square handmade wood trailer. While he made his written observations and estimates, he consumed three peanut butter and jelly sandwiches on white bread and a jug of coffee. That's all she ever saw him eat.

Maj was skeptical about what she would receive, if anything, in the way of estimates and drawings from the trio. Her worries proved groundless when, a week to the day after they'd begun, they presented her with an extensive packet of materials, professionally prepared and precise to the inch and dollar, and without even a shadow of a jelly or coffee stain.

Armed with their prints, reports, and estimates, and a worksheet of projected income she devised from a how-to book on hotel management, she went back to the bank and, with Noah's help and using the lodge as collateral, secured a loan to refurbish the West Wind.

She called for more than a dozen mail order catalogs for cookware, linens, and sporting equipment, and began making lists for every room in the lodge. In a separate folder she kept statistics and ideas for the other cottages to be restored at a later date.

When Noah could be with her, they worked companionably side-by-side. She felt connected to him, but wouldn't have been able to explain how if she'd been asked. Often she'd look up to locate him and find him looking back at her. His look, his presence, continued to make her feel weak in the knees at times, and make her pulse race whenever she was near him. Constantly she asked herself when those feelings swept over her, if they were because of him, because of her, or because of the chemistry between them.

Over a grilled cheese sandwich and a Coke at the kitchen table one Friday afternoon when

Noah was occupied with his own work, Maj went through her sheaf of notes and folders of magazine articles on restoration.

"The next thing is going to be furniture," she said to Fergie, and dropped her wire-rimmed round eyeglasses on a picture of a four-poster with a candlewick spread. "Even reproductions are expensive these days. I would love to see authentic period pieces that could tell the story of the West Wind for the last hundred years."

"I don't know where you'd start with that." Fergie scratched the wiry gray thatch on his head.

"The flea market's started again over at Big Tupper," Ada said, sitting down at the table and placing a palm over her chest. Maj noticed how tired she seemed to get lately, more than usual, after even a little exertion.

"There might be some of the old stuff up in the attic," Fergie said, as if the idea had just struck him. "Your granddad cleaned out a lot years ago, but could be there's still something useful."

"Great!" Maj said. "But I'm surprised that he cleaned anything out. Grandma always said he saved everything," she said, laughing.

"I didn't say he got rid of the stuff, I just said he cleaned it out." Fergie chuckled.

241

"People did that kind of thing back then," Ada said. "You never knew when you were going to need something. Money was tight in those days."

"Those days are back," Maj said.

"Not sure they ever left," Fergie said, getting up from the table and grabbing his jacket. "You know how to get the attic stairs down, honey?"

"Is it still that chain in the closet of the Astor room?"

Granddad liked to name the rooms after wealthy families who'd built luxurious camps in the mountains, but the Astor room was the most special to Maj. More open and spacious than the others, it boasted floor-to-ceiling windows with a balcony outside them.

"Yep. Nobody's been up there in years, so it'll be pretty dirty. Take that fog lantern up with you. You'll need the light."

"Where you off to?" Ada asked him. She seemed to keep her husband in her sight more often than usual, Maj observed, or want to know his whereabouts all the time.

"To find Noah. Remember that big cherry breakfront that used to be in the dining room? Says he uncovered a mountain of old canvas in the storage barn, and there it was. I sure

242

would like to see that again. I suppose all the glass will be busted, though." He went out the back door, still talking, thinking out loud.

With a bandanna over her head and the fog lantern in her hand, Maj went upstairs to the Astor room. Its oval brass nameplate was still there, tarnished, but almost a beacon of memory for her. She remembered how she used to make up stories of what would be in the attic above that room. Once she fantasized it as a ballroom, and all the famous rich people came to her own coming-out party.

She put her shoulder against the door, swollen from dampness and years of non-use, and pushed it open. Pushed it right off its hinges. She propped it against the wall in the hallway. Cobwebs, dust, peeling wallpaper, two water-stained bureaus, a mouse-chewed feather ticking, and a strong musty odor greeted her.

"I'll check the closet," she said out loud, as people often do when they're in an empty room and don't want to admit to fear of the unknown.

She hated the thought of opening the closet door, fearing some family of prehistoric creatures had moved in and somehow managed to survive years of evolution.

"Your imagination is working overtime,

243

Maj," she said to the empty room. But, just in case it wasn't, she knocked loudly on the door and listened long enough to be satisfied the closet was empty before opening it.

Inside, zippered bags of old clothes hung on a sagging wooden rod, and dust-covered cardboard storage boxes lined the back wall. Maj aimed the lantern overhead and saw the chain to the attic stairs hanging down. Hanging with it were thick spider webs and balls of dust. A shiver shook her shoulders. She'd never been keen on spiders.

She looked back out into the room for something to knock against the chain to dislodge some of the offensive webs, and spotted a discarded umbrella. Using it as a weapon, she swatted the chain, then backed out of the closet quickly. She repeated the act three times, until she was satisfied she could touch the chain without feeling creepy.

The spring-loaded wooden stairway creaked down after a few solid tugs on it using her full weight. "Good thing I hung on to that extra fifteen pounds." Peering up into what she thought must resemble the Black Hole of Calcutta, she could see nothing but a few veins of daylight shining through splits in the rafters and roof. All was silent.

"That's a good sign." She laughed. She didn't want to encounter squirrels, or mice, or, God forbid, rats.

Holding the lantern securely in front of her with one hand, and balancing herself on the rickety stairs with the other, she ascended into the darkness. As her head and shoulders cleared the attic floor, she braced her knees against a step and positioned the lantern so she could move it enough to explore the attic contents from a distance. She decided not to go walking around up there until someone could test the floorboards first.

"Ugh, what's that?" A fetid odor assaulted her nostrils, something she never remembered smelling before. She pulled the neckband of her sweatshirt up over her nose and pointed the lantern's light along the floor.

Dark mounds of canvas-covered objects jutting in strange shapes lined the space where the rafters sloped down to the eaves. No telling what was under there, but Maj felt her excitement rise as she realized it could be interesting old furniture.

She saw a heavy rocker in a corner, its rush seat hanging ragged to the floor. A steamer trunk stood propped partially open to the right of it. She remembered how her grandmother would sit in that rocker next to the kitchen fireplace, knitting afghans and watching pea soup simmer.

A child's tricycle and the remnants of a porch glider lay a few feet away. How many rainy days had she idled away on that glider? Too many to count. What else was there?

She fanned the light beam in an arc and heard a scratching noise. "What's that?" she whispered. She heard a squeaking sound, then several squeaking sounds. "Probably just tree branches rubbing against the roof."

Something that felt like a tiny breath of air whispered by her cheek and touched the top of her head. A dark shape passed through the cone of lantern light. Suddenly the flutter of wings filled the attic.

"Holy shit! Bats!"

Frantically, Maj scrambled backward down the shaking stairs, tripped on the next to the last step, and fell. Disentangling her foot, she got to her knees, grabbing at the staircase and hefting it as she rose. A couple of bats slipped through the opening and fluttered over her as she struggled with the staircase, pushing it back up toward the closet ceiling.

After what seemed an eternity, the spring caught and the staircase slammed up, tightly closed. She was afraid to look up, positive she'd slammed a herd of their furry bodies in the opening along with it.

The two bat escapees made lazy-eight swoops across the expanse of the room while Maj headed for the door.

"Hey, what'd you find up here, ghosts?" Noah's voice boomed from the hallway.

Maj shrieked. "You scared the shit out of me!" The word came out before she had time to think about it, and she clamped a hand over her offending mouth.

Noah made a sniffing noise into the air. "I guess so," he said, giving her an amused look.

"I'm sorry, but—look out!" She ducked, clamping both hands over head.

"Oh, yeah, you've got a couple of bats loose up here," he said calmly.

Maj shuddered. "I hate bats. They give me the willies." She shuddered again, out loud.

Noah put his hands on her back and pushed her into the hallway. Looking around, he spotted the door and, picking it up in front of him, started backing into the room.

"What—what are you doing?" Maj watched him, fright shading her face.

"Protecting you from a flock of crazed bats," he puffed, sliding the door into the opening. It

247

scraped along the gritty floor, the sound sending Maj even more shivers.

She heard Noah scuffling around the room, heard the attic stairway creak down, then creak up, heard a window opening, heard him making puffing sounds. And she thought she heard the bats squeaking angrily at the intruder.

"Some coming-out party," she mumbled, and the downy hair on the back of her neck stood up. Everything she'd ever heard about bats sped through her mind in rapid succession. They make nests in your hair; she tightened her bandanna. They bite your neck and suck your blood; she covered her carotid artery with her sweatshirt. They cast evil spells over you; she crossed herself even though she wasn't Catholic.

At last the unhinged door moved, and Noah emerged from the Astor room. He pushed the door back into place and tested it to make sure it would stay up. Then he brushed his palms together vigorously and looked over at her huddled against the door of the J. P. Morgan room.

"Fergie said you're looking for furniture."

Maj stared at him. How could he be so calm? Did he have the blood of slain bats on his hands? Did they even have blood? *Who cares?* She couldn't speak. Her eyes were riveted to his hands.

"Got more than you bargained for, I guess, hunh?" He laughed at her scowl. "The attic is full of bats. Great place for them."

"Yeah, just great. Glad we could be so hospitable." Maj failed to see anything positive about this form of wildlife sanctuary, let alone any humor in Noah's commentary. "The smell of them —" She shuddered again.

"Guano, and you've got a belfry full!" He laughed.

"Very funny. How does one . . . get rid of that kind of thing?"

"Wearing a gas mask and diving suit!"

"You're just full of it today, aren't you?"

"Not as full as you are!" He let out a long spate of laughter. When she didn't respond to his joke, he sobered slightly. "Don't worry, there are harmless ways of moving the bats out and cleaning up their droppings."

"Moving . . . ? You mean, you'd let them out alive to do . . . whatever it is bats do?" She rubbed her arms.

"Contribute to the balance of nature and the environment, yes."

"Well, you're a regular hero, aren't you? A caped crusader. Batman in disguise as a mild-mannered flying paramedic." She started to see some humor in the whole episode herself. "Of course, that EMT job is probably only a cover so you can get all the blood you want for yourself and your lice-infested furry friends!"

Noah laughed heartily, and, baring his teeth, made a lunge for her neck. At that moment an errant bat swooped down the hallway. Maj shrieked and ran for the stairway laughing.

"Holy guano, Robin!" Noah called, running after her. "Head for the Batmobile!"

In the kitchen a few minutes later Noah poured four tall glasses of tomato juice. "Drink your juice before it clots!" He affected a Dracula imitation, then bowed low as he set a glass in front of Maj. "Your Majesty."

"We are not amused," Maj came back in her haughtiest Queen Victoria attitude, stroking Clawed, who sat regally in her lap.

They had related the bat episode to Fergie and Ada, replete with appropriate shudders from Maj and detailed accounts of his heroics from Noah. Fergie and Ada responded accordingly, empathizing with Maj's distress and praising Noah for a job well done, protecting Maj and releasing at least one of the offenders.

"What does one call a . . . bunch of bats?"

Maj squeezed a lime wedge into her tomato juice. "A flock? A bevy? A coven?" She shuddered again.

"Swaaaarm," Noah muttered low.

"Disgusting," Maj countered.

"I've never wondered about that myself," Fergie said, teasing her suspiciously. "Why do you s'pose you do?"

"Well, they seemed like a thundering herd at the time." Maj laughed. "Suddenly I was just curious about it, that's all."

"You know what curiosity did to the cat," Fergie said, winking at her.

"Yes, I've heard," Maj said, covering Clawed's ears, her mood taking a turn toward the serious, "but sometimes being curious leads to important knowledge."

"And sometimes it's better not to know some things," Fergie came back. " 'Specially if it's bad and there's nothing you can do about it."

Maj let her thoughts wander away for a moment, thinking about the past, thinking about the present. Then she came back. "You could be right, Fergie." She caught Noah's brief pained look. "You could be right."

Chapter Ten

"I think it's time we took a break from this," Noah said early in the afternoon two days later. "My back is screaming for relief." He stood up straight, propped his hands against the small of his back, then arched and shifted his rib cage from side to side.

He'd taken on the toil with Maj and Fergie of refinishing the cherry breakfront they'd unearthed in the storage barn. Scraping off old finish, sanding, and replacing broken glass was tedious, arduous work, but Fergie was so thrilled to see the piece again after so many years that Maj and Noah had been putting great chunks of time into restoring it. Seeing the light in Fergie's face as the beauty of the piece emerged from under layers of old finish and dirt gave them almost hourly reward and kept them working.

On this day Noah noticed that Fergie's energy was waning, so he took it upon himself to cut the work time short.

Maj picked up his cue and stripped off a pair of yellow rubber gloves. "Me, too," she said, running a forearm across her brow. "My arms ache. And everything else aches, too. I've been getting up early and going out for a run before breakfast the last few mornings. I'm amazed to rediscover muscles I remember having a few years ago."

Noah studied her with an approving eye. Her cutoff jeans with ragged threads moved enticingly over her thighs, and an oversize T-shirt with a New York Marathon logo splashed across the front under swatches of paint that advertised the color of each bedroom in the lodge skimmed her body. Beat-up blue sneakers covered her bare feet. With her hair in a ponytail caught by a twist of flowered print fabric, she looked very inviting.

He marveled at the degree of stamina he'd managed to display for himself in not coming on to her like gangbusters after that night in his cabin. His admirable measure of strength was a test he supposed he must have passed, since every day he faced the intensity of his mounting attraction to Majesty.

It wasn't only lust, he knew that now. The

pace in which they were getting to know each other seemed controlled by some outside force. Maybe it was Majesty's force, and he hadn't figured out why sometimes she seemed to be as attracted to him as he was to her, yet at other times she put distance between them. Maybe it was about her husband. She didn't talk about him.

It would take an iceberg to miss what happened between them every time their hands brushed or their eyes met. But what was he going to do with these feelings anyway? He had his own complicated life to consider, no matter how much he liked to profess he had pared things down to the way he believed was the best for him.

"If you have to quit, you have to," Fergie said, stepping back to admire the breakfront as he did fifty times a day. "Young ones aren't made of strong stuff anymore."

"I'm not that young, Fergie." Noah laughed. "And I've been trying to keep up the work on my cabin as well, that is, when the Moffett Brothers aren't conning me into sanding ceilings or putting up sheetrock here. Not to mention that I have a business to run. Good thing I have a great crew. Things have picked up with the good weather. I sense a resurgence of building in the mountains."

"Tourists," Fergie muttered.

"Tourists are what'll keep you in business, too, old friend. Look at the work you've been putting in here since Maj got back! You need a break. You know what they say, all work and no play makes Jack a dull boy."

Fergie shot a wordless glance at Maj, who looked away.

Noah caught the exchange. "Did I say something wrong?"

"No, no, son," Fergie said, bending down with a slight groan to pick up soiled rags.

Noah watched the two of them avoiding eye contact with him. "If you want to keep working, I've got a few more hours left in this decrepit old body. Is that it? You both want to keep working?"

Maj came around the end of the breakfront wiping her hands on a faded print dishtowel. She knew she'd have to say it sometime, and there was no use in anyone feeling uncomfortable about such an unknowing slip. Fergie and Ada never spoke about her husband, and she knew they thought mention of him would upset her. It was high time she changed that.

"Jack was my husband's name," she said matter-of-factly.

"Oh, I'm sorry. I didn't know," Noah said sincerely.

"Of course you didn't. And it's really all right. It doesn't bother me to hear it." Fergie walked close to her, a pained expression on his face. "Really, Fergie. No one has to walk on eggshells, afraid to speak about him or mention his name. I've learned to handle his death." She'd never told him and Ada the rest of the story of her marriage on purpose. She saw no reason to.

"Are you sure, honey? It's only been a couple of years." Fergie's voice was full of love and sympathy.

"I'm very sure, Fergie. Trust me, please."

"Okay, then. So if you two are gonna wilt on me here, I guess I'll go make myself useful to Ada. Got a picture she wants me to hang over the fireplace in the main parlor. Then I guess we're going over to Tupper. Emma and George's daughter invited us."

"You won't be here for supper, then?" Maj wanted to know.

"Staying the night. Ada's got a doctor's appointment in the morning. Didn't make sense to make two trips."

"I don't know how you do it, Fergie," Noah said, sitting down on an overturned pail. "Got more energy than guys half your age."

"They don't make anything like they used to." Fergie winked at his friend. "If you need

256

me, you know where I am." He left the barn with Noah and Majesty looking at each other.

"What do you say we clean up and take the Stearman out for a spin, fly by the high peaks?" Noah asked her with a hopeful smile.

"You don't have to ask me twice." Maj dropped her cleaning rags and tore the ponytail twist from her hair, then hurried out of the barn.

Airborne twenty minutes later, again Maj was filled with a rush of sensations. Neither one of them spoke while they flew. The comforting song of the wind in the wing wires was sweet accompaniment to the communion of their spirits in tune with the mountains around them and the blue sky above.

The bright day was waning, showing glimpses of gathering clouds. They flew through time as if it were on their side. Past the Wolfjaws and Gothics Noah raised both arms overhead, signaling for Maj to take the stick. She did so gladly, feeling reborn with power in the palms of her hands.

Below, the magnificent peaks reached up to them in invitation to experience their ancient tales of eons of change. Their own shadow floated darker green over the lighter green of sun-tipped trees running up the mountains like gathered skirts to the bare stone peaks.

Maj marveled at how the Adirondacks could change with the waves of time and elements and yet remain the same from generation to generation.

Am I like they? The same yet different?

Just a few weeks ago she'd been Majesty Wilde in Manhattan, and now she was Majesty Wilde in the Adirondacks. But she was different inside now, and she knew it. It was as if her whole being were becoming reborn in spring along with the awakening earth and wildlife.

Noah pointed toward the northeast at a thickening cloud bank, then motioned for her to circle around and head back toward Big Moose. The wind picked up and sang a harsher song in the wires, and Maj clamped both hands around the stick and planted her feet against the pedals to keep the aircraft steady.

A sudden high-pitched zing sent a wing wire flying past Noah's head. He reached for it, but the wind whipped it into elusive flight around him. He swiped at it again and missed, and as the wind picked up velocity the wire came out of a second security pin and waved toward the propeller.

Maj grabbed the gosport tube and shouted over the roar of wind and engine. "It's getting too rough, I can't manage the plane!"

Not responding, Noah loosened his harness and started to raise himself out of the cockpit to reach the wildly flapping wire.

"Noah!" Maj shrieked, gripping the stick with one hand and trying to manage the gosport with the other. "What are you doing?"

She didn't have to ask that. She knew he was trying to reach the wire before it tangled in the prop, but fear had started to grip her senses and she was desperate to turn the controls back over to him.

Noah lunged and caught the wire, then lost it. The wind whipped harder around them.

Maj held the stick with both hands, struggling to keep the nose of the Stearman up. The wind took her breath away. The fuselage creaked, and she thought the wings were actually moving up and down like a bird's.

Noah grabbed the wire again and managed to wrap a length of it around his arm. As he was fitting himself back into his seat, the aircraft pitched, throwing him forward. His head hit a wood spar, and he fell back into the seat.

Glued to the controls, Maj fought the force of the wind against the Stearman. The valiant aircraft withstood the punishment like a warhorse. She couldn't tell if Noah was all right or not. He wasn't unconscious, but he seemed dazed. She wanted to reach for him, talk to him, but she could not take her eyes away from the altimeter and airspeed indicator in front of her and the mountain peaks around her.

Noah struggled for the tube and managed to shout enough for her to hear. "Let's get . . . out . . . of here!"

"That's what I'm trying to do!" Maj yelled back. "Only I don't know where I am. Are you all right?"

"Yes. Just . . . trying to keep . . . the wire tight."

She saw him fight to get another loop of it around his arm. Large cold raindrops pelted them.

"There!" He pointed to a lake off the right wing. "Go around, head into the wind . . . set her down there!"

"I don't—"

"You can!"

Rain came at them in sheets. The engine spluttered a miss. Water clouded Maj's goggles. Noah pointed directions with one hand, then grabbed the wire again to hold it fast.

"Rudder right!" Noah shouted.

Maj followed the order. The engine coughed another miss. The Stearman bumped through the air, buffeted by winds and currents as if it weighed no more than a piece of tumbleweed. Even strapped in tightly, Maj felt her backside lift off the seat as the aircraft dropped beneath her. Every nerve, muscle and bone in her body tensed, and the rush of adrenaline made her heart pound fast.

Her arms and shoulders working at peak strength, Maj held the aircraft as level as she could, descending, descending. The long lake lay like a naked finger stretching southwest to northeast. Rain slapped at them in torrents, soaking their clothes, gathering around their seats.

Noah tried several adjustments, but with the intensity of rain and wind the engine could not utilize the proper mixture of air and fuel. And then the great wood propeller wound down, no longer a dark smear in the path in front of them. Now it became languid, like a ceiling fan, slowing, slowing.

Stop.

The Stearman settled fast then, faster than Maj knew how to control.

"Keep the nose steady," Noah called. "I can handle the pedals. We're going in dead stick."

I can't see, Maj thought frantically, working to keep her panic at bay.

"Just feel it through," Noah called as if he read her mind. "We're almost down."

All Maj could feel was the force of nature tossing them around like a plastic baseball. Gorgeous blue sky had turned to menacing black, streaked with freezing needles of water. But the valiant Stearman pressed on at the bidding of her hands and Noah's feet.

"Hang on!" Noah shouted.

The aircraft hit the lake with a dull thud, a pitching and rocking, a splash against already churning water. The wind continued to whip them along erratically into tall weeds and grasses and branches that slapped their faces and chests. At last the aircraft came to rest against a bank of something they couldn't see.

Noah disentangled himself from the wing wire, and reached into a deep pocket in the side of the cockpit near his left leg. He extracted a five-cylinder flashlight. Getting out of his harness, he hoisted himself out of his seat and turned back to Maj.

"You all right?" he shouted through the storm's gathering force.

"I don't know," she shouted back.

"You can let go of the stick now." Noah leaned over toward her.

"Can't. I'm frozen to it."

Noah aimed the flashlight beam on her leather-gloved hands. They were gripped around the stick, fingers intertwined and locked. He stretched through the downpour and pried each of her fingers loose.

"Come on! Get yourself out of the harness."

Maj moved woodenly, but obeyed his bidding and released the straps. Noah searched for some rope he had stashed under the front seat, then jumped down and came to her assistance. She pushed her body up, then lifted one leg over the cockpit side, then the other, and slid down into his arms.

Noah set her on her feet, turned and waved the flashlight beam around them. "We'll secure the airplane as best we can!"

He looped a piece of rope around a leg above one float and handed it to her. Then he went around the other side of the aircraft and did the same with another length of rope. He aimed the flashlight beam toward the nose and the front of the floats.

"She's stuck in the mud. I hope that helps for a while! This way," he yelled, and they slogged through thigh-high weeds. "Find the nearest tree."

Maj followed him. Mud squished under her boots, making walking difficult, balance almost impossible. He motioned with the flashlight beam toward a young tree, and she stumbled for it. There the land felt more solid as it sloped up beneath her feet.

Noah slogged away to find another tree. As she wrapped the rope around the trunk and tied a strong knot, Maj kept her eyes on the dwindling beam of light that told her where he was. The light disappeared.

Maj panicked. "Noah!" She let go of the rope and started toward where she'd last seen the beam of light. "Noah!" she screamed against the raging storm. The rain and her tears stung her eyes, tasted gritty on her tongue.

Where is he? Is he hurt? Oh, God, will I be strong enough to help him? Please don't let him be hurt!

Then the beam of light came up directly to her face.

"Noah! Thank God. Are you all right?"

"Yes," he shouted. "I dropped the flashlight!" He waved the flashlight beam in an arc around them. "Stick close to me!" he called through the storm's relentless pounding, and started walking away from the lake.

"Like I was glued on!" she called back, getting ahold of her wits.

Soon they were in a forest, and the height of the trees cut the force of the wind and rain against them.

Noah walked, shining the flashlight methodically, first down in front of his steps and then into the distance ahead.

"There!" He stopped and she slammed into the back of him.

"What!"

"A lean-to!" He grabbed her hand and walked faster, dragging her through mud and brush. "Or what's left of one," he said, stopping.

Maj peered around his shoulder into the spotlighted object in front of them. Sheets of rain blew over a raised wood platform with back and side walls. The sloping roof had caved in at one end, and a stilt in one corner had broken, leaving that part of the floor resting in the mud.

"Well, it's not the Plaza, m'lady, but it is the only accommodation in town for the night." He stepped up onto the platform and pulled her in with him.

"The night?" Maj turned around and stared into the darkness. "Where are we?"

"Not sure exactly."

"Maybe there's a town near here."

"And maybe not. But I have no intention of wandering aimlessly through this storm to look for one."

"But we're soaked through. We'll freeze to death out here!"

"We're soaked, that's true. When the rain

lets up, I can build a fire. We won't freeze or die of advanced wet clothing."

"But what about animals?"

"They're not stupid enough to be out in this kind of weather. Come here."

Noah pulled her into the farthest corner of the lean-to and sat down on the wood floor. She dropped down next to him, and he put his arm around her, pulled her close to his chest, and wrapped his other arm around her.

"Better?" he asked over the loudly tapping rain.

She shuddered and wrapped her arms over his. "Oh . . . sh-sh-sure. M-much b-better."

They sat entwined for a long time while the rain and wind raged around them. It was surprisingly dry in their corner of the lean-to considering its obvious age and disrepair, and the strength of the storm.

Even more surprisingly, Maj relaxed and fell asleep wrapped in Noah's arms.

When she awoke, her head rested on his leather jacket and he was gone. The storm had passed. She sat up, the act requiring enormous reserves of strength, and knew her whole body felt cramped, stiff, sore, and chilled to the bone. And her neck and shoulders ached.

"Noah?" she asked into the quiet darkness. The rain had stopped, and the wind whispered

266

ancient secrets to the treetops. "Noah!" Her voice sounded on the verge of panic.

"Here!" She heard his boots making sucking noises in the mud as he came around the lean-to. He dumped a pile of something at her feet.

"What's that?"

"More posh accommodations for the night. You make up the bed and I'll make up a fire. Here's another flashlight." He flicked on a small beam, dropped it on the pile, and slogged away.

"Bed?" she inquired feebly.

She picked up the flashlight and scanned the pile of things in front of her. Short aluminum poles, a long pouch hand-stamped with the words "emergency shelter" on it, two folded Hudson Bay blankets, and a rolled sleeping bag. Where had he found those things?

The storm had washed the earth and forest around them to almost squeaky clean. The tall pines swayed against each other, creaking eerily. Small gusts of wind sent little showers of water out of the branches to drop on the lean-to roof, and sent up intermittent pungent scents of pine and mud. Raindrops tapped a gentle soothing rhythm on leaves around the campsite.

If it weren't for the fact that they were

stranded in an Adirondack mountain forest after dark, Maj thought the spot would be magical.

Noah came back as Maj was looking at the pouch. He shored up an old fire ring of stones crumbled by lack of use over a long span of time, and scraped out the middle with a small shovel.

"Dry wood is at a premium around here, but I managed to find some I think will burn." He opened a pack and took out a plastic bag containing matches, a half roll of toilet paper, candles, and some other things she couldn't see.

He picked up the flashlight and aimed it into the lean-to. Maj sat there with the blanket, sleeping bag, pouch, and poles around her just staring at him.

"If this were a buddy system for survival, one of us is not holding up her end of the arrangement." He pointed at the untouched pile.

"Don't tell me," she said, "you went to L. L. Bean and picked up a few things."

Noah laughed, setting the flashlight down and putting wood together for a fire.

"Well, perhaps a wood nymph was at work here, or Smokey the Bear? Where did all this stuff come from?"

"From me. I am an EMT, I am a mountain

pilot, I am a woodsman. These are simply staples."

"Staples. Of course. Where were they? Safely stored in a hollow tree?"

"My, my, for someone who's just been handed shelter, heat, and light in an emergency situation, you certainly are critical," he chided her.

Maj knew she seemed less than grateful for these things, but it suddenly all seemed contrived, arranged, as if he'd planned an overnight camping trip in the dark woods and she were his captive.

"Sorry, it just appears rather . . ."

"Calculating?"

"Well, to be honest, yes, it does."

"A bit suspicious, aren't you? I was never a Boy Scout, but I am a former Marine. Preparedness is our motto."

"So that's what *Semper Fidelis* means."

He grimaced. "Very loosely translated. I knew we'd fly the Stearman again, so I put some of my emergency gear in just in case we ran into trouble. Simple as that. No method to my madness."

He fanned a small flame, and soon the tinder caught and burned brightly, crackling as it heated under larger pieces. In the burnished glow Maj saw raindrops on his chambray shirt

269

spread darkly with the movement of his arms and shoulders, saw the outline of his backside in softly faded denim as he crouched next to the fire, watched droplets of water fall from his hair where it hung over his forehead in dark strands while he was intent in his work.

He stood up and stepped into the lean-to, tall, his imposing presence filling the small space. Maj fixed her eyes on his face. He stopped and settled his gaze on her. Something started happening in her blood and in the pit of her stomach. Something liquid like warm honey, and something gripping like a small animal trap designed only to capture.

"Did anyone ever tell you you look like John Wayne?" she asked dreamily.

He laughed. "As Davy Crockett or Rooster Cogburn?"

She laughed, too, and it caught in her throat. "Oh, much earlier than those."

"Did anyone ever tell you you don't follow orders very well?"

"What?"

"I see we still don't have a bed or a dry roof over our heads." He set about unfolding the small gray and blue nylon tent, inserting the poles and raising the dome, unrolling the sleeping bag, fitting it inside the tent and spreading it out, all the while sputtering for her benefit.

"How will I ever get everything done, what with dinner to prepare, laundry to dry, boots to clean. Primitive man's work is never done, it seems. Fight the dragons, bring home the brontosaurus steak, invent fire. Women have it so easy just lying around the cave all day oiling their hair and sharpening their fingernails."

Maj settled back against the damp wood of the lean-to, watching him, amused, enjoying the light banter amid the potentially dangerous circumstances. *Dangerous.* The word snagged in her mind. What was most dangerous, the storm, the state of the airplane, or the two of them alone together in the forest all night?

In a small tent. A very small tent.

"I like my brontosaurus medium. When will dinner be ready?" she said, trying to sound casual, blowing on her fingernails.

"As soon as I pop the corn and boil the water for cocoa."

"You're so thoughtful. My favorite two-course meal. Don't think I'll trade you to that Neanderthal woman on the other side of the mountain after all."

Noah threw a blanket over her head. "Get those wet clothes off, woman, and scoot over by the fire. Dinner is about to be served!"

She crawled into the tent and stripped off her damp clothes down to her underwear and set them outside on the lean-to floor next to her mud-laden boots. She sat for a moment in the silvery glow inside the tent and considered whether to remove her bra and panties. They were damp, but not uncomfortable. She decided to leave them on.

When she crawled out of the tent, Noah was nowhere to be seen. Then she heard something coming through the woods, and for a rigid moment thought it was a bear.

Noah emerged into the firelight wrapped in a blanket. She let out a relieved sigh.

"I see you've . . . slipped into something more comfortable," he said suggestively.

"Where'd you go?" she asked, trying but failing to ignore his comment.

"Gentlemen's powder room. The ladies' comfort station is to the right past the second maple sapling next to the white pine with the pile of wood chips at the base. Here." He handed her the roll of toilet paper, a bar of soap, and a small white towel. "Pretty posh as things go up here, right? Better put your boots on. You never know what might be on the trail."

Maj just looked at him. What could she say? Living became pretty elementary in such circumstances, she reckoned. She slipped bare feet into her damp boots, grimaced at the cold feel of them, and took the things from him.

"I'll just go powder my nose, then, and freshen up before dinner."

"Women!" Noah said into the trees. "Always primping!"

When she returned from a less than simple matter of normal toiletry in the dark woods — balancing a flashlight under her chin, trying to hold the blanket around her and not let it slip into whatever was on the ground, use the toilet paper, cover things over, wash her hands in a frigid stream, and not freeze to death in the process — Noah had their feast spread out on some short logs he'd set together in the form of a crude table.

Centering the spread was a lighted candle supported by a hole he'd carved in a fat stick, and a charred tin can holding a bouquet of tall green grasses and short trillium leaves. Their shirts hung off low tree branches near the fire, the arms draped back like loiterers.

He stood when she came near the fire. "May I seat you, madame?" he said, pulling a chunk of stump near the fire.

She set the toilet things in the lean-to next to the rest of their clothes which he'd arranged for drying, and lowered her aching body to the stump. Noah pulled up another stump and sat next to her. She caught his scent. Ivory soap mingled with the rain-washed outdoors and male warmth. She pulled her blanket closer around her trembling body.

"First course," he said, passing her warm slightly dried socks, and motioning to a log near the fire where she could rest her feet.

She pulled the socks on, ignoring their dampness, and welcoming their warmth.

He passed an aluminum pan with freshly popped corn nestled in an aluminum foil bowl atop it, and handed her a tin cup of hot chocolate.

"How gauche," she said haughtily, "no linens."

"Might I remind you once again that it's difficult to get good help these days, especially in this neck of the woods?"

"You mean your sectional sofa has not been delivered yet?"

"Correct. And the laundryman was a bit skimpy on the starch in my damask linens, so I refused to accept them.

"Huzzah!" She laughed. "It's hard work protecting oneself from victimizing conglomerates these days!"

"I'm so glad you appreciate the finer things in life," he said, clunking his mug against hers.

She sipped the cocoa and munched some

popcorn. "I do appreciate all of this," she said quietly, gesturing over the fire and back toward the tent in the lean-to. "I was pretty scared during the storm. I thought . . . I thought we might die."

"I was a bit concerned myself." He tried to sound offhanded. "But we're okay. And you were terrific up there."

Maj warmed as much under his praise as she did from the fire. "What about getting out of here?"

"We'll worry about that tomorrow. I'm glad Ada and Fergie aren't home to worry about it tonight. Ada would never let me take you flying again if she knew about this!"

"She does worry."

"Especially about you."

"I know. I never realized I'd have the feeling of unconditional love again at this stage of my life. It's almost as if I've started all over at the beginning of life."

"Incredible, isn't it? Did Jack make you feel that way? Unconditionally loved?"

Maj stared silently into the fire and let out a long breath through her nostrils.

"I'm sorry," Noah said. "I had no right to ask something so personal."

"No, it's all right, really. It's just that I've been forced to think about so much in my life since I came up here. My husband is probably the last subject to address."

Whoo, an owl called from somewhere away from them.

"Exactly!" She laughed nervously.

"Do you want to talk about him?"

"Do you want to hear about him?"

"Only if you want to talk about him." He turned on the stump and, beneath his blanket and through hers, she felt his arm on hers. "But more important, I want to know about you, Majesty, all about you."

"There's not much to know."

"Somehow I doubt that. After all, you learned to fly a biplane over mountains before you even had your first kiss I'll bet."

Maj raised her eyes quickly to his and felt a small smile of amusement play about her lips. She shivered when a cold finger of air insinuated itself down the opening of her blanket and settled between her breasts. She drew the blanket closer around her neck.

"How would you know when I got my first kiss?"

He looked at her as an artist would critically view a work in progress. "Hmm. You strike me as the kind of woman who began to bloom later in life than most. So I'd say you were hovering somewhere around, say, seventeen,

before you allowed any of your legions of suit-
ors close enough to steal a kiss."

"Legions of . . . ?" Maj laughed heartily.
"Trust me, you are no expert in assessing the
stages of a woman's life."

"Well, I shall take that as a challenge. The
gauntlet is down, m'lady, and I will prove to
you that while I may not be an expert, I can
quite accurately assess the stages of a woman's
life — correction . . . *this* female's life — and
what's more, I believe I might enhance the
present stage of this woman's life by bringing
to her at least some of the things she's longing
for."

Maj held his gaze through his speech to the
last words, then lowered her eyes quickly for a
moment before raising them and catching his
once more. "Well, sir," she said quietly, "you'd
have to be a mind reader to know what . . .
this woman is longing for, as you so eloquently
put it. And I doubt you are that."

"Try me." He looked directly into her eyes,
and Maj watched the slow movement of the
fire reflected along his strong jawline. "Tell me
about your life."

"Turnabout being fair play?"

"I always play fair."

Maj hesitated. Talking about the events in
her life up to then had been reserved solely for

Nan's ears. She didn't believe in discussing private things in public. And when could a woman be certain she could trust a man to understand personal details?

Trust was the key word. Just a couple of hours ago they'd trusted their lives in each other's hands. She'd long ago trusted her grandfather to protect her in the airplane, and never thought twice about it. She simply understood in her heart that he would.

Right now she wanted so much to believe she could trust Noah.

She drew in a deep breath, shivered, began. She told him everything, how she'd first come to the West Wind with her parents, and that her father was a pilot; how she'd met Jack at the prom the night her friend's tissue stuffing fell out of her dress; how he was right about her first kiss, it came from Jack that night; how they'd married young, had an active social life; how Jack was killed in a plane crash and she'd been working to pay off the bills; and how she came back to the West Wind just a few weeks ago.

"And the rest is such recent history, you know all about it," she finished.

He'd been staring into the fire as she spoke. "You're a gutsy lady, Majesty Wilde."

"Me? I've never thought so. Most of the

time I'm scared to death if I'm faced with something new. I'm surprised I'm even here. Well, I don't mean *here* here, although it is pretty surprising to think that we've landed a plane in a rainstorm and are sitting in front of a fire in the middle of the Adirondack forest wearing a pair of Hudson Bay blankets."

"I'll say!"

"I mean, I'm surprised I'm up here, and I'm the owner of the West Wind, and all the rest of it. Things changed so fast, I've felt I was spinning like a toy top."

"Things don't really change, we change." Noah poked the fire with a long stick.

"Another Decker pearl of wisdom?"

"I can't take credit for it. That's Thoreau again." He didn't say anything for several moments. "Why didn't you have children, Maj? I'm not judging, don't get me wrong. I'm just asking if it was by choice, or by fate, or health." He looked up beyond his shoulder to her face.

By choice. Fate. Maj turned his words over in her mind. Should she tell him about her fate, how the choice was made that she had no children?

She wondered what he'd think about her. Would his opinion that she was a "gutsy lady" change when he heard how she'd given in and

279

aborted her only child? How gutsy was that? She'd been weak and acquiescing, to her ever-lasting regret. No matter how much she and Nan talked through that time in her life, she knew in her heart she hadn't forgiven herself.

"You don't have to tell me if you don't want to," Noah said when she'd paused for a long time. "It isn't any of my business, actually. It was just something more I wanted to know about you."

"I think I do want to tell you, but you'll probably change your mind about your assessment of me. I'm afraid your accuracy record may be threatened."

"I'll take the chance."

Maj wrapped herself tightly in the blanket and hunched nearer the fire. And then she told the story to Noah, the story that lived like a cold, hard lump in the core of her being.

"Before we got married, Jack convinced me to have sex with him. Nowadays nobody thinks anything about that. But back then, well . . . I knew I'd get caught, knew it was wrong to have sex without being married. Jack said if I loved him I'd do it, and that would prove to him I really loved him."

Maj swirled the remains of her cocoa in the bottom of the mug. "I thought I was in love with him, but how do you ever know when, or

280

even if, you're in love? I was scared. I did it only once, and I couldn't figure out what all the controversy was about. It wasn't any fun. But then I discovered I was pregnant. I was really scared, and so was Jack. So we eloped. My mother was furious. Not so much because she couldn't have a big wedding for her only daughter, but because, I think, I married a pilot. Jack had been learning to fly, and eventually he became a corporate pilot."

"Your mother had something against pilots?" Noah gave her a glance and a small laugh.

Maj swallowed. "Dad was an airline pilot. Mother found out about several affairs he'd had. She was hurt deeply, but in true manner of the times, she stuck by him, silent and brave. I hated it, hated him for it, once I found out."

Noah added some more wood to the fire. "What about the baby?"

"Jack arranged for me to have an abortion. It wasn't a sordid back-alley kind of thing, although I certainly knew about those. His uncle was a doctor, and he did it in his brand-new office. He patted me on the shoulder, smiled so that I could see the artificially dark rose gums surrounding his false teeth, and told me I'd made the right decision." Her thoughts trailed back to a distant time, but her voice carried the pain of the memory as if the event had happened last week. "I didn't make any decision."

Noah watched her face as he settled back on the stump. Hearing the thickness in her voice made his gut churn, and he had to force his own voice through a throat tight with emotion. "You didn't want the abortion, did you?"

"No. I didn't. And since it was a nice sterile office with a doctor in a clean white coat using sterile medical tools, Jack expected me to get over it as if I'd had a tonsillectomy or something."

"But you didn't get over it, did you?"

"I felt guilty, sad, weak for letting him talk me into it. But I learned to live with it. It was the grown-up-married thing to do. Being grown-up caught me by surprise, I guess. Inside I still felt like a child. For the longest time I felt as if someone had taken away my favorite doll."

"Did you try to have a baby again after that?"

"Jack decided it wasn't the right time for a baby. We weren't ready for children yet. I realized, after a while, that there would never be the right time as far as he was concerned. There were too many trips, too many parties, too many things to buy." She let out a long sigh. "Too many other people who were more important."

"No child should have a parent who doesn't want to be one," Noah said into the distance.

Maj looked at him, wondering from which part of his life the comment was prompted. "You sound like you have personal experience with that."

Noah sat so still, Maj would not have known he was breathing if not for the small white mists of air emitted from his nostrils into the encroaching chill of the black night.

"Your husband treated you like your father did your mother, didn't he?" he said, his voice low, evading her question.

Maj drew her gaze back to the lowering fire. "Yes, only I didn't know about it at the time. I don't know if that's good or bad. I sometimes wonder if I was too naive to notice what was going on, or whether he was just very skillful in covering his activities."

"How did you find out?"

"Jack was killed in a plane crash. He was alone, bringing the company plane back empty. At his funeral"—her voice constricted and she swallowed audibly—"at his funeral a stunning woman appeared with a teenage boy. I asked her how she knew Jack, and she told me she was . . . the mother of his son, that boy."

Noah nodded, and uttered a small sound.

"The next year and a half went by in a blur of shock and hearings," Maj continued, "learning Jack left me with enormous debt and that Mustang, and seeing the boy's name as beneficiary on the life insurance. And then cold reality set in with the finality of hearing a judge pronounce the boy to be, without question, Jack's son. Since then all I've done is work to pay off my husband's debts."

Maj decided she was finished with the story. She kept her eyes on the fire, waiting. Waiting, she guessed, for Noah to say something she knew wouldn't change any of the events, and wondering what he might think about her now.

Noah said nothing for a long time. Then he moved toward Maj and put both arms around her, drawing her close.

"Now I know what the sadness means that I see in your eyes sometimes. And I know why I've felt you didn't trust me." He kissed the top of her hair. "Like I said, you're a gutsy lady."

Maj clamped her eyes shut. A shiver ran over her.

"And a cold lady!" Noah rubbed her arms. "I think it's time for you to get into that sleeping bag and get warm. I don't want you catching cold. Ada would never let me forget it."

284

"Wait a minute," she said with her hand against his arm. "You said you'd tell me your life story. I'm the one who's done all the talking here."

"I think that's best saved for another bedtime," he said quietly. "A night when you're having difficulty sleeping. I could bore you to sleep with the details."

"I don't bore easily."

"I think it's more important right now you get warm and get some rest. Tomorrow's going to be tough. I hope the Stearman is all right, and we can get it out of the mud."

He helped her to her feet. Maj gripped the blanket tightly. "You go in the tent first," he instructed. "I'll take care of the fire, and then I'll be in."

"In the . . . tent? You mean we're both going to . . . sleep in that tiny thing?"

"You wouldn't make me sleep out in the cold dark woods where some ferocious animal might drag me off, would you? Even if I am a dreaded pilot?"

He tried his best to look seriously concerned about how she'd control the fate of his welfare, but Maj saw the teasing in his eyes. And she knew she couldn't make him sleep outside for the sake of some ancient idea of propriety.

"Of course not. It's a matter of survival, isn't

it?" Maj tried to sound light. "Even if you are a pilot."

"Survival, yes. And warmth. Don't forget warmth."

"Warmth. Yes. Well, I'll just get into the tent now. I won't leave a light in the window, so you'll just have to find your way."

"I know my way," he said, "trust me."

"I do," she answered, and she believed she did.

Chapter Eleven

Inside the tent Maj wrapped herself in the blanket and lay down on the sleeping bag, spread open to act as a cushion over the lean-to floor. Damp chill had settled all through her and seemed to rattle inside her bones. She could see the vapor puffs of her breath in the waning glow of the fire through the nylon shell.

Turning on her side in the fetal position, she got as close to the side of the two-person tent as she could. The futile act created no more space than if she hadn't even tried—there was just enough room to accommodate one other average person. Just.

And Noah Decker was certainly more than the average person. Much more.

Outside, she could hear him washing the tin mugs, doing something with the fire, something in the lean-to with their clothes. The tent zipper went up in a swift slash, making her jump as if someone had suddenly unzipped her clothing. A shaft of frigid air came in and settled over her face, the only part of her anatomy not covered by the blanket. Noah crawled through the tent opening and zipped it down. Wrapping the blanket loosely around him, he lay next to her.

The tent atmosphere seemed to warm gradually with Noah's presence. Their blankets touched, and the heat from his body penetrated the thicknesses as if nothing more than air were between them.

He turned on his side, facing her back, and Maj felt his breath on her neck. A shiver coursed down her spine. In a moment she heard his even breathing.

He certainly fell asleep quickly. Exhausted by the day's events, no doubt. Why didn't she feel exhausted? Why did she feel keyed up, like a tightly coiled spring ready to burst apart in a twist of uncontrolled curls? How was it he didn't feel the kind of tension she felt?

The quiet settled around her, a thick quiet she never ceased to marvel at since she'd been back in the Adirondacks. And then she heard a cricket chirp. Another answered. More responded, and soon she thought they must all be lined up outside her side of the tent. She pictured them seated and warming up like an orchestra in their little black suits.

A loon wailed from somewhere on the lake. Its partner chimed in answer. Above the tent, tree branches rubbed together in the wind, creating an eerie song of communion. An owl asked the inevitable question, asked it again, then again. No answer came from the forest or from Maj.

She tried to relax, willed herself to think this was a perfectly natural arrangement between two adults. Two people had been stranded in a raging storm, their transportation out of the mountains crippled. They were fortunate to have shelter for the night. Perfectly natural. Maj felt imperfect and unnatural, and disturbed when she recognized those feelings.

The howl of a coyote underscored a profound loneliness she'd suppressed for so very long. How could anyone be lonely in a place like Manhattan? Easy, she thought. What good was being surrounded by millions of people if you weren't connected to a special one?

She'd learned to live with herself and be satisfied with her life. In fact, after Jack she'd enjoyed her solitude. But coming back to the West Wind and the Fergusons had shown her how much she was missing.

And now there was Noah Decker. He'd landed in her life with all the subtlety of a supersonic transport, and she felt like an air traffic controller in a tiny airport who didn't know what to do with such a piece of a equipment.

She shuddered as another chill swept over her.

Noah stirred and moved close to her, fitting his knees to the back of her knees, his stomach to the small of her back, his chest to her shoulders, his cheek to the top of her hair. His groin to the curve of her buttocks.

Perfectly natural, two bodies fitting together like that.

He brought an arm out of his blanket and slipped it over her waist. He slipped his other arm under her shoulder down inside her blanket along her arm, and fit his body into all her curves, the blankets between them.

"Are you getting warmer now?" he whispered in her ear.

Maj shuddered again. This time she knew it wasn't from the cold. "I don't know yet," she whispered back.

"Body heat is the best remedy for this kind of cold." He breathed in ragged rhythm with her.

His comment felt as if it should be right. She felt as if she trusted him. Why? She didn't know anything about him. No, that wasn't quite true. She did know he was intelligent, honestly cared about Fergie and Ada, worked hard and companionably with her and Fergie, had been a Marine pilot, had been a stunt pilot.

Had a daughter.

What about a wife? Past or present tense. That was supposed to matter, especially in a situation like this one.

Maj's chilled body thawed, and in the growing physical warmth between them, it fell against Noah's. All at once that seemed like the most natural feeling she'd experienced since she'd become an adult. Amid the tangle of blankets she felt cradled by him, warmed. She snuggled into the blankets and in his arms.

He uttered a sigh of contentment. She turned her head slightly; he lifted his a little. She opened her eyes; he opened his. In the waning glow of the firelight, their heavy-lidded gaze held for only a heartbeat before closing at the moment their lips met.

It was a feeling kiss, a moving of lips gently against each other, tasting, tentatively exploring with the tips of tongues, and then turning hot, wet, lavish. He moaned, gathering her closer against him.

Her body felt languid, her limbs heavy. Time decelerated to slow motion, and she felt suspended above herself and Noah, watching them meld beneath the blankets into one aching, pressing need.

His hand inside her blanket rested along her rib cage while he held her mouth captive with

291

his own. He let his hand travel like a feather over her smooth skin up to the fullness of her breast. He cupped the globe, softly kneading, then rubbing his thumb tantalizingly over the nipple, enticing it to a hard bud.

New feelings swept over her. Desire, most certainly. Desire for this man, this man's hands, body, mouth, and more. He ran his hand over the roundness of her hip, down her thigh to her knee, then up the front of her thigh to the soft mound.

They didn't speak, didn't have to, for the little moans escaping each of them told them all they needed to know. He ran a finger along her opening, then stopped. She moved, pressing against his fingers, commanding him to continue.

He reached for her hand, pulled it across her body, and rested it upon him. Her quick intake of breath showed he stirred her the way she was stirring him. And then they stroked, explored, learned the shape and responses of each other.

She pressed against him, her need clearly communicated. But he held back. He wanted to pleasure this woman the way she should be pleasured, and wanted to revel in pleasure from her. Sensual greed consumed him. The texture of her skin, the curves of her form, the moist silkiness he felt inside her, the fresh air and womanly scent of her, the picture he fantasized of her sex-drugged face beneath him. He couldn't stop, didn't want to stop any of it.

The way she responded told him she was feeling the same way.

Maj stroked him, took liberties with her hands over his body. Any inhibitions she'd learned during her physical life before this moment shattered, and her hunger for Noah gnawed until her insides burned. To touch him, smell him, hear his raspy breathing amid his desire for her, *for her,* and to know the breadth of that desire, overwhelmed her.

She reached up out of the blanket, plunged her hands into his hair, and pulled his head down. With a deep breath and a moan she claimed his mouth, capturing his lower lip in both her own, consuming him.

With a groan he ripped the blankets away and, supporting himself on one arm, shifted her hips until she was under him, knees bent, thighs wide apart. He lowered himself against her, poised for a moment at her opening, then eased inside. As she welcomed him eagerly, he paused halfway, opened his eyes and looked down upon her face turning languidly back and forth in the final glow of the firelight.

She let out a hard breath as he plunged deep, then lowered his arms and rested his lips against her ear.

"Take all of me and don't let go," he whispered through clenched teeth.

Instinctively she raised her hips and entwined her legs around him over his back, hooking her ankles. Her own response shocked her. She'd never done that before. And she wasn't embarrassed.

They rocked together, she silent, he moaning with pleasure. He rained kisses over the sensitive cord at the side of her neck. She raked her fingers up and down along the expanse of his back and buried her face in the hollow of his shoulder.

They moved together as one, working to get ever closer, ever deeper. She slid her hands down his back and grasped his hard, muscular buttocks, straining to pull him deeper. Her teeth nipped at his shoulder as he ground into her.

"Oh, God," he uttered against her ear, "I can't hold on any longer."

Maj wanted him to hold on forever, wanted to move against him, taking all she could get from him. Hunger. That was the most overwhelming emotion coursing through her at that moment. Ravenous, physical, mental, emotional, sensual hunger, and Noah fed that deep, intense hunger with exactly the right sustenance.

He pressed deep, arched, then shuddered in release. She pressed against him, letting him fill her, wanting to hold on to him and all he was giving her.

He fell against her and wrapped his arms under her, holding her so closely, she sensed herself his lifeline. She clasped him with her arms and legs and pulled him even closer. He reached back and pulled the blankets up over them, enveloping them in a cocoon of warmth and the spicy scent of their lovemaking.

He slid then to the side, starting to ease out of her.

"No," she said dreamily, "don't go. It feels so good."

He slid down behind her, turning her on her side with her back against his chest, and pulled her buttocks against him where he was wet with her juices as much as with his own. "I want to make you feel this good, too."

"I do already."

"There's more I can give you."

"You don't have to," she whispered.

"Yes, I do," he whispered back. "Let me have the thrill of giving you all the pleasure you deserve."

He slid an arm under her and cupped her lower breast. With his other hand he strummed his fingers over her thigh, lower, until he connected with the place where she felt completely alive. He explored her until he found the magical spot that controlled every nerve ending. She dropped her head back against his shoulder. He lowered his head and took her other nipple into his mouth. Moving his hips against her buttocks, he set a rhythm of their bodies together, fondled one breast and sucked the other, while relentlessly moving his fingers inside her.

Behind her she felt him hard along the back of her thigh, felt the tip of him rest against the base of her opening, where his fingers strummed a rhythm she was drawn to with magnetic force.

She moaned, raised her arm up to encircle his neck, bury her fingers in his hair and pull him farther into the fullness of her breast. He opened his mouth and took in as much of her as he could. And then the turbulence gathered momentum low inside her, gained intensity, surged, and took off buoyed by the chemistry and power of the two of them together.

When Noah entered her again, Maj's physical and mental emotions were exposed, and they flew in tandem into their own personal space beyond reality. Maj letting go, Noah giving in. Her to all her reserves, defenses. Him to the aching lust for her he'd been holding back.

She wanted him to stop. She wanted him

never to stop. She couldn't get enough. She was getting too much. She wanted to hold it all in, yet the pressure was so great she was frantic to let it go.

And then with her eyes closed to hold her fantasy, they soared above the clouds on wings of abandon, she the craft and he the pilot, in a cataclysmic rise. They poised at the peak of their ascent, and then rolled over to soar down through clouds, to level off and fly the horizon toward the sun.

As they descended to earth they lay with limbs entwined, their skin clinging with heat and body moisture, pulses slowing to rest, chests heaving for air. She sank against him, emitting an elongated "ohhh" in a raspy whisper.

Noah wrapped them both in the warmth of the blankets, and they drifted off together with the heat of their closeness and the scent of their lovemaking hovering around them.

In her dreams John Wayne in a leather jacket stepped out of the Stearman and walked toward her, a long white silk scarf trailing behind him in the breeze. He emerged from an azure mist, came to her, stripping off his leather helmet, dark hair fluttering in the breeze, brown eyes, filled with lust, that sparkled like diamonds.

He swept her up in his strong arms and carried her to a cave, set her down on a bed of thick feathers and kissed every inch of her skin. And then she sat up, slipped his jacket from his shoulders, unbuttoned his shirt to reveal another one, black and silky with a golden Batman silhouette across the chest. She loosened his belt, opened his trousers. . . .

Maj's eyes flew open. Above her a gray nylon dome shone in natural light. She stirred, and felt the skin of one buttock peel away from Noah's thigh. He sighed low, and cupped his hand more closely around her breast. Every moment of their lovemaking passed through her mind as she relived the flight.

Noah opened his eyes. He leaned up and saw Maj staring overhead.

"Good morning," he whispered, and kissed her lightly.

"It is morning, isn't it?" she said dreamily.

"I think so. Or maybe it's next week. I don't know, and I don't care. As long as it's this moment."

She leaned her head back and kissed him deeply.

"You're all right," he said as a proven statement rather than a concerned question.

"I'm extremely all right."

"I'm glad. I wanted to please you, make you happy."

"I'm a bit disappointed about one thing."

He sat up and looked down at her, honest worry on his face. "What?"

"I can't believe I had to wait this long for *that!*"

"What do you mean?"

"You were right."

"About what?"

"I am a late bloomer."

"How's that?"

"This is the first time I've ever experienced . . . the ultimate . . . making love."

"You mean, you've never before . . . ?"

"No."

"No one ever made sure you got as much pleasure out of it as he did?"

"There was only one, and his own pleasure was uppermost in his mind."

"Then he missed out on as much pleasure as you did."

"What do you mean?" She cocked her head.

"I mean it thrilled me to see and feel your pleasure, thrilled me to know you reacted that way to me, to us together."

"Certainly taught me a brand-new meaning for the term *happy camper!*"

He laughed the kind of feel-good laugh she'd come to love.

She slithered over on top of him. "Can we do it

299

again so I can watch you getting pleasure from me?"

"Well—" He paused.

"Well what?" She straightened her elbows and leaned up straight over her hands, looking shocked.

"Well, it's a nasty job, but somebody's got to do it."

"You . . . !"

"Yes, me," he whispered, "and you, and glorious us. Come here." He wrapped his hands in her hair, cupped her head, and drew her down to his demanding mouth.

She sat astride him and he fondled her breasts and she watched him watching his own hands. Then he slid them down her rib cage and cupped her hips, lifted her, and settled her down upon him. She rocked against him as he slid his hands back up to her breasts.

Noah watched her through a haze of lust as she closed her eyes and dropped her head, letting her tousled hair fall over her shoulders and down her back. He moved against her, bent his knees and lifted his hips, and she rode him in rhythm to their heightened desire.

And then she grasped the back of his hands over her breasts and held him, letting a long moan escape her lips. He let himself release everything, and they slammed against each other in the intense desire to assuage the ache inside them both.

When their needs were fulfilled, each let their emotions ease down one by one, as if the pain of it all at once would be shattering. Noah slid his hands around her back, pulled her down into the womb of their nest, and wrapped the blankets around them. He rocked her in his arms and said nothing. Maj was too overcome with emotion to speak, almost even to breathe.

One blinding thought flashed into her mind— *Mother was wrong!*

Morning beat relentlessly against the tent, and Noah stirred. Maj lay atop him, her face nestled into his chest.

"I hate to be the one to say this," he muttered, "but we should see if we can get out of here. We have to check the airplane."

"Do we have to?" She sighed sleepily.

"We have to."

"Un-unh, let's just stay right here and make love again."

"Well, you certainly do live up to your name, don't you?"

She leaned upon her elbow. "If you say anything about purple mountains, so help me . . ." She gripped his hair in a playful tease.

"I wouldn't dream of it. All I was going to say is that you are a wanton woman, and you're aptly named — Wilde. Now, get off me, woman, so I can get about the business of a manly rescue of your fair self!"

"And what if I command you to stay right where you are?"

"Then I shall disobey your queenly command, your majesty, and strip your regal body of its tent, thereby exposing you to any foraging animal in the forest!"

"You wouldn't dare!"

"I would dare!"

"Before I've had my coffee?"

"You're not getting any coffee."

"You wouldn't be that disobedient!"

"Watch me!" He rolled her off him, unzipped the tent, got out, released the clips from the frame poles, and dropped the tent on her before she barely knew what happened.

"Why, you . . . !"

"Now, now, no less than kingly names for your brave caveman! It wouldn't become your queenly self." He lifted the flap of the tent and threw some clothes inside. "Don your robes, your majesty, you're about to indulge in real labor!"

Maj scrambled out of the blankets and tent a few minutes later. Noah had disappeared, probably into the woods to the gentlemen's comfort station. She worked at getting dressed. She was

302

freezing and shivering badly, and her fingers felt numb. She couldn't get her bra hooked. She struggled, standing in jeans and boots, naked from the waist up, skin rippling with goose bumps.

"May I be of some assistance?"

Maj spun around. Noah stood, fully dressed right to his leather jacket, leaning against a tree watching her with an amused grin.

"Noah Decker, are you spying on me?" she said with mock indignation.

"No, ma'am, just enjoying the view," he answered, not moving a muscle. He watched her nipples respond to the cold by pointing straight out.

"Well, perhaps you *could* be of some assistance," she said with a coquettishness that surprised her.

"With pleasure," he said, pushing away from the tree and sauntering toward her.

She pulled the front-hook bra around her, holding the cups away from her breasts. He opened his jacket and walked to her until his chest pressed against hers. He wrapped the jacket around her back and kissed her. Then he released her lips and, holding her against him, looked down into her eyes.

"Did that help?" he said softly, with a seductive timbre.

"Immensely," she replied, gazing at him with her eyes half closed.

"I knew it would."

"Pretty sure of yourself, aren't you?"

He clasped her head against his shoulder. "I wasn't before, but now I am," he whispered.

Maj could only hold him. She was so filled with every sensation she thought it was possible to feel, that words would have shattered the moment.

He leaned back then, brought the bra cups around her breasts, and hooked the clasp in the valley between them. Then he lowered his head and kissed the soft mounds tenderly. When he looked up into her eyes, neither of them could speak for a moment. At last he broke the silence.

"Reality reigns now, your highness. Your chariot is stuck in the mud. It'll take both of us to get it out. We'd better get moving."

"What, no breakfast? I'm starving. I'd even eat brontosaurus leftovers."

"We're out of fresh kill. You kept me too busy last night and this morning to attend to things like survival."

She leveled her gaze on him and said in seriousness, "Frankly, I thought what we did had everything to do with survival. Mine, at least."

"You weren't alone."

"No, I wasn't."

He motioned her silently to come with him to the Stearman.

"I can't believe I'm doing this," Maj muttered a half-hour later as she mushed through ankle-high marshy sod, her hands gripped under the tail section of the aircraft.

"You?" Noah said from the front. He slogged through thigh-high weeds and muck, ropes through the struts of the airplane, pulling it toward open water. "I feel like Humphrey Bogart in *The African Queen*."

"Don't expect me to pull the leeches off you like Katharine Hepburn did," she called back. "And we're all out of salt anyway."

"And here I thought you wanted me for my body, that is, if there's anything left of it when the black flies get through with it." He swatted at the back of his neck.

"Okay, okay, I'll take care of the leeches, but I'm powerless against these flies." She waved a hand around her head, trying to fend off the pesky biting insects.

"I knew I could bring you to your knees."

"You affected more than my knees," she grunted against the aircraft, pushing with what little strength she had left.

"I'll take that as a compliment."

He tugged at the Stearman once more, and it floated free. "The quicker we're airborne, the quicker we'll get away from these flies," he said, motioning her to get into the aircraft and swatting above his head.

"I'm a mess," Maj said weakly. "How can I go back to the West Wind looking like this?"

"We'll stop at my cabin first. You can clean up, and maybe we'll beat Ada and Fergie back to the lodge."

The old workhorse Stearman protested the early morning start, but with a cough and wheeze there was ignition, taxi, and liftoff as if nothing of any importance had happened the night before.

At least nothing more than blinding rain and destructive wind.

In his cabin Noah heated water so they could wash up, and gave Maj a pair of his jeans and a shirt. Behind the curtain that served as a temporary door to the bathroom he was building, they laughed and played in a basin of soapy water in front of an antique gilt-framed mirror. Suds flew everywhere. Bubbles floated in the air and they made silly games of catching them with their tongues when they weren't catching other things with their tongues.

Sleek chest to slippery breasts, they kissed and held and touched each other with as much

306

air of discovery as they had a few hours earlier in the tent.

"If we don't stop this," Maj said against his lips, "I will never get back to the lodge before Ada and Fergie."

"And I will suffer a reprimand for certain."

"For certain."

"Then get dressed, woman!" He turned her around and gave her a playful pat on her backside.

Maj gave him a towel snap on his, and scurried out of the tiny bathroom before he could retaliate.

While Noah finished bathing, Maj put on her bra and his shirt. Buttoning it, she strolled around the room surveying his progress.

Bookshelves lined both sides of the fireplace now. Maj scanned them. Evident were volumes by Thoreau, Dreiser, Zane Grey and B. M. Bower; Adirondack history books by Durant, Colvin, and Hochschild; books on stunt flying, antique aircraft restoration, and wilderness survival. And the complete works of both Brownings. Maj lifted her eyebrows in wonder. Poetry?

A wrought iron floor lamp with an ivory cut-paper shade stood next to a deep burgundy print wing chair flanking the fireplace. Framed and matted, wall-hung photographs showed bits and pieces of Noah's life in his stunt-flying days, and as a child in the Adirondacks with what looked to her to be family members.

Maj smiled back at the pictures, wishing she'd known him then.

A square yellow-pine dining table centered the kitchen alcove. Hanging precariously over the center of it was a wood and black wrought iron chandelier in the process of being wired. An Adirondack twig lamp and side tables stood in a line along one wall as if waiting for their turn to be placed.

Maj climbed the open stairway to the sleeping loft. A cedar post bed occupied one end, while at the other a half-constructed closet held Noah's clothes. Maj smiled as she touched a stack of underwear on a low shelf. His briefs were folded in perfect squares, no doubt a skill learned in the Marine Corps.

His home still looked to be in the state of creation, and Maj compared her state to that of the rustic cabin.

An unfinished pine dresser stood between two windows. Atop it lay a comb, pocket change, a bandanna, and a photograph of Noah, his arm draped around the shoulder of a teenage girl with long blond hair. Maj surmised the photograph to be of his daughter.

She wondered who had been on the other side of the camera lens.

"Hey! Where'd you go?" Noah's voice sounded around the cabin.

"Up here!" Maj bent over the loft rail and peered down at him.

"Nice view from down here." He smiled, taking obvious assessment of her bare legs emerging from his shirttail.

"I'd love to say the view is better up close and personal, but I think it's best left unconsidered."

"Oh, I don't know about that," he said, raising his eyebrows and starting up the stairs.

"Noah, we can't!" Maj giggled.

"We can, too, and we've proved that!"

"I mean, we can't *now*."

He reached her, grasped her under her naked buttocks, lifted then dropped her down on the bed. He kissed her long and with a thoroughness they both enjoyed.

"Mmmm," she murmured.

"Hm-hmm," he responded, pulling a patchwork quilt over them.

And they both knew where they were going. She closed her eyes and opened her body. He closed his eyes and entered her. They rocked together in comfortable union as if they'd been together like this since the beginning of their memories, and were still in awe of how much they loved being together, whether this was the first time or the hundredth time.

Maj ascended to new heights, then softly drifted down deeper into her own depths, where knowledge of pleasure was a seed to be nurtured and used to give back.

She was falling in love with this man.

This must be love. Watery-kneed excitement, rapid pulse, fluttery stomach—the same things she'd felt in high school at the moment of her first infatuation. Incredible to think that the intervening thirty-five years hadn't dulled acute recollection of the sense memory. Only now, every cell in her body, mind, and emotions seemed even more aware, open to trust, to new experiences, to a new life she never thought was possible in any human being. She was experiencing rebirth, and would cherish and savor the moment.

Noah pulled her to him and held her close. "Ah, Majesty, what you do to me." He jumped, as if poked with something sharp.

"What do I do to you?" she purred.

He kissed her throat. "Things I've never felt before."

"Do all former Marines say things like that?"

"I can't speak for all former Marines. Each one of us is unique unto himself."

"Oh, brother, does that sound like a recruitment poster!"

"I speak only the truth." He kissed her again.

"I mean it when I say I'm feeling things I've never felt with anyone else. Like right this moment." His voice carried a hint of pain.

"What are you feeling right this moment?"

"Like someone's watching us. And is it possible you've suddenly sprouted extremely long arms and very sharp nails and are, even as we speak, sinking those nails into my behind?"

"I beg your pardon!"

"Ow! What the hell . . . ?"

Maj lifted her head and peered past the curve of his shoulder, over the hollow of his lower back, then up the slope of his firm, round buttocks beneath the quilt.

"Someone *is* watching us!" She let out a long, tinkling laugh and dropped her head back into the pillow.

Noah twisted around. "Orville!"

The indignant feline sat poised above his buttocks, kneading deeply through the patchwork, flexing his claws and connecting with sensitive flesh. He leveled a yellow almond-shaped gaze at Noah, then lowered his lids to half-mast.

"Do you suppose he was there the whole time we . . . ?" Maj shattered into another spate of laughter.

"It wouldn't surprise me." Noah bounced the cat off him. "Voyeur." He accused Orville. The cat jumped to the floor with a cranky, deep-throated meow.

Maj clamped a hand over her mouth. She'd laughed over Orville's auspicious entrance, and now she worried Noah would think she was laughing at him.

"I'm sorry I laughed, Noah. It was only because of Orville, nothing else. Really."

Noah looked back at Maj and chuckled. "It's all right to laugh in bed, you know."

She cocked her head to the side as if she'd just heard a piece of knowledge new to her. "Hmm. All right. I just didn't want you to think I was laughing at the way you—"

Noah laughed. "Performed? Is that what you were going to say?" He kissed her lightly when she nodded. "If you feel so good in bed with me that you want to laugh, for whatever reason, then don't hold back. All I want is to make you happy during our times like this."

She pulled his head down to her chest and sucked in a breath. "Oh, Noah, I do, more than you will probably ever realize. I just don't want to hurt your feelings."

"You won't. My ego is very much intact. And as I said, I've never felt all these things with anyone else."

She stroked the back of his hair. "You . . . you've been married, of course."

He sat up then. "Yes. I want to talk about that with you. Talk about a lot of things."

She sat up next to him and dangled her feet over the edge of the bed. "The bedtime story you told me about?"

"Yes. But I don't want to be in a hurry when we start to talk. There's so much to tell you. And right now I have to get you back to the West Wind, so get dressed before I lose what impressive control I'm displaying at this moment and ravish you shamefully." He kissed her neck playfully.

"You? Display control?" Maj leaned back in mock amazement.

Noah leaned back on one elbow and studied her profile. He laced the fingers of his other hand through hers and let his gaze drift past her into the space beyond their physical one.

I want to keep this woman in my life. Imagine that! I want to laugh with her, discover with her, live with her, love with her.

I don't want to lose her.

I'm afraid to tell her.

The unmistakable sound of tires skidding over the gravel drive leading to the cabin startled them both.

"Fergie?" Maj breathed.

"Maybe," Noah said, grabbing a pair of jeans. "Oh, God, I don't want him to see us like

313

this." Maj scrambled to find something to wear. The jeans he'd given her were below on the wing chair by the fireplace.

Noah started to run down the stairs barefoot, his chest naked. Maj followed close behind, hoping to get to the jeans before the door opened.

Too late.

A young woman stepped into the cabin, dropped a suitcase on the floor. Maj's heart started a deafening pounding in her ears. The girl brushed her long blond hair out of her face as she stood up. Her pale features changed dramatically from anticipation to shock.

"Daddy?"

Chapter Twelve

"Kimmie," Noah started toward his daughter, arms outstretched, "what a wonderful surprise! You're earlier than I expected."

"I can see that. Daddy . . . what's going on?"

Maj picked up the jeans from the chair and started toward the bathroom. "Um, excuse me. I'll just go in here." She stepped quickly behind the curtain.

"Kimmie honey . . ."

"Never mind. I *know* what's going on here, and it's obvious I've arrived at the wrong time." Kimmie's big blue eyes filled with tears. She swiped at them, then bent down to retrieve her suitcase.

"Kimmie, just give me a minute to explain, honey." Noah tried to reach her.

"Please" — Kimmie raised her hand — "I've

had all the explanations I can take. My loving mother Adrienne is conveniently not at home, even though she knew when I was through school."

On the other side of the bathroom curtain Maj heard Kimmie's words. *Adrienne.* So that was her name.

"And now my dear father is busy with some . . . some . . ." Kimmie's face reddened, and angry tears streamed down, marring her porcelain cheeks.

Maj came out of the bathroom barefoot, Noah's jeans rolled up at her ankles, his shirt tucked in and blousing around her waist. Kimmie eyed her with disdain.

". . . slut."

"Kimmie!" Noah grabbed her arm. "That was uncalled for, young lady."

Kimmie stepped back as Noah's scolding words hit her like a slap in the face.

"Well, what is called for, Father dear? I'm damned if I know anymore. I have two parents who live on opposite ends of the country, no home with either one of them because *she* doesn't want me and *he* has a girlfriend. Why didn't you tell me, so I wouldn't come up here and embarrass myself? I'm the stupid one, the naive one. I thought I'd come up and see you for a few days before I started

316

my summer job, but—"

"Kimmie, come on now, honey. I'm so glad to see you! It's great you're here." Noah tried to smooth her hair with his hand, but she drew her head back sharply.

"Great! Just great! You both think you're so cool. Neither one of you has time for me, the daughter you created. Or was I just a mistake in your otherwise perfect lives?"

Noah tried to slip his arm around her shoulders. "Honey, please calm down and let me explain."

Kimmie wrenched out of his grasp. "I don't want to hear anything you have to say right now. Especially not in front of . . . whoever *she* is. I thought I knew you, Daddy." She started to cry again. "I thought you were the one person in my life I could count on."

"You can count on me, Kimmie, and you know that. I believe you've always known that."

"It was all an act!" She hurled her words at her father. "I was just playing perfect little girl. I always had the feeling you'd leave me someday. And then you did leave, didn't you?"

Noah's mouth twisted in pain. "If you're referring to when I left the house, that was after you left for boarding school, Kimmie. You know that," he said evenly. "But I never stopped being your father, never left *you*."

317

"Yeah, but after you left the house I felt like I could never go home again, like there wasn't a home to go to. Didn't you know that?" She swiped angrily at her tears. "But I didn't have anywhere else to go, did I? So I had to go there. The place was like a museum. Nobody home, if you can call it that, except me and the servants. Adrienne was off with her daddy somewhere. Somewhere I couldn't be. And you were off somewhere else, being selfish, Adrienne said. She said you didn't think of anybody but yourself. And for some damned reason I reminded her of you. I knew it by the way she treated me, as if I were some distant relative to be tolerated, like everything was all my fault. I didn't understand why she did that. But you could have told me why, couldn't you, Daddy?" She shifted her eyes toward Maj.

Maj heard the girl's stinging words, saw how they affected Noah. She felt intrusive listening to Kimmie spill such painful thoughts to her father, and speak of the mother she'd been wondering about since she first met Noah. She felt Kimmie's anguish, in a reverse way. It touched her heart where she'd been holding the secret of her own baby for so long. The conversation she'd had with Noah about it was still fresh in her mind.

Maj knew her presence upset Kimmie further. Nothing about why she was in Noah's cabin dressed in his clothes could be explained rationally right now.

"I'm leaving now," she said, gathering her jacket and dirty clothes. "You two need to talk privately." She stopped and looked at the young woman. "I'm truly sorry, Kimmie, that we had to meet this way. I wish I could say or do something that would let you listen and understand. My being here isn't exactly what you think."

"You can't say anything I want to hear."

"Perhaps not right now, but—"

"Never," Kimmie whispered through clenched teeth. "But no need for you to leave. I'm going back down to the West Wind lodge. There's a nice old couple there that may let me stay overnight while I figure out what to do next." She turned her attention toward Noah. "They seemed to think a lot of you when I told them who I was. Looks like they don't really know you, either, do they?"

Kimmie slammed out of the cabin, got into her car, and burned rubber driving away.

Noah reached Maj and clutched her against him. "God, I'm sorry you had to hear that, sorry she aimed so much anger at you. It's me she meant to hurt."

319

Maj held him close, rocked him in her arms. "I'm sorry there was the need for her to say it at all. She's hurting so much herself, Noah, and she's frustrated. She doesn't know how to get rid of her feelings, that's all."

Noah leaned back and looked deeply into her eyes. "How do you know so much?" he asked with tenderness.

Maj sighed. "I've been there."

Noah held her close again.

"You'd better go and try to talk to her."

"I'll drive you back to the West Wind."

"No, I think I'd like to walk right now. You go on without me." She started to open the door. "Perhaps it might be wise to get dressed first, however." She threw him a kiss, and closed the door behind her.

Maj ran along the narrow mountain road, listening to the pad of her running shoes hit the pavement. The steady rhythm sent a comforting sameness to her jumbled emotions.

She'd managed to get back to the West Wind, enter through the front door, and go down the hall to her room without Ada and Fergie—or Kimmie—seeing her. She'd thrown off her clothes—Noah's clothes—and flung them on the floor. When her underwear followed, the unmistakable scent of their love-making had filled her.

Her mind reeled. As much as she'd been calm for Noah after Kimmie's outburst in the cabin, she was upset and embarrassed for herself. She'd never been in such a situation, and it unnerved her. Thinking back to the days when she'd faced Jack's son and his mother across a courtroom table, she wondered if that woman had felt as mortified as she felt today.

She'd hurried around the room, gathering her running clothes. Clean underwear first. Jogging bra next, to flatten and firmly hold her still-sensitive breasts. White T-shirt and red nylon shorts with side slits, low white socks, and blue and white running shoes. Elastic headband to keep her hair out of her eyes and the sweat from running down her forehead. She fully intended to work up a good sweat, work off her embarrassment and frustration.

The day was clear and cloudless, the sun in a stall directly overheard poised for a slow westward descent. Crisp mountain breezes picked up and set full-leafed maple trees to rustling.

Maj's mind churned and her pace picked up. She couldn't get her breath to work efficiently. She gasped. Her chest hurt, her head hurt, and, exhausted already, she slowed.

She knew she'd started too fast, and now suffered with a stitch in her side and labored breathing. She could hear the coach's words at the track club she and Jack had belonged to, telling her that starting out too fast could get a person hurt. Vaguely she thought that might be good advice to apply to relationships.

She walked then, allowing her lungs to take in oxygen, allowing her nerves to calm. Allowing her mind to think.

Maj walked, for how long she couldn't determine, but enough to remind her body of its former responses, and to remember the coach's other words about giving herself a second chance by starting all over, thinking clearly, and starting out slowly and smoothly. More sage advice?

She began to run again, this time relaxed and easy, until she settled into her own rhythm and could put her feet on automatic pilot. From experience she knew thoughts flowed more freely from a mind expanded through physical exercise.

The familiar pungent scent of balsam wafted over her as she pumped her arms through the mountain air. *Noah smells like mountains, outdoors, campfires, comfort.*

She took an incline, aware of the extra

power she summoned to reach the apex without breaking stride, pleased that her own power came through for her.

I've loved the challenge that taking over the West Wind has presented to me. I'll be working at it a long time, but I'm beginning to understand I have what it takes to succeed.

She rounded a bend where dense reforestation threatened to overtake the road's narrow shoulder, and spotted a yellow and black butterfly lying on its side, one wing rising and lowering slowly. She stopped, bent down, and tenderly lifted it to a low-hanging evergreen branch. It exercised both wings then, and, as if to express its gratitude, flew off to a nearby branch. There it sat in sunlight filtered through lacy leaves, testing its wings again.

Maj smiled and resumed running.

I know it's meant a great deal to Ada and Fergie to have me there taking over things. It's meant a great deal to me to be with them, too. They've given me an opportunity to try my wings, and they've been right there to pick me up in case I fall. Along with Granddad's spirit, they've launched me into a chance for a new life.

She turned down a side road, thinking it would take her back toward the West Wind. Instead, the road went from gravel to dirt and grass and then to meadow. She saw no way to get around it in the direction she wished to go.

Dead end. I didn't expect this. No route signs or directions. I'll have to go back. Maybe there was something I didn't see.

Returning to the main road, Maj surveyed the landscape, then started back the way she'd come, running on the opposite side.

Funny how the same scene can appear to be so different when viewed from another angle.

Rounding another bend, she met Noah running toward her. She slowed, stopped, bent over, and breathed rapidly. He ran up to her and stopped.

"I thought you were going to the lodge to talk with your daughter," Maj said between breaths, rubbing the back of one thigh.

"I was too tense to go right away," Noah answered between his own heaving breaths, shifting kinks out of his rib cage. "I might have said something to her I'd regret later. And she needed time to cool off, too. I suddenly felt like running. Haven't done it in ages." He surveyed her running attire and smiled. "I might ask the same of you."

"Same thing."

She surveyed him back, from shirtless torso, over royal blue nylon running shorts with slits high on the hips, over long, muscular legs with a dusting of light brown hair, to sockless feet in blue running shoes with neon orange stripes. The shorts enhanced his muscular backside. Her hands still sensed the hard, rounded feel of it.

"Are you as bushed as I am?" he asked with a laugh.

She smiled back. "I'd never admit it."

"True. That would be a sign of your senior years over me."

"I prefer to think of them as superior years, having nothing to do with age."

"Of course you do. Well, then, do you think the reason we're breathless and hurting right now is that we're out of shape and had rather a . . . vigorous, shall we say, evening of activity last night?" He narrowed teasing eyes.

"Out of shape for which? The running, or the vigorous activity?"

"As I remember it, we can admit to both, can't we?"

"There goes the superiority myth!" Maj smiled into his eyes.

It was an odd moment, both of them standing, gasping for breath and sweating, swapping snappy banter, to realize that was she falling in love with Noah Decker. Cancel that. *Had* fallen love with him.

She tried to determine which was the exact

moment it happened. The only scene that appeared and reappeared in her mind was the one when he stepped out of the mist, looking like John Wayne in pilot's attire, after bumping the dock with his airplane.

The *first* moment? Did love at first sight actually happen? And to women her age? The notion seemed ridiculous. Maybe *lust* at first sight was more to the point.

"Got another mile left in those tired bones?" he chided her.

"If you've got one in that worn-out chassis, I can promise you I'll keep up!"

"Come on, then. See if you can catch this mean machine before I leave you in the dust!" Noah bragged. He started down an abandoned logging road.

"Here's a taste of real true grit, Rooster!" she called as she summoned some speed and passed him.

"Oh, yeah?" He caught up with her and gave her a pat on the rump as he sped by.

"Hey, none of the locker-room stuff!" she puffed. Catching up with him again, she gave him a resounding smack on his flanks. "Unless I get to do it, too!"

"You have my permission, anytime."

He caught his breath and hit his stride as she did the same, and they ran in companion-

326

able silence, matching rhythms and inhaling the last scents of spring and the first breaths of summer.

The abandoned road brought them back to the West Wind road and, as if their thoughts were attuned, they slowed their pace to a walk.

"I suppose we should head back," he said, breaking the exquisite silence.

"I suppose."

"Thanks for not talking about it."

Maj knew what he meant. There was no need for either of them to mention the scene at the cabin. They would talk about it sometime. Sometime soon.

"See you at the lodge?" she asked.

"Soon as I get cleaned up. Won't take me too long to get back to the cabin, that is, if I can muster another few ounces of energy!"

"I believe you can," she whispered, and started down the road.

"Wait a minute!"

She turned back. "What?"

"You can't leave just like that without a proper runner's goodbye?"

"I wasn't aware there was a proper runner's goodbye."

"Of course there is. I believe it's even sanctioned by the Athletic Congress of the United States."

"This is some outrageous Marine deployment, isn't it?" Maj eyed him suspiciously.

"Marines have been known to be outrageous," he said with seductiveness as he walked slowly toward her. "Especially this one."

"What—"

The rest of Maj's question was cut off as Noah drew her quickly into the circle of his arms and pressed her perspiring torso against his equally damp one, and captured her lips in his. She slipped her arms under his and up his back, and her fingers clung to his shoulders.

Slowly he let go of her and leaned back. She kept her eyes closed, totally lost in the fuzzy glow of the moment.

"Mmm, you taste salty," he murmured, tracing the moist V of her T-shirt between her breasts.

"And you taste like . . . more," she murmured dreamily. She pressed against him and bestowed a kiss of her own.

Noah drew his lips away from hers reluctantly. He leaned back in the cradle of her arms, then dropped his head to kiss the tip of her nose.

"Much as I would like to stay here all day in the sun and fun with you, I think I can delay the inevitable no longer. I'd better go."

Maj tilted her head. "Your daughter scares

328

the hell out of you, doesn't she?"

"Indeed she does."

"I don't understand how that can be."

"I know. You wouldn't think a package that probably weighs ninety-five pounds fully clothed and soaking wet could be so formidable, could you?"

"Especially not to the father she's adored and who adores her."

Noah hesitated a moment, and Maj had the feeling he was biting back words, words to the effect that the reason she didn't understand was she'd never been a parent.

"I've let her down. I didn't realize how much until now." His voice carried hurt, despair. "That's an awful thing. I never meant to . . ."

"Noah, we haven't talked about . . . Kimmie's mother," Maj began. "I don't mean to pry, but I've wondered about her, of course."

Noah dropped his head back and searched the sky for a moment. When he returned his gaze to her face, she saw more pain in his eyes.

"I know. It's my fault. We've been having so much fun together, and we've been so busy. That's a lame excuse, and I know it."

He slipped his arms around her and held her so tightly, Maj's breath went out of her.

"Truth is," he went on, "I haven't felt ready

to talk about my . . . marriage. Sounds weak, I guess, but I've been"—he swallowed—"afraid to talk about it. And then we were growing so close, and . . ."

Maj pushed her back against his arms. "Why afraid? Nobody knows better than I how bad some marriages can be. I've told you my story, and you understood. You can tell me yours, and I'll understand."

He gazed into her eyes a very long time without speaking. Then she said, "I'm not so sure you will."

"Try me."

He held her again. "I will. Just not yet, okay? I think Kimmie's going to need a lot of attention right now." He kissed her and searched her face, then stepped back, and looked her up and down. "Well, you'll be a sight for comment when you get back to the lodge."

"Why?" she asked slowly, looking down at herself. "People always look pretty ragged after a hard run."

"Yes, but do they always have two perfect sweat circles right over their two perfect breasts?" He was chuckling now.

Maj grabbed her T-shirt around the middle with both hands and pulled it out like a shelf so she could see it better.

330

"Oh, for heaven's sake! Look what you did!"

"What *I* did? Have you forgotten, you wanton hussy, that you were the one who grabbed me shamelessly to lay a goodbye kiss on me? I guess it's true what they say."

"And what do *they* say?"

"That the memory is the second thing to go!" He kissed her and took off on a run up the road in the direction of his cabin.

"You've got one coming, Rooster!" she called after him, laughing.

"I'll see you keep your promise," he called back, waving, and then he disappeared below the rise.

Maj walked briskly, then slowed as she neared the lodge, allowing her body the cooldown it desperately needed. Blue jays squawked at one another among high branches, then squawked at her when she passed beneath them. She breathed in the freshness of the darkening green and golden day, and basked in the sheer pleasure of being a part of it.

Back in the lodge, pleased that she'd accomplished it once again without anyone seeing her, Maj was glad the Frenchman had finished her new room on the main floor with a private bath. She'd thought for a while he might never get to it. A shower was going to feel divine.

331

She stripped off her sweaty running clothes, caught a terry robe from a hook in the closet, and stuffed her feet into a pair of rubber flip-flops.

She took a long drink of cold water, then got into the shower and stood in the pounding spray for a long, therapeutic time. The Frenchman had outdone himself with her bathroom, even if the Moffett Brothers had thought her ideas were outlandish. Treated cedar shakes lined three walls, a skylight overhead was curtained with hanging plants, and the clawfoot tub was enclosed by a half circle of brass hung with a white Battenburg lace curtain.

Sheer mountain heaven, she thought, letting soft spray fall over her face.

As she towel-dried hair and body, she remembered Noah's hands and mouth running over her, remembered how beautiful he made her feel, the way his touch expressed appreciation for her.

She dressed in a pair of blue- and black-flowered leggings and a long blue T-shirt, the last clothing purchases she'd made while still at the ad agency.

She stepped in front of a full-length oval mirror framed and supported by an oak stand, and took a long look. Her legs looked good in the leggings, and with the T-shirt floating over them she looked slimmer than she believed she was. With no makeup and wet hair, it would be difficult for someone to tell she was over fifty, or over thirty-five for that matter.

"Not bad for an old broad," she said, smiling into the mirror.

She slipped into soft leather huaraches, fluffed out her damp hair with a pick, took a deep breath, and headed down to the kitchen.

The murmur of voices could be heard in the hallway as Maj neared the kitchen door. She stopped a moment. By the soothing sound of Ada's voice, and the concerned vague responses in Fergie's, she surmised Kimmie had unburdened herself on the old couple. The secret she hadn't wanted to share with them yet was out now.

Maj was as afraid as she'd been when she was a teenager coming home the first night after having sex with Jack. She was positive her parents would know exactly what she'd been doing just by looking at her. But they'd been asleep when she'd let herself in.

Funny how, no matter how old you got to be, you continued to do things you were still afraid your elders would disapprove of if they found out. Does anyone ever truly grow up? Maybe we're always suspended in some form of adolescence.

Kimmie's back was to her when Maj entered the kitchen. Fergie and Ada looked up, and there was not an accusatory glance from either of them. Kimmie turned around then, and seeing Maj, spun back to the Fergusons.

"That's her! What is *she* doing here?"

Maj was positive she saw an amused glint flash momentarily in Fergie's eyes. But his voice was serious.

"She's the proprietor of the West Wind. It appears you're her guest."

"But I thought . . . how can that be?" Kimmie seemed out of breath.

Maj stood still for a moment. There was no reason to hide the fact that she'd been with Noah, since his daughter had caught them and, she suspected, had told Fergie and Ada all about it. She went to Kimmie and held out her right hand.

"Hello again, Kimmie. I'm Majesty Wilde. I'm sorry about how we met earlier, but I'm glad we've been given another chance."

Kimmie said nothing, but when the silence in the room grew too awkward to ignore, she relented. "Kimberly," she corrected Maj icily, and did not offer her hand in greeting. "Kimberly Decker. Only my father calls me by that baby name."

"Fathers tend to do that, Kimberly." Maj

334

smiled and clasped her hands behind her back. "I think they want to always keep their daughters little girls. My grandfather was that way, much to my mother's consternation." She knew she was babbling, and why. She felt off balance, nervous in the presence of Kimberly Decker. She hoped sharing a similar experience might serve to put her on common ground with the girl, but it soon became clear Kimberly would offer her no quarter.

"Lucky you. My mother couldn't care less."

"Maybe she just has a different way of expressing her concern for you. I'm sure she wants you to mature into a confident young woman."

"What a lot of bullshit that is. I suppose you're the perfect mother and have all the answers for your kids."

Maj saw the look pass between Ada and Fergie. She wasn't certain if it was reaction to Kimberly's expletive, or her reference to Maj's motherhood.

"I don't have any children," Maj said quietly.

"Then what gives you the right to spout off like some hot-shit expert shrink, then?"

Again Fergie and Ada exchanged looks. "Here now, young lady," Fergie put in, "I don't think it's necessary to use foul language."

Kimberly turned back to them. "Foul lan-

335

guage?" She sounded surprised, and then her snippy tone softened. "I'm sorry. I'm not aware of it half the time. People I hang out with use those words, and worse, so I guess I forget it might offend somebody."

Maj could see that underneath the tough exterior lived a lonely, frightened little girl. A nice girl who wanted a nice life with nice parents. Funny how things happen, she thought, as if the planets tipped askew at the moment of someone's birth, and then the baby ended up with the wrong mother.

Maj's heart went out to Kimberly. She wanted to put her arms around her, talk to her, listen to her, soothe her.

Mother her.

The last thought rocked Maj. She moved to the stove and put the kettle on to boil for tea to cover her nervousness.

The sound of truck tires on gravel split the tension permeating the kitchen's atmosphere.

"Here's Noah," Fergie said, heading out the kitchen door to meet him.

"I don't want to see him yet," Kimberly said, standing. "Is there a room available for the night?" she asked Ada. "I can pay. Do you take credit cards?"

Maj turned around. "Yes, there is a room available for you."

Maj could see the reluctance in Kimberly's body when she turned to face her. "Thank you," she said without a trace of thaw toward Maj.

"We're not set up yet to take credit cards, but I would be happy if you'd accept our hospitality and spend the night free of charge."

"I'm not an orphan. I said I can pay, and I will. I assume you'll take a check?" Again Kimberly's voice was cold.

"Of course. If you prefer to pay—"

"I prefer. Would you tell me where the room is, please?"

Maj acutely felt Kimberly's urgency to leave the kitchen before Noah came in. She was feeling a little like that herself, probably because of the awkward embarrassment that she assumed would overtake her. Maybe it was best that Kimberly have her way and let some time pass before she saw Noah again. She took the lead toward the hallway.

"Right this way."

"There's no need for you to take me up there. I'm not a child. Just give me directions. I can find it." Kimberly picked up her suitcase and stood in the doorway.

"I prefer to usher my adult guests to their rooms, if you don't mind." Maj tried to sound businesslike.

Reluctantly, Kimberly nodded in silent acquiescence and allowed Maj to lead her up the wide stairs to the second floor.

When Maj came back downstairs, Noah was seated at the kitchen table, drinking a mug of tea. He stood up when she entered the room. She caught the appraising scan he gave her, and it unsettled her further.

"Kimmie all right?" he asked, his voice thick with emotion.

"She will be." Maj nodded. "I put her in the Astor room. It's the most finished of any of the others."

"Fit for a princess," Fergie volunteered.

"Perfect. She is a princess, isn't she? She's prettier than ever." Noah looked down, then back up sheepishly. "I suppose I'm acting like a bragging father. She's always been my little princess."

"My guess is she'd prefer to be just your daughter." Maj poured a cup of tea for herself, suddenly sorry she voiced her opinion. How Noah and . . . his wife . . . handled their daughter was no business of hers.

There, she'd admitted it. *Wife.* She realized she'd been avoiding even thinking the word, as if she and Noah had been teenagers, virgins without any past up to the moment they'd made love.

Noah sat down when she did. A helpless look swept over his handsome features. "I know," he whispered. "I'm as much at fault about that as . . ."

Maj saw his head dip over his mug and thought he could use some mothering himself.

"I'm really sorry about the things Kimmie said to you earlier." He searched Maj's face.

Fergie picked up his cap and clamped it over his wiry hair. "Ada and I have some groceries to get, so we'll go now."

"No, Fergie, please stay," Maj said "There's nothing we—I want to keep from you. Noah and I were forced to land the Stearman—"

"Noah told us what happened, honey," Fergie interrupted, "after Kimmie had told us she . . . met you at the cabin."

"I hope you can understand about that. I wouldn't want you and Ada to think less of me for . . ."

Fergie's leathery face grew ruddy. "Well, now"—he scratched his head and busied himself at the sink—"she didn't tell us too much, I mean, not everything, you know. And there's no need for you to, either."

Fergie knows everything.

"Well, I for one think Noah could use a thrashing," Ada said quickly. "Taking you flying in a storm. I'd take him over my knee if

339

he wasn't so big and ornery!" She limped to Maj and hugged her around the shoulders.

"We're still going to go get groceries," Fergie put in. "Young girls are always starving. We need extras like those chip things, and Coke, and whole milk. And you young ones need privacy right now. We're giving it to you, so take it!" he ordered gruffly, but Maj heard the love in his voice.

Ada shrugged into a white sweater, draped the double handles of her straw purse over her arm, and let Fergie help her down the porch stairs.

Maj smiled lovingly at the backs of the older couple as they retreated. At the slam of a door from upstairs, she lifted her eyes toward the sound, then drew them around to Noah. Her smile faded.

"So much for privacy."

"I know," Noah said, his eyes intent on her face, "I'm sorry. I didn't know Kimmie would be coming so soon."

"I didn't mean that the way it sounded," Maj said quickly. "I'm glad your daughter is here. It will give me the chance to get to know her, and to perhaps know you better through her."

Noah fixed his gaze into the depths of the mug as he swirled its contents.

Maj inclined her head toward him, attempting to pull his gaze back to her. "Or would you rather I didn't?"

He lifted his head quickly. "On the contrary. I think I want you to know me better than anyone ever has."

After the space of two heartbeats, he leaned across the table and kissed her lightly but lingeringly.

The ticking of the school clock in the hallway seemed to clang like a steam radiator for a lifetime before Maj could whisper, "You took the words right out of my mouth."

Neither of them moved then, locked in a moment of discovery, eager for further exploration.

And then the spell was broken with the sound of Kimberly clunking down the stairs.

Noah stood up quickly, scraping his chair across the kitchen linoleum with the force of his calves. He was busy at the sink, washing out his cup, then drying it with a white dishtowel when his daughter came in.

"Oh," Kimberly said glumly, *you're* still here." Her remark was aimed directly at Maj.

"Yes, I am," Maj said, "this is my home."

Noah turned then. "Kimmie, how would you like to go for a walk with me?"

"In the woods?"

Maj noted that Kimberly sounded as if

walking in a fragrant forest on a bright day was something akin to being forced to scrub all the toilets in Grand Central Station.

"In the woods. We need to talk."

Kimberly shrugged and sent him a look that told him he should understand he was forcing her to do something against her will. Maj sensed exactly the opposite. She believed Kimmie didn't want to admit how much she wanted her father to talk to her.

"You'll need to change out of those shoes. Those things won't stand up in this country." He noted the things she had on her feet looked like cowboy boots that had been sawed off at the ankles.

"These cost a hundred and thirty dollars," Kimberly sniffed.

"That's a couple of months groceries for me and Orville," Noah came back.

Maj stepped in, attempting to ease the situation before it worsened. "I've always wanted a pair of those," she said, eyeing Kimberly's shoes appreciatively. "I saw them in Bloomingdale's in New York. Is that where you got them?"

For the first time, Kimberly looked at Maj as if she weren't the lowlife she'd originally decided. Then quickly her demeanor changed.

"No, L.A. We're always several steps ahead

342

of New York," she sniffed again.

Before Noah could come back with the admonition Maj knew from the look on his face he was ready to expound, she said, "That's what I've heard. But they'll be ruined if you wear them on a hike. Did you bring sneakers with you? If not, I can lend you a pair that you can get muddy."

"No, thank you," Kimberly said stiffly. "I brought cross-trainers." She turned then and clunked back upstairs.

"What the hell does she need cross-trainers for?" Noah whispered loudly. "She doesn't know the meaning of physical exercise."

"Something tells me she'll need them when she goes into the ring with you, slugger." Maj patted his cheek. "Have a pleasant walk, that is, *if* you can still put one foot in front of the other, old-timer!"

She headed down the back hall to her office, sashaying just out of reach of Noah's snapping towel.

343

Chapter Thirteen

Halfway through Kimberly Decker's announced week-long stay with her father, she made another announcement that her job in Saratoga didn't start until the third week in June, and she'd stay on a few more days, if that was all right with everybody. "Everybody" included himself and Fergie and Ada, Noah noticed, as the girl's cornflower-blue eyes skimmed over Maj.

Maj didn't seem terribly upset by the deliberate snub. He noticed that, too. And a lot of other things.

With Kimberly at the lodge, Noah decided to stay there every night instead of returning to his cabin as he had been doing recently. It would give him more time with his daughter, he said. The Moffett Brothers had finished the room he'd been using before Maj came. His cabin was not in any way ready for anyone to live in other than himself. Certainly not anyone like his pampered daughter.

Even with her fluctuating moods, Noah liked the notion of living in a home with her again—teasing her over breakfast, making her go outside in the afternoons for boat rides or walks. Before she left, he wanted to take her up in the Stearman if Maj okayed it, and show her the mountains in a way she'd never forget.

Kimmie seemed so out of touch with basic values, and he blamed himself for at least part of the problem. He hoped it wasn't too late to reverse the trend. If she turned out like Adrienne, self-centered and spoiled and money hungry, he would always blame himself. Being with her day and night at the lodge would give him the opportunity, he hoped, to influence her thinking and open new worlds to her.

Often he found himself wishing Maj could have been Kimmie's mother.

Maj.

Face it, Decker, you like living at the lodge because she's here, too. You like seeing her first thing in the morning, watching her on the dock drinking her coffee at sunrise. And you like seeing her the last moment at night when she sits in the parlor curled with a novel, her forehead resting on a palm.

He noticed something new about Maj every day. The way she lifted her hair and let a breeze from an open window fan her neck as she put the finishing touches on the breakfront they'd been working on for weeks; the discipline she displayed silently by running almost every morning, rain or shine, then stretching afterward on the front parlor floor with Clawed sitting comfortably on her stomach; the shape of her hands, small and capable, and the way her fingers curled under her chin when she was thinking.

And she'd never made him feel he had to choose between Kimmie and her or divide his time equally between them. He felt no pressure from her. But he was damn well feeling pressure from himself. Much as he loved being with his daughter, he wanted time alone with Maj.

There was more to be said between them. More to be experienced together. And he was eager to do both.

Toward the end of Kimmie's stay, Noah could stand it no longer. He had to see Maj alone.

Two mornings before Kimmie was to go back to Saratoga, Noah took a cup of coffee and went down to the dock. Maj was seated in a metal chair, the one she'd painted a bright red, a folded towel under her. Clawed was hanging over the edge of the dock, waiting to pounce upon a young sunfish should it dare to come into his sight.

" 'Morning," he said as he stepped onto the dock. He hadn't wanted to disturb her before that, just wanted to watch her hair move in the morning breeze, shine in the rising sun. He just wanted to watch her living, breathing.

He couldn't remember the moment when, in his mind, Maj had changed from a sharp-tongued Manhattanite into a soft-spoken integral part of the life of the lake and woods and mountains.

And the life of Noah Decker.

Maj turned quickly, and her quick smile and welcoming gaze moved him.

" 'Morning," she said brightly, looking at her watch. "Oh, it's time for breakfast, isn't it? I've been daydreaming out here and the time got away from me."

He drew up a blue-painted chair close to hers and sat down.

"Don't be in a hurry. Fergie's putting the handles and knobs on the breakfront — I'm sure I'll find my back somewhere under that monstrosity today, lumbering up the stairs — and

Ada's hemming the new curtains she made for the garden room, as you call it."

"And Kimberly?"

"Where else? Still in bed, sleeping."

"She's probably catching up. I hear students don't sleep much at college."

"The way she's been sleeping, she should be caught up for the next ten years!"

"She'll be down in time for breakfast."

"That's another thing. She's eating like she grew up in the poorhouse."

"Maybe she likes having someone prepare it for her," Maj smiled.

"I know she does," Noah answered quietly. "Don't expect her to ever tell you, but I believe she's beginning to think you might not be the enemy after all."

"I hope so. I like her. She does work hard at keeping a barrier between us, though. Perhaps she thinks I'm a threat to her relationship with you."

"Why would she think that? I'm her father."

Maj directed her gaze over the lake to the trees beyond. "Being female is much more complicated than you realize, and relationships can't be explained in such a simple statement of fact as that."

Noah shook his head. "Maybe not. But I

notice her barriers, as you call them, don't stop her from eating all the meals you prepare. You're a great cook, you know. Or should I say chef? Do you plan to do any of the cooking when the place opens for business?"

"I've been thinking about that, actually. I believe I'll do some special things for the guests."

"You're always doing special things for the guests." He reached over and closed his hand over hers, then brushed a kiss across her lips. "I've missed you."

Her gaze fluttered as she looked around to see if anyone caught them, then settled on his face. She let out a small breath. "I've missed you, too."

"What do you say we remedy that?"

"How? It's a little difficult . . ."

"Will you go out for dinner with me tonight?"

"Out? For dinner?" She leaned back and gave him a skeptical look.

"Yes. Out for dinner. Like a date. Can't you tell I'm asking you out on a date?" He grinned at her.

"A date? What's that?" she laughed.

"Something they used to do in prehistoric

times. I thought we might try to revive the concept."

"Sort of like reinventing the wheel?"

"You might say that. Might you also say you'll do it? Go out on a date with me, I mean?"

Her lower lip quivered as she tried to suppress a smile. "Yes, I'll do it. Go out on a date with you, I mean."

"Hot damn! Pick you up at seven, okay?" he laughed.

"Okay. Where will we go?"

"Leave that to me. I'll take care of everything."

"My hero," she said falsetto, batting her eyelashes.

"And don't you forget it! First Gerald Morris, then ferocious bats, a daring aerial rescue, and now an actual date. Will I never cease to amaze you?"

She didn't say anything for a long moment, just watched his face. "I hope not," she said, her voice quietly serious. She looked at her watch. "I'd better get breakfast going before the natives grow restless."

They walked together up the lawn toward the porch, shoulder brushing shoulder. A lock of her hair blew past his ear like an intimate whisper, and it was all he could do to keep from picking her up and carrying her into the woods, where he could kiss her the way he was aching to do.

As she climbed the stairs ahead of him, he bent his head and nipped her backside through her jeans.

"Hey!" She turned around quickly and caught his sheepish look. "What do you think you're doing?"

"Sampling dinner."

"Shh! For heaven's sake, what if someone heard you?"

"Wouldn't bother me in the least."

"It would mortify me!"

"You're too sensitive."

"And you're too fresh!"

"And you love it!" He grabbed her belt buckle and drew her close to him.

"And I love it," came her whispered echo.

He whirled her around. "Now, get in there, woman, and cook my breakfast. The man's hungry!"

"You might get it yourself once in a while, buster!" she retorted playfully.

"That's woman's work," he replied in his best macho voice.

"The hell it is!" she came back, grabbing

his shirt collar.

"Oh-ho, so you think you can use men's words to convince me, do you?"

"What?"

"Get into the kitchen!" He opened the door and they tussled, laughing and gasping for breath.

Kimberly stood near the coffeepot, watching them. Her look told them she did not approve of their behavior. Noah held out his cup.

"Say, daughter, pour your old father a cup of coffee, would you please?"

Kimberly sent a look to Maj that would have flash-frozen a side of beef. "Of course, Daddy, it would be my pleasure." She took his cup and filled it, and didn't bother to offer any to Maj.

"Don't bother to refill mine," Maj said lightly. "I'm trying to control my caffeine intake."

Noah watched her and marveled still that she showed no malice toward his daughter's obvious barb. He watched her get out a frying pan and the waffle iron and start breakfast.

Somehow she always managed to arrange breakfast so that everyone was present at the same time. He marveled at that, too. What didn't he marvel at about her? How she managed to fit the meals in around Fergie's list of chores, Ada's fussing with decoration of the latest room the Moffetts had refinished, her own morning run, his daily check-in at the emergency station and his office, and Kimmie's sleeping habits astounded him.

When they were all seated around the breakfast table talking about their plans for the day, or new ideas, or even once when Kimmie ventured to tell something about a despised instructor, Noah felt very much at home.

And very much a part of a family.

She'd never admit it, he knew, but Kimmie was absorbing it all, and he could see her frown lines smoothing, her chip-on-the-shoulder attitude crumbling.

Maj was always pleasant to Kimmie, no matter how curt or downright rude the girl was to her. She seemed so patient with her. She'd have made a wonderful mother, he declared to himself. Wistfully he daydreamed that Maj was Kimmie's mother, and the thoughts made a new emptiness gnaw in his gut.

"Maj and I won't be here for dinner this evening," Noah ventured.

"That's all right . . ." Ada started.

"Why not?" Kimmie looked sharply toward him.

"We've made some plans for the evening." Why was he so nervous? This was his young daughter he was talking to. He reminded himself that he was the parent, yet he felt as if he were a kid asking his parents if he could go out with a girl.

"Well, now, that's fine," Fergie said.

"What will I do?" Kimmie's voice edged near a whine.

"We'll be here, honey," Ada said, smiling at her. "The three of us will take supper together."

Noah saw her eyes narrow, knew she didn't like the idea of being alone with the Fergusons. She'd never been good with older people. He was proud of her for keeping her thoughts to herself for once.

They spent the day working around the lodge. Except for Kimmie, who lazed in a hammock under the trees near the carriage barn.

Noah had one emergency call to locate a lost hiker. It took him the better part of the afternoon to find him, unhurt except for a sprained ankle. He was glad of that. For a while he fretted he wouldn't be back in time for his date with Maj, but he wouldn't have given up until he'd found the lost hiker.

Funny how fearless he could be about that while he was very fearful of talking about Adrienne to Maj. He wouldn't be her hero anymore once she knew he was married, he was positive of that. And he wanted to remain her hero. He hadn't done anything about his marital status before because of Kimmie. At least that's what he'd thought was the reason. And until now, until Maj, nothing and no one had ever been important enough to him to change things. The whole situation was beginning to knot his insides. There had to be a right time to make everything right for everybody. All he'd ever wanted was to simplify his life, and now it was more complicated than ever.

At a quarter to seven Noah appraised himself in the round mirror atop an oak chest in his room. He'd combed his hair twice but couldn't seem to get it to do what he wanted. He'd had a haircut a week and a half before, so that wasn't it. He splashed a little Pierre Cardin cologne below his jawline, then went back to his hair.

Then in the mirror he noticed Kimmie leaning against the doorjamb behind him. Her

355

hair fell long on one side in a perfect blond sheet, and she wore slim jeans, cut perfectly to enhance her almost too-slim figure, a black turtleneck under a hand-embroidered sweater studded with pearls, and those cowboy boots. She was a beautiful girl, he thought, very much like her mother. He wondered how much of himself was a part of his daughter as well.

Noah mentally calculated how much that outfit must have cost, and figured with that amount of money he could install a cabinet and closet in his cabin's bathroom. Another fault of his, since he hadn't been around to teach her about more important things in life than clothes.

"Hi, honey. Sorry I didn't see you. How long have you been there?"

"Long enough," she said with a disdainful scowl.

Noah turned around. "Do I look all right?"

"Fine," she said evenly. "New shirt? I don't remember you ever wearing anything like that."

Noah smoothed his hand over the fine cotton purple plaid shirt, and picked a tiny bit of lint from his pale gray trousers. "That's because you saw me only in regulation stuffed-shirt white. I threw those out long ago. What do you think of this tie?" He held a midnight-blue tie dusted with pale mauve dots against his chest."

"Fine," she said again.

"Try to be a little more enthusiastic, dear," Noah chided her. "I'm soliciting your valued opinion."

"As if you really wanted it," she muttered.

"Yes, I do want it. Come on, Kimmie, what's the matter? I thought things were going well between us. I've been having a great time since you got here. I thought you were, too."

"Could you call me Kimberly, please? I'm not a kid anymore."

Noah gave her a smile full of love. "I know you're not, honey. *Kimberly.* That feels like a foreign name to me. You've been Kimmie forever."

Kimberly bit her lower lip. "Do you really have to go out tonight, Daddy?"

Noah smiled. "Yes, I do." Did he ever!

"But what am I going to do around here alone?"

"You won't be alone. Fergie and Ada are here. You'll have supper with them, and you can read or watch television."

"Oh, sure, they love those stupid game shows. There isn't even a VCR here."

"That's one of the attractions of mountain living."

"What? Being cut off from real civilization?"

"You're exaggerating just a bit." Noah put the tie on, turned back to the mirror, and started knotting it. Disliking the finished product, he untied it and started all over again.

"Really, Daddy, you're acting like a kid, the way you're all nervous. You'd think this was your first date, or something."

"It feels like it, honey." Noah smiled.

"That's a bit hypocritical, isn't it, considering you've already slept with her?"

Noah clenched his teeth, determined not to give her a cutting remark about how what he did in his private life was none of her business. But he wouldn't sugar-coat the truth either.

"Yes, that's true. Maj and I have made love."

Kimberly plopped down on the end of the bed. "Made love. You make it sound so nice and proper."

"It was nice. And personal, if you don't mind."

Smoothing his tie down the front of his shirt, Noah turned back to his daughter.

358

"But what about Adrienne?" Kimberly pouted.

"What about your mother?" Noah felt as if he had to remind Kimberly that Adrienne was her mother. But not as often as he'd had to remind Adrienne that she had a daughter she should be paying attention to.

"Don't you feel guilty about it?"

"Not in the least." Noah sat down on the bed next to her and looped an arm around her shoulders. "I know it's been hard on you, honey, the way your mother and I have been living apart. But, believe me, this way is better than before."

"Why?" Kimberly's tiny voice came from a constricted throat. "At least we had kind of a home together."

"For me it was only a home while you were in it. Once you were gone, it was just a house to me, a big, rambling showplace for other people to *ooh* and *aah* over. I didn't care about it one bit."

"Adrienne does," Kimberly said.

"Yes, she does," he sighed.

"More than she cares about me."

"Now, honey, I think that's a little too harsh for you to say. Your mother has a difficult time showing her feelings. It's just Adrienne's way."

"More than she cared about you, too. That's true, isn't it, Daddy? That's why you don't live with her anymore, isn't it?"

Noah was silent for a moment. "I'm sorry it can't be better for you, honey."

"I always felt bad when I saw her push you away, or heard her yelling at you. I wanted to make it up to you. I could, Daddy, if you'd let me."

Noah turned toward his daughter, sliding a knee up on the bed and resting his weight over one hip. He took her hand.

"I apologize to you for all the things that upset you while I was living in California with you. You didn't deserve to be unhappy about anything. You were only a child. But, honey, as much as I appreciate what you say about wanting to make everything up to me, you can't do it. I have to do that myself. That's what I've been trying to do since I left there."

"Did you and . . . my mother love each other once? Before I was born?" Kimberly's voice quavered.

"Yes, we did."

"Then what happened so you didn't anymore?"

Noah thought a long time. Where did the blame go when any marriage crumbled? He knew what was wrong with the marriage, but he didn't know the moment when it started to go wrong. It was as if he woke up one morning and everything about the relationship didn't work anymore. How do you tell that one to your daughter?

"I think . . . we simply grew apart, that's all."

"That's all?" Tears started down Kimberly's cheeks, gathering strength. "Daddy, she must have done something wrong, or you must have. Adrienne says it's all your fault that the two of you aren't together. She says you had someone else on the side. And now I see she was right!"

Anger rose to Noah's throat, but he kept it at bay. He couldn't tell his daughter that her mother had many affairs after Kimberly was born, and was shifting her own guilt onto him.

"If you're referring to Majesty Wilde, I will say only that I met her a few weeks ago. I didn't know her till then."

"Oh, Daddy, why don't you fix things up with Adrienne and go back home. Make everything like it was before?" She dropped her head against his chest and sobbed.

When her crying had subsided, Noah sat her up straight and looked deep into her eyes.

"Kimberly, you're becoming an adult. It's not an easy job, believe me. I'm going to give you some hard truth. Regardless of how much it hurts, truth is the best thing. Okay?"

"Okay, Daddy," Kimberly said in a child's voice.

"I can't go back to Adrienne. I don't love her anymore, and she doesn't love me. And we were both unhappy the way things were before. I think you were unhappy then, too, weren't you?"

Kimberly didn't speak.

"It's all right for you to say it. You can admit you were unhappy."

"I still am," she whispered.

"I know you are, honey," he said, rubbing her back, "and I wish I knew how to change that for you."

"You can."

"How?"

She leaned back and looked up at him through reddened eyes. "Let me live with you. Let me make a home for you, the way it should have been."

"You can't do that, honey. It's not fair to you. You have your own life to live. And only you can make it what you want it to be."

"I want to be with you."

"And I want you to be with me. Wherever my home is, that's your home, too, as long as you want it."

"Then let's go back to California."

"My home is here, Kimberly," he said firmly.

"It's because of *her*, isn't it."

"Not in the beginning. But now, now I don't know what will happen with Maj and me. It's too soon. But I do know we care a lot about each other, and I want to take the chance to find out if there can be more."

"But what about me?"

"You, my darling daughter, the light of my life, will always be a part of me, and I'd want you to share in my future wherever it is and whoever it's with."

Kimberly frowned, and dropped her head against Noah's chest again. "She's nothing like Adrienne."

"That's right, she's not." Noah rejoiced in his heart over the differences.

"And she will never be my mother. No matter what, I won't call her that."

And that's a shame. "Whoa, girl! That's rushing things a bit! I'm only going out on a date with the woman, not walking down the aisle, you know."

"Yes, but you've already had the honeymoon, haven't you, Daddy?"

Noah felt the conversation turning back to the bitterness of the beginning of it, and decided not to comment on it. He did decide then to speak about something that had been bothering him since she'd arrived.

"This is not a criticism of you, Kimberly, but do you think you could you call me Dad, or Father, or Pop, or anything except Daddy? We're both too old for that term."

"But Adrienne calls her father Daddy."

"Exactly."

Kimberly laughed feebly. "Oh, I see what you mean."

Noah nodded smiling at her. "I hope so."

"That will seem like a foreign word for me, too."

"I know, *Kimberly*."

"Me, too, *Father*."

"Wow, does that sound old! Now, I've got to get out of here or I'll be late to pick up my date."

Reluctantly, Kimberly eased out of Noah's arms. "It's not like she's on the other side of the city, you know. She's only one floor down."

"I know, but"—he shrugged on a navy linen sport coat— "being late makes a bad impression."

"And you wouldn't want to do that, now, would you?" she said sarcastically.

Noah chucked her under the chin and kissed her forehead. "No, I would not. I'll see you later." He stepped out into the hallway.

Kimberly scuffed out behind him. "What time will you be back?"

"Don't wait up!" he called over his shoulder. He was eagerly going down the stairs and didn't see the look of anger and disappointment cloud his daughter's face.

At Maj's door, Noah paused before knocking. He did feel a little like an awkward teenager on a first date. But he also felt like a whole man, excited about spending an evening with the one special woman.

He knocked lightly. The door opened and Noah sucked in his breath.

"Hi," she said simply.

Her hair was curled loosely and fell in dark gold curves at her shoulders. She wore a violet and dark green flowered cotton knit dress, with a wide neckline that plunged to a V, revealing just enough of the soft roundness of her breasts. Short-sleeved and fitted at the waist, the dress rounded into a smooth hipline and ended in soft fullness at midcalf. Tan leather strappy high-heeled sandals and large gold hoop earrings completed her outfit.

"Hi," he replied, drawing it out while settling his gaze over her. "You look beautiful."

Maj smiled a shy thank-you. "So do you," she breathed.

He kissed her lingeringly without touching her with his hands. Her lips were reluctant to release his.

"I'd much rather stay in tonight," he whispered, "but it would be a shame for you not to be seen by the public at large." Holding her hand over her head, he twirled her around slowly until she faced him again. "I can guarantee these Adirondackers have never seen a more beautiful woman."

"Noah, please, you're making me blush." Maj fanned herself with a hand.

"And it becomes you," he whispered. "Shall we?" He took her hand and led her down the hallway to the front door.

He took her to a cozy restaurant on one of the Fulton Chain lakes called the Lake House Tavern, where the waitresses wore eclectic uniforms consisting of khaki shorts, poet shirts, mobcaps, tan pantyhose, and leather sandals. Both Maj and Noah chuckled in amusement once, then never noticed them again.

They were seated on the porch overlooking the lake at one of six candlelit tables. The menu was handwritten on a chalkboard brought by the hostess and propped on a chair next to their table. Noah ordered wine after conferring with Maj.

Every one of his senses seemed acutely aware. He watched the candlelight dance over her face, first lighting then shadowing the contours of her cheeks and jawline, making her hair appear to have a life of its own. The scent of her perfume reminded him of the first time he took her to his cabin. The sounds of the other diners were muted in the background under the recorded strains of Vivaldi's *Four Seasons*. Beyond her stretched the dark expanse of lake, the meandering edge of it becoming more defined as lights came on in cottages and restaurants.

He reached across the table and took both her hands in his. They were cool, but warmed almost immediately at his touch. He couldn't seem to get enough of looking at her, searching her eyes as she looked and searched back.

A waitress with a dyed rust-red French-braided hairdo returned with the wine bottle, pulling him out of his reverie. She showed him the label, deftly uncorked the bottle with a winged chrome opener, and splashed a little into the stemmed glass in front of him. He made a flamboyant show of swirling the wine around the bowl of the glass, checking the color against the flickering candlelight, then tasting it, rolling it around on his tongue before letting it slip down his throat. The waitress stood with a deadpan expression, waiting for him to decide.

"Impudent little bouquet, but not too saucy." He feigned seriousness as he spoke to Maj.

"Does that mean yes or no?" the waitress asked impatiently.

"Why, yes, of course, my good woman. This is one of the finest wines the Finger Lakes has to offer. Pour away."

The waitress obliged, but showed her annoyance by twitching clamped lips as if she sported a Charlie Chaplin mustache above them.

Maj and Noah touched glasses. "To tonight," he toasted, "and to the future." They drank of each other as much as of the wine. The rust-haired waitress stopped by their table several times to see if they were ready to order. Twice they ignored her, and once they shook their heads.

"Kitchen closes at nine," she announced, pad in hand when they hadn't ordered by eight-thirty.

Noah tore his gaze away from Maj's face long enough to give the order. "We'll have the fish."

"Baked, broiled, or fried."

Noah looked at Maj. "Broiled?" She nodded. "Broiled," he told the waitress.

"Baked potato, french fries, home fries, or tavern rice."

"Baked," Noah and Maj said in unison.

"Butter, or sour cream and chives?"

"Both," they said again, and started to laugh.

The waitress clearly found nothing amusing about their united responses. "What kind of dressing for your salads?"

Noah looked at Maj, and as if they knew the next question might be fun, she nodded at him, and he asked, "What kind do you have?"

The waitress let out a long sigh, then took in a deep breath. "House, French, regular Italian, creamy Italian, creamy bleu cheese, chunky bleu cheese, ranch regular or light, oil and vinegar." She waited, pencil poised over pad.

Maj and Noah eyed each other. "I can't

369

make up my mind," she said, "what are you going to have?"

"I'm not sure." Noah toyed with the idea of asking the waitress to run through the list again but thought that might be going over the top just a bit in the aggravation department. He looked up at her. "What's in the house?"

"Parmesan cheese, garlic, and black pepper."

"I will if you will," Noah said to Maj.

"Wouldn't do for only one of us to have garlic." She smiled at the waitress, who appeared very unamused. "I will, too."

Noah looked back at the waitress. "That's two house—"

"I got it," she snapped, and pocketed her pad and pencil, then hauled the chalkboard away.

"Must have had a bad day," Noah observed.

"I'm sure I'll find out soon enough that it's difficult to deal with the public," Maj said.

"I thought we were nice."

"I thought we drove her crazy!"

"I defer to—"

"My superior intelligence?" Maj inclined her head.

"Your superior everything"—he leaned toward her—"which I hope to partake of after dinner. Don't order dessert."

"Well, sir, you certainly do presume rather a lot." Maj affected her best haughty demeanor.

"As if you don't, my lady!"

"Conceded," she said, touching her glass to his.

Their salads arrived in less than a glassful of wine, and the fish two mouthfuls later.

"I think she's in a hurry to get out of here," Noah whispered.

"Maybe she's got a heavy date."

"Probably going to the submarine races."

"She'll be disappointed," Maj teased. "There aren't any submarines around here."

"If she's smart, she won't mention that to him."

In Noah's Buick on the way to his cabin, which is where they both knew they'd be going after dinner, Maj watched him as he drove, humming to himself.

"You were bad, back there," she chided him.

"What did I do?" Noah feigned innocence.

"Asking that waitress to list the desserts when you knew she was in a hurry to leave and we weren't planning on having any anyway."

"How was I to know they had eleven flavors of ice cream, seven assorted sundaes, nine tortes and cakes, and six cobblers and pies?"

"When she announced the Mississippi mud pie, I knew she was thinking how much she wanted to throw it in your face!"

"That was pretty obvious," he chuckled. "I had to ask. It was the polite thing to do for my date. You might have changed your mind about wanting dessert."

"No danger of that happening," she murmured. "I never used to order dessert before. Suddenly I've developed an insatiable sweet tooth."

Noah stepped on the gas. "I have just the thing to take care of that."

And Maj knew he did.

Maj nestled against Noah in his bed, their curves and contours fitting each other head to foot. Her limbs felt languid, her eyelids heavy, and every other part of her thoroughly and satisfyingly spent.

Orville, wiser now, purred contentedly on the braid rug next to the bed.

"We're good together," Noah whispered into her hair, "aren't we?"

"Mmm-hmm," she responded dreamily. "I never would have guessed it."

He squeezed his eyes to look down past his nose to her face. "You mean you doubted my artful abilities?"

"No. Mine." She snuggled closer.

He wrapped his arms around her more tightly. "That's the last thing you have to worry about. You are a wonderful, sensitive lover."

"You're a nice lover, too," she sighed.

"Nice? I'm nice? What an insult!"

Maj raised on one elbow, leaned over him, and looked into his warm brown eyes. "Why is nice an insult? I think it's a . . . well, nice thing to say about somebody."

"Oh, you do, do you?"

"Yes, I do."

"Well, I don't want to be nice."

"What's wrong with being nice? What would you rather be?"

He thought for a moment. "Sexy, sensuous, stimulating, incredibly gifted in bringing you pleasure, able to move heaven and earth for you." He caressed her breast where it was pressed against his chest as he talked.

"You are all of those," she said seductively, capturing his lower lip in both of hers and letting it out slowly.

"I thought you said I was nice."

"Yes. You're all those things, and that's nice."

He catapulted up and flipped her onto her back. "How would you like a second helping of nice dessert?"

"What about the calories?" she said with a fake whine.

"We'll work 'em off!"

And they did.

Chapter Fourteen

When Maj returned from her run the next morning, she was almost to the bathroom door when she noticed it: a bouquet of violets in a white-speckled blue tin mug sitting on her bedside table.

Noah.

When had he done that? He must have brought them in while she was running. She picked up the mug and pressed the violets to her nose and closed her eyes. They felt velvety against her skin, and smelled like early summer, earthy and warm. Just like Noah.

Violets in a mug. Simple. Romantic like old romance was supposed to be. She'd have to tell Nan about this. Nan the skeptic who said romance was dead. No. What she said was there weren't any romantic men around anymore. Maj smiled all through her shower, thinking how Noah had dispelled the myth.

Over breakfast she and Noah sent meaning-
ful glances each other's way, while Ada and
Fergie and Kimberly chatted with more anima-
tion than Maj had noticed among the three
before.

"She is a smart one, that daughter of yours,"
Fergie told Noah. "Knew most all them answers
on the quiz show last night."

"They were easy questions," Kimberly said,
lazily arranging a few remaining Cheerios in an
abstract pattern in her cereal bowl.

Maj noticed a measurable change in the girl's
attitude. She could tell she enjoyed Fergie's
praise, but didn't want to show it. Kimberly
had difficulty accepting compliments. When did
it start, the moment when a child's self-esteem
was threatened? As often as she and Nan had
talked about just that, neither one of them had
come up with a satisfactory answer.

"No, they were not easy," Ada defended Kimberly. "All that Shakespeare stuff you knew, and
geography, and most everything in the pot-
pourri category."

"One of my teachers says I have a head full
of useless information," Kimberly said.

"You should get on one of those game
shows," Fergie gushed. "You'd win a lot of money.
Then tell that stuck-up teacher what-for!"

"You two knew all that stuff about the movie

376

stars and the big bands. How did you remember all that?"

Maj warmed inside. Kimberly sounded as if she meant the compliment, and as if she really wanted Fergie to tell her how they knew so much about those things.

"That was easy," Ada answered. "We grew up with it. Fergie took me to the movies on our first date. Remember that?" She looked toward her husband.

"Oh, yeah?" Kimberly put down her juice glass. "What'd you see?"

"*The Sheik* with Rudolph Valentino." Ada sighed. "I nearly swooned when he burst into her tent."

"That was the idea," Fergie said, feigning a lecherous voice.

Ada poked him. "Go on with you."

"Speaking of dates," Kimberly started, looking at Noah.

"What else did you do last night?" he interrupted quickly, "besides show off your brain power?"

"We played Flinch," Fergie said.

"Flinch," Maj said, sipping hot coffee. "I haven't played that card game since I was a kid. I didn't know you could still get it."

"Can't," Ada said. "We saved ours. Bought it over at Big Moose years ago."

377

"Must be an antique by now," Noah laughed.

"They told me all about the history of this place," Kimberly said, forgetting her earlier question. "We looked at old pictures and stuff. It must have been great back then, coming up here in the winter by horse-drawn sleigh."

"You wouldn't think so if you'd come across that corduroy road in those days."

"Corduroy?" Kimberly asked.

"Logs. Like to jolt the kidneys right out of a body!" Fergie scratched his head, remembering.

"I wouldn't have cared," Kimberly said dreamily. "Those full skirts, and the bearskin throw, and a beaver muff . . . just think about arriving here in such style. Right out of a Currier and Ives drawing. Too bad things have to change."

"Well, now, lookit here, missy," Fergie said, "I'll make you a promise. You come back here in the winter and I guarantee I'll have the old sleigh out and ready to go on a ride. Plenty of people around here with horses I could borrow. Not sure about the bearskin and beaver muff, but would part of the picture do?"

"Would it ever! Can you do that? Do you still have the sleigh?" Kimberly looked like an excited child opening a Christmas present.

"You bet we do, child."

Noah groaned. "Another piece of history for

378

me to refinish. Will it never end?"

"Quit complaining. You love doing it, and you know it," Ada scolded good-naturedly.

"Sure I do. Look at these hands. Takes me an hour just to bleach the stains out of them, thanks to Fergie and his furniture."

"You never complained when you redid that old airplane," Fergie chided him. "Kept it a secret all that time. 'Cept for the day you had red paint all over you, even in your hair, and you never once said a word about it. That's what gave it away. In fact, you was humming the whole time you worked on it. Except for the time when you dropped the wrench on your foot and you said—"

"Never mind what I said. Speaking of the Stearman, Maj, would you mind if I took Kimmie, ah, Kimberly up for a ride in it today? Looks calm and clear."

"Of course not, go ahead."

"You want to go, Kimberly?" Noah asked.

"I think I should let my breakfast settle first."

"Good idea."

Later in the afternoon, after Noah had taken her flying over the mountains and she'd clicked off almost a whole roll of film in her camera, Kimberly asked, "Why did you ask her if it was all right if you took me for a ride in the airplane?"

379

"It's her airplane."

"Hers?"

"Yes. Why are you so surprised?"

"I don't know. She just didn't seem like the kind—"

"You don't know a lot about Maj, honey. I wish you'd have taken the time to get to know her while you were here."

"Why? What difference does it make?"

"It makes a big difference to me. You're both important to me."

"You're not getting all soft about her, are you? In any case, I'm leaving tomorrow morning, and it won't matter anyway."

"You'll be back, won't you? I really hope you'll come back here, Kimberly. Everybody likes you. And I miss you."

"Everybody?"

"Yes, everybody."

"Well . . ."

"You'll be back."

"I'll think about it. Maybe for Christmas. Think the sleigh will be ready by then?"

"The sleigh." Noah groaned.

They spent a pleasant evening together. Noah barbecued chicken for dinner, and afterward they went into the parlor, where Fergie had a huge jigsaw puzzle going on a square mahogany table. After a while Maj went to the kitchen to prepare dessert. Noah followed as soon as he could make an easy departure from the group.

"It's been fun tonight," she said, cutting chocolate brownie squares and setting them on stoneware plates.

He came up behind her and slipped his arms around her waist. "You've made a lot of fun things happen in my life," he whispered in her ear.

"And you in mine," she whispered back. "Whipped cream?" She held one of two red and white cans over a brownie, her finger pressing the nozzle.

"Sure."

She turned and squirted some on his nose, then burst out laughing.

"Oh, I suppose you think that's funny, don't you?"

"Yep!" she giggled.

He wrested the can away from her. "Well, what do you think of this?" He squirted two little puffs on her shirt right over where he knew her nipples rested in her bra.

"Hysterical!" She let go with a spate of laughter. Grabbing the can back, she said, "And what do you think of this?" She pulled the waistband of his jeans out, tipped the nozzle inside, and pressed a long, full puff.

"That is not funny, Miss Smartie, that is war!"

He grabbed for the can and missed. Maj shrieked and ducked under his outstretched arm. He made a lunge and caught her around the waist. She kept the can far out in front of her so he couldn't reach it. They were struggling against each other, and laughing and panting heavily when he swung her around.

Kimberly stood just inside the door, scowling.

Their laughter died away, and their panting subsided. Nervously Maj wiped the smeared whipped cream from her shirt.

"We were—" she started to say, then stifled a giggle.

"Playing," Noah said seriously. "We were playing, actually. Weren't we, Maj?" He burst out laughing, and grabbed the can out of her hands in a last battle move.

"Give me that," she muttered under a laugh. "Yes, playing, that's what we were doing."

"Why don't you two grow up?" Kimberly gave them each a disdainful look, the longest of which lingered on Maj.

"We tried that. It wasn't any fun, so we decided to start over," Noah laughed, wiping his nose with a dishtowel and trying to hide the wet spot forming over his pants front.

"You ought to control yourselves." Kimberly

382

ignored his teasing. "You're acting like silly teenagers."

"Will you listen to Mrs. Methuselah over there?" Noah looked at Maj, then back to his daughter. "You're entirely too serious for a nineteen-year-old. You should try acting like a silly teenager sometime. It would be good for you, especially since you still are a teenager. If you're even the least bit silly, you've been hiding it very well."

"Noah, maybe you shouldn't . . ." Maj began.

Noah started stalking Kimberly, whipped cream can in hand. Kimberly saw what he had in mind, and started backing away. Noah circled the table fast. Kimberly dodged, holding up her hands.

"No, no, no, don't do it. My hair—"

"What about your hair, your pretty, perfect hair? It's washable, isn't it? Get silly, Kimberly! I know you can do it!" Noah goaded her.

"Come on, Daddy, don't do anything." Kimberly circled the table.

"Aha! You called me Daddy! Proof that you're still a child, and quite possibly a silly one at that!" Noah pressed the nozzle. Whipped cream squirted out in a long, snaky squiggle and landed on Kimberly's hair and shoulder.

"Dad-dy!" Kimberly dodged, and a laugh

threatened to turn up the corners of her straight mouth.

"Whaaat?" Noah mimicked her tone. He squirted again. This time a stream of whipped cream went from her nose to her chin.

"This isn't fair! I don't have a weapon!" Kimberly started to laugh in spite of herself.

"Whipped-cream torpedo at twelve o'clock high!" Maj called to her from the opposite end of the table, holding up the other red and white can, making ready to toss it.

Kimberly looked toward her, surprised at the offer, and more surprised when Noah let her have it with a pouf of the sticky stuff on top of her head. She stuck out two hands and Maj tossed the can to her.

"Reinforcements!" Kimberly yelled.

Noah feigned fear and started backing away as his daughter advanced on him, nozzle pointed directly at his face, trigger finger at the ready.

"You wouldn't do that to your old man, would you?" Noah was laughing so hard he could barely get the words out.

"Oh, wouldn't I?" Kimberly shouted back.

"His hair!" Maj shouted. "Get his hair! He hates anything to mess it up!"

"Are you saying 'like father like daughter'?" Noah's surprise at her comment stopped him.

"Right!" Maj pounded the table.

"Right!" Kimberly shouted back, unaware that she and Maj had just become allies.

"Hey! Two against one, that's not fair!" Noah spun around the table, trying to get Maj as a shield.

"All's fair in love and war!" Maj laughed, easily eluding him.

"This is definitely war!" He lunged toward his daughter.

"En garde!" Kimberly held out the can like a sword.

"Touché!" Noah squirted her squarely in the neck.

"Parry! Thrust!" Kimberly shot a puff into his hair and one in his stomach.

"Olé!" Maj called from her vantage point by the back door.

Noah stopped and looked at her. "This is a duel, not a bullfight!"

"All depends on how you look at it," Maj laughed.

"Oh, it does, does it? Well, take this, *toro!*" He pressed the nozzle and landed a splatter of whipped cream across her face.

Maj wiped her eyes. "Unfair advantage," she laughed, grabbing a towel to clean off her face. "But so is this!" She sprang toward him and had the towel looped through his arms and his

385

hands pulled behind his back before he had the wherewithal to prevent it. The whipped cream can fell to the floor. She tied a knot around his wrists and plopped him onto the kitchen stool before he knew what hit him.

"Where'd you learn that?" Kimberly seemed to be actually in awe of Maj's move.

"Personal defense class," Maj said, brushing her palms with satisfaction. "I lived in Manhattan."

"Okay, okay, I give up," Noah laughed breathlessly. "Untie me."

"Not before you pay for your imprudent actions," Kimberly announced.

"Wait a minute. I'm the father here, you're the kid, remember?"

"War ages a person," Kimberly came back with a grand attempt at seriousness. She turned toward Maj and lowered her voice. "Is he or is he not a prisoner of war?"

"He is that, general," Maj saluted Kimberly. "Torture him. He's all yours. Be ruthless."

"Aye, aye," Kimberly said.

"I'm going to tell Ada and Fergie on you," Noah whined.

"Go ahead," Maj sniffed. "They're our commanders-in-chief."

"The traitors," he muttered.

Fifteen minutes later Kimberly went to the

parlor, where Ada and Fergie sat poring over the puzzle.

"Dessert is served in the salon, your highnesses," she said, sounding ever so pompous, and then she curtsied.

"What's this?" Fergie said over his shoulder.

"It's a special treat expertly concocted by the team of Majesty and Myself."

"Is that the new caterer?" Ada winked.

"You'll love this," Kimberly giggled.

Ada and Fergie followed her to the kitchen. They stopped in the doorway, mouths open before they dissolved in laughter.

Maj and Kimberly locked inner arms, and with their outer arms outstretched, palms up toward Noah, said in unison, "Ta-dah! The West Wind specialty—giant banana split!"

Noah sat dejectedly at the table, a dishtowel draped around his neck. A crown of whipped cream encircled his head, resembling a pouffy cap. Over that was sprinkled chopped nuts. A cherry perched at the very peak of the white swirls. A cream mustache melted over his upper lip, and he licked each little stream that trickled toward his mouth. The tops of his ears supported tiny puffs of cream sprinkled with varicolored candy shot. He held a peeled banana in each hand.

"Photo opportunity!" Kimberly went to the

sideboard, where she'd left her camera. "Everyone gather round the dessert for a group shot!"

They did, and Kimberly took the photograph with Noah licking his whipped-cream mustache, Fergie and Ada grinning with pure happiness, and Maj with a big spoon poised over Noah's head.

"Would you care for a taste?" Maj asked Ada.

"Oh, dear, no, thank you. He's too pretty to spoil. I'll just take one of these." She picked up a plate with a brownie on it, and took a fork. "Fergie?"

"Same here," he answered, laughing, and picked up a plate and fork. "I got this thing about finding hairs in my dessert."

"I must apologize." Kimberly stifled a laugh. "The hotel is fresh out of whipped cream this evening. But I hope you'll find this delicate chocolate confection more exquisite to the palate."

"Oh, to be sure," Fergie said, then exploded with laughter.

It was catching, and soon Ada was laughing, and Maj and Kimberly, too, who were so weak they leaned on each other's shoulders.

"Very funny. You all think you're very funny, don't you?" Noah said evenly. "But someday, when you least expect it, I shall exact my revenge."

In his heart and mind Noah rejoiced at the whole episode. As Maj and Kimberly began cleaning up the kitchen, he noticed an excitement in his daughter he hadn't seen before. She'd just had some pure unadulterated fun, albeit at his expense, but it was worth every minute he endured to see her laughing and having an uninhibited good time.

He could tell by her face now that she'd forgotten her animosity against Maj, at least for the moment, and the two of them had worked together to do him in as if they'd been partners for years. Emotion welled up inside him and he had to keep swallowing to hold it back.

He loved his daughter so much, he ached with it. He hadn't remembered seeing her laugh so hard since the time she mastered the tricycle.

He wiped what was left of the mustache away with an index finger, then sucked off the cream as he caught Maj's eye. She smiled from across the kitchen, and he saw the color in her face deepen. She came to him with paper towels and started wiping the sundae remains from his hair, laughing as she cleaned him up.

When had he fallen in love with her? He wasn't shocked as the question burst in his mind like a rocket on a movie screen. Somehow he wanted to know the precise moment.

Then he realized something blinding. There'd been so many beautiful moments between them. He knew he'd fallen in love with her over and over with each one of them. And he wanted the moments never to stop coming.

You'd better do something about this, Decker. You want this woman in your life forever, and you know it.

"Did you see the moon tonight?" Maj was saying as she stood by the back screen door. "Anybody for going down on the dock to watch it on the water?"

"How about it, Kimberly? Want to walk down there with us?" Noah had finished cleaning off the table and was drying his hands.

Kimberly shifted her gaze between them, and Noah saw the uncertainty return. Now that the silliness had subsided, she behaved as if she remembered she didn't like Maj. It became an uneasy truce once again.

She shrugged her shoulders. "Sure, why not?"

Over the water the moon hung like a perfect silver dollar, its creamy reflection undulating with the subtle movement of breeze-swept black lake water.

"It looks close enough to touch," Kimberly said in hushed awe. "And look at that!"

All around the moon's reflection were shimmering tiny points of light, floating as if some sky grower had sown diamond seeds in free abandon across the water off the end of the dock.

"That's the diamond patch," Maj offered. "Granddad always told me the diamond patch was a good omen. If I was patient and waited long enough, the diamonds would float to my dock and I'd have good fortune for the next year."

"Did his prediction ever come true?" Kimberly asked without looking at Maj.

"I guess I never waited long enough then. I've grown up and I think I have more patience now."

"You think maybe diamonds will float to your dock this year?" Noah said with a cryptic note in his voice.

"I'll just have to wait and see."

"Yah! What was that?" Kimberly shrieked and ducked her head.

Maj ducked then, and held her hands over her hair. "Oh, no, not again!"

"What is it? It's dive-bombing me!" Kimberly backed off the dock.

"Bats!" Maj yelled, following her.

"Ugh, I hate bats! I'm going inside." Kimberly started for the back porch, fluttering her hands over her head. "Yow! Why do they always go for hair? They're so creepy."

391

Noah stood in the same place on the dock, laughing and watching Maj and Kimberly head for shelter.

"What's so funny, Dad? I don't see anything to laugh about," Kimberly called over her shoulder without stopping.

"We've been through a previous bat episode." Maj refrained from telling Kimberly that the previous bat episode had taken place in the very room in which she'd been sleeping.

Noah ran up behind the two and draped arms around their shoulders as they started up the steps. "Once again the Caped Crusader to the rescue! Holy bug-infested wings, Robins, I seem to be on call twenty-four hours a day!"

"Batman returns," Maj said, dissolving with laughter.

"More like batty man," Kimberly giggled.

"Don't start, daughter!" Noah gave her light smack on the rump as they entered the kitchen. "Remember, I'm spoiling for revenge, and you've still got another night here!"

"Oh, please, your disgustingness, please be lenient on this poor subject," Kimberly pleaded like a minion. "I promise to be nothing but worshipful from this moment on."

"I'm glad you know your place," Noah replied with feigned sternness.

"That is, till next time!" Kimberly giggled

and started up the stairs to her room. "G'night, everybody."

They all chorused a good-night to her.

Maj and Noah were still looking at each other, smiling, when Kimberly came halfway down the stairway. "And thanks for the good time." A few seconds later they heard her door close.

"That's a good kid you got there, Noah," Fergie said, yawning and making preparations to head for bed.

"Nice girl," Ada concurred. "She's been a pleasure to have around."

"Sure has." Noah's face crinkled with the smile of a proud father. "I'd almost forgotten how good it could feel."

Ada and Fergie went off to bed still talking about how smart Kimberly was.

Maj had retreated to the kitchen and was busying herself with the final cleanup. Noah sensed something had upset her, and he followed her.

Maj turned around then, and he saw her eyes were moist with fresh tears.

"What happened? Did Kimmie do something to upset you?"

"On the contrary," she said thickly, "she made me very happy tonight."

Noah inclined his head. "I understand," he

393

whispered, and put his arms around her.

"Just being with her tells me once again just how much I've missed not having a child of my own. I thought I'd resolved all that inside myself." She pressed her cheek against his comforting chest. *And being held by you makes me know what else I've missed.*

Noah wrapped his arms tighter around her. *Holding you like this makes me know how much I've missed in my life.*

"I wish she and I could be friends," Maj said into his shirt.

"Maybe someday you can be."

"I'm not so sure about that."

"Why?" He leaned back to look into her eyes.

"You heard her the other day. She wants a home with both parents in it. If you look as if you're . . . seeing somebody else, her dream will be shattered."

"She shouldn't have that dream, anyway." Noah stroked Maj's hair.

"But she does have it."

"Sometimes dreams are shattered. She's young. I've tried to explain to her how things are with me. She'll understand someday."

"Meaning us old folks can't have dreams?" Maj leaned back in the circle of his arms and looked up at him.

"I think it's best not to."

394

"Why not?"

"Somebody will always come along and destroy it. If you never have dreams in the first place, no one can hurt you."

"I didn't know you were such a cynic."

"I'm a realist. A tired realist. Being a banana split and a caped crusader all in one night has exhausted me."

"I know what you mean. That old adage about youth being wasted on the young may not hold up anymore. It takes a lot of energy to be young." Yawning, Maj flipped the light switch off.

"Sure does. Aren't you glad we're never going to get any younger?"

"Sure am." She slipped her arms around his neck and kissed him good night. "I'd hate to have to go back to the time when I didn't know about all this." And then she kissed him so the memory of it would last all night.

Chapter Fifteen

After Kimberly went back to Saratoga, summer arrived in full force. Noah's company work increased, as it always did during the summer months, and he was away from the West Wind a great deal.

Maj was determined the lodge would be ready to open by Labor Day. The related cottages would not be ready, but the main lodge would be, and she was working the grousing Moffett Brothers, the nontalkative Frenchman, and herself hard to accomplish that goal.

She designed new brochures and had them printed, placed ads in major newspapers and magazines, and ordered an airplane banner made to fly behind the Stearman on opening day. Then she sent out letters of invitation to former colleagues and friends.

In the midst of his own frantic schedule, somehow Noah managed to find a way to leave flowers for Maj, or chocolate kisses, or notes, and she smiled in anticipation each time she sensed he'd done something.

Once he left her a pilot's log book in her underwear drawer. On the few occasions when they managed to fit in thirty minutes to an hour of flying, she took great delight in logging her time in the book, and he took pride in initialing the column reserved for the flight instructor.

One night Maj discovered a note under her pillow. Inside were the words from a Browning poem:

Grow old along with me!
The best is yet to be.
The last of life for which the first was made . . .

N.

Did that mean what she thought it meant? She liked thinking Noah was courting her in an old-fashioned manner with his flowers and candy and log books. But was this note . . . a marriage proposal? Did she want it to be a marriage proposal?

During their times together, they seemed to grow closer emotionally, mentally, and certainly physically. Maj was continually amazed at how much that part of their relationship varied. Just when she thought there couldn't be anything more to discover in their lovemaking, Noah showed her something else. Her emotions skyrocketed. And then she began to think of new things of her own, much to his delight and their mutual enjoyment.

What she and Noah had together was more than a marriage. It was a true connection of two souls and minds and bodies, and no ceremony could validate that any more than it already was between them.

Early on the morning of the Fourth of July, Noah burst into the West Wind kitchen just as Maj was pouring her first cup of coffee.

"I've entered us both in the race," he announced, kissing her on the cheek.

"Race? What race?"

"The International Mountain Road Race down in Pinewood. Eleven o'clock this morning, so don't eat too much breakfast."

"I can't compete in a race, Noah. I'm not that good." Maj went out on the porch with her coffee and sat down on the top step.

"It's only a five kilometer race. You can do that," Noah said, dropping down beside her. "Would you look at that sky? It'll be a scorcher later today. Clear night for the fireworks, and perfect for a morning run."

"What does that translate into in feet or yards?"

"A little over three miles. You can do it! It'll be fun!"

"Three miles! I run to keep fit, not to race. I've seen road races and marathons on television, and nobody looks like they're having fun. In fact, they look like they're drawing their last breath. That's not for me. Besides, I'd be embarrassed if I came in last."

"You wouldn't come in last, trust me. People of all ages, shapes, and sizes run that race every year just for the fun of it. Not to mention the free hot dogs and beer afterward. There are a bunch of prizes for each age group. Horace Mason won the over-eighty prize last year."

Maj saw Noah narrow his eyes toward her. "You made that up!" she accused, laughing. "Horace couldn't run three miles and be alive to tell about it afterward!"

"I am not making that up! He did!"

"How many over-eighty runners were there?"

"Well, just Horace, but that's not the point. He didn't run the whole way, he walked some of it, but he completed the five kilometers and he was the only one over eighty to do it, so he won the prize."

Maj sent a skeptical glance his way. "Are you really going to run in this race?"

"Yep. What's the matter? Afraid I'll beat you?" He drained his coffee cup and watched her face for the answer he knew was coming.

"Beat me! Ha! I've seen you run, remember? You're not material for the Marine Corps marathon."

"I never ran that thing. But I've picked up a few five- and eight-kilometer-race prizes in my day. Meet me in front of Danbury's at nine-thirty. Gotta run. Don't be late!"

"But . . . !"

"Right!" he called over his shoulder. "Get that cute butt in gear! See you there!"

At exactly nine-thirty Maj walked up and down in front of Danbury's Hardware wearing her running shoes, blue shorts, and a white T-shirt with an American flag printed on the front. Her hair was pulled back in a ponytail, and around her forehead she wore a navy blue sweatband printed with white stars. Several people walked by her with friendly greetings and told her they were glad she'd entered the race. They'd be cheering her on from the sidewalk, they said.

Maj was mulling over what she knew would be her inevitable embarrassment at the finish line, when she spotted Noah coming toward her, a wide grin lighting his face.

"It's about time you got here," she whispered. "I feel conspicuous standing here dressed like this. People are staring at me."

"They should be staring at you. You look gorgeous. And you look nervous. Relax."

"I can't relax. Hey, you look pretty gorgeous yourself." Maj made a frank appraisal of him from the top of his hair, where the sun made copper glints, past his broad chest under a blue T-shirt that said "I Survived Big Moose Road" on it, over his thin navy shorts, down muscular, lightly tanned legs to his white running shoes.

"You"—he leaned close to her face—"are a shameless hussy looking at me that way right here in front of God and Danbury's Hardware. Let's go warm up."

"I'm plenty warm already." She smiled to herself, oddly proud that she'd had the nerve to say something like that. Being in love at her age gave a woman courage, she decided. Or maybe it made her foolhardy. In any case, she liked it.

They stretched out and did a warm-up jog. A panel of race judges consisted of the Moffett

401

Brothers, sweating in shirts and ties, one horse-faced girl named Faye, and her widowed mother, the stern-faced librarian named Penelope Hawkins. They checked off the entrants' names and gave out white sheets printed with black numbers which they instructed everyone to pin on their shirts.

"There's more people entered in this race than live in the whole town," Maj observed as she stood next to Noah at the starting line with about sixty or so other runners. "But how can they call it 'international'?"

"Canadians come down for it. There's runners here from all over New York and even Vermont. This is a popular event."

One of the Moffetts held a starting pistol over his head and shouted, "Ready!"

Maj looked over her shoulder at the sound of several pairs of shoes settling on the pavement. Horace Mason stood behind her and winked.

"Set!" shouted Moffett.

Bodies leaned forward. Maj's stomach growled.

"I can't believe I let you talk me into this," she muttered out of the right side of her mouth to Noah.

Bang!

At the report of the pistol the block of runners took off in a herd, Maj and Noah pressed among them.

"Don't push it yet," Noah said, running in rhythm with Maj's steps.

"Who's pushing? Look at that! Six-year-old kids are passing us! This is embarrassing!"

"They're over forty years younger than us, they're supposed to pass us. It's the natural order of things."

The pack thinned out as runners sprinted in front or lagged in back. At a turn at the mile-and-a-half mark, a wiry man with white-streaked short gray hair held a stopwatch and called out each runner's time as they passed.

"Fourteen thirty," he said without looking up as Noah ran past him.

"Thanks, Luther," Noah breezed.

"Fourteen thirty-two," he said as Maj passed, and she heard him rattle off more numbers as the pack ran by.

"What does that mean?" Maj puffed.

"It means we'd better horse it on the way back or we won't make it in under thirty." Noah sounded hardly winded at all.

"I'm over fifty! How can I be expected to come in under thirty?"

"Because you're in better shape than a lot of

people in this race. So stop talking and pump your arms!"

Maj pumped.

At the next turn there was a table set up with pitchers and cups of water. A woman stood near it holding a garden hose. Noah grabbed a cup of water as he passed, downed it, and threw the cup to the ground. The woman sprayed him with water from the hose.

Water! Like one lost in a desert, Maj grabbed a cup, tried to gulp it and keep running, but spilled most of it down her chest. The coolness felt good. But the spray of hose water was a cold shock on the back of her neck, and it took her a few seconds to regain equilibrium.

She wiped water and her hair out of her eyes. Her mouth grew dry. She wanted to spit so badly she could hardly keep from doing it. Her chest ached. Her legs felt as if they weighed a ton each.

Noah spat along side the road, and Maj noticed that he hadn't been the first. He looked at his watch.

"Pour it on! You can make it in twenty-eight!" he said to her.

"I've got to spit!"

"What?"

"I've got to spit!" Maj said thickly. *And I've got to go to the bathroom badly!*

"So spit!" Noah said.

"Won't — *puff* — it — *wheeze* — look — *puff* — bad if I do?"

"Runners spit. It's expected. Go ahead. You'll feel better."

She did, and she did feel better. Vaguely she wondered if anyone would step in it, slip and fall, then blame it on her in front of the crowd of spectators.

Ahead, the race course narrowed to a lane marked with strings bearing waving pennants in orange and yellow. Beyond that stretched a banner between two poles marked FINISH LINE. On the other side of that Maj saw a big cooler and several stacks of cups. Water. *Please let there be a bathroom.*

"Okay now," Noah coached. "You're gonna do it. You're looking strong. Pump your arms. Relax. Breathe."

"Shut — *puff* — up!" she wheezed.

"Go for it!" Noah shouted from behind.

With a burst of energy Maj did go for it, through the lane with the pennant flags and under the banner. The finish-line timer said, "Twenty-eight nineteen!"

On the other side of the finish line Maj

405

walked slowly, breathed hard, bent over, shook her legs, breathed some more, went to the cooler for water. A crowd of sweaty runners stood around a picnic table, drinking water and sucking oranges. Maj heard a ringing in her ears, then several fragmented sentences as runners inquired about others' running times.

Noah was beside her then, pressing his hot, perspiring body against hers. "You were great! You did it in under twenty-nine minutes! What a terrific first race! Wasn't that fun?"

Maj lifted a weary gaze to him and whispered one word, "Bathroom."

Noah pointed to a pair of pale green portable toilet facilities on the far side of the field. To Maj they looked as if they were another five kilometers from where she stood, but she managed to walk to them without falling down. Inside the one marked Girls she thought she might keel over from the enclosed heat. *Fun* was not the word she would have used to describe her present state.

When she returned to the finish line, Penelope Hawkins was announcing names and times, and Faye handed out prizes to the winners. The overall winning man and woman each received a trophy. Other age group winners were picking up prizes of gear bags, gift certificates

406

from the Coffee Cup and Danbury's Hardware, visors, and sweatbands.

Horace Mason won the prize again for his age group. It was a bag full of donations from Shafer's Pharmacy, which Horace promptly spread out for all to see. Maj laughed with the rest as Horace displayed denture adhesive, laxatives, itch powder, and hair dye. And a certificate for dinner for two at the Big Moose Inn.

"For the category of men forty-five and over, except for Horace Mason," Penelope announced, "the winner at twenty-eight twenty-six is Noah Decker!"

There was a round of applause as Noah accepted the prize. Maj jumped up and down and squealed like an excited child.

"Noah! That's terrific! Let me see what you got!" She tried to peek inside the plastic bag he carried.

"Wait," Noah whispered.

"For the category of women fifty and over," Penelope said, "the winner is Majesty Wilde with twenty-eight nineteen!"

Another round of applause. Maj stood next to Noah, stunned, unable to move. Noah whistled and patted her on the back. "Go get your prize, champ!" he whispered in her ear, and gave her an affectionate push on the shoulder.

In a daze, a smile plastered on her face, Maj walked to the prize table and accepted a similar plastic bag from Faye.

When she walked back to Noah, she was still smiling.

"I did it! I actually ran in a race and won! I can't believe it!"

"I can," Noah said. "I knew you could!"

She looked around at the crowd of runners. "Wait a minute. Just how many women over fifty ran this race, anyway?"

"What difference does that make?"

"Well, if I had no competitors in my age group, how can anyone say I won?"

"You ran like a competitor, and you finished, and nobody beat you. That's all that counts. Be proud of yourself. You deserve it."

"Heyyy," she said when an idea occurred to her. "I beat you, didn't I?"

"Well, not so anyone would notice."

"I noticed! And you did to! I told you I could beat you, and I did!" She laughed, linking her arm with his.

Echoes of a distant past floated past her conscious mind. No teenage girl of her generation would have allowed herself to beat the boy she had a crush on. And she never could have said a thing like that to Jack, or even allow herself to best him.

Noah guided her to a shady spot beneath some maple trees in the park, and they opened their prizes. Inside the bags were long-sleeved T-shirts, his in red and hers in black. They each held them up by the shoulders.

On each was printed a phrase: SENECTUDO ET PERFIDIA ARTEM ET IUVENTATEM SUPERANT!

"What does that mean?" She looked up at Noah, perplexed.

"Here's the translation," Noah said, pulling a sheet of paper out of his bag.

He showed it to her, and they laughed as they both read the phrase out loud.

"Old age and treachery will outlast youth and skill!"

Noah smiled broadly.

"Don't you dare say it, Noah Decker!"

"Say what?" he said coyly.

"You know very well what."

"I wouldn't dream of mentioning the fact that you are older than I am, and that you ran a better time than I did, and that you represent the first of that phrase and I represent the last. I'd never say anything like that."

"You are an incorrigible human being!" Playfully she socked him on the shoulder with the shirt.

"And you are the lady I love spending time with."

"And I love . . . being with you, too.

A girl of her generation would never reveal her feelings too soon, Maj remembered. But she was beginning to burst with them. If he didn't say something pretty soon, she was going to have to throw that stale 1950s caution to the refreshing 1990s mountain winds and just tell him she loved him.

But, oh, how good it felt to be living so pleasantly, filled with fun, with work she loved, with results of her ideas and labors she could see. Life without conflict — her life almost in reverse, that's what was happening.

These are the best of times, and I'm better than ever.

August crept to a close, and the frenzy of putting the final touches on the lodge consumed Maj's days during the last week. At night, if she didn't see Noah, she retired early and read until her eyes closed, which sometimes took no longer than five or ten minutes.

Noah burst into the kitchen one morning when Maj was alone trying to find something for breakfast that appealed to her.

"My crew finally gave me the morning off!"

He planted a playful kiss on her lips. "What a bunch of whip crackers they are! Where's Ada and Fergie?" He stopped and took a closer look at her face. "Aren't you feeling well? You're looking a little green around the gills."

"Thank you, and a pleasant good morning to you, too." She sat down slowly and examined a piece of wheat toast. Unappealing. She dropped it back on the plate. "They're at Tupper Lake. Doctor's appointment."

"Seriously. You sick?" He felt her forehead with the backs of his fingers.

"I don't think so. Just tired, I guess."

"You've been working too hard and at a pace that would put a crew of ten-year-olds to shame." He poured a cup of coffee. "What do you say you take the day off, too? We could take the Stearman up. That is, if your stomach can stand it."

Maj lifted her head slowly. "That sounds like a great idea."

"Naturally. I thought of it." Noah downed the toast.

"Naturally. I yield to your great mind. Let's take the Stearman."

"And a picnic?"

Maj brightened. "That would be wonderful! Except I couldn't afford to be stuck again

411

someplace. There's too much to do around here before opening next weekend."

"Don't worry, we won't get stuck."

"Famous last words. I'll change my clothes. Check the fridge for lunch food. There's a soft pack you can use in the far cupboard."

"Yes, sir!"

When they were airborne, Noah, in the front seat, lifted his arms overhead, signaling her to take over the controls. Maj took them joyfully, for the incredible sense of control and freedom still overwhelmed her each time she felt the stick in her hand and the pedals under her feet.

As the Stearman cut through the air and Maj watched the back of Noah's head turning one way or the other as he took in the scenery below and beyond, the sense of oneness she was still absorbing surrounded her. Like the fragments of an unnamed but familiar song, the feeling curled around and set her humming contentedly.

She was so good at landings and takeoffs now, Noah often relinquished his role of instructor. The day was warm and sunny, the air clear with little turbulence. They landed on Sixth Lake, moored the plane, and opened their picnic on a stretch of partially shaded

412

shoreline.

In the few hours they could spare each other out of their busy day, the communication they used was mostly of the senses—breathing in the scent of clear fragrant air, grateful they were breathing it together; watching several species of birds spending the time searching for and capturing their own food; listening to the ducks that came near their picnic site chatter to one other in low, comfortable tones, or quack outright in demand of any crumbs they might share; touching grass blades, leaves, stones; tasting cold chicken, potato salad, iced tea, and each other.

The moments were over all too soon, and they packed up and took off again. When they alighted on Big Moose Lake and taxied to the West Wind dock, Noah jumped out and shouted over the roar.

"Time you soloed, Captain! Take her around for a couple of touch and gos!"

"No!" she shouted back. "I'm not ready yet."

"You're ready as you'll ever be. You can do it, and you know it."

Maj's fingers tightened around the stick. Her pulse raced. Her heart pounded. Her stomach clutched. Her mind reeled. Her hands perspired. Her fingers froze. Her knees stiffened.

Her feet went numb, and she couldn't feel the pedals beneath them. Her ears rang with the high pitch of the engine. Her sight blurred through the gray smear of the propeller cutting through the air.

I've forgotten everything.

Checklist. Takeoff checklist! What am I supposed to do? She couldn't think. She couldn't hear. She couldn't remember. She was in a trance, a fog, a coma.

Awakening came to her after she'd taxied down the lake, turned around, and headed into the wind — speed accelerating; stick pulling back; Noah waving from the dock; lake, land and trees falling away beneath her.

She was off!

Soaring! Solo!

Alone in the sky, alone with herself, alone with her own power and talent.

In love with life, in love with flying, in love with a man who lifted her high enough to catch on to her real spirit and soar with it on her own. This moment was the greatest, most satisfying moment in her entire life.

Oh, to follow the horizon until it fell away to the great beyond, to fly straight on until morning.

Bringing reality back into the cockpit, Maj

piloted the aircraft in a long lazy-eight back to Big Moose. She brought it down steadily, skimmed the water past the West Wind dock, and lifted the Stearman again over the trees like a giant insect eluding a flock of kingbirds. Another lazy eight, then she brought the aircraft back to the water and landed it smoothly.

Noah was there to guide the aircraft along the dock. When she cut the engine, he moved quickly around, securing the tie-downs. Maj jumped down to the dock. Her knees seemed suddenly to have turned to jelly, and she collapsed.

"Maj!" Noah ran to her. "What happened?" He lifted her shoulders and straightened her around so she sat leaning against him.

Dazed and a little shaken, Maj looked up at him. "I don't know. One moment it was a thrill and the next I heard ringing in my ears and then fell."

"Too much excitement, I think. But, God, lady, you were wonderful up there! I watched until you disappeared beyond the mountain. Your touch and gos were smooth and solid. You're a great pilot!"

"It was wonderful, Noah," Maj said with weariness in her voice. "What an incredible feeling. I didn't know I could do it."

"I knew you could," he said with pride. "Well, I hoped you could, anyway."

"Were you worried about me?"

"What, me worry? Nah!"

"Really? You believed I could do it all along? You didn't question it?"

Noah sat silent for a moment, hugging her against him.

"Noah?" She looked up at him.

"Okay, so my palms got a little sweaty. Nothing to fret about."

"Aha! You were worried about me."

"Not because I didn't think you were capable of going solo. I was worried because I didn't want anything . . . to happen to you."

Maj dropped her head to his chest and hugged him tightly. "Let me get my log book so you can make the entry I've always wanted. 'Solo!' "

"There's one more thing you have to do before I can sign off on today's lesson."

"What?"

"Actually I'm the one who has to do it. Stand up."

She did, a little wobbly. "Noah, I don't think I can do anything else today."

"You can do this. Wait here."

He went into the carriage barn and returned

416

several minutes later, carrying a large pair of shears.

"What are those for?"

"You'll see."

He pulled her blue chambray shirt out of her jeans and held out one of the long front tails. Then, to her horror, he sliced a big chunk off the end of it and handed it to her.

"What in the world did you do that for?"

"It's a tradition. Now you've officially soloed. You're a pilot."

"Ruining a good shirt makes me a pilot?"

"Like I said, it's a tradition. I've clipped your tail, and now you're on your own."

An amused grin started on one corner of her lips and spread up to her eyes, which shone as she looked at him.

"You're thinking something nasty, I can tell," he said, cocking his head.

She nodded. "Right you are. I was just thinking that you have indeed clipped my tail, on more than one occasion."

"What a dirty mind you have, Ms. Wilde!" He kissed her. "But I like the way you think. Especially since it parallels my own thoughts. And now I'd like to present you with the kind of award you so richly deserve."

"I'm afraid to ask what that might be. Do

417

you plan to cut my jeans off me, too?"

"In a manner of speaking. See if you can read my mind now!"

He lifted her in his arms and ran up the porch steps like Rhett Butler bearing Scarlett O'Hara, and into the house.

In her room he lowered her to the bed, tenderly removed her clothes, and stripped off his own, then gathered her naked body against him. With exquisite slowness he made love to her, and with heated desire she responded. This was the first time they'd made love in her bed, and she knew the feel of it would fuel her fantasies in the busy days ahead.

When they were lying exhausted in each other's arms, Noah sighed deeply and lazily caressed her breast. Maj sighed against him. He squeezed a little harder, and she flinched.

"I'm sorry, did I hurt you?" he asked with deep concern.

"No. I just felt something twinge a little, that's all."

"Where?" He moved his fingers to one spot. When she sucked in a small sharp breath, he pressed a little harder. "Right there. That's where it hurts, doesn't it?"

"Just a little. Nothing to worry about."

Noah palpated in the area of discomfort,

then his fingers stopped. He let out a long breath. "I feel a lump there," he said after a long pause.

Maj lay still for several minutes. "Where?"

"Here." He moved her hand to the area.

She felt around it and found the thickness. "Yes, I feel it, too."

"Better have it checked out," he said low in his throat.

"It's probably nothing. But I will have it looked at." Her voice sounded nonchalant, but her mind churned. She made a mental note to call the new gynecologist, over in Long Lake, she'd read about in the newspaper and make an appointment.

After Noah left that afternoon, Maj sat on the dock, watching the water and thinking. She let a nagging thought she'd relegated to the back of her mind come forward.

She'd missed her period this month.

At first she'd chalked it up to overwork and stress, but in the last week she'd been feeling exhausted even after a night's rest, and her stomach felt queasy in the morning.

Was it possible she could be pregnant? Emotions slammed inside her.

Joy.

Panic.

Fear.

She hadn't said a word to Noah about it when the thought first nagged her. They'd never discussed birth control, but it hadn't worried her. He probably assumed she couldn't get pregnant, thought that at her age she'd already been through menopause.

And it had never occurred to her that at age fifty-one she could possibly conceive.

Maybe that was playing ostrich. Maj knew full well that a regularly menstruating woman could get pregnant. Somehow she'd never thought it would actually happen to her, especially at this late date. She'd long ago buried the dreams of having a child.

At least she thought she'd buried them.

Chapter Sixteen

Maj made a doctor's appointment for the Thursday morning before the lodge's grand reopening day. Dr. Langford, a tall brunette woman Maj guessed to be about her own age, took down her vital statistics and medical history with an interest and efficiency Maj admired.

Maj was perched on the end of the examining table dressed in the always unattractive open-backed white cotton hospital gown. The doctor chatted amiably, saying how glad she was to hear that the West Wind would reopen. Then she resumed her medical questioning.

"Are you still getting your periods?"

"Yes, except for last month." Maj answered, controlling her nervousness.

"Do you remember approximately when your mother started menopause?"

"She'd just passed her fifty-second birthday."

Dr. Langford looked surprised. "Interesting that you can remember so accurately."

"It's just one of those things I remember." *My father was having an affair with a thirty-five-year-old corporate executive, and mother was an emotional wreck, that's how I can remember so accurately.*

Dr. Langford removed her glasses and turned in her swivel chair to face her patient.

"Now, Majesty — what an interesting name — how can I help you today?"

Maj took in a deep breath. "I've discovered a lump in my breast, and while I'm sure it's nothing, I just want it checked out."

"Of course. Let's have a look. When was your last mammogram?" She proceeded with the examination.

"A little over a year ago. In Manhattan."

"You're due. If you have time today, I'll call the hospital and schedule one for you. Would you call your doctor in New York and ask for last year's report to be sent to me?"

Maj agreed to both. Dr. Langford continued with her complete gynecological exam and called in the mammogram order.

"I believe this lump you've discovered is fibrocystic in nature. While they aren't threatening, these lumps can be painful and do multiply. In women over fifty, we like to check them yearly with mammography as well as with examination. Do you regularly check your breasts for lumps?"

"Sometimes. I confess I'm not consistent with it."

"And that's how you found this one?"

"Not exactly. My, ah . . ." How should she refer to Noah? "It was during lovemaking."

Dr. Langford's smile was brief. "Are you and your partner exclusive? No other partners?"

Maj felt her face heat. "Yes," she answered almost inaudibly. Funny, but she'd never suspected Noah might have other sexual partners. She'd certainly had experience like that with her father and husband. Curious, all of a sudden she wondered why she'd never questioned Noah's exclusivity with her.

"Good!" Dr. Langford was saying. "Many women your age think they are too old for sex. I tell them that's a myth. They can experience good healthy sex for as long as they want to. Appropriately engaged in, it's good for your health and well-being. If it still works, use it, that's my advice!"

Maj laughed. "You sound like a friend of mine. That's the first thing she asks me whenever we speak."

Dr. Langford smiled again. "I hasten to add it's important to know your partner and to practice safe sex. When is your next period due?" she asked as she checked Maj's blood pressure.

"It would have been this Sunday if it was as regular as it's always been. But, as I said, I missed the one last month."

Dr. Langford noted the fact in Maj's new record.

"Doctor, could I be . . . is it possible I might be pregnant?" Maj felt like a timid girl asking the question.

"Have you used any protection during intercourse?"

"No." She felt a little embarrassed answering.

"As long as you're menstruating and producing estrogen, and you have a vigorous intact male partner, well, then, yes, it is possible for you to become pregnant."

Joy spread through Maj, and Dr. Langford continued quickly. "However, carrying to term at your age is risky to both you and the fetus. In some cases we recommend aborting the fetus as an option."

"That's out of the question," Maj said firmly. "It's not an option for me."

Dr. Langford made another note in Maj's record. "Well, this conversation is premature anyway. I'll conduct some tests, and we'll wait and see what happens during the time of your next period. Then we'll consider what steps to take, if any. In the meantime, I think you're letting yourself get run-down. Pay more attention to your health. Okay?"

Maj agreed. After the doctor drew some blood, Maj left the office and drove to the hospital for the mammogram.

On the way back to the West Wind, her thoughts took as many twists and turns as the mountain road. The idea she might be pregnant was at once electrifying and frightening. Questions nagged her as she drove Noah's old Buick. *Should I tell Noah? What would his reaction be? I won't say anything yet.*

Friday morning of the Labor Day weekend, Maj hung a No Vacancy sign at the end of the long lodge drive, and happy tears crept down her cheeks.

Noah had given up his room at the West Wind, and planned to spend the holiday nights at his cabin. Maj knew he felt as much pride in her accomplishments as she had come to feel herself, and that knowledge strengthened her feelings for him.

He questioned her about her visit with the doctor, and she told him parts of the discussion with Dr. Langford, and said she'd have the results from the mammogram in a few days. But that's all she told him. She wanted to keep thoughts about the possible pregnancy to herself for as long as she could.

She knew she was guarding the feeling. If indeed she was pregnant, she wanted to savor this personal time between herself and her baby.

At midnight on Friday, long after Fergie and Ada had retired and the guests had finally stopped arriving, Maj was turning down lamps in the front parlor when she heard the door open and someone drop a suitcase on the braided rug. Whoever it was must have missed the No Vacancy sign out front. She walked to the reception area and saw the latecomer. Her eyes widened.

"Nan! For heaven's sake, how'd you get here?"

"The way I feel right now, I think I got here by mule train. How does anyone ever find this place without an Indian guide? Come here and hug me before I dissolve."

Maj was already on the way with outstretched arms. The two friends hugged a long time.

"Why didn't you tell me you were coming?" Maj asked. "I hope you're alone. We're sold out for the weekend. You're going to have to bunk in with me."

"I decided at the last minute to drive up here. I was lucky to get a rental truck so I

426

could bring the rest of your furniture to you."

"You drove a rental truck?"

"Yes. And I did it alone. Radio-Shack Dave turned out to have a major system glitch. That's the last time I do business with those people."

"I'm sorry it didn't work out."

"Don't be. That would have been one more marriage down the tubes." Nan rubbed the back of her neck and rotated her shoulders. "Got any Scotch?"

She shrugged out of a russet-colored blanket coat and dropped it over her suitcase. Then she pulled an olive-green crewneck wool sweater up over her head and dropped it on top of the coat, revealing a black turtleneck.

"What are you dressed for" — Maj eyed her from snow boots and woolen socks up heavy-weight trousers to her face — "sled dog races? It's still summer, you know."

"I wanted to be prepared for anything. I figured you must have turned into Nanook of the North. I haven't heard much from you lately, so naturally I thought you'd become a living snowperson up here in the New York Alps."

Maj looked down a little sheepishly. "I have been kind of busy."

"So I gathered. Where is Duke, anyway?"

"Noah. He's down at his cabin."

"Where is it?"

"A couple of miles down the road."

"Long way away to keep your Scotch, kid."

"Oh," Maj laughed. "I'll get it. Come on into the lounge. What do you think of my place?

Nan dropped down in an Adirondack chair in a corner. She adjusted her backside two or three times, propped an elbow on one arm, dropped it back down to her side, and leaned against the tilted wooden back.

"Uncomfortable."

Behind the small bar Maj popped a cup of water in a microwave oven to heat for tea, then poured Scotch over a glass with two ice cubes in it. "How can you say that? I think the place is cozy and very comfortable."

"I mean this chair. How in God's name does anybody get out of these things?" Nan was inching herself forward on the chair seat and managing only to force her shoulders down the back.

Maj laughed. The microwave dinged. She took out the cup of water and dangled a tea bag in it.

"You're out of shape. Adirondackers are a hearty bunch. They find those chairs perfect."

Nan propelled her body out of the chair with a burst of energy, and accepted the glass in Maj's outstretched hand.

428

As usual, the irreverent Nan had instantly settled comfortably on an overstuffed couch in front of the fireplace, and Maj dropped into one of the matching chairs flanking its massive stone facade. An Adirondack-style coffee table, legs made of interwoven twigs, was between them. A stuffed lynx with a permanent open-mouthed snarl revealing sharp teeth stretched along the mantel, and the newly cleaned bear cub stood near the hearth, resembling a begging dog.

"So, tell me everything. How are you? You're thinner, aren't you? Are you happy? Have you had sex yet?"

Maj smiled. "Fine. A little tired. I am. Yes. Yes. There, I've answered all your questions. Now tell me about you."

"Cute. There's nothing to tell about me. I have no life. I really am desperate. For a minute there I thought that one-eyed bear was winking at me! I live vicariously through my clients. Even with all their problems, at least they're not boring."

"And neither are you. It's so good to see you, Nan. I've missed you."

"You've been too busy to miss me," Nan sniffed teasingly.

"Not so! There've been plenty of times I wished I could sit down with you over a cup of tea and just talk."

"Your wish just came true. Talk." She peered through the low light into Maj's face. "You look a little pale. Are you feeling all right?"

"I'm bushed, that's all. The work has been intense. Remember how long it took me after Jack died to figure out how to keep a check-book? I'd always handed over my paycheck to him and he took care of everything. I didn't know anything about money."

"Big mistake. But you know that."

"I knew it after Jack died. No woman should ever allow that to happen. Anyway, multiply that struggle by a hundred, and you know what I've had to learn since the lodge fell into my hands. Not just money, but insurance, taxes, li-censes, ordering of supplies so I don't end up with a thousand washcloths and no towels, roof-ing, wiring, plumbing. Bat removal."

"Bats? You have bats here?" Nan stiffened her shoulders and shifted her eyes around the beams in the ceiling.

"They won't bother you if you don't bother them."

"They won't hear a squeak, trust me. And I'd better not hear one from them." Nan shivered. "Friendly little place, isn't it?

"Yes, it is. It's the best thing that ever hap-pened to me," Maj gushed. "Things are going very well. Must be I learned a lot more at the ad agency than I realized. The West Wind is booked solid every weekend through New Year's Day, and I'm able to make a substantial payment on my loan. It's scary how good it's been for me. My formerly pessimistic self would be wondering now when the other shoe was going to drop."

Nan propped her head on her elbow and studied Maj. "So, are you gonna tell me about him, or what? Not that I don't want to hear about your successful business venture, of course. So let's cut to the good stuff, okay? And don't think I missed that last yes you gave means you've had sex. I'm too quick for that."

"Okay, what do you want to know?" Maj set down her cup. Might as well get this over with. There'd be no sleep tonight if she didn't answer all of Nan's questions.

"All there is to tell. Leave out none of the gory details."

Maj spent the next hour telling her friend about Noah Decker from the moment he splashed down at the dock through the time the tree dropped on the Mustang and how they later sold it to Gerald Morris, through their evening at the firemen's field day and his cabin, about his surprise with her grandfather's airplane, through Kimberly's visit. Then she basked in Nan's applause over her solo and she told her every detail to the moment the West Wind opened.

"What about the girl's mother?" Nan asked when Maj had finished.

"What about her?"

"Dead? Divorced?"

Maj hesitated. "Adrienne isn't dead, I know that. Noah says he doesn't feel ready to talk about her."

"Adrienne, eh? Sounds rich and bitchy, doesn't she?"

Maj didn't respond.

"I can see that's a subject you've both been avoiding," Nan observed. "Trust me, don't avoid it forever. One way to learn about a man is to find out how he was with his mother and with his last wife or girlfriend. Valuable information that has direct bearing on your relationship with him."

"Don't get clinical on me."

"Wouldn't dream of it. There's more, isn't there?"

This was one time Maj didn't want Nan to be her usual perceptive self. She sighed.

"Well, there's the possibility there may be one tiny complication," she offered.

"How tiny?" Nan narrowed her doelike eyes.

"Baby tiny."

"Baby? What baby?" Nan waited a moment. Maj thought she saw her mind click. "You're pregnant. Good God, Maj, that's awful!"

"*Maybe* I'm pregnant. And if I am, I don't think it's awful at all. I think it's wonderful. A miracle."

"I guess you would," Nan said. "What does your doctor say about all this?"

Maj told Nan the story of her visit with Dr. Langford. "So I'll talk with her in a few days, and then I'll know for sure."

"And what does Mr. Decker think about all this?"

"I haven't told him."

"I see."

"I will when it's the right time."

"I know I don't have to tell you that having a baby at your age is a helluva risk."

"No, you don't have to tell me. I know. But if I am pregnant, I'll take the risk."

Nan sighed. "You certainly have changed into a very determined woman since you've been up here in this rarefied air."

"That's a good change, isn't it?" Maj laughed.

"Certainly, if you use it well."

"What better use can there be than for a child?"

"I can't talk you out of this pregnancy, can I?"

"If there is one, no, you can't. If there isn't one, then there's nothing to talk me out of."

"You've become logical, too. You won't need me anymore. I'll be obsolete, turned out to pasture," Nan wailed with appropriate melodramatic gestures.

"I'll always need you, my friend," Maj laughed. "And you in a pasture? What a concept!"

"Mind-boggling, isn't it?" Nan stood up and stretched.

"What's mind-boggling?" Noah asked, stepping into the lounge.

Nan spun around in mid-stretch. "You are, that's safe to say. Are you spoken for, or might you be running around free, just waiting to be trapped by a skillful hunter?"

Maj watched Noah's smile turn into a delighted grin, and wondered how long he'd been standing there.

"Maj, help me, how do I answer that question?" He looked toward her with a cryptic smile.

"Nan, I'd like you to meet Noah Decker. Noah, my friend Nan Doyle from New York."

"Ah, yes," Noah said warmly, clasping her outstretched hand. "I've heard a lot about you."

"Boy, have I heard about you! Yes, sir, I've heard a lot about you." Nan clasped his

434

hand in both of hers.

Noah's smile grew warmer. "If it's good, then it's true. If it's bad, who is the person spreading those lies?"

"Mmm," Nan murmured, "not bad, Maj, not bad at all."

"I didn't hear you come in, Noah. Have you been here long?" Maj asked, concealing her concern about how much of their conversation he may have heard.

"Just came in. I thought I heard your voice, so I just followed the vocal trail. I hope I haven't interrupted anything."

"Yes, you did," Nan said, settling back on the couch. "But feel free to interrupt me anytime."

"I had no idea New Yorkers were so friendly," Noah teased.

"They're not," Nan came back. "I'm from Brooklyn."

"Would you like something to drink, Noah?" Maj interrupted their banter.

"I'll get a beer." He peered over her cup. "Refill on the tea? What about you, Nan?"

Maj shook her head.

Nan held out her empty glass. "Scotch and two ice cubes, please."

Noah came back carrying Nan's glass and a bottle of Molson's Golden ale. He opened the top and took a long drink that consumed almost half the bottle in one swallow.

Maj suddenly felt very sleepy. Much as she wanted to stay and chat with her best friend and Noah, she was fighting to keep her eyes open and couldn't concentrate on the conversation. She stood up.

"I hope you two won't mind, but I have to get to bed. I have twenty-two breakfasts to prepare in the morning, and I need some sleep."

Noah stood up and touched her arm. "You feeling all right?"

She nodded, "Just exhausted. Last room down this back hall on the left is mine, Nan. There's a twin bed in an alcove in there, and a private bath."

"Where is it?" Nan stood and peered around the parlor door.

"I know where it is. I'll show you when you're ready to go to bed," Noah volunteered.

"Isn't that lovely?" Nan said sweetly. "You know where it is. I'm going to enjoy some conversation with you."

Noah turned a ruddier shade and looked helplessly toward Maj.

"You're on your own"—Maj waved on her way down the hall—"and you're in there with the champ!"

* * *

436

The phone rang early Tuesday morning while Maj and the Fergusons were cleaning up from the weekend guests. Maj grabbed it at the reception desk before Ada or Fergie could answer it. If it were Dr. Langford, she wanted the conversation to be completely private.

"Good morning, darling, it's me!" Nan shouted into the phone.

Maj held the phone away from her ear. "Hi, Nan. Please don't shout. I've got a killer of a headache."

"Sorry. After I saw where your place was, I figured the phone line between civilization and there could use some help. I had a great weekend in the mountains. Have you heard from the doctor?"

"Not yet. I thought your call might be from her."

"Call me as soon as you know, will you?"

"I will. Nan, I'm sorry we didn't have more time together."

"You were busy. I understand, and I entertained myself quite well."

"Yes, with Noah," Maj chided her friend.

"A bit jealous, are we?"

"Not in the least. I trust you."

"I hope you trust him, too," Nan said seriously. "He's a very special man, and you make a cute couple. I'd hate to see him loose in

437

Manhattan with all these flesh hunters down here. Me included!"

"I can see being up here in the wilderness didn't dull your colorful way of looking at things."

"On the contrary! I asked Noah to be on the lookout for a number of slightly depressed mountainfolk. I'm thinking of moving north to set up practice."

"You're kidding!"

"Am not! If there's more around like him, I could start this weekend!"

"Nan, you are . . ." Words failed Maj.

"Your best friend. Call me when you know, okay, hon?"

"I will, Nan. It was great to see you, even if we didn't have a lot of time together. You'll come back, won't you?"

"Try and keep me away. See ya', hon. Oh, and save the whales!"

"Save the . . . ?" The click in her ear told Maj Nan had said goodbye.

The phone rang immediately after she hung up. Maj answered quickly, anticipating Dr. Langford's voice.

"Hi!" Noah said. "I'm at the Coffee Cup. Need anything from the hardware or grocery store?"

"No," Maj answered quickly, too quickly.

438

"Something wrong?" Noah sounded concerned. "Did you hear from the doctor?"

"Not yet. Just tired from the weekend, I guess."

"I should think so. Hey, your friend Nan is a pistol. I stayed up with her until almost four both Friday and Saturday nights."

"I'm glad you were here, Noah. I wouldn't have made it. Nan is a real night owl."

"I'll say. She'd have gone on until dawn if I hadn't left when I did. She's great. And she thinks the world of you."

"She thinks that of you, too. She thinks we make a cute couple. Cute. Can you believe that? Us? Cute?"

"I don't know about you, but I've never been cute. I've been gangly and goofy, but never cute."

"Me either."

"Oh, before I forget, I've got a letter here from Kimberly. She wants to come up for Christmas vacation. Imagine that! We haven't been together at Christmas since she was a kid."

"I'm happy for you," Maj said.

There was a brief pause at the other end of the line. "I hope so. It means a lot to me that she wants to spend that time with me. I always thought she preferred sunny California over snowy New York."

Maj tried to put some lightness into her voice. "I'll bet she still prefers California, but something tells me the sun in her life these days is you."

"Thanks, Maj. I needed to hear that. See you tonight."

"Fine. 'Bye."

Maj dropped the phone in its cradle, then stared at it, willing it to ring. But it didn't again until almost noon. She beat Fergie to answer it, and he looked at her with a curious grin.

Dr. Langford was on the other end at last. "Well, Majesty, I have good news for you."

Maj's heart leapt to her throat and pulsed there relentlessly.

"Your mammogram showed fibrocystic masses as we thought, but nothing that could be questionable. I'm pleased with the results."

"What about . . . ?" Maj ventured.

"A possible pregnancy? No, you aren't pregnant. But it is possible you're onset menopausal. I suggest you take precautions during intercourse from now on. Anything else you want to talk about?"

"No, I guess not. Thanks, Dr. Langford."

When Maj replaced the phone set, her emotions flip-flopped between disappointment and relief. She'd call Nan later and let her know, but as for Noah, there was no need to tell him anything about it.

She'd savored the feeling alone, the sensation of being pregnant. *Having a baby.* She'd guarded her feelings closely, as if she'd been afraid they'd escape. With one phone call those glorious feelings dissolved.

Life is so fragile. Maj dropped down on the stairway, and seated on the second to bottom step, she covered her face with both hands. The sobs did not come forth. They welled up from her depths but locked themselves in her throat until she started to choke on them. Her ears rang, her neck muscles stiffened.

She shook her head to release the tension and sorrow that gripped her mind. An arm slipped around her shoulders and she jumped at the touch.

"Ada."

The older woman bent with a groan and sat down on the step next to Maj. She gathered her into her arms as if she were a daughter with a broken heart needing a mother's assurance. Maj clung to her but didn't cry.

"This, too, shall pass," Ada said, rubbing Maj's back and kissing the top of her head. "Time heals all wounds."

Maj looked into the woman's loving face and

wondered if Ada knew somehow what she'd been going through the last few days. *She couldn't know.* But her intuitions were strong, Maj could feel that. Ada's intuitions were very strong.

"Thank you, Ada," Maj said, kissing the wrinkled cheek. "And I have so much work to do, so much to think about, I won't have time to brood about anything else, right?"

"Hard work is good for a body," Ada said, laboriously pushing herself off the stair, "and good for the soul. But it doesn't always stop the mind from thinking. The mind heals the mind." She patted Maj's head and walked away.

Maj watched Ada walk down the hallway. She seemed to have aged a great deal over the summer. She didn't look well; she was pale and drawn, her limp more pronounced than usual.

Life is so fragile.

Maj's thoughts tumbled when she considered the loss of her baby from long ago, and today the loss of her baby that never was. And Ada. The vital, energetic Ada of long ago replaced by the frail Ada of today.

Time was as much an enemy as it was an ally.

That night when Noah arrived late, the first thing he wanted to know was if she'd heard from the doctor.

"Yes, I did. She had the results of the mammogram and said the lump was nothing to worry about."

Relief was evident in Noah's face. "I knew you were worried, and, well, the truth is, I was scared to death."

"You were?"

He drew her into his arms. "I never want to lose you, Maj. I feel somehow that together we've both had a chance at a new and good life. I don't want you to be sick, or unhappy, or hurt, or anything, because . . ."

He pulled her closer to him, and she felt the erratic beating of his heart and the slight trembling in his arms and chest.

"Because?" she whispered.

"Because . . . I love you, Majesty," he said hoarsely.

"Noah . . ." Maj's breath caught in her throat.

He leaned back to look at her, and the light in his eyes corroborated the words on his lips. "And it's all right if you don't know what you're feeling about me, it really is. I just . . . I just couldn't hold it back anymore."

"If you let me get a word in . . . I love you, Noah," she whispered, "loved you for so long." The tension of her own holding-back of the words until now dissolved when his mouth closed over hers in the most soul-touching kiss they'd ever given each other.

October crept in with red and gold dotting the formerly deep green landscape, and the air grew noticeably crisp. The first dusting of snow came in early November, and by Thanksgiving a quilt of white turned the surrounding land into a lacy winter wonderland.

The West Wind buzzed with activity as guests came and went. Maj marveled at the steady flow of skiers, snowshoers, and winter hikers. She hadn't felt the usual marked difference between summer vacation and the resumption of school as she had in Manhattan. Fortunately for the West Wind and her own financial well-being, one tourist season had overlapped another.

Determined to have her morning coffee down on the dock for as long as she could, Maj layered on clothes and gloves and waded through shin-high snow in late November. The snow had a crusty top to it, and in the early hour after daybreak the sound of her boots breaking through it echoed around the trees and cottages.

A winter hush lay over Big Moose Lake, broken only by an eerie whisper. Ice making.

The final freeze-up was happening right before her eyes and ears, beautiful yet perilous in the speed of its primal strength.

On the dock she smiled at the curved line of silver that protruded through the snow at the edge of the lake. Fergie had turned an aluminum rowboat upside down during late autumn, and the distinctive hump was the only indication of it.

Summer-lush shrubs planted by Maj's grandfather at the back of the lodge now hung heavy with snow and icicles, threatening to break with the very next flake. Moisture in the air could be seen with the naked eye as tiny iridescent crystals. The inside of her nose frosted with each intake of air.

She lifted her eyes to scan the snow-blanketed ancient Adirondacks, covered again by a miniature form of the thick ice sheets that had carved them more than fifty million years before. Standing there in the brittle November morning, Maj felt secure, like an infant in the arms of an old, old grandparent.

The lake sparkled with jewellike facets. The diamond patch had come to her dock to stay awhile. Its prediction had come true. Maj believed good fortune had come to her for certain in the form of the West Wind and the Fergusons.

445

And Noah Decker.

Noah loved her. She loved Noah. The words and the knowledge meant as more now than they had when she was young. Correction, *younger*. They were more exciting, more uplifting.

She knew she and Noah appreciated this new state of sensual communication more than ever before in their lives. Maj reveled in simply *feeling* it all. Feeling the superb sense of being alive and being in love. How fortunate to have the chance, recognize the worth of it, savor the experience.

Chapter Seventeen

Kimberly Decker arrived at suppertime on a mid-December Friday evening. She slammed through the kitchen door, wet with snow from hatless head to sneakered feet, her coat open with only a yellow cotton cropped sweater and jeans beneath, and no gloves.

"Is my father here?" she asked Maj in an irritated voice.

"Hi, Kimberly, welcome back," Maj said with a cheerfulness that she noticed seemed to make Kimberly recoil.

"Is he?"

"No, but I think he will be in about an hour."

"Great. My car is in a snowdrift at the end of the drive. Why I came to this godforsaken place is beyond me. Why he stays here is a good question, too." She shivered, and tears started down her face.

"Here." Maj pulled a rocking chair with a colorful hand-crocheted afghan draped over the back next to the wood stove. "Get those wet things off and get warm. The water's hot for tea."

Kimberly dissolved in tears then. Maj went to her and silently helped her out of her coat. For a moment she thought about putting her arms around the girl, but she refrained from the urge. Somehow she sensed asking any questions or making physical contact would make matters worse. There seemed to be more than a stuck car bothering her.

Maj guided her to the rocking chair, wrapped the afghan around her, then prepared a mug of Earl Grey tea for her. She'd noticed from Kimberly's last visit that she'd brought her own Earl Grey tea bags, and she'd made a note to be sure to have some on hand for her next visit.

Kimberly blew her nose in a crumpled tissue from her pocket and accepted the mug silently. She wrapped both hands around it and shivered.

Noah burst through the back door, startling them both.

"Is Kimmie here?" Worry lined his face. Maj pointed toward the wood stove. "Oh, baby, are you all right? I saw your car . . ."

Noah crossed to her, knelt down next to the rocking chair, and hugged his daughter. Kimberly burst into tears.

"Kimmie honey, don't worry," he soothed her, totally forgetting he wasn't supposed to use that baby name, as she called it, "we'll get your car out."

Kimberly's tears flowed harder, and Noah sent a look of helplessness toward Maj, who shook her head with a silent "I don't know" on her lips.

After a beef stew and dumpling dinner, they went into the front parlor, where the big stone fireplace gave off fragrance and warmth. Fergie had a ten foot fir tree propped in a red and green metal holder and was pouring water from an aluminum farm bucket into it. Several boxes marked "Xmas decors" sat near the tree.

"Fergie puts the lights on first," Ada said, "and then the star on top. And then we can all put the decorations on."

Fergie stood back and admired the tree. "It'll feel good to have a Christmas tree up again."

"Haven't you been putting one up every year?" Maj asked.

"Didn't seem to be a reason to," Ada said, "up till now." She looked at Maj with so much love in her eyes that Maj felt a lump in her throat. "And with Kimberly here, too, that just makes it all the more reason to have it."

Fergie opened the carton containing the lights, pulled out a pile resembling green spaghetti, and groaned. "Look at this." Light strings with large pointed colored bulbs in black sockets were twisted together in a maze of wires and plugs.

Noah laughed. "Here, give those to me. Kimmie and I are good at unraveling. We have years of practice, don't we, honey?"

Kimberly smiled wanly and nodded. Maj noticed that was the first flicker of light in her eyes since she'd arrived.

"I've never seen lights like these," Kimberly said, rolling a blue frosted pear-shaped bulb between her fingers.

"That's because no one has made those since World War Two," Noah teased Ada.

"They cost a lot of money," Ada answered, "and as long as they work, why spend more for those flimsy things they're putting out now?"

"Tell me, Ada, do you still save Christmas wrapping paper and ribbons like you used to?" Maj asked.

"Save them?" Kimberly spoke up. "Why

450

would anyone save used paper and ribbons?"

"Because they were hard to come by during the war," Ada told her. "Everything was needed for the war effort. Money was tight. We made do, and we used over. People could learn a lesson from that today," she said nodding.

"It's a throwaway society," Maj agreed.

"I'll say," Fergie put in. "It's tough to be old these days. Soon as you're not useful, they stick you away somewhere 'cause they don't know what to do with you otherwise. Makes old people fearful."

"Something you don't have to think about." Noah winked at his friend. "You exhaust me sometimes. I'll be old before you ever will!"

"Nothing to do but keep a-goin' as my mother used to say," Ada said. "If you stop, you die."

"I think it's become tougher to be old, poor, or a child in these times," Maj said. "It seems, at least from the news, that those are the throwaways in some places."

Kimberly's tears came back. She excused herself and went to the kitchen. Noah followed and found her leaning with her forehead against the back door, sobbing.

"Honey, what is it? Do you miss home? Is that it? You want me to put you on a plane

for California so you're home for Christmas?"
He rubbed her shoulders.

Kimberly spun around. "Home?" she
shouted. "I don't have a home! I'm one of
those throwaways she talked about!"

"Kimmie, that's not so." Noah tried to put
his arms around her. "You have a home with
me wherever I am, you know that."

Kimberly pushed him away. "Here? You call
this a home? It's a hotel, for God's sake.
There are other people living here."

"And there's love in this place and a homey
feeling to it because of those people. And you
know I've built the cabin."

"That's not a home. That's a *cabin*, a place
for a — a hermit, or something. I can't stay
there."

"But, honey, I'm making it into a home for
us. You can live there with me if you want
to."

Noah's voice carried a growing frustration
that Maj heard as she entered the kitchen. She
touched Noah on the shoulder. "I think something else is bothering her, Noah."

"Is that right, Kimmie?" He lifted his
daughter's face with a finger under her chin.

"Who cares?" Kimmie answered sullenly.

"I do, princess," Noah whispered.

Kimberly started to laugh. "Princess! Ha! Well, here's one for you, dear Father, your perfect princess got herself pregnant! What do you think of that? Isn't that a riot?" She swiped angrily at the tears streaming down her face.

"What . . . ?" Noah stepped back.

"See? I'm not perfect after all, am I? Want to throw me out? Adrienne did. She said it would be too embarrassing to have me home for Christmas, what with the big party she was throwing and everything. And she wouldn't want Daddy to know about it. *Her* daddy, of course."

Kimberly's sobs racked her thin body, and she started to run out of the room. Noah caught her. She spun around.

"Do I have a room here or not? Is it rented?" Her voice was filled with panic.

Maj stepped in then. "Of course you have a room, Kimberly. Nobody wants to throw you away. Not anybody here, anyway." She wanted to throw her arms around the girl, tell her everything would be all right. Just as she'd wanted her own mother to do when this happened to her. But she didn't tell her mother. And she had never been comforted.

"What about the father of the baby?" Noah

asked quietly.

"He doesn't know. I don't love him anyway. It was stupid of me to get pregnant. Stupid of me to have sex with him in the first place. I don't even know why I did it. I was being so stupid."

"No, you weren't," Maj said gently. "What happened happened. It just did. Don't blame yourself."

"Well, I'm going to get rid of it," Kimberly said, pacing the kitchen.

"What?" Maj's eyes followed her. "Why? Don't you want the child?"

"It's not a child yet. It's a . . . it's a fetus. Nothing. I'll find a doctor up here who'll do it."

"Are you saying you don't want this baby?" Maj's throat tightened as she watched Kimberly.

Kimberly stopped. "I'm not ready for a child. I don't even think I can be a mother ever. But especially not now. I don't know where I am half the time. I don't mean in *place*, I mean where I am in my head. A baby would only complicate my life."

Noah watched the two women squaring off. He stepped in the middle. "Kimberly, wait a minute. You need to think about this when you're calmer. Then you can make a more rational decision." He tried to put his arms around her, but she pushed him away.

"You can't make me have this baby, so don't even think about it." Kimberly trembled violently.

"I'm not suggesting that, honey. But I am suggesting we seek some counseling before you do anything you might regret later."

"I've done that. I went to a clinic. They gave me some stuff to read."

Maj gripped the back of a kitchen chair and rocked back and forth. "But did they talk to you about it, explore your feelings with you, talk about your options?" She'd had to speak. She was experiencing deep-down panic. There must be a way for her to stop this from happening. A feeling of desolate helplessness was rising in her, overtaking her, and she could not think of something that would stop it.

Kimberly spun around. The panic in her eyes mirrored the pain and panic in Maj's chest. "What options? You mean have it and then give it away? God, don't you read the papers? Perverts get kids and then abuse them. The worse thing I could do is have it and give it away!"

"That's selfish!" Maj lashed at her. "That

child didn't ask to be conceived. You did that, and you have a responsibility to it. There are honest, loving people who are desperate for a child, and here you are saying you don't want it so you're just going to get rid of it."

"I didn't ask to be conceived either, but look what they got!" Kimberly lashed back, pointing at Noah.

"I'm sure they thought they had a beautiful daughter."

"That's how much you know."

"What I do know is that now they've got a spoiled brat who can think only of herself, can't accept responsibility for—" Maj's eyes filled. The tears burned and she bit them back along with any further words.

Noah went to Maj then. "Kimberly, please sit down over by the fire, and don't move till I come back." He put his arm around Maj and drew her out of the kitchen and into the lounge.

He sat down on the sofa, drew her down next to him, and cradled her in his arms. She wept softly against his chest. He tried to speak, but no words came out for several minutes. Then he gently stroked her hair and spoke quietly, trying to soothe her wounded soul.

"I know what's going on inside you, and I understand. You had no choice back then when you had an abortion. It wasn't your fault, but I think you haven't forgiven yourself for what happened, or something. I know you must still be hurting. I don't know—"

She lifted her tear-stained face. "No, Noah, you don't know. You couldn't. It still hurts like hell. And it will hurt Kimberly, too. She'll never get over this if she goes through with it."

"And maybe she'd never get over it if she doesn't. I don't know. But maybe she'll be able to get beyond it with love and understanding and support."

"Do you really think abortion is the answer to an unwanted pregnancy?"

"In some cases, yes, I do. Maj, if she decided she wanted to keep this baby, I'd be thrilled! Don't you know that? If it was you and me and we were twenty years younger, I'd be so happy, I'd be hanging off these chandeliers!"

Maj's face blanched at his last words. But Noah continued before she could say anything, and maybe that was best.

"But it's not us," he went on, "it's Kimberly. Maybe it's different being a mother than it is a father. All I know is I love my daughter and

I'm hurting right along with her right now. She believes she doesn't want to have a baby yet. Not now. And I know I have to support her decision and help her. I'm sorry, but I want to do what's best for her, and no one else. I hope you try to understand."

Maj stood up then and went to the fireplace. She turned on him. "Listen to what you're saying, Noah! For God's sake, what if Adrienne had had an abortion? You wouldn't have that child you're loving right now!"

Noah clenched his fists. From the look on his face Maj thought he was angry enough with her to start screaming. Instead, he stood up slowly, flashed a gaze full of pain toward her, then spoke evenly.

"I think Kimberly is right, Maj. If she's not ready to bring a child into her life right now, then she shouldn't."

"How can you say a thing like that? This is a helpless life we're talking about here. A life that didn't ask to be created. You've been trained to save lives! How can you let your own daughter throw one away, just like that, as if it was . . . was another piece of scrap?"

"Maj," Noah said patiently, "I just think this is Kimmie's decision. She's the one who'd have to take care of a child, and she's in no

458

position to do that right now."

"Then let *me* take care of it!" Maj shouted back.

"Maj, be reasonable here. You're letting your own feelings get in the way of clear thinking."

"Clear thinking?" Maj cried. "What's so clear about this? Kimberly hasn't even considered alternatives other than abortion. It's up to you to explain those to her."

"You heard her. She knows what those are. She believes there is no other option for her. She's a smart, modern young woman."

"She's a pregnant young girl! She's carrying a life inside her, a life she's considering snuffing out."

"That's her choice to consider!"

"Stop it! Stop it!" Kimberly screamed, tearing into the room. "You're fighting over me like two cats with a dead mouse! *I'll* decide what I'm going to do. It's my body, my life!"

"Kimberly," Maj said calmer now, "please listen to me."

"Why should I listen to you? You're not my mother."

Maj winced as if she'd been slapped. She watched Noah's face. She could see he wasn't going to speak. "Kimberly, your father and

I—" she started, but was immediately cut off by the girl.

"My father and you what? Are you going to tell me you're sleeping with him? I know that. You're sleeping with a married man, so what makes you think you've got anything to say I'd be interested in hearing?"

Maj snapped her head around and fixed her gaze on Noah, whose face had gone ashen.

"Married . . . *married?*" Maj swallowed hard, holding back a flood of recriminations.

"Maj, please, not now. I told you I had a lot to talk to you about. I should have done it before this, but now is not the time. . . ."

Kimberly burst into sobs and sank onto the sofa.

"It's true, isn't it?" Maj whispered thickly, and headed for the hallway before she started to cry, too.

"Maj, please, wait a minute," Noah begged.

"What's it all been about, Noah? All this time spent, I mean." Maj spun around, trembling, her eyes glistening with unshed tears.

"Something beautiful between two people who came to care for each other," Noah said quietly.

"What does 'care for' mean, Noah? Or am I the only one here with an old-fashioned way of defining and understanding things?"

"You know what I mean. Please don't play games with me now."

"Games? Me? God, from what I've experienced, men are the masters at games, at least where women are concerned!"

Noah stepped close to her, grabbed her shoulders, and gazed at her with glass-hard eyes. "Now you are being unreasonable. I'm not playing games with you. What's happened between us means as much to me as it has to you. At least I believed it meant a lot to you. What did you think happened between us?"

Maj wrenched herself from his grasp. "I thought we were falling in love," she choked out, "but all we've been doing is having an affair! Only I didn't know it. Serves me right for acting like a silly teenager."

Maj turned back to the girl. "Kimberly, think about what you're planning to do. You're making a decision that will affect you the rest of your life, believe me."

Kimberly lifted her head. Her face and eyes were red and swollen. "This is none of your business," she said through clenched teeth. "I'm going to have the abortion, and nothing you can say will stop me."

Maj turned to Noah. She felt a crumbling

within her, as if her internal fortitude had been penetrated by an old and hated enemy, and she was powerless to fight back.

"She's right," Noah said evenly. "I'm sorry. I know her decision hurts you, because . . . Well, I understand."

"Good for you!" Maj flung at him. "You understand. Well, let me tell you, Mr. Decker, you don't understand anything. Especially not truth and honesty. The only thing you understand is how to hurt, and hurt deeply."

She turned and ran from the kitchen, past Ada and Fergie, who were just coming out of the parlor, down the hallway to her room. She flung herself across her bed and stemmed the tide of tears that threatened to flow.

Damn him! Damn them all! They're all alike, every single one of them. Dad, Jack, and now Noah. How does a woman know she can trust any man?

How in hell could I possibly think about — God, falling in love — at this stage of my life? I've been acting like a silly schoolgirl going ga-ga over a cute boy. Nowadays girls come right out and tell a guy they want to have sex with him. And if they get pregnant, they simply have an abortion. Forget and go on, that's their motto. That's not me!

She rolled over on her back and flung her forearm over her head. If there was to be a future for them, there was no chance of it now. Noah was married. Very much married.

She sat up on the edge of the bed. *Pull yourself together, Wilde. Fergie and Ada will never understand this. You'll get through it on your own. You can fly that airplane alone, you can run this lodge alone, and you can live your life alone. You don't need more men to foul things up.*

A light knock came to her door. "Majesty?" Noah asked. "Can I can come in? We need to talk."

"I don't think there's anything to say right now."

He opened the door and came in anyway. Maj sucked in a deep breath and swallowed hard.

"Please . . . let me explain." Noah sat down next to her.

"I don't think you can," she said. "What Kimberly thinks about me . . . you should have told me, told her. I don't know."

"I wanted to tell her. But I wanted to be certain about what was between us. This was too important. I'd be proud to tell her about you, about us."

"There is no us, Noah."

"I thought there was." His pleading eyes searched hers.

463

Maj stared down at her hands as she gathered courage to ask the question she already knew the answer to. "Are you . . . married, Noah? I mean," she added with a hopeful note, "are you separated, or anything?"

"Yes, I'm married. Separated, but not legally. Emotionally and physically, we've been separated since Kimmie was born. And by distance since she left for school. Adrienne never wanted children.

"She blamed me for making her go through the pain of childbirth. She hated being a mother. She told me she didn't have the instinct for it, and I told her that was nonsense. Everybody has the parenting instinct."

Maj gave a wry little laugh, thinking she was agreeing with Adrienne. "She may have been right about that."

"I know that now. And I think Kimmie must have felt it, too. There was always tension between Adrienne and me, trying to keep up a front for the child. Except that I think it was a front Adrienne wanted to keep up for her father more than it was for the child. Her father doted on Kimmie when she was little. Adrienne got jealous of his attention being diverted away from her. That made things worse for her, and she blamed me even more. But she successfully constructed a wide gulf between her father and Kimmie, so she has what she's always wanted, her father's exclusive attention."

Noah ran a hand through his hair. "Once I asked her to move away. We'd take Kimmie, get out of the rat race, maybe come back here. She laughed in my face. The Adirondacks were the last place she wanted to live. She told me to go if I wanted to, and I would have, but I didn't want to leave Kimmie in the house with a mother who didn't pay any attention to her."

"Why didn't you just leave and take the child with you?"

"I would have had to fight Adrienne's father. Even though he lavished Adrienne with everything she wanted, Kimmie was still a possession of his, in a way. And in those days no court would have ever given custody to me. Extricating myself from Adrienne meant extricating myself from the company, and that meant I wouldn't have any income to support myself, let alone a child."

"But you did leave eventually. Alone."

"Yes. Once Kimmie was in school, I just said goodbye one day and walked away. All I wanted for me, us, was to be on our own. Oh, we had good times in the early days. But once I went into the company, we had social obligations that made our life a whirlwind. Adrienne and I were the beautiful couple, and there was a set of rules that went along with that distinction. She loved it. I hated it."

Noah paused. He was remembering all that he'd wanted to forget. "When we were first married, Adrienne wanted to do nothing except travel, buy things. When I reminded her we needed to work to make money for those things, she asked Daddy to give me a job. He did. A vice presidency. I didn't deserve that so soon, and I didn't want it in the first place. But I discovered later it was what Adrienne and her father had wanted all along."

"Did you want children?" Maj asked.

"Yes, I did. But I was too naive to be aware of what Adrienne thought about it, I guess. When she discovered she was pregnant, she wanted to have an abortion. I was shocked that she felt that way. I prevented her from going through with it. She never let me forget it. She began having affairs after the baby was born. I think she felt her femininity had been compromised. I knew about the affairs. It hurt me, made me angry. But I felt guilty about forcing her to keep the baby. I should have let her have her way, I guess. I just don't want the same thing to happen to Kimberly. When or if she has children, I hope she'll truly want them and mother them and give them a father who will truly father them."

A wave of emotion crossed Noah's features. "I love Kimberly, but I haven't been a father to her. Not the father she should have had. I feel gutless sometimes."

"Don't. You gave Kimberly life, and you have the chance now to help her move on with hers and make it better."

"Can I do that?"

"Yes, you can. I believe that."

"I appreciate your confidence, Maj." He slid his hand across the bed and took hers.

His touch made Maj's insides turn over again. *Damn him! Why does he have that power?* "Why didn't you ever get a divorce? Do you still love . . . Adrienne?" She made herself say the name again, made the person real to her.

"I told myself that it was in Kimmie's best interest that we stay married. When I left, Adrienne told her family I was traveling a lot for the business. When I didn't come back, her father gave Adrienne the vice presidency, which is what she wanted anyway. I guess both of us just never got around to doing something about a divorce."

Maj jerked her hand out from under Noah's. Noah grabbed it back in his.

"I know that sounds feeble. No, I don't love Adrienne. I sometimes wonder if either one of us loved the other. We were young, impetuous, when we got together. I think now that biological urges had more to do with it than love." He watched Maj's face. "You've taught me what it is to love. And like you, I can't believe I had to wait this long to learn that. I know that doesn't alter the fact that I'm still legally married.

"Maybe I thought somewhere in the back of my mind that it would never happen to me, so I didn't think being divorced mattered. Maybe I thought Kimberly would be hurt more if we were divorced. Hell, I don't know what or even if I thought about it at all. Then when I knew what had happened between us, I guess I was afraid to tell you. I didn't want this to happen, what's happening now. Maybe I was trying to find out if what we had was real—I had no idea how to recognize real love other than from watching my parents. And how do we ever know if our parents are really in love? Do they hide their feelings from us? And do we ever think about our parents' relationship

468

until we get to be this age?"

Maj pulled her hand out of his again. She pushed away from the bed and stood up. "I'm sorry things happened between us," she said almost inaudibly.

Noah jerked his head up. "Why? I'm not. Can you honestly say you regret that we've made love? Do you regret how wonderful you know we are together? Do you regret that we've fallen in love?"

Maj spun around, her cheeks hot, her lower lip trembling. "Yes . . . when one of us is married to someone else. . . ."

Noah stood up slowly. "Now I understand."

Maj let out the breath slowly.

"You think I'm like your father, and your husband, don't you?" Noah's voice grew hard. "Married and fooling around. That's it, isn't it?"

"Isn't that exactly what happened, Noah? I'm not going to allow myself to go through that again. My father, Jack, the abortion . . ."

"You can't take care of the hurts of the past by trying to make up for them in the present with someone else! You can't expect Kimmie to do things for herself the way you wished you could have done them. Maj, you've got to stop living in the past."

"Me living in the past! What about you? I think the fact that you have never divorced is a way of avoiding commitment to any other woman."

Noah let out a long breath. "I'm not them, Maj. How could you even think I could be capable of doing something like that?"

"I've come to' realize how foolish I've been, how much I don't know you at all, how quickly I allowed things to progress."

"Stop blaming yourself as if you've committed some kind of crime."

"For God's sake, Noah, how can you explain it in any other way? It's very plain to me." Maj swallowed repeatedly, working to keep her surging emotions at bay.

Noah stood up. "The only crime may be in the speed in which we got together. Although I don't honestly see it that way. It all happened so fast . . . I don't know how. From that first moment we met out there"—he motioned toward the lake beyond—"or maybe it was the day we sold the Mustang to Morris, or the time I first showed you the Stearman. Hell, I don't know. All I've been able to think about was you."

"Me? Or some inexperienced, stupid woman you could have sex with and then dump?"

Noah stared hard and long before speaking calmly. He had difficulty controlling the tremor in his voice. "I want to believe you don't mean that. You're upset and saying hurtful things."

"I wish I could apologize, but I can't. I wish I thought differently about what you did, but I don't," Maj admitted quietly.

"What *I* did!" Noah's voice choked. "Don't you mean what *we* did?"

"All right! I'm just as much at fault as you are." Her voice grew soft. "Probably the fact that you were a father was one of the things that attracted me to you."

Noah leaned back, stopped by her last comment. "I thought being a father was a turnoff to women."

"Not to this one." Maj clamped her eyes shut, willing back insistent tears. "I kept ignoring the fact that it's usual for the father to have had a wife."

Noah sighed. "I have no answer for you that will satisfy. I wish to God I did. I wanted to tell you about it. But then we were having such a wonderful time together, I didn't want to lose it, didn't want to lose you. I guess I was just caught up in the glow that seemed to surround me whenever we were together. I felt like a teenager again. I started checking for acne every night."

He grinned at her, trying to lighten her mood, but her countenance darkened. She stood with her hands clenching at her sides.

"Perhaps that was our problem, then," she said quietly. "But we won't have it anymore. We're adults, and it's time at least one of us made an adult decision here."

"What kind of decision, Maj?" Noah was afraid to hear her answer.

Maj lifted her chin. "We won't see each other again, at least not in any other way except business."

"Maj, please, we can get through this. Let's just talk about it rationally. You know something has happened between us. Something good and strong, and—"

"And wrong! At least for me. You're a married man, Noah, and it's time one of us remembered that. If not for us, then for your daughter, and for Ada and Fergie."

Noah reached for her arm, but she was too quick for him to make contact. "What about us and what we want? What about making a decision for you? For me?"

Maj bit her lower lip. "That's what I am doing."

472

"By tearing us apart?"

"I . . . isn't that the right thing to do?"

"It probably is, for a lot of other people's benefit. But not for us. I think we both know the right thing for us is to be together."

"But there are so many things against it. . . ."

"I know. It seems the older we get, the greater the obstacles become, or maybe we give them more importance than the young do. Interesting how age changes one's perception of obstacles, isn't it? Presumably with age we're supposed to know how to solve all our problems. We're grown-up. Adults. We're supposed to act like adults and face our problems in an adult manner. Trouble is, being adult is singularly personal with singular difficulties and singular ways of handling them.

"If we love each other, Maj, then we love each other for the sum total of who each of us is and what made us this way. I never thought of that until just now, right before I'm to turn the half-century mark.

"But now that I look at you, know you, know us together, I'm glad I've finally grown up."

He went to her and turned her face toward him. "I'm sorry I have to end this discussion right now. I have to attend to Kimberly. Don't close any doors on us, sweetheart. Even though you've proved you can fly solo now, think about how much we've shared dual."

Tenderly he slipped his arms around her. Her arms draped loosely around his waist. Numbness rendered her unable to speak or move. He kissed her hair, then tore himself away from her and walked out of the room.

She watched his retreating back and knew a desolation that gripped her heart and soul such as she'd never known.

Chapter Eighteen

Christmas Eve was the worst night of Majesty's life.

Noah spent the evening with Kimberly in the hospital. She'd had the abortion, and some physical complications coupled with her depressed state of mind had caused the doctor to require she stay in the hospital for a few days.

Ada and Fergie were in the parlor by the fire, talking. At first Maj had been reluctant to let Noah tell the Fergusons why he and Kimberly wouldn't be there that night. Ada had not been feeling well all week. It wasn't like her to complain about her ailments, but she'd been plagued by headaches and dizziness. She had a doctor's appointment scheduled for two days after Christmas.

Even so, Noah felt it was better to tell them the truth. The Fergusons knew something was very wrong. When he told them, they said they understood, but Maj believed they probably didn't, not really.

As she looked at the shimmering Christmas tree in the corner of the parlor, Maj sighed. "Christmas is for children, I think. I have no energy for it anymore."

"Where'd the energy come from to bake all them Christmas cookies, then?" Fergie winked at her. "Or did the elves do it?"

"It's not Christmas without six dozen leftover bell- and star-shaped cookies." Maj smiled back. "And that recycled fruitcake. Where did that come from, anyway?"

"We've lost track of who gave it to us, haven't we, Ada?" Fergie looked over at his wife. "It was so long ago."

"Christmas is for everybody," Ada said weakly, curled up on the couch with an afghan over her. "Grown-ups, too. It means new life."

"It's hard to think about new life," Maj said, "when so many lives never quite make it." She thought about Kimberly, and her own baby, and a sadness settled deep inside her.

And she thought about Noah, and the thoughts weighed heavily during a season that was supposed to be about joy and light.

"Those are things to think about, understand, and pass," Ada responded. "This is the season to recelebrate life, no matter what age you begin the celebration."

A joyous thought, Maj acknowledged. Ada was so wise in a simple fashion about the complications of life. She always made things seem so clear.

That night Ada suffered a massive stroke.

At the hospital Christmas night Maj had felt the faintest squeeze from Ada's hand to hers. It was tiny enough, but she and Fergie rejoiced.

Noah came by Ada's room almost hourly. On Christmas night when Kimberly was asleep, he came and sat with Maj and Fergie after the medical team left. Ada was being kept alive by a life-support system, not by that once-bright light in all their lives.

Maj sat by her bed day and night for two days. The doctors involved her and Fergie in constant discussions and updates. Ada's speech was gone, and she was paralyzed on one side and barely responding on the other. They risked operating to remove pressure in her brain, but the damage was too extensive and the surgery was of little help.

Then Ada went into cardiac arrest, but the expert medical team brought her back. The indomitable spirit that was Ada hung on to every second of life, it seemed to Maj, no matter how strong the forces against her.

The third day after Christmas Noah suggested they think about removing the life support. Fergie refused, and Maj found him praying in the chapel that afternoon. He'd never been a praying man because he'd never believe in any god, but Maj knew he was trying everything to bring back his wife, his life, their life as it once was.

When the doctors pronounced no hope of recovery, Maj and Noah and Fergie were together around Ada, the three people she loved the most. Life support was removed. Each kissed her one last time, and she slipped away from them peacefully. When Fergie could tear himself away, Noah went with him to make the necessary arrangements while Maj stayed with Ada, unable to let her go quite that soon.

Maj's sorrow was relentless in every part of her. The three had comforted one another as best as it was possible to comfort someone who'd lost someone precious to them.

"Celebrate life," Ada had told her, but here she was mourning her death.

Maj's strength shattered and, alone, she let her tears flow freely. Tears for Ada. Tears for Fergie, who wouldn't know what to do with himself after more than fifty years of loving and living with one woman. Tears for her mother, who was sad so much of her life. Tears for Kimberly. Tears for her own baby, who never was.

Tears for herself.

Ada's words came to her again. *Celebrate life.* Two nurses came in and spoke quietly to her. They would take care of Ada now.

Maj lifted her head, wiped her tears, and steeled herself to go to Kimberly's room.

Kimberly was dressed and packed, waiting for Noah to pick her up. Her face registered surprise when Maj walked in.

"Hi," she said quietly.

"Hi," Maj returned, not quite knowing whether to sit or stand.

"Daddy told me they brought Ada in. How is she?" Kimberly asked.

"She didn't make it," Maj whispered.

Kimberly stood stiffly, fingering the sterile white hospital linens on the bed. Her eyes filled, and tears started to flow.

"I don't understand things like this," she choked. "Ada was good to everybody. She never did anything wrong. She never hurt anybody. Why did she have to die?"

Maj saw Kimberly try to hold back her sobs, but they broke loose. She went to her then, not caring if the girl would reject her or not. She put her arms around her and held her close. Falteringly, Kimberly's arms went around Maj's back.

"I don't know, Kimberly. I've asked myself that over and over. She was old, and I guess . . ."

"Don't tell me it was her time, because I don't believe that!" Kimberly's voice was muffled against Maj's sweater.

"I don't believe that, either. But I guess for some people that's enough of an answer," Maj said.

Kimberly leaned back, but she didn't let go of Maj. "Doctors can do anything, can't they? At least I thought so. If they can take away life, why can't they give it back?"

Then Maj lost what little reserved strength she had, and her own tears came hard. This time it was Kimberly's turn to comfort Maj. She hugged her, rubbed Maj's back, and patted her hair.

Neither one of them saw Noah stop just outside the door.

"I'm sorry I said terrible things to you, Maj. I didn't mean them, really," Kimberly sobbed. "I guess I've just been so angry at my parents for splitting up and leaving me. I think I know now they didn't do it to me. At least not Dad. He didn't mean to hurt me. I know he wouldn't deliberately hurt anybody. He just did it in the act of being himself."

Maj leaned back and brushed a hair from

Kimberly's cheek. They walked to the window, their arms draped loosely around each other's waists, and watched the snow fall.

"I want to tell you something," Maj began, "and I hope you'll understand. When I was just about your age I got married. I got married because I was pregnant. Women did that in those days."

"I thought you didn't have any children." Kimberly looked at her.

"I had an abortion."

Kimberly's face registered surprise. "But why? You were married."

Maj told the story about her life before and following the abortion. "I felt helpless then, Kimberly, believed I didn't have any choices. It was the most difficult thing I've ever had to do in my life. I never got over the loss. I blamed my husband for making me go through it, and I blamed myself for being weak. I guess that's why I was so upset when you were talking about having an abortion. I believed you had choices and you weren't examining them all. You could have had the baby I couldn't have."

Kimberly rubbed Maj's back again. "You're right. Women do have more choices now than they ever had. But that doesn't always make our lives any easier. I know I must have sounded like a spoiled brat to you, but I had already decided on the abortion by the time I got here. It was the hardest decision I've ever made in my life, too, and it was killing me to think I was killing a baby. My baby. Maybe I wanted someone to try to talk me out of it, I don't know. I wanted to hurt somebody as badly as I was hurting, so I hurt you with what I said. I was beginning to hate myself because I was feeling so guilty."

"Oh, Kimmie, I'm so sorry you were going through that," Maj said, smoothing the back of the girl's hair. "I'm sorry, I meant to say Kimberly."

"That's okay. Sometimes I still want to be Kimmie. I still want to be a little girl."

"Me, too," Maj confessed.

"Really?"

"Really. I guess you never get over that sometimes, no matter how old you get to be. You never get over needing to be mothered sometimes. Ada was doing that for me these last few months, and in a way I feel I've lost my mother all over again."

"I know a little of what that feels like, I think," Kimberly said. "I mean, my mother's not dead, but our relationship is. If it was ever alive." Her voice trailed into another private sorrow.

"I'm sorry you were so alone when you went

through this," Kimberly said when she'd composed herself. "At least I had Dad. I understand why you were so upset now. This experience has changed me, as I guess it must have changed you. Those little lives we were fortunate to have inside us, even for so short a time, gave us something to grow on. And we must do that and move on, or they will have existed in vain. No good will come of dwelling on what happened to either one of us."

Maj turned to look at her straight on. "I've felt so terrible for so long because of what I did."

"I'm not saying I don't feel terrible. I think I'll grieve a long time. But I believe I made the right decision. And I'm different inside now. I'll be much more conscious of the decisions that affect my life, and someone else's, from now on." Kimberly mopped her face with a tissue. "I wish there'd been time for me to know Ada better."

"Me, too," Maj said, and her tears started again. "She was a wonderful, warm lady. I've learned a great deal about how to be an adult from her. She told me something very important before she died, something I think you'd understand now."

"What?" Kimberly asked, handing Maj a tissue.

"She said it's not too late to recelebrate life, no matter how old you are."

"Recelebrate life," Kimberly mused. "That's the best advice I've ever heard. I'm glad I knew Ada for even a short time. We're lucky, aren't we? We've both had a chance to start over. I'm going to make my life count for something from now on."

"How'd you get so wise so early?" Maj laughed lightly.

"I've had a lot of . . . ah, interesting teachers. And you helped me just now."

Maj wiped her eyes. "And I owe you a great deal of thanks, too."

"For what?"

"You've shown me I can put my grief over my lost baby to rest at last. I feel as if I've been moving through a fog. On automatic pilot. But I think I'll follow your example and take control of my life. You don't think it's too late for an old broad like me, do you?" she laughed.

"Old?" Kimberly came back. "When I first saw you, I thought you were maybe in your thirties. Dad told me your age. I never would have believed you're old enough to be my—" She stopped and looked down.

"Your mother," Maj said quietly. "I would have felt honored if I'd been privileged to be your mother, Kimberly. You are an impressive young woman."

"So are you." Kimberly's face colored slightly. "Dad says—"

"Never mind what Dad says." Noah let his presence be known then.

"Dad! I didn't hear you come in." Kimberly walked into his open arms.

"Hello, Noah," Maj said with a self-conscious attempt at trying to make her hair and face look presentable.

"Hello, Majesty," he said over Kimberly's shoulder. "I've just left Fergie in the waiting room. He's ready to leave whenever you are."

"How is he? I'm very worried about him."

"I think he'll be all right. As long as he has you and the West Wind," Noah assured her.

"He'll have us both as long as I can draw a breath," Maj vowed. Nervously she searched her purse for another tissue. "Will you both be back at the lodge tonight?"

Kimberly closed and zippered her suitcase. There was an awkward silence before Noah answered. "Actually, we're leaving for California tonight."

"Oh," Maj said. A heaviness settled in her stomach.

"I have . . . business to take care of there,

and Kimberly wants to see her mother," he said thickly.

"Oh," Maj said again.

"Thanks for everything, Maj," Kimberly said, starting for the door. "I've had some time to think about something I'll want to discuss with you.

"What's that?"

"I'm thinking about seeing if I can transfer to Cornell."

"What?" Noah was clearly surprised. "I thought you were happy at Skidmore."

"I have been. But I understand Cornell has a hot hotel management school, and I've begun to think seriously about what I want to do with my life."

"Well, don't that beat all?" Noah mimicked Horace Mason for Maj's benefit.

"I was wondering," Kimberly hedged for a brief moment, "if you might consider having a summer apprentice tagging along behind you, driving you crazy. Isn't that a request too attractive to refuse?"

Maj was struck dumb. Kimberly's words were a balm to her injured spirit. She went to Kimberly and the two hugged closely, Kimberly putting as much warmth into the embrace as she was.

"Well, in the words of someone whose opinion I value highly, it's a nasty job, and I'll be happy to do it. You've got yourself a summer apprenticeship. Be prepared to work your butt off!"

"Great!" Kimberly was genuinely pleased. "I'll write to you from school, okay?"

"Yes, that would be great. Keep me posted." Maj tried to hold back the emotion of the goodbye.

"I'll meet you in the waiting room, Dad." Then Kimberly was gone.

Maj and Noah stood several feet apart, their gazes locked. She was determined there would be no more tears for him to see.

"Maj, I want to thank you for how you've been with Kimberly."

"I'm sorry I said anything about her decision. She had every right to make her own choice, and you were right to support her. She's a very nice young woman, your daughter. You're lucky."

"I know. I've come to learn just how very fortunate I am."

The silence hung like thick fog between them.

If Maj were to define just what brought about this gulf between them now, she could not fully name Noah or herself, or even Kimberly. Not even the faceless Adrienne. But it was there, almost palpable, and she could not find the means or strength at that moment to cut across it.

"Well, I guess I'd better go. I'm sorry I won't be here for Ada's funeral," he said.

"There isn't going to be one. Those were her wishes. She wanted to be cremated and her ashes spread over the lake by the West Wind."

"I could do that for you sometime from my airplane."

"Thanks for the offer, but thanks to you, too, I'll be able to do it myself from the Stearman next spring."

"That's right. You can fly solo now."

"Yes, I can."

He passed a pair of brown leather gloves back and forth between his hands several times. "Well . . ."

Maj turned back toward the window. Why did she feel she was mourning yet another death?

"Have a safe trip," she managed to say evenly.

"We will. Maj?"

"Yes?"

"I'll be back."

"I know." But she wasn't certain she believed him. Not then.

"Happy New Year."

"You, too."

He didn't speak again, but she knew he was still in the room.

And then she knew when he wasn't.

In the weeks that followed, weeks that stretched into long winter months, Maj and Fergie kept busy at the lodge. They worked on the insides of the adjacent cottages, getting the Moffetts to finish the insulation and interior stone work on the fireplaces.

Maj heard from Kimberly twice. Her transfer application had been accepted and she was making the move to Cornell. She asked questions about the West Wind and the Stearman, and asked after Fergie's welfare. She wrote that her father was very busy, but they were enjoying getting to know each other again.

Noah called from California once and talked to Fergie on a day when Maj was in town buying supplies. Fergie seemed to have learned no details about what Noah was doing, but he did tell her Noah wished to be remembered to her.

Remembered to her.

As if she had to be reminded of him. He was in every corner of the West Wind, every tree, in the air, in the sun whenever it came through the cloud cover, in her room at night.

In the little blue tin mug and the stuffed chartreuse dinosaur.

In her mind, and heart, and soul.

She answered Kimberly's letters. She filled a basket with marshmallow candy chicks, chocolate-creme-filled sugar eggs, jelly beans, and rabbit-shaped cookies, and mailed it to her for Easter.

One day in early April Maj came up from the dock with her empty coffee cup, thinking about starting breakfast. As she got to the back steps she noticed the violet bloom of a brave little crocus pushing out of the snow.

Spring!

There was hope after all that a relentless Adirondack winter would be bested by the softness of spring's arrival.

The phone rang incessantly from then on. While the Moffetts argued between them about tar and sand versus roofing shingles, the Frenchman managed to reroof four of the cottages with a method he would only say was an old French-Canadian secret. They looked nice, but Fergie said the job wasn't done until after the spring rain test. Maj was grateful to have the cottages open to accommodate their swelling clientele.

"You did it," Fergie said on the first weekend they were filled up. "You brought the place back to the way it was."

"We did it, Fergie, you, Noah, me, the Moffetts and the Frenchman. And Ada. I wish she could see it now."

"I believe she can." Fergie turned away and blew his nose in his ever-present bandanna. "Soon as the ice is gone, let's take her ashes out."

"We will."

Spring warmed the earth and made the scents from balsam and pine and lake almost aphrodisiacal. Birds nested. Sunfish and perch were busy making their own nests at the water's edge. Damsel flies clustered over the water, re-creating their species by the hundreds. Tulips and daffodils bloomed in bright red, yellow, and pink, their heads waving on tall spikes in the warming breezes.

And the black flies threatened to drive some of the patrons away from the Adirondack streams and lakes.

Maj was able to take her morning coffee to the dock just a few minutes earlier each day.

One morning in late April she took a towel and plopped down on a metal chair on the dock. Fog lay in pewter-colored clouds around the West Wind as the temperatures of air and lake and earth adjusted to one another.

Once again the loons spoke to her as they

had a year before. She wished them a silent happy anniversary. Maj sipped her coffee and reflected on last year at this time, remembering how it had all started with the drone of an airplane motor.

She let the memories of all the events filter through her mind, from the moment she'd met Noah till the moment he'd left after Ada's death.

How she missed Ada.

How she missed Noah.

She couldn't shake the feeling that perhaps she hadn't given their relationship a real chance to develop. But she'd been right, hadn't she, to say she wouldn't let herself be involved with a married man?

How married was he, after all?

In name only. There wasn't a real marriage underneath.

Legally, he's tied to her.

Emotionally, physically, mentally he wasn't.

Maybe he is now.

Maybe not.

Maj forced back tears and tried to see above the fog bank. Black tips of trees were just beginning to poke through.

Why should it have made a difference, the fact that he was legally married to someone else? If they hadn't been living together for many years, was it still a real marriage? With vows that could be violated?

Maj wrestled with the questions, grappled with her own answers.

If—when—Noah came back, she vowed she wouldn't ask him anything about his life in California. It didn't matter anymore. What mattered was that two people, two lonely people, had found each other and had discovered they each had something to offer the other, something that filled the emptiness inside, something that gave them so much more as individuals, and even more together. How could anything that mutually powerful be wrong?

The sun began to warm the air, and Maj lifted her eyes toward it, squinting through the fog at the hazy outline of its brightening glow.

An airplane engine droned in the distance. Blue jays squawked in the trees. The airplane came closer. The blue jays flew away.

Maj's senses sharpened. The whir of the airplane's engine became louder, closer. She stood up. Then came a splash, and a whoosh of water under the dock. The plane's engine roared. Maj backed off the dock onto the grass.

She heard a bump against the dock, and the creak of boards tearing from pilings. The engine shut down, and all was quiet save the rolling waves against the shore.

Was this a dream? Déjà vu all over again?

Stunned, Maj backed slowly away from the dock and up the lawn. She heard feet on the dock. Heard the scrape of pontoons against the stony shoreline.

She stopped. Waited.

And then he was there.

John Wayne, stepping out of her foggy dream once again.

No.

Noah Decker, and he was stepping into Majesty Wilde's clear spring morning. Again.

Chapter Nineteen

Noah!

Coming out of the fog in his leather jacket and white scarf. Noah, heading toward her. Noah, smiling that sexy John Wayne — real sexy Noah Decker — smile.

Maj dropped her coffee mug.

This time she was running, or she thought she was running. Maybe she was flying into his arms.

He picked her up, swung her around, set her down, and kissed her until she thought she'd faint without a breath of air. He released her lips.

"Isn't this where we came in?" His voice was raspy in her ear.

She opened her eyes and looked up into the love-filled depths of his. "I don't know. Refresh my memory," she whispered back.

He stepped back from her, cleared his throat,

and held out his right hand. "How do you do? I'm Noah Decker. Some people might say I'm not a bad guy to know. But then again, some others might—"

She stopped him with her lips.

Reluctantly, their mouths separated.

"I'm sorry . . ." she started.

". . . I didn't write," he finished. "I wanted . . ."

". . . to call you, hear your voice, but I . . ." Maj searched for the right words.

". . . couldn't because I knew if I heard your voice, I wouldn't be able to stay long enough to take care of unfinished business."

"And did you—take care of unfinished business, I mean?"

Noah slipped his arm around her waist and drew them together, hip to hip, as they walked up the rolling lawn to the back porch.

Before he could answer, Fergie was swinging through the screen door, a look of welcome astonishment pleating the skin around his eyes.

"Well, my stars, look who's back! When I heard that airplane, I says to myself, that's Noah come back, and we'll probably have to fix the dock again. And I was right!"

Noah dropped his arm from around Maj's waist and sprinted up the steps to embrace his old friend. "How are you, Fergie? You're look-

496

ing sprightly as ever!"

"I get along, son. God, you're a sight for these old eyes. You've been missed, Noah, you've been missed. And not only by me." He winked at Maj.

"You've been missed, too." Noah thumped Fergie on the back. "Both of you." He, too, winked at Maj. "Breakfast ready? I'm starved."

"I was just about to start it," Maj said, ascending the steps.

"Let me do it," Noah said, holding the door open for both Maj and Fergie. When he stepped into the kitchen, he looked around with a pleased smile.

"Like it?" Maj asked, her hand sweeping around the newly remodeled kitchen.

Noah's eyes skimmed over the gleaming range, stainless steel refrigerator, oak cabinetry with ecru countertops, deep-red tiled floor, and newly painted ivory walls. The wood stove was still in the corner, but the back wall had been bricked. The old rocker with the same afghan Ada had crocheted stood next to it.

Noah whistled. "This is fantastic! I didn't know the Moffetts had it in them!"

Maj laughed. "Frankly, neither did they!"

"Majesty was like a foreman out here issuing orders to those two, and not taking any guff from either of them," Fergie put in. "The

497

Frenchman didn't say a word, but I never saw him work so fast in my life! Sure was a pleasure to see them three work!"

"Well," Noah laughed, "I can see now who it is I want working in my company. With these kinds of results, I could rebuild the town inside of a couple of years!"

"Does that mean . . . you're back for good?" Maj asked.

"Yes, it does."

Maj's pulse raced.

"Yippee!" It was Fergie's turn to thump Noah on the back. "I knew you couldn't stay away from these mountains for long."

"It wasn't only the mountains, Fergie."

Fergie's sharp eyes snapped from Noah to Maj and back again. He turned toward the shed door, took down his jacket from a peg, and pulled his cap on his head.

"You don't have to bother getting breakfast for me, Maj honey. I got a hankering for one of those McBiscuit things. Guess I'll go meet Luther and Abe for coffee. Need anything from Pinewood?"

Maj and Noah stood locked in a long, lingering gaze. "I don't need a thing," she said at last.

"Neither do I," Noah said.

"That appears to be so," Fergie said with his

hand on the back door handle. "Back later, say one o'clock or so. Don't worry about me."

Neither Maj nor Noah spoke or moved.

"No danger of that," Fergie muttered, and left the kitchen.

The two of them stood rooted to their spots with the table between them. When the sound of Fergie's truck died away, Noah spoke.

"Are you hungry?"

"Not for breakfast," Maj said dreamily.

"Me neither."

He walked around the table, reached her side, and slipped his arm around her waist. He guided her out of the kitchen and down the hallway to her room. Once inside, he shut the door behind them.

"I've been dreaming about this moment," he whispered, undressing her slowly.

"So have I," she whispered in response, pushing his jacket away from his shoulders and carefully unbuttoning his shirt.

Her jeans were pushed down over her legs and she stepped out of them. His shirt fell to the floor, followed by his jeans. Her shirt was next, then her bra. They stood pelvis to pelvis with only a barrier of white cotton and blue lace separating the mounting heat between them.

"I'm a nervous wreck, as if it were our first

time." He dropped his head back and closed his eyes.

"Me, too," she said, laying a palm on the center of his chest. She slid her hand up over his shoulder and cupped the back of his neck. "But I want you now more than I've ever wanted you." She drew his head down, kissed him lightly, then caught his bottom lip in both of hers.

His arms shot around her, catching her and crushing her breasts to his chest. His mouth ground into hers, and she moaned with the sheer pleasure of it. She looped both arms around his neck and clung to his lips with demanding force.

He pulled his lips away and buried them in the hair over her ear. "I've missed you, Maj, missed this. You smell so good, like a warm, vibrant woman. Sometimes, at the strangest moments, I remembered how much I loved the very aroma of you."

"I've missed you so much, Noah." She let her hands slide lightly down his upper arms, then to his ribs and hips. "And I've thought of making love with you so much, I thought I'd die from the longing."

She moved one hand slowly across and caressed him through his soft white cotton underwear. He let out a long sigh, and she felt the heat of him push hard against her hand. He closed his eyes and tilted his head back, then slid his hands inside her blue lace panties and cupped the soft roundness of her backside.

They parted and finished undressing in a rush. She crawled onto the bed and waited on her knees for him to follow. In all her years she'd never felt for a man what she was feeling so acutely with Noah. Desire, yes. All-out lust and all-consuming love. She wanted him completely, and any other encumbrance he might have no longer mattered to her one whit.

That admission shot her emotions to the dizzying height her physical desire had already reached.

And then they pressed together, hotly and joyfully, touching, stroking, studying, tasting, learning the rise and fall, curves and hollows of each other all over again. They pushed each other to the limits of desire and restraint, savoring their reunion for as long as was humanly possible.

Noah turned her on her back and poised above her, a knee on each side of her hips. She slid her hands up the front of his thighs and caught his hips, watching his face as she guided him over her, then pressed him down until he was deep and strong inside her.

He caught her hands and raised them over

her head. She closed her eyes and arched as he pressed harder against her. He lowered his lips over her breasts, kissed one nipple, and nuzzled it with his cheek before moving to the other.

She heard him breathing quickly, felt him move inside her, felt her nipples ache. She opened her eyes and found him watching her, a wondrous sensuality softening his features.

"You are so beautiful, Majesty," he whispered, "even more beautiful than in my fantasies these last long months." He tightened his thighs against her hips. "Get closer," he ordered, "closer, get closer."

"Noah, I . . ." She arched against him, raising her knees so her feet lay flat on the bed, drawing him in completely. The ragged stirring in her depths, the soul-shattering force she'd felt only in the arms of this man, started forward with the momentum of an incoming tide. "I can't hold back anymore," she whispered, throat arching.

"I can't either," he said huskily.

He pulled away slightly and she rose to meet him, and murmured in pleasure as the waves of pure sensation washed through her. He echoed her sounds, and she opened her eyes to see the muscles tense along his throat and upper arms. His eyes closed, his head bowed, and then she felt his shattering release pulsing inside her.

This was a total mating ritual of bodies, minds, and spirits. Complete communion.

Later, in the afterglow of each other and the first warm rays of late morning sun streaking over their naked bodies, they lay nestled together like spoons, she in front of him, he with his knees drawn up under hers, his arm across her midriff. Maj let out a long, audible sigh.

"My sentiments exactly," he said near her ear. He leaned over and looked at her face. "You're smiling."

"Yes, I am," she said lightly.

"Is that the smile of a woman named Majesty who's just been royally satisfied by her man?"

"Mmm-hmm," she closed her eyes.

"What are you thinking?"

"I'm thinking I've lived more than half my life before I found out how it really ought to be between a man and a woman."

"What do you mean, more than half your life?" he said, letting his tongue roam lazily along her jawline. "We're not even middle-aged yet."

She shifted her head to look up at him. "Oh, yeah? I'm almost fifty-two years old. How many hundred-and-four-year-old women do you know?"

"Don't confuse me with math. Can you honestly say that what just happened between us was the true behavior of middle-aged people?"

"God, I hope so!" Maj laughed.

"Me, too!" He flopped on his back and stretched his long legs beside her. "Let's make a promise to each other right now."

"Okay, what kind of promise?"

"That we turn into a dirty old man and dirty old woman at the same time so we can keep being shameful on warm spring mornings."

"It's a deal. Let's hope we have a lot of springs to test this promise!"

He sat up and propped some pillows against the headboard. She sat up and snuggled next to him. He pulled the sheet up over them and studied the outline of their bodies beneath it.

"It's been a helluva Ferris wheel ride, Majesty Wilde."

She nodded. "I feel like I've learned how to walk all over again." She thought for a moment. "And run. And fly!"

"And I'm getting on with my life. You pointed out before that I wasn't doing that."

"Noah, I'm sorry I said all those things to you. You were right. I was blaming you for the things my father and husband did. I couldn't take out my resentment on them, and so I aimed it all at you. And I've finally learned that it doesn't matter to me that you're legally

504

married. Life's too short to—"

"I think we both had some excess baggage we were carrying when we first met," Noah interrupted, picking up her hair and letting if filter through his fingers. "I want you to know that I've begun letting a lot of that go."

She looked up at him. "What do you mean?"

"Adrienne and I signed separation papers, so it's only a matter of time before the divorce is final. You were right, too. By not doing anything about a divorce I was keeping myself from becoming attached to anyone else. That way I couldn't be hurt and I couldn't hurt anyone else. Hanging in that kind of limbo isn't living. It's just existing. When I met you, I wanted to live life to the fullest."

Maj relaxed against him. Even though she'd allowed herself to believe it wouldn't matter if he was married or not as long as they were together, she was glad he would soon be no longer attached to someone else.

"I'm glad we happened to each other," she said. "When I think back to a year ago . . . well, I'm a very different person than I was then. I came up here full of fears. Fear of making a change, fear of being on my own, fear of taking care of others. You gave me confidence to make a complete change. You gave me confidence to solo in that wonderful old aircraft

505

and in this wonderful life."

"Are you happy?"

"Happier than I've been since I was a child. Happier with me. I couldn't have done it without you."

"Yes, you could. You just needed a little nudge." He wrapped both his arms around her. "How do you feel about marriage?"

That question came like a bolt out of the blue, Maj thought. What did she think about marriage? It was a good question.

"I try not to think about it," she laughed. Maybe a flip answer was the best one for the moment.

"I used to be that way, too. But I've changed my mind now."

"And what do you think now?"

He sat up, lowered her head back to the pillows, and gazed into her face with a love so vast she could read it in his eyes.

"I think now I want to ask you to marry me, and I want you to say yes."

Maj gazed at him a long time before answering. "You don't have to say that, Noah, because you think it's what I want to hear. I guess I must have seemed an old-fashioned prude to you when I said I couldn't be involved with a married man. But I've become more modern now. It's the nineties. We don't need a legal document to validate us as a committed couple. I don't have to have you tied to me by law to make me know we're faithful to each other."

"I'm not asking you to marry me because it's what you want to hear," he said quickly. "It's what I want to hear, too. I know we don't need a ceremony to bind us together for the rest of our lives. I believe we will be forever bound from this day forward. We don't need the ceremony, but I want it anyway. Will you agree?"

A warm smile spread from her lips to her moist eyes. She nodded. "It's tough being a nineties woman, but I like it so far. Even so, I'm old-fashioned enough to want a wedding ceremony, too."

He kissed her and jumped up. "Don't go anywhere. Stay right there."

"What?"

"You'll see."

He picked up his jacket and rummaged through an inside pocket. He came back to the bed and knelt down beside it.

"Majesty Wilde, will you marry me, Noah Decker, even though I kneel before you naked as a jay bird in the pine trees?" He held out a black-velvet-covered ring box. "Until it's legal for me to place a wedding band on your finger, I hope you'll accept this token of my love for you and my good intentions. And I think you'll find it's a memento of all that we've shared."

Maj's lips parted. She sat up, threw the sheet off, and dropped her feet to the floor. Still seated on the bed, she accepted the box.

Thrilled and teary-eyed, she opened it. There, poised above a black velvet holder, was a gold Batman ring with shining red glass eyes.

Noah searched her face. "I love you, Maj, want to spend the rest of my life running with you, flying with you, and eventually doddering with you, just living with you. What do you say?"

Maj swallowed. "I, Majesty Wilde, love you, Noah Decker, sitting here on a bed both of us naked as jay birds in the pine trees, accept with all my heart your proposal for marriage."

For a moment neither one of them moved. Then Noah carefully removed the ring from the box and slipped it on the third finger of her left hand. It was too large and slipped a little to the side. He turned her palm over and squeezed the open prongs of the underside of the ring until they came together in a perfect fit.

"Look," he said, "it's completely adjustable."

"Perfect," she said, "just like us."

"Us," he echoed, kissing the back of her hand while the eyes of the Caped Crusader shone hopefully beyond them.

FEEL THE FIRE IN CAROL FINCH'S ROMANCES!

BELOVED BETRAYAL   (2346, $3.95)
 Sabrina Spencer donned a gray wig and veiled hat before blackmailing rugged Ridge Tanner into guiding her to Fort Canby. But the costume soon became her prison—the beauty had fallen head over heels in love!

LOVE'S HIDDEN TREASURE   (2980, $4.50)
 Shandra d'Evereux felt her heart throb beneath the stolen map she'd hidden in her bodice when Nolan Elliot swept her out onto the veranda. It was hard to concentrate on her mission with that wily rogue around!

MONTANA MOONFIRE   (3263, $4.95)
 Just as debutante Victoria Flemming-Cassidy was about to marry an oh-so-suitable mate, the towering preacher, Dru Sullivan flung her over his shoulder and headed West! Suddenly, Tori realized she had been given the best present for a bride: a night of passion with a real man!

THUNDER'S TENDER TOUCH   (2809, $4.50)
 Refined Piper Malone needed bounty-hunter, Vince Logan to recover her swindled inheritance. She thought she could coolly dismiss him after he did the job, but she never counted on the hot flood of desire she felt whenever he was near!